LET ME SLEEP

LAURA J. SILLETT

Edited by Rebecca Millar
Typeset by Phillip Gessert
Cover design by Jude D'Souza
Cover image from iStock

'Blow thy horn, hunter' excerpt by William Cornysh

ISBN: 978-1-7399649-0-0 (print)
ISBN: 978-1-7399649-1-7 (ebook)

To the me who wrote this.
Be brave. You get there.

TABLE OF
CONTENTS

EXODUS

I THOUGHT HEAVEN would be different.

They sell you stories in church. Pearly gates, angels, peace and light for eternity. But there are no happy endings here.

Time and hope have forgotten this place, and me with it.

In the beginning, I'd tried to escape.

I ran, searched, begged, pleaded, my fists bleeding from pounding on walls. Broken and damned, I sank to my knees, screamed pure fury at my prison, and the echoes screamed back at me.

Escape... that brief flicker of hope had soon died.

Pictures of a past life haunt me.

A dark-haired woman, bewitching, unreachable, running from me.

A clock ticking in time with the flash of a nearby light.

Fire searing across the horizon.

Two numbers surrounded by black... *2* and *3*.

Tick. Flash.

A building on fire.

Huge fingers squeezed tight around a pale throat.

Tick. Flash.

A baby playing in a pool of crimson. Its cold, blue eyes seeking me out; the grin sending chills up my spine.

Tick. Flash.

On repeat. Again and again and again.

Maybe I didn't deserve heaven.

The first sound in an age of silence, and it was one of fear.

The woman's scream pierced through the nothingness, like fingernails down a chalkboard. Curled up in a corner, I jammed my hands over my ears, grimacing at the pitch of the sound. But blocking the noise out was impossible when it was just as loud inside my head.

I pawed at the slippery walls and staggered to my feet, swaying unsteadily as my eyes readjusted to the grey expanse.

'Who's there?' I shouted. My words bounced off multiple surfaces and returned to my ears.

I stepped one foot in front of the other, concentrating hard on repeating the motion. My hands felt their way along the wall, moving quicker as my search gathered pace. I broke into a run as the scream began to die.

'No, don't go!' I choked, rounding a corner to find a different yet identical corridor. 'Don't be afraid. I'm coming to help you.'

If I kept repeating it, surely she would understand, she would wait?

Preoccupied as I was with the terrified girl, I didn't notice that the door I was barrelling towards wasn't closed. I crashed through it as yawning darkness swallowed the scream whole.

'Don't leave me!'

My shriek carried me from nothing into bright light, and for the first time in forever I realised my voice was being answered.

'Nico?'

The voice that broke through the murky haze was urgent, but thick with relief. Even with my eyes closed, I could sense its owner was hovering over me, and sure enough, two large hands closed around my shoulders, shaking me back to life.

'Nic,' he whispered. 'Wake up for me.'

I groaned. Reaching up to my face, the dead weight of a half-numb hand smacked into my cheek, discovering a jumbled web of plastic wires and tubes. These things had no reason to be here. I tugged at them.

'No you don't. Hanna!' he called, pinning down my arms.

Running footsteps signalled the arrival of an additional person, a hesitant touch strapping each limb until I couldn't move.

I needed my sight. Forcing open heavy eyelids, glued together from lack of use, my gaze found a whole new and blurry world.

It was all too much, too soon.

Shades of colour and new sounds overwhelmed my senses, bringing home the reality that I'd finally escaped that place. Relief flushed the adrenaline from my body, chest muscles forcing the sob from my throat before I could stop it.

I turned my head to the wall, ashamed of my tears.

The tall man hesitated, clearly trying to get some words out, before hasty footsteps thudded from the room, followed shortly after by the lighter footfall of the girl.

My eyes scanned the chilly room, and claustrophobia snuck over me. The space was small, and heavy with a gloom that leached from the wet stone of all the walls. There were no windows; the only light was shining feebly from a dusty bulb hanging from the ceiling and from a couple of candles on a nearby dresser. Straggly ferns and discoloured moss crept through crevices in the ceiling.

It wasn't a room, it was a cave.

Panic had steadily risen in the ten minutes it took for the tall man to return, with the idea of escape winning the fight or flight battle in my head, as I attempted to wrestle free of my restraints. The opening of the door announced his arrival; a second set of footsteps told me he wasn't alone. I tugged frantically at the restraints.

'Where the hell am I?' I hissed, my voice weak and in need of water.

'Easy, Nic, we're here to help,' the tall man said.

Selecting the chair that looked least likely to fall apart, the new man put it at a safe distance from the bed. 'You had us worried, old friend. Gerrin hasn't left your side in two months.'

Not taking his eyes off me, he gestured to the tall man standing behind the chair who was smiling hopefully at me.

I stared back.

The seated man sighed and glanced at this Gerrin, whose expression had fallen. 'You still don't remember us.'

It was a statement, not a question. These people knew me, and the feeling wasn't mutual. I shook my head, the tears threatening to make an unwelcome reappearance.

'What happened?' I croaked.

No one answered.

The next few days tried my patience.

Locked in the small room, but no longer restrained, my visitors were restricted and few. Either Gerrin or the nurse girl, Hanna, was with me at all times, but sidestepped any questions I threw at them. The other man went by the name of Cosbi, and I was sure that everyone considered him to be in charge.

After a full week of being cooped up in the tiny cave, my irritation was bubbling.

'I understand your frustration, Nico,' Cosbi had said, after I'd confronted him for the hundredth time about letting me out. 'But if you're not patient, we jeopardise your recovery. Promise me you'll stay here for now.'

I scowled at the older man. I imagined he'd been strong in his youth; though shorter than me, his build was stocky and solid. The significant greying of his formerly black hair suggested that he was probably approaching his mid-sixties, the years marked by several scars on his weathered face, tokens of some unknown battle. Kind, dark eyes were trained on my face, awaiting my promise. And with no argument springing to mind, I found myself agreeing.

Running a hand across his beard, he nodded and stood.

'Wait,' I called. 'I want to ask you something. About Gerrin.'

He hesitated in the doorway and sighed. 'You want to know what he is to you.'

It'd been impossible not to see the likeness between myself and the tall man, despite the difference in hair colour. It'd been on my mind since I'd first been given a mirror.

'Yes.'

He exhaled and smiled, watching me carefully. 'How could I keep it from you when you're so alike? Gerrin is your brother.'

Despite promising to rest and get better, peaceful sleep just wouldn't come. Although a lot weaker, physically, my health was faultless, but I was finding the psychological effects of being unconscious for two months more difficult to deal with.

I dreamt of that place often.

Emptiness was all that my sleeping mind knew, and it went to increasingly desperate levels of insomnia to avoid it. Stolen moments of rest were haunted by the flashbacks I'd seen while unconscious, and the resulting nightmares often brought Hanna running.

I would lie awake until late, remembering the horrors of being stuck unconscious and replaying that woman's scream over and over in my head, clearer than my own voice and more painful than any physical injury. Reclusive, I wallowed in tiredness and frustration as my attempts to remember anything failed. As my imprisonment ticked by without success, I discovered only one thing about myself—I was a man with a temper.

Sitting in the corner of my room one morning, staring at the ceiling, once again I willed something, just a tiny piece of information, to come back. But there was nothing. Nothing but her scream.

In the blissful moment of silence that followed, a breath across my ear whispered, '*Baby, don't do this to yourself.*'

I buckled as a sharp pain shot through my tired heart. Her soft voice was dangerous enough to my slim grip on sanity, but her words tipped me over the edge.

I launched myself to my feet and hurled a chair across the room, channelling physical strength from the torment. Pillows and medical crap scattered as the bed was upended, glass smashing against rock and needles rolling across the floor. I ripped a bedpost from its socket and swiped it at anything within reach—lights, chairs, plates, mirrors.

Shouts outside the door suggested that my outburst wasn't going unnoticed. Ignoring them, I picked up my basin and hurled it, the water giving the rickety medicine cabinet a good dousing.

The door handle rattled and several hesitant bodies tried to squeeze through the door at once.

'Get out!' I roared, propelling the bedpost at the gap.

Two men ducked, but the post hit one and just missed another. A string of swear words tumbled out in a thick Scottish accent as the door slammed shut in a hurry.

'Nico!' Gerrin shouted. 'What the fuck are you doing?'

But my mind was full of her, and on the wrong side of rational. I got a hand on the medicine cabinet and heaved until it fell, the prolonged

. crashes allowing someone to slip through the door
˷ed.

.ing hard, I rounded on him, ignoring that family resemblance. I
.d a shaking fist back.

'Nic, it's me,' Gerrin said, raising his hands in surprised surrender. 'You
know me, right?'

'Of course I don't fucking know you.' I grabbed a glass and threw it at
him. 'I don't know anyone. I can't remember anything. I want out of this
sodding place.'

He dodged the missile and approached. 'Calm down, Nic. Whatever
this is, I can help you. Talk to me.'

'I've been trying to talk to you for days—you won't tell me a bloody
thing.'

'OK, OK, fair point, that's my fault, but I'm here now. Let me help
you.'

'I don't need help, I need her to stop.'

'You need who to stop?'

I forced my hands over my ears as the scream rang out, and I winced in
pain. 'Why can't anyone else hear it?'

'Nico, hear wha—'

I threw my fist at him, a weak flail at best. He caught my punch easily
and turned me round, my back against his chest, holding my arms tight. I
struggled, pointlessly, furiously, but my legs gave out, and we slid, as one
heap, down the wall and hit the floor. Amongst the glass and water, I half
screamed, half sobbed.

'Stop,' he ordered, one arm tight around my chest. 'Stop this now.'

I tried to fight, but the only resistance my body would offer was
emotion. The energy ebbed and the tears poured. His grip didn't loosen.

'Stop her screaming,' I begged.

'I'm here,' he whispered, clasping my fist in his.

Seconds later, a needle pierced my arm and cold liquid forced its way
through my veins, flooding my body. I looked up at the blurry, troubled
face of Hanna before collapsing into drugged unconsciousness.

GENESIS

H E WAS EVERYTHING a little brother could want.
   He said the coolest things; he taught me all the awesome stuff.
He was as strong as Superman; the bullies knew not to touch me.
He was my hero; he made the monsters go away at night.
I would've given my BMX to be him.
Wherever he went, I followed. He called me his little shadow. That day
was no different, and he smiled back at me as I shyly traced his footsteps
into the hayloft.

'You heard it too, right, little shadow?' he said.

I nodded. 'Monsters?'

'I've told you before, there's no such thing. Right, kiddo?'

'But maybe we should get Daddy.'

'I wanna look.'

He crept forwards as I shuffled behind, clinging to the toggles of his
anorak. He was so brave.

'*No.* He's not ready for anything like that. He just flipped... not stable...
I'm telling you it's too soon.'

My head was pounding as my eyes cranked open a fraction, and I
reached a clammy palm to my head. Then it came flooding back.

'Monsters!'

'Nic?' Gerrin said, dropping to his knees at my side. 'Monsters? What
is it?'

'There was... something... a barn... I was a child. You were older. We
heard a noise. I thought it was monsters. You used to call me—'

'Little shadow,' Gerrin finished with a grin. 'You followed me bloody
everywhere.' He turned to Cosbi. 'You see? He's starting to remember by
himself.'

'Childhood memories are useless to us, Gerrin,' Cosbi said. 'Time is against us. Gabriel, tell him.'

'The drugs are helping, Gerrin,' confirmed a man in the corner. 'They're acting as a catalyst.'

'He's not ready for this.'

'Unfortunately, we have no choice. We'll go ahead as agreed,' Cosbi said.

Gerrin looked mutinous, but surprisingly, didn't argue further.

'Nico,' Cosbi began, pulling up a chair by my side. 'It's time you understood what's going on.'

ENEMIES

'I OWE YOU answers, so please, go ahead and ask your questions.'
My eyes widened. Finally.

'What is this place?'

Cosbi gestured to his surroundings. 'You must've gathered by now that we're underground. A large and complex network of caves, to be precise.'

'Underground, where?'

'Somewhere in the south-west, I believe. Although no one's seen a map in years.'

I pulled a face. 'Why?'

'Maps are hard to come by. Underground for safety.'

'So you're all hiding out or something? Has it gone a bit apocalyptic out there?' I said.

It was a joke, but no one smiled.

'This place is our protection, our sanctuary, and now our home,' Cosbi said. 'We've lived as refugees underground for several years. Each of us ran from our homes, and each of us somehow found our way here. Many have joined us over time. The mountains offer a certain degree of protection and we inevitably cross paths with those needing refuge.'

'Protection from what?'

A sad smile crossed Cosbi's face. 'From ourselves, Nico. The human race is programmed to self-destruct. Faith, race, gender—we never could find a way to exist together. The world fought itself, friend against friend, brother against brother. And, as is usually the case, the worst of humanity tended to survive. Murderers, gangs, rapists, each of us has run from someone out there. Seven years on, and still no one knows how to stop.'

'And there are people like that... around here?' I asked.

'There's a large encampment nearby, a lot of brutal foreigners, that we have to be careful of. They know we're here and have tried many times to get in. It's only safe outside when we're certain they aren't around.'

'So you have lookouts?'

'Lookouts, yes, and guards, joiners, cooks, teachers. We work as a community—everyone has a task.'

I paused briefly. 'Why am *I* here?'

'You and Gerrin made it here almost four years ago, looking rather worse for wear if I recall correctly.'

Gerrin grinned.

'How on earth do you survive?' I said.

'We're mostly self-sufficient,' Cosbi said. 'We've a sustainable hydroelectric power source, a stream running through the caves that provides our water supply and we grow our own food just outside, where the guards can keep an eye on it. Anything else we need, we trade or take from abandoned houses.'

'These people outside, can't you just fight back? You know, so you can live normally?'

Cosbi turned to Gerrin. 'Let the others in.'

Gerrin opened the door and in trooped four men, only two of whom looked remotely happy to be there. Looking at the line-up, it was clear which of them I'd hit with the bedpost. His nose was swollen and bloody, his dislike aimed squarely at me. I glared back.

Turning in his seat, Cosbi tapped an airborne finger along the row of men stood cramped together against the far wall. 'Lee, Parker, Chase, Ash. Show him what the outsiders mean to you.'

One by one, the four men rolled up sleeves, pulled up trouser legs, raised their shirts and pulled aside their collars, revealing linear scars, circular scars, branding scars, and even a missing finger. So many scars.

'Gerrin,' Cosbi prompted.

Dutifully, Gerrin pulled on the neck of his T-shirt, revealing two small, healed bullet wounds right next to his heart.

'How...?' I asked.

'Wrong place, wrong time,' he said with a shrug.

'Do you see what we're facing, Nico?' Cosbi said.

There was one thing I did see. That I was getting a hell of a lot of attention when everyone had far bigger things to focus on.

'I assume I'm part of the solution here?'

'To the point, as ever,' Cosbi said with a smile. 'Your memory loss wasn't accidental. Two months ago, you suffered an almost fatal head injury. A deliberate one.'

'You mean someone did this to me?'

'It was my fault—I should've seen it coming. I had some evidence that one of our own was colluding with the dangerous gang outside, and I asked you to keep an eye on them.'

'Spy on them?' I said.

He rolled his eyes. 'If you will. We think you were attacked because you overheard something you shouldn't have.'

'A secret?'

Cosbi nodded. 'Exactly. There's a significant threat to our home should that information fall into the wrong hands.'

I paused, processing the huge pile of information that had just been dumped on my head.

'I know it's a lot to take in,' Cosbi added.

'It's been hard watching you suffer alone, Nic,' Gerrin chimed in. 'But believe me, I wouldn't be telling you any of this if I didn't have to.'

'Why not?'

'Some things should just happen naturally. But we do need to find her, before it's too late.'

'*Her?*' I said, almost choking on the word. 'A girl did this to me?'

The man with the bloody nose couldn't keep his damn face straight.

'A very capable woman,' Cosbi corrected. 'Capable enough to be long gone with everything she knows.'

'Why?'

'No one knows for certain. We think she was probably a plant, to find a way of letting the others in. Of the few friends she had here, you were once her closest. But she made sure that anything you knew would never see the light of day.'

'Her name?' I asked.

'Elena.'

Elena. Didn't ring any bells.

'Why won't they just leave you in peace?' I asked.

'They want to survive, Nico. So they want everything we have,' Cosbi said. 'Time is no longer on our side. We have to know what you overheard, before she tells them the way in.'

He paused, turning to ask an unspoken question of Gerrin, who remained still for a few seconds before nodding.

'For the safety of everyone here, we need you to remember,' Cosbi said.

I frowned, not understanding what he was asking of me. I couldn't force myself to get better.

'We think the drugs we used to sedate you after your injury were starting to help your memories return. We injected you with the same thing after your outburst earlier...'

'... and I remembered,' I said.

'You must want your old life back,' Cosbi prompted.

It was true. I was a desperate man who needed to know who he was. So desperate, in fact, that it took a few moments for his intent to sink in. My eyes widened in horror. I shook my head, nausea creeping up my chest as Cosbi finally said it.

'We need to put you back to sleep.'

My heart stalled.

Anything but that.

LEVERAGE

'N o...'

It was a drawn-out whisper that escaped my mouth, blood draining from my face at an alarming rate as I stared back at them.

My body quickly reacted to what my mind couldn't process. And like someone had flicked the switch on my air supply, there suddenly wasn't enough oxygen in this clammy room.

I closed my eyes against the thunderous ringing in my ears and tried to slow my increasingly erratic breathing. My brain soon caught up with events.

'You can't... make me—' I rasped, my chest heaving.

But the words failed against the weight forcing down on my chest. My heart thumped against the pressure in defiance.

Opening my eyes only confirmed that I'd lost control. Black spots littered my vision and everything in the room slid out of focus.

Several thuds sounded as bodies rushed forwards. I could no longer see who they were. People were shouting, stamping.

'Fetch Gabriel back, now. Hanna?' Cosbi said.

'He's in shock.'

'Nic?'

'... on his side. One, two, three.'

The unwelcome motion of being heaved sideways by several sets of arms brought me back to reality for a split second, and I opened my eyes long enough to vomit over the side of the bed before my head slammed back into the pillow, swallowed in darkness.

'Oh God, Nico, please forgive me.'

I couldn't see her behind me. I could see nothing but my own reflection in the mirror, dark and distorted by a huge, jagged crack down the centre.

'*Nico, say something, please.*'

She was begging. I didn't care. I didn't want to speak to her.

Her scream rang out. High-pitched, pained, spine-chillingly frightened. It froze the blood in my veins as I turned to see her.

My eyes opened to greet the dark rock of the ceiling. With a jaded sigh, I rubbed my hands over my sweaty face.

Again. That was four times in the last two days.

My feelings towards the faceless woman were confusing. My pity for her, the need to stop her pain, was being eaten away by the most irrational surges of anger.

But then again, irrational anger seemed to be a speciality of mine. Hanna had been my only visitor in the last two days, and only then it was to bring in food. The others were avoiding me, probably afraid that anything they said would either send me crazy or make me faint. I couldn't say I blamed them.

I instinctively felt, rather than saw, the movement in the shadows over by the door. Hanna was standing there, staring.

'Oh!' She gasped as our eyes locked, before dropping her gaze and muttering her remaining words at the floor. 'You were talking.'

A smile tugged at the corners of my mouth. 'Bad dream,' I said, running a hand through my unruly hair and sitting up. The damp snap in the air of the wintry caves bit at my bare chest. 'What time is it?'

'Six thirty. What were you dreaming?'

'Nothing worth telling.'

She struck a match to light more candles on the dresser. Alternating orange flickers and black shadows found her biting her lower lip, and there was a moment of hesitation before she joined me on the edge of the bed. Hands fidgeted in her lap. 'Try me.'

I glanced sideways in surprise. I knew nothing about her, but this forwardness seemed out of character.

She was a pretty thing, not striking, but maybe that'd come with age. A mass of red corkscrew curls almost hid her freckled face, which shone with teenage innocence. Warm hazel eyes fluttered bashfully up to watch me as my gaze took in her appearance, a blush touching her cheeks under the scrutiny.

I sighed. 'A woman, begging, screaming... I can't ever see her though.'

Concern filled her eyes as they darted across my face. 'It scares you?'

I shook my head. 'She doesn't scare me, she hurts me.'

'Is that the reason you won't help us? Because of her?' she blurted out, then clamped her hand over her mouth. 'I'm sorry, that's none of my business.'

'It's fine, don't worry.'

Nervous fingers left her mouth and snuck over into my lap, seeking and finding my hand. 'You can tell me anything.'

'She's not the reason,' I said, frowning down at our entwined hands, and trying to think of a way of removing mine.

'But your reaction when Cosbi mentioned... it... I mean, well, you know, it must be something pretty awful.'

'My head was a bad place to be in those two months. I don't want to go back there anytime soon.'

'Bad? As in nightmares?'

'No, there was just... me. Nothing but me. Can you imagine thinking you're dead and that's what forever looks like?'

From her puzzled expression, I knew that she couldn't. Even given time, it would be impossible for them to understand what I'd been through.

'You should trust Cosbi—he can help you,' she said.

I shook my head. 'No one can.'

My abrupt answer killed the conversation and Hanna chewed her lip like she'd said something wrong, staring awkwardly down at our hands.

'How long have you been looking after me?' I asked.

'Since you got hurt,' she said, seizing the lifeline gratefully. 'You were always nice to me, so when Cosbi asked for someone, I volunteered.'

'You're here a lot though, don't your family miss you?'

'I only have my father, and he's—'

Whatever her father was, I never got to hear. Gerrin's overly noisy entrance into the room at that moment gave me the perfect excuse to escape her grasp, but not before he saw. Startled at the interruption, Hanna stumbled to her feet and fled from the room.

'Bit young for you, isn't she?' Gerrin said with a smirk, nodding in the direction in which Hanna's red curls had just disappeared.

I threw my pillow at him. 'She's not my type. At least, I don't think she is.'

He laughed at my puzzled expression. 'Be careful then, Nic, 'cause I think you're hers.'

I scowled. 'You done avoiding me then? Before seven in the morning too, what's the occasion?'

He aimed a grin at me and lounged against the wall. 'Get out of bed the wrong side or something, Nic?'

I didn't bother responding. Feeling the cold, I dragged myself off the mattress and pulled on a sweatshirt, eyeballing him.

He rolled his eyes. 'I wanted to talk to you. Cosbi agreed, as long as I didn't say anything that would make you go all crazy again.' He winked at me and bit into the apple he was carrying.

I regretted not having a second pillow to throw at him. 'Didn't think you'd need his permission to do anything.'

'I trust him—he knows what's best for you.'

I looked at him with scepticism. 'You've come to ask me to change my mind?'

He said nothing, but crunched the severed apple chunk.

'Thanks for coming to see how I am,' I snapped.

'I did come to see how you are.'

'Well, you shouldn't have bothered—I'm fantastic and I'm not doing it. Now go.'

'Are you throwing me out, Nic?' he said, looking unsure whether to be irritated or amused.

I shrugged. 'If you've nothing better to say.'

'You never did have any patience,' he said, trying hard not to laugh. 'I actually had something I wanted to show you.'

He delved into his jeans pocket as he crossed the room. Nestled between two fingers of his re-emerging hand was a tatty square of card, the folds of which were well worn. Gerrin paused to look at the exposed image before handing it to me.

Sinking back onto the bed, I studied the offering. Beneath my fingers was a very old photograph, but its age had stolen nothing from the love story.

The couple who smiled happily out at me as they hugged were from another time, another world—one where the sun shone and the trees blossomed. The woman was a beauty. White material skimmed the long grass as she flashed a smile for her unknown audience. A weave of daisies sat on her long dark hair, the strands caught in an infinite invisible breeze around a flawless Mediterranean complexion. Her brown eyes were lit with such warmth as she laid her head on the chest of the man in her arms.

My eyes wandered across the page, breath catching as I studied the man's features. There was no other way to describe what I saw, other than it was like seeing an older Gerrin staring out of the photo. The expected frost of such stark blue eyes was melted by the look of adoration on his face. She was his world.

Gerrin sat next to me and leaned over my shoulder, his index finger introducing me to the two people. 'Oliver and Rosa Jakes.'

'Are they...?' I said, but my mouth was unable to form the words.

'Our parents, yes.'

My thumb skimmed over the silky surface of the old Polaroid, my touch resting on her face. 'She's very beautiful.'

'She was.'

'Was?'

But I knew my question was redundant. The fact that the photograph was necessary meant that my parents were, one way or another, beyond reach.

Gerrin's quiet swallow told me more about him than I'd learned in three weeks. All the bravado had gone, the cocksure rogue nowhere to be seen. 'They died, five years ago today. That's why it was important for me to speak to you.'

They died.

I repeated the words over in my mind, applying them to the smiling faces in the picture and trying to summon a memory of them. But as usual, I came up empty and was left only with the shame of knowing I should be sorrier.

'Oh,' I muttered. 'I shouldn't have snapped.'

'You couldn't have known.' His finger tapped next to my thumb on the picture. 'She was Italian—we moved there when you were thirteen, to her family's old farm. We came back to England after they died, to see if any of Dad's family were still alive.'

'How did they die?' I said, regretting my interest as his face fell.

'The fighting, Cosbi didn't tell you how bad it was. Where we lived, we were well out of it for a while, but trouble found us in the end. We were in town when it happened. When we got back, there wasn't much left of our home.'

'How did we get back here?'

'Running, stole a boat, hiding when we hit problems. We were in bad shape when Parker found us near here.'

'Bad shape, as in...' I said, pointing to the location of the gun wounds.

'Yes.'

I frowned. 'You don't think I'm being a dick, do you? Not doing what Cosbi wants?'

Gerrin folded the photograph and put it back in his pocket. 'Your wellbeing is my priority, Nic, not what Cosbi wants. I wish I understood what you're so afraid of, but I guess you'll tell me in time.'

'Wouldn't it be easier just to let me out? Surely my memory would come back quicker if I saw where I used to live?'

Gerrin shook his head. 'There are some things you need to remember... to understand on your own, before you see the people you used to know.'

'Then I'm going to be in here a long time.'

He sighed. 'Will you promise me one thing?'

'What?'

'Take a few minutes today to think about it. But whatever path you decide to take, I'll be right here at your side. Nothing will hurt you while I'm here. You understand?'

I nodded.

'Get some rest,' he said.

'Gerrin?' I called, just before he disappeared through the door.

'Yeah?'

'I just wanted to say thank you... for earlier. For pulling me back from the edge.'

He smiled. 'We've always pulled each other back, Nico.'

It was like something from a war film.

People were running everywhere, their screams interrupted by ear-splitting crashes. Lumps of earth were flying in every direction; patches of blood stained the ground.

The man beside me hit the deck as a blast rocked the ground less than ten metres from where we were scrambling to safety. I froze, staring at the site of the explosion, unable to move. An arm reached up from the dirt, caught my jacket, and pulled me off my feet.

Face down in the grass, my arms flew to cover my head from missiles as a shower of stone rained down. I turned to face my rescuer and saw Gerrin shouting something. But the ringing in my ears was too loud.

He pointed in front of us. I lifted my head and saw figures fleeing towards some nearby hills. Clambering to my feet, I sprinted with him, grabbing his T-shirt.

Someone was chasing us. One by one, the people behind had their petrified screams silenced as a gun was discharged until only a few frantic escapees remained.

I didn't notice the branch lying on the floor until my foot was lodged beneath it. My body lurched forwards and I unintentionally collided with the floor for the second time in a minute.

Shit.

Gerrin skidded to a halt as I tried to free my foot. Hearing quickening footsteps behind, my head whipped around to discover the identity of my pursuer, my fists balling in anticipation.

Panting in fear, a woman dodged out from behind a rock and stumbled towards where I was kneeling, her body exhausted and her face completely bloodied.

I reached out a hand to help her. She reached for me too, her fingers almost clasping mine when the shot hit. Her face registered surprise, her lips forming an 'Oh' as her eyes rolled back into her skull.

'No!' I screamed, lunging forwards to pick her up.

'Come on, Nico!' Gerrin's words broke through the ringing as he tugged at my arm. 'Leave her! For God's sake, you can't help her now.'

I struggled to my feet and backed away, transfixed by the dying woman.

Gerrin and I froze simultaneously at the click of the gun.

The second before it fired felt like a lifetime, the only lifetime we had left. As the two shots sounded, the figure next to me launched itself in front of my body before I could shout to stop him. Gerrin recoiled as the bullets punctured his chest, staggered backwards and collapsed, trapping my legs between him and the ground.

I closed my eyes and lay perfectly still until the enemy had passed, thinking they'd eliminated both of their targets.

'Gerrin!' I gasped. 'Damn you, Gerrin!'

I broke down and sobbed as I shoved at his motionless body.

I couldn't move him. He'd always been bigger than me. I heaved and pushed, desperation pumping through my veins.

I refused to let him die.

There was a low-lying tree branch just inches away. I reached out and locked my fingers around it. Pushing Gerrin with my feet, I pulled myself free of his weight. Shaking from the effort, I scrambled to his side and used my filthy jacket to stem the flow of blood.

'You're OK, it's going to be OK. Oh God...'

I'd made the mistake of looking down. My hands, arms and chest were covered in blood. Forcing back rising nausea, I pressed two fingers to his neck.

Nothing.

I moved my shaking hand.

Nothing.

Frantically I searched, moving my hand around his neck, his chest, wrists, anywhere.

And then, I found it.

'Yes. Stay with me... stay with me, Gerrin.'

I heard my voice in the distance like it was someone else speaking, and the whole picture slipped out of focus.

'Over there, see the smoke?' one of them said.

American... I thought, fighting to bring my heaving chest under control. Sinking back against a nearby tree trunk, I rested for a few moments, dragging precious air into my lungs.

'Sounded like a bit of a bloodbath.'

I opened my eyes and slumped forwards, hands on knees, listening as carefully to their conversation as my noisy breathing would allow.

'Food again, you think?'

'Probably, they don't let many get away.'

I looked down at my feet. Gerrin was lying there, unconscious and barely alive. I had no other choice. I either took a chance on them or he would die out here.

Grabbing hold of his wrists, I dragged him from the protection of the thicket. It was slow, painful progress, just as it had been for the last half-mile. Gerrin was too heavy to carry.

My strength abandoned me as I broke free of the trees and sank to my knees.

'Help!' I rasped in the direction of the two men. But my throat was parched, and they weren't looking in my direction.

They turned and began to walk the opposite way, deep in conversation. Tears sprang to my eyes. This was my last chance.

Licking my dry lips, I summoned every last ounce of fight I had. 'Help us!' I shouted.

Two heads whipped around. The last thing I remembered before my head hit the cold grass was hearing pounding, running footsteps skidding to a halt.

'He's dead beat,' a fuzzy American accent said, and a hand gently smacked my face.

'This guy's been shot—he needs a doctor.'

'Survivors, eh?'

'Yeah, Cosbi will have 'em. Go for help, Parker.'

One set of footsteps ran away, then the pop of a bottle cap sounded and the faint trickle of running liquid.

Gerrin let out a weak groan.

I didn't even remember falling asleep.

'Gerrin!' I shouted before I'd even opened my eyes. Scanning the room, I spotted Hanna frozen by the door. 'I need to see him, *now.*'

Nodding in alarm, she scuttled away. Several minutes later, he returned with her, completely out of breath and not dressed, given that it was the middle of the night. His sleep-messed hair couldn't hide the anxiety on his face.

'What's wrong?' he said.

I pointed at his heart. 'One of those bullets was meant for me. You saved my life.'

'You remember?'

I nodded. There was only one way I could think of to repay this impossible debt. A thrill of fear ran through my body as I prepared for what I was about to do.

'Gerrin?'

'Yeah?'

'I'll do it,' I whispered. 'I'll do it for you.'

He ran a hand over his tired eyes and through his loose hair before my words sank through the haze of interrupted sleep.

And for the first time in memory, my brother looked afraid.

BACKWARDS

WHAT A SHIT thing time is, running away without a thought for those who want it to slow down.

On learning that I'd given in, Cosbi had wasted no time making plans. It'd taken two days to find the equipment and set up the anaesthetic, and now the hours remaining until I had to keep my promise were slipping by at an alarming rate.

I was petrified. Thoughts of getting trapped in that place again were banished before they rocked my nerve. I owed Gerrin my life and everything in it.

'Almost time,' Cosbi said.

'How do you even know this is going to work?' I complained, pacing a groove in the floor.

'Unfortunately, we don't,' an unknown man said as he unravelled tubes and broke fresh needles from their sachets. 'But I'm much more optimistic knowing that it's worked once.'

'Nico, Gabriel, our doctor,' Cosbi said.

I nodded a curt greeting and obeyed Hanna's wordless request for me to lie down.

'I need to put a tube in your arm so we can control the drug through a drip,' she explained. Strapping a tourniquet around my bicep, she doused a piece of cotton with alcohol and sterilised the skin around the bulging veins at the crook of my elbow. 'This will probably sting a bit.'

I winced as the sharp stainless-steel tip broke through my skin.

'Now then, Nico,' Gabriel said, connecting the line to a drip suspended on a makeshift stand. 'We'll be using an anaesthetic, as I'm sure Cosbi has already explained. You've agreed to this procedure?'

'Yes.'

'Wonderful. To begin with, we'll try phases of around five hours, and if that goes well, the time will probably be doubled. You'll wake within minutes of the drug being discontinued.'

'Is there any chance it could go wrong?' I said. 'I mean, I couldn't get stuck...'

He shook his head. 'You've had this medication before, with no issues.'

The podgy, balding doctor pushed his glasses back up his nose and retreated from my line of sight, allowing me a glimpse of a sullen-looking Gerrin propped up against the wall. One heel kicking glumly at the rock, hands stuffed deep in his pockets, he was frowning at the floor.

'Gerrin, you OK?' I said.

He looked up, and the frown darkened. 'Are you sure about this?'

'Absolutely,' I lied.

'Then there's something you should know,' he said. 'It might've ended badly, but you used to have time for Elena. Don't let her in your head again.'

'Gerrin,' Cosbi warned.

'I'm always here for you,' he added, and resumed his silent feud with the floor.

'Are you ready, Nico?' Gabriel said.

My confusion vanished as fear surged through me; I fought back the need to hyperventilate.

'Good luck, Nico,' Cosbi said.

'I need you to count backwards from ten,' Gabriel instructed, injecting a syringe of cloudy-looking liquid into the tube in my arm.

'Ten, nine...' I whispered.

Hanna squeezed my hand.

'Eight, seven...'

The words were coming slower. They were difficult to form.

'Six...'

Insurmountable gravity pulled my eyelids down, sealing off the world outside.

'Fi...'

The voices around me rumbled on, but I could no longer understand them.

After an age of staring through darkness, praying to emerge from limbo, my surroundings began to change. Light infiltrated the black, blanching the tone until it had reached a very familiar grey. It was like watching the sun rise in monochrome.

Emptiness reclaimed me and I dropped like a stone to the floor.

I was back.

A sickening sense of déja vu paralysed me for some time.

But I needed to move.

Stumbling towards one of the useless exits, I grasped for the handle just as the smooth wall swallowed the door. The same thing happened ten times over before I lost my temper and hammered pointlessly on the surface.

'Hello?'

I spun around. Finally, there was life in this hole.

'What're you doing back here?'

The voice had an edge of panic to it.

I took off in her direction. I charged down every path I could find, shouting promises of help.

I hadn't heard the voice in a long time when I eventually slowed. On the brink of giving up hope, I rounded a corner and found myself in a vast white room.

It was already occupied.

Sheltering in the corner furthest from me was an agitated young woman. Her long, dark hair was knotted and dirty, but it didn't hide that her shoulders were trembling uncontrollably. She had the crazed look of a trapped animal, scouring the room for a way out and cowering from an unidentified danger.

Concerned for her, I scanned the room to see what she was afraid of, my eyes settling on the second person—a tall, solid-looking man. His long blonde hair fell forwards, hiding his face. His body language was all aggression, and it was directed straight at her.

'What're you doing back here?' the woman whispered.

The man laughed. 'You know the answer to that. You were only supposed to listen, not throw yourself at him, you silly little bitch.'

Something was definitely wrong with the scene in front of me, but I couldn't put my finger on it. I moved closer, curious, but wary of being noticed. I was about ten metres away when I stopped dead.

I knew these people.

'Mum?' I whispered, looking from one to the other. 'Dad?'

They glared at each other, either unaware of my presence or refusing to acknowledge it.

'Couldn't help yourself, could you?' he sneered, advancing and smiling as she tensed in response. 'I saw you.'

'I didn't! I wouldn't do that! I was only doing what I was told...' She broke down and sobbed. 'Please don't hurt me.'

I looked into the face of my father, expecting to see some remorse, but there was nothing but cruelty.

He closed in despite her desperate pleas, goading her with the deliberate pace. I rushed forward, putting out my hand to stop him, but he walked straight through it.

I was nothing more than a ghost here.

Both she and I held our breath as we waited for his move. He dragged it out painfully, but inevitably it came. A huge fist shot out and seized her by the throat, pinning her to the wall. She screwed up her eyes in pain and gasped for breath as her hands grappled pointlessly with the tight grip.

'You'd better figure out which side you're on.'

Her face contorted into disgust as she struggled against his power, a stifled squeal of fear coming from her throat. Realising the seriousness of her situation, my mother summoned all of her strength and kneed him full force in the groin.

My father let out a howl of murderous rage as she slumped against the wall, breathless and shaking. Knowing she only had seconds to make her getaway before the inevitable retaliation, she clawed along the wall towards the exit. But those few seconds were not enough.

Catching her by a trailing arm, he dragged her around and drew back his hand.

'No!' I shouted.

The sound of the sharp slap resounded around the room, the strength behind it enough to send her crashing to the floor. Sobbing and cowering, she lay there as he stood over her.

'Just remember what I can do if you don't behave!' he roared.

She flinched and curled into a ball, begging to be left alone. Teeth bared and panting, my seething father seemed to think better of it and stormed from the room.

No sooner had he gone than the woman raised her head from the floor. Her cheek was already beginning to colour an angry, swollen red, sparkling from fresh tears. Wiping her eyes on her sleeve, she scrambled to her feet and ran in the opposite direction, the sound of her run punctured by broken moans.

I had to make sure she was all right.

I raced out of the room in pursuit, following her down corridor after corridor, the hem of her dress flitting around the bends. We reached a long path just as she was beginning to outrun me. There were only three doors, and she wrenched open the furthest, diving through the gap and leaving me alone.

I approached with caution; this exit was different. Aged, discoloured oak had swollen with years of rainwater to fill the gap, and it was not disappearing as I approached. There was something else too. Two numbers had been branded into the wood with red-hot metal.

2 and *3*.

A drawn-out sob escaped from a crack underneath.

My fingers closed on the handle, twisting until the door swung free of its frame. Grateful that this world was finally responding, I pushed the weight, hearing the wood swing open into the space beyond with an impossibly loud creak.

Inside the room was pitch black and reeked of stale water. Running my hand along the wall told me that smooth grey had given way to coarse wet rock. One step at a time, I crept into the engulfing darkness, towards where she was lying. The crying changed to an almost strangled choking.

'Don't be afraid,' I whispered, feeling the way with my hands. 'I came to see if you were OK.'

'Is it really you?'

'You can hear me?'

The sparse light trickling through the door lightened the shadows of the room and threw into focus a crumpled shape on the floor.

I inched forwards. 'I saw what he did, are you—'

My sentence broke off. No sooner had I crouched at her side and offered a hand than she'd raised her head. This was not the same woman.

Sure, she looked similar and the hair colour was the same, but it definitely wasn't my mother.

And this girl hadn't been crying.

Retracting my offer of help too quickly, I wobbled and lost my balance, falling backwards onto the cold stone floor.

Her triumphant dark eyes burnt into mine, a curious sense of dread falling over me when she opened her mouth. My heart didn't want to hear what she had to say.

'Hello, Nico.'

ELENA

I KNEW IT was her.

Her glare was exposing, making me more vulnerable as each second passed. I scrambled backwards to put some distance between us.

She cocked her head to one side. 'Welcome back, Nico.'

I grasped the uneven surface of the wall behind, tightening my grip until sharp rock bit into my skin.

She wouldn't have been out of place in a slum. Her long dark hair was tangled and clumped, clinging to her grimy face and looking like it hadn't seen water for a long time. The dress she was wearing was so ripped that it was barely doing its job, clinging desperately to curves of tanned flesh. The calm breath rising from her mouth froze as it entered the damp air, visible as it spread through the space between us.

'Why don't you come and take a closer look?' she said, licking her tongue around rough, cracked lips.

I gagged.

The moments ticked by as we stared at each other, the silence broken only by water dripping from the ceiling and the sounds of two people breathing, their rhythms out of time.

I glanced at the door.

'Going already?' Breaking the deadlock, she crawled slowly towards me. 'You know, I hope you suffered for what you did. I really hope it *hurt*.'

'Stay the hell away from me,' I hissed.

'It speaks. Still scared of me, Nico?'

'In your dreams.'

'Coward.' She snorted.

Without thinking, I kicked my heel hard at the floor and sent a shower of loose stones raining down on her. 'Don't you dare laugh at me.'

'Pathetic. I see your temper hasn't improved.'

'What do you want?'

Tracking me with furious eyes, she straightened up and stood. I followed.

'Want? From you?' she spat. 'You never had anything I wanted.'

'Then why are you here?'

'Good question,' she said, casting her eyes around our arena. 'Why this room? Kinda sick, don't you think?'

'You have a problem with this room?'

'No, Nico. Not me.'

'Meaning?'

But she just shrugged and smirked. 'Given your chosen destination for this emotional reunion, and the fact that you've turned me into this...' she said, gesturing downwards in disgust. 'I'd say someone's feeling guilty. You want answers from me? Apologise.'

I gaped.

'Go on, Nico. Beg for my forgiveness on your knees in the dirt.'

I laughed in disbelief. 'I've done nothing to be sorry for.'

'Then what are you so afraid of, *Judas*?'

'You're a traitor and a liar, Elena,' I sneered. Apparently not one to back down, I went in for the kill. 'Hypocrite.'

'Son of a bitch!' she screamed, her voice thundering through the hollow room as she stormed towards me. 'Get out!'

I caught hold of her arm as it swiped through the air.

And then the scream rang out.

Pain engulfed me and I dropped to my knees.

Ever had one of those dreams where you're falling? Tumbling into blackness so quickly you're afraid you're going to hit the ground, hard?

I wasn't in a hospital bed anymore. Nor was I in that grey place. The space surrounding me was all cragged rock with decaying wooden doors.

The darkness that extended in front, disrupted at points by wall-mounted torches fluttering in the draught, was unfamiliar to me. The feeling of cold was alien too. My bare feet stood in puddles, the freezing water nipping at my skin as it flowed from crevices in the walls. The path was deserted, but wouldn't be for long.

Without time to think, I decided hiding was the best option. Pressing myself into a nook, I made my shape as inconspicuous as possible before two people rounded the corner.

One of the men, if he could be described as that, was a stranger to me. He looked ridiculous, tottering along next to his companion, who stood at least a foot and a half taller. With his scrawny body, upturned nose and small, greedy eyes, he reminded me of a weasel. Time and gravity hadn't been kind to his face, the skin beneath the eyes and chin sagging from trying to fight the inevitable. His hair had given up too; what was left of it was a greying black, curling greasily around his squashed neck.

'You think I care?' Gerrin snorted.

The weasel man tittered and licked his thin, wet lips. 'Not yet, Mr Jakes, no. But Mr Cosbi will be wanting to know about this.'

'So? She's the one in trouble, go pester her.'

'I've already paid the lovely lady a visit, of course, sir.'

'Then you have what you want. Take a hike.'

Gerrin strode away. Weasel panicked and scampered after him, squeezing himself in front of Gerrin and having to walk backwards to get his attention.

'I guess Mr Cosbi might let you off. Why take that chance though, Mr Jakes?'

Gerrin stopped and glared at him. 'How much did you see?'

'Enough. And I wasn't the only one.'

Gerrin took a threatening step forward. 'Have you got people spying on me?'

'No, no. The other Mr Jakes was there, sir. In the shadows, sir.'

To my surprise, Gerrin laughed.

'Come on, Foley, you can do better than that. He didn't see anything I didn't want him to see, and he won't say anything.'

Weasel Man—this Foley, it seemed—gawped. 'How did you know he'd be there?'

'Keep your nose out,' Gerrin warned. 'And stay away from Nico—this is between me and him.'

My ears pricked up at the mention of my name.

'And if I did tell?'

'You're either very brave or very stupid, Foley. Where do you think blackmailing me is going to get you?'

'Mr Cosbi really doesn't like rule-breaking. And you know people will pay well for what I know. But I like you, Mr Jakes, so just a small donation and you don't have to worry about a thing. My lips are sealed.'

Gerrin snapped and grabbed a fistful of the man's musty coat, lifting him clean off the floor. 'Shall we play a little game, Foley?'

Foley whimpered as his legs flailed ridiculously through the air.

'Let's forget this conversation ever happened. You'll go crawl back into whatever hole you came from, keep your mouth shut, and I'll let you live. Deal?'

Foley nodded frantically.

'Glad you've seen sense,' Gerrin said, lowering him to the ground and smoothing the ruffled clothes with the back of his hand. 'Nice doing business with you.'

The man screwed up his sly eyes and took off in the opposite direction.

'Halfwit,' Gerrin muttered.

I blinked and opened my eyes to a rainbow of colours scattered around the room.

'Wake up, Nico. Welcome back,' a voice said.

A hand offering help appeared through the deluge of colour, and I grasped it. The smiling face behind the gesture dragged back the remnants of my last dream, and I searched Gerrin's eyes for any sign of the coldness he'd shown towards Weasel Man. But there was nothing but relief there.

'What's wrong?' he asked immediately.

'Nothing,' I lied, looking around the room. 'What's with the entourage?'

'Just in case,' Cosbi said.

'In case I lost it again,' I finished his sentence with a roll of my eyes.

'I need to check him,' a small voice muttered. I hadn't seen Hanna hiding in the shadows.

'Of course,' Cosbi said.

Hanna's sight was directed inoffensively at the floor as the group left, her face tucked almost defensively in a cocoon of red curls.

'Hey,' I said when she'd crept from her hiding place.

'Hi,' she replied, detaching various tubes.

An awkward silence filled the room.

'You're fine,' she stated, leaving without another word.

'What's up with her?' I said, frowning at the returning Cosbi and Gerrin.

'We all have off days,' Cosbi said. 'I'll check in on her later, make sure she's OK.'

'Elena had... dark eyes, dark hair. Bit of a temper?' I asked, screwing up my eyes as I tried to remember.

'A lot of a temper,' Gerrin corrected. 'You remembered her?'

'I don't think I remembered. She was more like a dream. A really angry dream.'

'In your head, she probably has every right to be angry,' Cosbi said. 'When you were watching her, she had to be convinced that you were a friend, that you cared. Perhaps you were too good a liar.'

'Was I right to betray her?' I asked.

'Never question that, Nico,' Cosbi said. 'You were trying to save lives.'

'Was there anything else, Nic?' Gerrin asked.

'What's in room twenty-three?'

Cosbi paused on his way out. 'Bad memories, Nico. There's a time and a place for those.'

I frowned.

Gerrin clicked the door in place, and waited until Cosbi's footsteps had faded away. 'You have more questions for me?'

'You know me well,' I said.

He took a seat. 'Fire away.'

'I remember... you were in trouble. Well, you were going to be if Cosbi found out, you and a woman. A small man was trying to blackmail you. Sorry, that probably doesn't make much sense.'

Gerrin rolled his eyes. 'Yeah. Foley. Only a few people knew about Elena and that you were spying on her. Foley caught on and was in danger of blowing your cover and the whole plan.'

'You threatened him.'

'Only way to stop him blabbing to someone. Pain in the arse.'

'And Elena, were we really friends? I don't see it.'

'Believe it or not, yes. I always thought you were morbidly curious about her. She was fascinating to you in a way.'

'Did I have a death wish?'

Gerrin laughed. 'Quite possibly.'

I hesitated, deciding how best to approach my last question. 'You know what you said about our parents?'

'Yeah?'

'Well, are you sure... I mean, were you telling me the truth?'

He looked at me in surprise. 'Every word, why?'

'I saw something that didn't fit with what you said.'

'Well, what did you see?'

'They were fighting. He was angry at something she'd done— something to do with throwing herself at another man. He hit her.'

A look of horror stole across Gerrin's face, and he backed away like he was escaping the Devil incarnate.

'Gerrin?' I asked.

'I told you not to let her in your head. That never happened. They weren't like that.'

'Jeez, OK, I was only as—'

'You must've mixed it up with a memory of someone else.'

'I know what I saw.'

'You know nothing.' He snarled, pointing a finger at me.

'Gerrin, what the—'

Like he was about to face trial by firing squad, Gerrin rushed for the safety of the corridor, just as Hanna walked in carrying breakfast.

Concentrating on balancing the liquid in the teetering cup, she didn't look up until she heard the boom of Gerrin's thumping steps. There was a flash of unconstrained panic, and her hands flew up to stop a scream from escaping. Without a prop against gravity, the tray performed an arc towards the floor, the contents smashing and slopping across the rock.

Gerrin strode past without so much as an apology, leaving the poor girl standing there, trembling from head to toe.

'Oh God!' She gasped, stooping down to collect the pieces of food and bowl now littering my room, but her hands were shaking too much.

I was at her side as quickly as my legs would move, wrapping my arm around her shoulders. 'Hey. What's wrong?'

She said nothing, there was just fast breathing.

I tried tucking her hair behind her ear.

Shaking her head, she threw off my arm. 'Get off, it's nothing! He just surprised me is all.'

'It's not nothing—you're shaking.'

I reached for her face, but she slapped my hand away.

'Don't touch me, Nico!' she cried.

'I was just trying to help,' I said.

'Don't. I don't need you to. Just… give me some space.'

Holding up my hands in exasperated defeat, I retreated, noticing that someone had left clean clothes on the bed. I took my time getting dressed, but Hanna was still there when I'd finished, on her hands and knees collecting what she'd dropped.

I stood with my hands wedged in my jeans pockets, watching her. Knowing it was impossible to avoid me any longer, she straightened up and wiped her hands down her front.

'Walk?' I asked.

'You're not allowed out.'

'Only around the medical bay.'

She hesitated. 'Come on then.'

The medical bay contained four rooms linked by a small, circular corridor completely shut off by a heavy oak door. Beyond that was out of bounds for me. A garish mixture of artificial and natural light sources were scattered about the walls.

Hanna insisted on walking to my left, some distance away.

'What's the deal with this place then?' I asked. 'Has it all been built?'

'War tunnels,' she answered. 'Adapted from how they were found, to make them habitable. Cosbi had the doors and locks fitted a couple of years ago, and all the furniture has been taken from places nearby. Some people brought things with them too.'

'Whereabouts is your room?'

'Near the exit. My father is there, but he's not very well. And he's not in the best temper most of the time. I mostly sleep in the room next to yours.'

'How about friends, boyfriend?'

Her line of sight took a dive, and she shook her head, absently rolling a locket around her neck between thumb and forefinger. 'No, no one special.'

'And you're the only nurse here?'

'I'm the only one allowed here at the moment. All the others have jobs in the main bit.'

We walked five whole laps of the deserted loop before we came to a natural stop outside my room. More relaxed, Hanna was chattering away about the caves when my brain finally realised what was on my door.

'Twenty-five...' I whispered.

'What is it?' Hanna said.

'The rooms are numbered.'

'They have been since the doors were put on.'

I jogged down the corridor to the next room.

26.

27.

I ran the circumference of the path looking for a particular number, Hanna scurrying along behind, demanding an explanation.

24.

'Dammit,' I muttered.

'What're you looking for?'

'Twenty-three. Why isn't it here?'

'It's down there,' she whispered, pointing to the large door that I was banned from opening.

'I want to see what's in there.' I grabbed her hand. 'You can show me the way.'

But she resisted. 'I can't, I can't go there with you.'

'Why not? No one's watching.'

'Nico, stop, you'll get me in trouble.'

'I won't tell anyone.'

'You're not allowed.'

'I'm a grown man.'

'Please, please stop,' she begged.

But I didn't want to listen; all I wanted was to find that room.

'Nico, *stop!*'

I dropped Hanna's hand as the screamed 'stop' bounced around me, and she sank back against the wall.

'Enough!' I snapped.

I seized her arm and propelled her through the door of my room before the noise brought everyone running. Checking the corridor and barricading us in, I rounded on her, expecting answers. But she was too busy combing at her hair to notice, the red curls now covering most of her face.

'Are you going to tell me what's going on?' I said.

She stopped messing and stared at me, stared like I was a threat.

'This is ridiculous, Hanna. The way you were earlier, and now this.'

She stayed frozen, seemingly incapable of talking.

'Hanna, it's just me. I'm your friend.' I reached for her, carelessly forgetting how she'd reacted to that before.

'No!' she screamed, trying to bite my hand. '*No!* Get off me!'

I pinned her arms behind her back before she hurt both of us. 'For God's sake, Hanna, calm down!'

She yanked her head away, her hair falling from her cheek. It was the side she'd been keeping hidden. Knowing I'd already seen, all the fight left her. Visible there, extending all the way from her eyebrow, across her cheekbone and down towards her nose, was a deep purple bruise.

A solitary tear slid from her eye, leaving a glistening trail of innocence across the colourful violence.

CONFESSION

'What on earth...?'

Feeling ashamed for snapping, I relaxed my grip. It was one hell of a bruise, but it seemed all the worse on the face of such a caring woman.

'Hanna?' I prompted. 'How did this happen?'

My voice pulled her back. More tears streaked down the path left by the first.

'Does it look that bad?' she whispered.

'Well, it definitely needs an ice pack.'

'Gabriel told me to put a compress on it.'

'You've seen the doctor?'

She nodded.

'Don't even try telling me you walked into a door—I'm not that stupid.'

'Not a door. I fell.'

I rolled my eyes.

'Really, Nico. Have you seen the floor? I had a bowl of water in my hands and went face first into the wall.'

'So, no one else was involved?'

'Of course not.'

'And Gabriel believed that?'

'Not everyone is as suspicious as you.'

She couldn't fob me off that easily. 'So explain why you just nearly chewed through my hand.'

'Come on.' She groaned, finally looking up. 'Would you want anyone seeing you looking like this?'

'You realise how stupid that sounds, right?'

She pouted. 'Well, let's throw you into the wall and see how you feel about people seeing *your* face.'

I sighed. 'Has Cosbi seen?'

'No,' she muttered, sliding along the wall, trying to keep as much air between us as possible. 'I'd better go, I'm supposed to be working.'

I caught hold of her arm. She shied from the movement, and I again felt a pang of regret about my heavy-handedness. 'I know a wall didn't do that.'

She sighed. 'Let it go, Nico.'

I could go no further. Whoever she was protecting, she was prepared to go all out for. I opened the door and let her pass.

'Need some privacy?' Gerrin hollered.

Hanna let out a tiny surprised shriek and jumped away like the floor surrounding me was lava. I glared at him.

He was in hysterics by the time he reached us. 'Seriously, the looks on your faces!'

'I've got to go,' Hanna squeaked and ran off.

'So what were you two up to?' Gerrin asked.

'Just talking.'

He looked at me with a sceptical grin. 'So you weren't... busy then?'

'Busy? Oh come on.'

'What? She likes you, she's doing a shit job of hiding it.'

'We're just friends. And it's none of your damn business.'

He held up his hands and smirked.

'You've cheered up anyway. Got over your tantrum?' I said.

That wiped the smug smile off his face. 'We'll have to agree to disagree on that one, Nic,' he said. 'I shouldn't have lost my temper, but you don't know what you were saying about Mum and Dad. You'll understand when you remember.'

I shook my head. I'd remembered enough about my parents.

It was the only time she'd ever screamed in fear. It began quietly but soared as the drugs pulled me further and further under, back into room 23.

I opened my eyes.

A shadow stood before the young woman, aggression and hatred pulsing from its skin.

Tearing her transfixed stare from the threat, she bolted for the exit.

Sauntering to the door, it seized her long hair and dragged her back to the spot she'd just abandoned. Frightened gasps of effort punctuated each thump of a small balled fist against dark arms.

The figure reached out and tenderly wiped tears from her cheeks.

It paused, I froze. The eye of the storm.

My cry of horror rang out as its hands leapt to attention, fingers binding, tightly encircling, thumbs concentrating all of its strength against her vulnerable throat.

Darkness. Silence.

The memory disappeared.

I gasped in a breath.

The rotting wooden door of 23 loomed out of nothing, sticking out like a sore thumb against the grey.

Elena.

She'd appeared last time because I needed help. She was an illusion, an echo, a memory. *My* memory. I was scared enough to try it.

'Elena?'

The whole place was eerie, too silent by far. The hairs on my arms stood up at the deadly calm stealing through the air. Something was coming.

'Where are you?' I whispered.

It started as abruptly as ever. The sound pierced my eardrums and stabbed at my heart. I was on my knees instantly, all of my strength focused on keeping out the pain.

I couldn't hear it happen again.

Sacrificing one ear, I peeled a hand from the side of my head and pounded on the solid wood. 'Elena!'

'Apologise.'

'I'm sorry!'

'What for?'

'Dammit, you know I can't remember!'

My scream fused with hers as the pitch took a semitone hike, the sharpened note taking me to an all new level of agony. 'For God's sake, let me in!'

'Apologise.'

The woman—she needed me. I was powerless.

I hammered on the door. '*Please!*'

'Say it.'

Decibels were no obstacle for the noise, and it cranked up to maximum. I could take no more. 'I'm sorry I told them where you were!'

The door flew open and a hand grabbed hold of my T-shirt as I half fell across the threshold. The scream ceased the second the exit was sealed.

Sudden peace calmed my racing heart. I dragged my shaking body to its feet and faced my enemy. She stood in the filthy remains of her dress, staring at me, frozen in the position of her last movement.

'I'm sorry I told them where you were,' I repeated in the barest of whispers. Saying it was like a release. I *had* done something I was ashamed of.

CAIN

No one would stop me this time.

I was free to stand; there were no restraints tying me to the bed. I pulled on clothes but remained barefoot—I'd be quieter that way.

I looked at my watch. Two in the morning. Everyone would be asleep by now.

I crept to the door and flattened myself against the wall, peering into the pitch black outside. Empty. They always cut the lights at twelve.

The guard was asleep. The unfortunate man had fallen off his chair and there was a stench of alcohol hanging in the air around his gawping mouth. Whoever he was, it'd been a bad idea to leave him within reach of a bottle of brandy, with several hours to kill.

I knew the path without thinking, all the way to room number 2 in the main cave system.

Candlelight bled out into the darkness along the corridor, the rustling of paper filtering to my ears as sheets were separated.

Taking advantage of my barefoot approach, I managed to creep close enough to peer through the crevice that the open hinge had left. Perched on his desk chair, excess flesh oozing over the sides of the strained wooden seat, the sweaty man was writing furiously, his balding head shining like a beacon.

Curiosity got the better of me.

If the broad loins had been kept in check with the odd piece of fruit over the years, maybe he would've managed to leave his seat before I had my hand over his revolting mouth. As it was, he only managed two words.

'What the—'

I grabbed the nearest object, a thick glass jug, and shattered it over his head. His lolling skull slumped forwards and blood flowed across his unfinished letter. Out cold or dead—who cared?

I snatched the paper from under four fat sausage-fingers.

DATE: January 2031

NAME: Nico Jakes.
STATUS: Solitary confinement.
RECOMMENDATION: Volatile member of the community.
Recommend interrogation and—

The recommendation sentence trailed into a scrawling mess at around the point I'd smashed the glassware into his brains. Pulling open his jaw, I stuffed his recommendations for me exactly where they belonged and grabbed a knife lying on the desk.

I took the curved passageway at a run, excitement coursing through me. The door I was searching for appeared on my left through the gaping darkness. Taking a torch from its wall bracket and setting it alight, with a steady palm I freed the door from its frame and entered room 22.

Swiping the flame through the air, my target became visible. Arrogantly sprawled on his bed, he was half-naked and dead to the world, his sleep blissfully free of screams. But not for much longer.

I was hurting, and I was angry, and only one thing was going to make it better.

Setting down the torch, I walked to the bed, hatred pulsing through my blood at the sight of him. Raising the knife high above my head, I whispered my last words to him.

'Watch your back in hell. I'll be seeing you there real soon.'

Cold blue eyes flew open as I brought my fist down with all the force I could muster, sinking the silver blade of the knife into the exposed skin of Gerrin's chest.

STAY

I COULDN'T HAVE, could I?

He was alive and well last night. It was just a sick dream.

'So, you couldn't see who the figure was?'

I looked down at my hands for the hundredth time that morning. Still no blood.

'Nico?'

Cosbi wouldn't be here if something had happened. But Gerrin's absence was making me panic.

'It attacked a woman?'

I frowned. I hadn't wanted to mention the shadowy figure and the woman at all, but it was either that or confess to the dream about Gerrin. I'd woken up screaming and had to explain it somehow.

'Yeah,' I muttered.

How would I be able to look him in the eye? I certainly couldn't talk to him about it; imagine how that conversation would go.

'Hey, bro, sleep well last night?'

'Well, I stabbed you in the chest, but apart from that, great.'

'Nico?'

My concentration reluctantly swung back to Cosbi. 'I don't know who it was, or what it was... or even if it was real. Her scream though.'

'You hear it often?'

I nodded.

'And have you remembered anything more of Elena?'

'I saw her, but no memories. Sorry.'

'No need to apologise,' Cosbi said. 'Nico, I feel like I haven't been entirely honest with you about Elena. Saying you two were once close friends was a slight misrepresentation. She did once have... shall we say, a certain *physical* interest in you.'

'She... what? Are you kidding?' I scoffed.

'There's no need to be modest.'

My mouth must've resembled that of a goldfish. 'Are you listening to yourself? She hates me.'

I stood and paced to the other side of the room, both angry and disgusted with myself. My thoughts had taken a worrying turn into what it would be like with her, how that disgusting wretch would feel under my hands.

'I'm sorry, I'm making you uncomfortable,' Cosbi said.

'Do you need anything else, or can I go?'

'By all means, we can speak some more later.'

The memory of the expression on his face was haunting me. Pupils were glazed by early death, crushed with disappointment at my treachery. Two motionless hands were frozen in the hopeless act of stemming the river of liquid pouring from his heart.

'Whoa, where's the fire?' Gerrin said as he and I collided in the corridor.

I shook the image of the dead eyes from my mind and met the worried stare of the very real ones. Just a dream.

'Sorry. I was just coming to check... that you were...'

'That I'm what?'

'Erm... still here.'

'Is that all?' he said. 'I swear you'll be the death of me, Nic.'

I groaned inwardly, my conscience smarting at his choice of words.

'I was just on my way to see you, didn't realise the time,' he said. 'Did you want something?'

'Just to... chat?' I improvised.

'You were running hell for leather out of your room just to chat?'

'Oh. No, I guess not.'

'Out with it then.'

I hesitated. 'Have I ever... killed someone?'

His expression darkened. 'There's loads of ways of killing someone, Nic, what do you mean?'

'In cold blood, I guess.'

'You stand up for the people you love, but like that? No.'

Concerned at my line of questioning, Gerrin pressed for more details, but he was sounding stranger by the second. Red lights pricked at the back of my eyes, each flash accompanied by a shooting stab of pain. I squinted at him.

He took me by the shoulders, mistaking my discomfort for guilt. 'The fact that you're asking means you care. Good people don't kill in cold blood.'

I dropped my head into my hands, fingers trying to massage away the agony scorching across my forehead.

'Who was it?' Gerrin said.

'Who was what?'

'You dreamt you killed someone—who was it?'

I blinked; I was sweating far too much. 'Stranger. No one I recognised.'

'How did you do it?'

'Knife.'

'What did they do?'

Staying upright was proving tricky as my surroundings whirled around me. I guided my back against the wall.

'What did they do to you?' Gerrin pressed.

'I... I can't remember.'

Close to blacking out, I gasped at breaths and tried to focus on Gerrin's voice...

... 'This community room is fucking huge,' Gerrin said.

'Ye tois. Cosbi wants to speak tae ye both, now,' Ash said.

I looked up and saw the lanky Scot standing just metres away, watching us with a spiteful sneer.

'Ever heard of please?' Gerrin said.

'It was no' a request.'

We glanced sideways, wordlessly asking the same question of each other. Cosbi wanted our answer and we knew we'd have to give it sooner or later.

'Watch your fucking mouth in future,' Gerrin snarled as we strode past.

Ash's mouth curled into a smirk at the threat. The prat had some real delusions about his strength, blind overconfidence trumping the puny evidence. He wasn't God's gift to women in the looks department either—sleazy, greasy, with an eyebrow piercing someone had once told me was popular in the nineties.

A slim teenage girl in the distance glanced up as we approached, pulled her cardigan tight around her body and disappeared through the nearest door. Gerrin's fingers twitched in and out of balled fists. Cosbi would do his best to change our minds about leaving; we both knew it.

The vast rabbit warren twisted, turned and stretched in every direction as we traipsed the lengthy route. The path was familiar enough to me, but Gerrin hadn't been this far down yet.

I hadn't needed Gabriel to tell me how lucky he was to be alive, with the bullets only missing his heart by millimetres. I'd spent a tortured month at his bedside, heart breaking with the guilt of knowing it was my fault that he'd been shot outside. Often I thought it was only pure stubbornness that got him through, or maybe some stupid need to protect me.

'I'll be seein' ye around, boys,' the Scot drawled, knocking on Cosbi's door before tipping his head in sarcastic farewell.

'Come in.'

Not many people had been in here, but the rumours about his room weren't wrong. Apart from the community room, it was probably the largest space down here, lit by several ceiling bulbs. The flickering lights fell on Cosbi, reading glasses perched on the end of his nose as he flicked through a leather-bound book on a worn brown sofa.

'Where on earth did you get that?' I said, gawping at the first sofa I'd seen in years.

Cosbi smiled. 'Occasionally, Parker and Chase are lucky enough to come across trucks trading goods when they're out scavenging. We pay in food usually.'

'You wanted to see us?' Gerrin said.

'To business, of course, Gerrin,' he said. 'I hope you're fully recovered now?'

Gerrin nodded.

'It was a close call,' Cosbi said, reaching towards a bottle and three glasses. Sloshing amber liquid into them, he pointed to Gerrin's chest. 'It was a selfless thing you did, but you wouldn't have survived out there.'

'I'm aware of that,' Gerrin muttered, clearly more interested in swilling his drink around than anything Cosbi had to say.

'And you, Nico,' he said, turning next to me. 'Your brother wouldn't be here without you, dragging him over half a mile.'

I snorted and took a large slug of my drink to suppress a sarcastic comment. Gerrin wouldn't have been hurt at all if it wasn't for me.

'Is there a point to this meeting?' Gerrin said.

'There most certainly is,' Cosbi said, reclining with a smile. 'I was just trying to point out that you need us, and we need you.'

It was what we'd expected. Since our arrival, Cosbi hadn't been shy in voicing his wish for us to stay, rather than continue our journey north.

'Why do you need us?' Gerrin asked.

'Safety in numbers, and we can never have too many pairs of hands. Everyone here has a role—we all work together to keep our way of life safe. I always try to convince passers-by to stay.'

'It's just more mouths to feed.'

'Our supply is sound.'

'What's in it for us?'

'I would've thought it obvious,' he said. 'I can offer you food, shelter and safety—somewhere for you to build new lives. Why take the risk of travelling on and finding nothing?'

'And if we decide to leave?' Gerrin asked.

'Of course, you're free to go if you want, but I can't say I wouldn't be disappointed.'

Unfortunately for him, we'd made up our minds before we stepped foot through the door. With a quick exchange of unspoken agreement, we downed the dregs and rose to leave.

'Thanks for the offer, but we need to keep going,' Gerrin said.

Cosbi smiled. 'Of course, you must do what you think best.'

'We'll be on our way in the morning.'

'Can I just ask—is the decision to leave a mutual one?' Cosbi said, looking directly at me.

I felt Gerrin bristle with anger.

'My way lies with my brother,' I said. 'I trust whatever he decides.'

'Well, you know where I am if that changes.'

I had to get Gerrin out of there.

'You'll need supplies to make your journey,' Cosbi continued. 'Come see me first thing.'

I nodded my thanks and heaved Gerrin away from the sofa, propelling him back across the huge room and out through the door...

'... Nic?'

Someone was smacking my face.

'Nic? Nico.'

'What?'

Gerrin was waving his hand back and forth in front of my eyes. 'You OK?'

'Is everything all right?' a female voice whispered.

'He's out of it—go find Cosbi.'

Fighting the ache of nausea in my stomach, I grabbed the sleeve of Gerrin's T-shirt and dragged him out of earshot.

'Calm the hell down,' I hissed. 'We're leaving tomorrow, don't start causing trouble now.'

'Nic, what're you talking—'

'Don't get on the wrong side of him.'

'What? The wrong side of who?'

'Stop being so damn slow!'

The urgency behind my thoughts ebbed as I argued. I was puzzling at the sudden change in location when the return of the pain in my head hit me like a sledgehammer, knocking me off balance. 'We're still here.' I gasped. 'Why didn't we leave?'

'Right, that's it. I'm taking you back.'

Propped up by Gerrin, the familiar walls of my medical room were soon surrounding me.

'What happened?' Cosbi said as he strode in.

'He went blank for a couple of minutes, couldn't get anything out of him,' Gerrin said. 'He's been talking nonsense ever since.'

'Not nonsense,' I muttered. 'Was trying to stop you hitting Cosbi.'

'See?'

I greeted my bed gladly, burying my face in the pillow to banish the agonising bluish glare of the light overhead. A large weight depressed the mattress at my side.

'Nico, do you know where you are?' Gabriel said.

'I'm not stupid,' I garbled through the pillow.

'Turn over for me.'

I prised myself from the sheets, my head pounding with anger at the movement. Seeing Gabriel waiting with a bright torch, I clamped my hand tight over my eyes.

'I told you all this was a bad idea,' Gerrin raged.

Cosbi muttered something indistinct in reply.

'Look at the bloody state of him!' Gerrin shouted.

'Shut up, Gerrin!' I snapped.

'Light hurts your eyes?' Gabriel asked.

I nodded, wincing at my own stupidity. Nodding was bad.

'And your head?'

'Splitting.'

The mattress sprang back a few inches, and the sound of rustling came from across the room.

'Migraine,' Gabriel announced. 'Has he suffered from them before?'

'Not that I know of,' Gerrin answered.

'It could've been brought on by anything. Stress, tiredness, anxiety—'

'Flashback,' I groaned from behind my hands.

'You saw something?' Cosbi said.

'That would explain why he was away with the fairies,' Gerrin said. 'And why he told me we were leaving.'

'Leaving? The two of you were thinking of going years ago.'

'His memory of recent events is improving,' Gabriel said.

'At what cost though?' Gerrin said.

'What're you giving him, Gabriel?' Cosbi asked.

'Painkillers and sleeping pills. Looks like he could use both.'

Gabriel insisted on everyone leaving me in peace while the sleeping tablets kicked in. I crossed over to the mirror. It was nothing a good night's sleep wouldn't fix. I splashed cold water on my pale skin and rubbed at the tiredness in my bloodshot eyes, washing down the tablets with a glass of water. I sought out the comfort of the bed, enveloping myself in blissful quiet.

Left alone in the dark, my mind wandered.

Years later, we were still here. Gerrin had been so set on leaving. What'd happened to make him change his mind?

A snapshot of Cosbi lounging on his sofa snuck into my head, his fingers tightened around a brandy glass. Then a ruined farmhouse. The bullets hitting Gerrin square in the chest. A stunning girl with wavy blonde hair, opening a door as I went to knock on it. The weasel man meeting with Gerrin's temper. Those lifeless blue eyes and all that blood...

'What's up with poor baby Nico today?' Elena taunted from the shadows of 23. 'Has someone got no friends?'

She wouldn't leave me be. I was starting to think that being alone in this place hadn't been so bad after all.

I blocked her out and tried to focus on remembering, but there was only myself, knife in hand, seen through the ice-blue mirror of his eyes. The last dream was haunting me.

'Did nasty Elena hurt your feelings?'

I huffed in frustration.

There was a pause before the barest of whispers came from the corner. 'Did it feel good, murdering him?'

Dread stole over me, pricking at the hairs on my arms. My head twisted in her direction. 'What did you say?'

'*Murderer.*'

As filthy as the day I met her, she trod barefoot across the merciless crags of rock and came into the light.

'You... know?' I whispered.

'You wanted to kill him, more than you've ever wanted anything. And it felt *so damn good.*'

'It was just a dream.'

'Dreams can be more real than reality.'

'How do you know abou—'

'I know you better than him. Always have. Poor clueless Gerrin has no idea that he isn't safe to be alone with his homicidal baby brother.'

'Stop it!' I snapped.

'Didn't you mean to, Nico? Didn't you plan it? Who steals a knife if they don't intend to use it?'

I could do nothing but stare. She knew everything.

'How did you feel?' she pressed.

'Like I had nothing left to lose,' I whispered.

'You're still a dangerous man, eh, Blue Eyes?'

My heart sank. 'Help me. Help me remember.'

Her lips hooked up. 'To understand the end, you have to go back to the beginning.'

'Tree log, dead ahead!' I yelled over my shoulder, laughing as Gerrin didn't get the warning in time and tripped, pouring a string of foul language into the humid Italian air.

'Get back here, sneaky fucker!'

He'd claim I'd cheated once we reached the house. He wasn't going to win this race—judging by the odd, infrequent thumps on the undergrowth behind me, he would be hopping for the rest of the journey.

I broke free of the forest's shelter, not half a mile from home, and waited for the invalid to catch up. Red-faced, with bags of money and animal feed slung low on his back, he limped into the field five minutes later.

He threw me a resentful look and slumped on a nearby stile. 'Cheater.'

'Sore loser,' I mocked, tossing a cypress cone at him. 'You're too heavy to beat me.'

'But I can kick your arse when you stop.'

'Hope you didn't drop any money when you fell.'

'Sacrificed my foot for it.'

'Idiot,' I said with a laugh. 'Come on, dinner'll be nearly ready.'

Still huffing from the run, his short hair clinging to his sweaty forehead, Gerrin clambered to his feet.

'You'd better not let Mum hear you swearing like that,' I said as we stalked back down the hill towards home. 'You know she doesn't like it.'

'Nic, I'm fucking twenty—'

I turned, wondering why he'd broken off his typically coarse sentence, and caught him staring over my head. His face transformed as I watched, from carefree to terrified. Before I could even ask what was wrong, the bags had thudded to the ground and he was sprinting past me, pain no longer hampering his progress.

Knowing there was only one thing in the valley of fields behind, I followed his line of sight. There below me, its state unmistakable from the plume of dark smoke winding through the sultry air, were the blazing remains of an old farmhouse.

'*No...*' I breathed.

I tried to catch him up; I tried shouting his name as my arms pumped and my legs raced, propelling me down the hill. But he seemed to have found an inhuman speed from the depths of his panic.

I managed to get a hand on his shoulder as he wrenched open the wrought iron gate to the back orchard. 'What's happened?'

'Let me go, Nico!' he shouted, ripping my hand from his vest.

'I'm coming with you.'

'Like hell you are. You stay here until I call.'

'Gerrin—'

'Stay here!'

And with that he shot through the gate, leaving me staring at the wreckage of what'd been our house. All I could do was watch the rising cloud of ash and pray to God that they hadn't been in there.

Ten minutes passed before I could stand it no longer. Vaulting the gate without bothering to open it, I sprinted across the debris-strewn field, searching for any sign of my three family members.

I saw him when I rounded the stone wall into the back courtyard. On his knees in the wild grass, Gerrin's gaze was fixed at the level of the house, the only sign of life the jolted movement of his breaths.

Once again I followed his eye line, and once again, I saw something I didn't want to.

Just visible through the cloud of smoking grey, almost buried beneath a pile of rubble, were two hands clasped in union. Firelight twinkled off a dust-covered gold wedding band, a trickle of blood dripping from the slender finger into the licking flames below.

AUTOSCOPY

I SKIDDED TO a halt on the pebble beach, tossing two backpacks and a gun inside the old wooden rowing boat, the momentum almost sending me in head first after them.

'Here!' I shouted, grabbing the oars from the trunk of a nearby tree.

We'd managed to outrun the crowd, and Gerrin was firing warning shots at anyone daring to come close, trying to deter them from swamping or stealing our escape craft. People were dancing around the bullets, trying to find a way through. The noise of the gun drowned out my voice.

'*Gerrin!*'

He turned and sprinted towards me, just as the front line of men in camouflage appeared on the horizon.

There was a huge crash and fireworks shot into the sky, raining down silver sparks, as the boat house on the beach exploded into flames.

Gerrin's eyes widened like a rabbit in headlights. He fell to his knees, hands over his ears, seemingly unable to move.

I stumbled back up the beach.

'Come on!' I urged.

But he stayed put, limbs trembling.

'That's not home, Gerrin,' I said. 'They weren't in there. Come back to me now.'

Still he didn't move.

I knelt in front of him and thrust my hand in front his face.

Slowly, he looked up. Shakily, he reached for my hand and clasped it with his own.

'Come back,' I said.

He nodded and allowed himself to be pulled to his feet. We dived for the boat and pushed off into the channel, Gerrin hitting out at the approaching crowd threatening to drag us under as I rowed us out to safety.

For the first time in weeks, I wanted to forget. But the image of my parents' entwined, lifeless hands was emblazoned in my memory, never again to be unseen.

'I can't even imagine having to live through that again,' Gerrin said, shaking his head.

'The first time was bad enough,' I said.

'I tried to stop you seeing.'

'I know, but they were my family too.'

'You were a headstrong kid,' Gerrin said. 'Mum and Dad tried for hours every day to get you off your bloody bike and in the bath.'

I smiled. 'I think I miss them.'

He put his hand on my shoulder. 'Me too, Nic. If I could take that memory from you, I would.'

Frightened by what it could produce, my memory shut down completely. And that wasn't even the worst of it. Concerned by the increasing severity of the migraines, Gabriel had threatened to put a stop to the whole experiment before I caused myself permanent damage.

But I craved the drug. Sleep was difficult without it, and the few moments of exhilaration after I woke were somehow worth the hours spent in Elena's company. And admitting that to Gabriel was the surest way of never getting it again.

Fortunately for me, it seemed that whatever Cosbi wanted, Cosbi got. And that meant the continuation of the experiment, which left me free to plan how I was going to get to room 23.

I'd waited until midnight before trying my luck.

Cranking my door open a fraction allowed me an unrestricted view of the path weaving away from my door and the freedom it offered. There was also a man perched right in the middle of it. I quickly ducked back in.

'Sod this,' the Scot muttered as the chair scraped backwards and boots thudded away.

Ash.

'... think he is?'

The booted thuds turned and came back.

'... no' a fuckin' guard dog.'

He stopped outside the door.

'... wide-o needs bringin' down a peg or two.'

He finished his solitary argument by aiming a kick at the chair, which jumped a few feet down the corridor with a noisy clatter.

'Oi, idiot!'

'Oh, fuck off, Jakes.'

'Fancy shutting the hell up?' Gerrin said, footsteps entering the medical bay from the main corridor. 'Or are you trying to wake the whole place?'

'Aren't ye missing yer beauty sleep, pretty boy?'

'Haven't I told you to watch your mouth?'

'Or what?'

'Or Cosbi and I might have to have a little chat.'

'Wait 'til he finds out what you've had me daein' toni—'

'It was Cosbi's order for you to be on watch tonight,' Gerrin interrupted.

'Why?' was the eventual petulant reply.

'Why you? No idea. But you know why we need someone here.'

'That ah do, blondie.' There was a smile in Ash's voice as he raised his volume. 'So maybe ah'll just let him out—'

'Shut it, now.'

Approaching steps signalled my cue to leave. Leaping back into bed, I wedged my eyes shut, trying to ignore the chink of light that rested on them as the door was held open. I held my breath, not daring to move until Gerrin's curiosity was satisfied.

'You're one lucky son of a bitch,' he said to Ash. 'That would've been game over for you. You wake him or let him out, it'll be the last thing you ever do.'

Conceding defeat for the night, I settled myself down for a few hours of unexpected, disappointing sleep.

A guard.

Elena had called me a dangerous man. I wasn't. Was I?

Breath poured like smoke from my mouth as the warmth condensed in the damp air.

'*Damn,* stupid door!'

My attention snapped to the right, where a slim young woman was wrestling with the handle of a door marked with a coarse *20*, a huge cardboard box balanced precariously between hand and raised knee.

If she was doing her own furniture removals, then she was hardly dressed for it. A quick glance down took in a small skirt that skimmed her thighs as she struggled with her cargo, and a clingy T-shirt pulled tight over the top.

'Open, you bloody... stupid... son of a—' She cut off her own sentence with an exasperated snarl, flicking strands of silky dark hair out of her pretty face.

'Ye awrite there, doll?'

I rolled my eyes as the irritating owner of the Glaswegian accent came jogging down the corridor, shoving past a group of disgruntled women carrying folded clothes, a gratified smirk on his face as he drank in the numerous charms of his damsel in distress.

'Tha' looks heavy. Would ye like some help?'

She furiously rounded on the offer, glaring at the Scot like he'd caused the sticky door lock. Her eyes caught my gaze like the chocolate-brown irises were black holes, drawing me in. I'd know that expression anywhere.

'Woah, ah come in peace,' Ash said, holding up his hands.

Elena's face relaxed into an apologetic frown. 'Sorry, bad day.'

'Lit me get that for ye,' he said, arms snaking around the box.

'Oh, thanks.'

Now box-free, she took out her annoyance with both hands and the door yielded. 'A couple of guys were meant to be giving me a hand.'

'I've got a free half hour—ah can help if ye like?'

'If you're sure you don't mind?'

'It's no' bother. If it's the lads ah think it is, they would no' ha' been much help anyway.'

Elena laughed and took possession of the box. 'Did Cosbi send me a couple of wimps?'

Ash's jaw hooked up into an ugly, crooked smile. 'Is it just these?' he asked, pointing to three remaining boxes strewn down the corridor.

'Yes, thanks.'

'Oi, idiot!'

I turned to see another man stalking up the corridor, his stubbled jaw clenched tight in dislike. As he passed by me, the light threw his features into sharp relief and my breath caught in my throat. The man was blue-eyed, dark-haired, tall and athletic.

The man was... me.

A younger me.

'Speaking of wimps...' drawled the Scot.

'What're you doing here?' Younger Me snapped.

'Doing yer job, by the looks of it.'

'Well, I'm here now, so you can bugger off.'

'Did yer mother no' teach ye manners, Jakes?'

The man went to open his mouth again, but was interrupted by someone hollering. 'Nico! Gerrin needs you at the front. Someone's outside!'

Younger me looked torn between the danger outside and not leaving Elena alone with such a scumbag.

'Go,' Elena volunteered. 'This guy can help me.'

Ash smirked.

'I'll be fifteen minutes,' Younger Me promised and ran off with more than one backward glance.

'Never seen you roon' these parts a'fore,' Ash continued.

'Oh, sorry, I'm Elena.'

'Ash,' he replied, reaching out to shake the hand that'd appeared from the side of the box.

With the shutting of the door, whatever was happening in the room was beyond my reach, and the landscape slid momentarily out of focus, blurry rock surrounding me until a yell dragged the memory back into clarity.

Younger me was back outside Elena's room, hand poised and ready to knock, when the door flew open and a stumbling Ash was propelled through it with a yelp of pain. Younger me moved quickly, neatly sidestepping the action with a look of amused surprise on his face.

Clutching at his groin, a snarling Ash turned, not prepared to accept such humiliation. 'Bitch! Fuckin' tease!' he roared, wincing as the movement jolted his injured crotch. 'Bendin' over in a skirt like that, wi' that arse.'

Elena's eyes were alight with fire, nostrils flared. 'You think you can just take what you want, even when a woman says no? *Twice!*'

The amusement vanished from the face of Younger Me, and there was a deadly softness to his voice when he spoke. 'You tried to force her?'

'The wee whore was leadin' me on!' Ash spat.

Younger me didn't even have time to respond before Elena stormed forwards, drew back her fist and thumped Ash in the eye. The Scot landed heavily on his backside and looked utterly flabbergasted for several moments, now pawing at both his wounded face and groin.

Struggling to stifle a laugh, Younger Me plonked Ash back on his feet with a rough grip on his T-shirt. 'I suggest you learn when a woman isn't interested. Which in your case must be most of the time.'

Offended, Ash took an ill-timed and poorly balanced swing at Younger Me's face, which was easily dodged, leaving the Scot to crash headfirst into the wall behind.

'Leave. Now,' Younger Me said. 'And if I catch you here again, there's not a single bone in your body I won't break. Got it?'

Ash clutched at his head and backed away. 'Ye tois deserve each other. Enjoy yer fuckin' tart, Jakes.'

The two people left in the corridor were both silent, tense; two complete strangers awkward in each other's presence, having been introduced in the most bizarre of circumstances.

Finally, Younger Me heaved an angry sigh and his shoulders relaxed slightly. 'Are you OK?'

'Yes.'

'Are you hurt?'

'No.'

He nodded, and the awkward silence returned.

Water dripped through the uncomfortable vacuum.

'I could use a drink, how about you?' he offered as he made a move to head down the corridor.

'Don't go!' Elena blurted out, looking mortified as soon as she'd said it.

'I'll be two minutes, I swear.'

After a moment's thought, she nodded.

He reappeared as promised within two minutes, bearing a large bottle, two tumblers and a packet of pre-rolled cigarettes. He knocked on the door and entered, and this time I was free to follow.

Elena had changed in his absence, the unwanted evidence of Ash's attentions now lying forgotten in the bin. He poured two healthy measures of the spirit and handed one over, along with a cigarette. He struck two matches, one for her, one for him, and clouds of smoke poured into the air.

'Thanks,' she murmured, taking a drag.

'You've hurt your hand,' he observed.

I could see it too. By the firelight, her knuckles were beginning to swell and bruise.

'It was worth it,' she said with a shrug.

Despite the situation, the two of them broke into a giggle.

'Cracking punch,' he said with a grin.

'Nice dodging,' she shot back.

He tipped his head at the glass. 'Drink.'

She followed the advice, her face screwing up at the sharp taste. 'Oh, that's nasty.'

They both burst into laughter again.

'Nico Jakes,' he said, holding out his hand.

'Elena Martinez,' she replied, shaking it.

'I can stay tonight, if you'd feel easier?' he asked, before hurriedly correcting himself. 'On the floor I mean, of course.'

'That's kind of you, but I can't expect you to sleep down there.'

'It's fine, I'll go grab the mattress off my bed—I live right across the hall, room Twenty-one.'

'We're neighbours?' Elena beamed.

I watched them for several moments.

My being there had been pointless. She hadn't needed me; in fact, I doubted she'd needed anyone for a very long time. And despite myself, all I could think was, *Christ, what a woman.*

JAILBREAK

I WAS SO preoccupied that evening that I almost forgot to check if there was a guard.

This newfound admiration for Elena had thrown me off balance. Denying any attraction had come easily when talking to Cosbi, but dwelling on the issue had made me less certain. Had she loved me? Had I loved her? The prospect no longer seemed quite so ridiculous.

And then there was Ash. I couldn't linger on that subject too long—the thought of him prowling unchecked made my blood boil. With men like that living here, I found Hanna's anxiety perfectly reasonable.

A flash of his filthy hands on Elena shot through my head.

My boot lashed out and caught an unfortunate table leg, the wood shuddering in protest. Stuffing my fists in my pockets seemed to work, if only by stopping me from throwing open the door and finding the bastard.

The door. The thought of it was enough to bring the plan back into my head, and I realised with a rush of anticipation that it must be nearing midnight.

Something felt different tonight.

The door inched open. My body squeezed through the gap.

No one.

The chair sat in the usual spot, but it'd been abandoned, now the sole witness to the secret comings and goings of the night caves.

Even stranger than the lack of guard was the large oak door separating me from my former home. It stood wide open.

It was almost like someone wanted me to do this.

Stealing away, my path lit only by the occasional struck match from the box in my hand, I hoped that, just like in my dream, my journey would be uninterrupted. The success of this mission would determine whether or not I could ever try it again.

It took ten minutes to travel the long corridor. For stealth reasons,

before the flame ate through the matchstick and burnt my fingers, I managed a glimpse of my surroundings, my skin prickling at what I saw.

Clothes, shoes, books and pictures lay abandoned or hung lifelessly in places they never normally would've been. Cupboards and wardrobes had vomited their contents onto the floor, having been flipped upside down. The mirror had been smashed, the bed frame broken.

I felt my way to where I knew her dresser had been and found a candle and lighter after ferreting on the floor. The dancing flame was a welcome relief to my eyes after straining to see for the past half hour, and it confirmed what I'd seen in the brief match light.

My fingers brushed over the debris, occasionally overturning objects that looked vaguely interesting. But there were no clues about what'd happened here.

I'd almost decided my instinct to visit the old room of my enemy had been wrong when I spotted a charred patch of rock in the corner. Amongst a few rags of burnt clothing and some cold pieces of wood, pieces of white flecked the kindling.

Crouching down, I picked through the sooty remains, retrieving several pieces of half-burnt paper. One fragment had been covered with a drawing, a map of sorts, but it was unrecognisable. The only other evidence looked like a list of names beneath a date, but only the edge had survived being set alight.

Whoever had lit the fire had done so in a hurry; something in those papers had needed to be hidden.

My head was starting to pound with the effort of concentrating in the gloom. I knew the feeling, and knew I had to move quickly; it was a long way to get back before I could surrender to the migraine. I stuffed the scraps of paper in my trouser pocket and blew out the candle.

It was already starting. My surroundings were spinning, a dancing medley of darkness, rock, floor and ceiling. Clamping my eyelids shut, I felt my way out of the room.

I made it three steps down the corridor before it hit, more ruthless and sudden than ever before. With a loud ringing in my ears, earth and sky inverted, and I fell to the floor.

No, not here. This couldn't happen here.

The pounding of my heartbeat was imprinted on the inside of my eyelids, blood forcing itself too quickly through my head. Blindly, I grasped at what I thought must be the wall, trying to find a way up.

'What're you doing down here?'

His voice had a familiar sternness to it.

The agony eased away like the sea tide leaving the shore, leaving me free to use my eyes. Like I needed them to know who'd found me.

BREADCRUMBS

'WHAT'RE YOU DOING down here?' Gerrin repeated. 'Nico?'
Legs splayed across the corridor, I was sitting with my back
against the wall outside 20, bouncing a ball off the wall opposite.

'What does it bloody look like I'm doing?' I said, sighing as his blank
expression didn't budge. 'I'm waiting for that girl—the one Cosbi told us
to help.'

'Oh shit, yeah. Change of plan—emergency meeting and you're late.
Didn't you get the message?'

'No, what meeting?'

'Sodding Shaun, useless. Room one, soon as you can.'

'Might as well come now—God knows how long she'll be.' I threw out
my hand, and he used it to haul me to my feet.

'So, is this your secret?' he asked.

'Huh?'

'Camping outside their rooms until they can't ignore you anymore?
You're only nineteen—you've learned quickly.'

I cuffed him over the back of the head.

'Ow! What? You would've been long gone if it was a bloke moving in.'

We burst into laughter and tramped down to Cosbi's room.

One month after arriving at the caves...

A SMART RAP on my door was closely followed by Cosbi's head around
the side of it. 'Liking the new room?'

'It's only for a month,' I replied, not bothering to stop unpacking and
look at him.

'You're feeling let down, I get it.'

I shoved my empty rucksack under the double bed upgrade I'd been given and positioned the photo of my parents in pride of place on the bedside cabinet. As always.

'It's not so bad here, is it?' he said.

I snorted.

'Perhaps if you took the time to get to know us a little better—'

I turned on him. 'What did you say to him?'

Uninvited, he closed the door behind him and went to sit on my bed.

'Gerrin? He came to collect the supplies you requested, we chatted, about many things, and he left—without nearly hitting me this time.'

'Chatted about what?'

He sighed. 'Nico, you saw for yourself how determined he was to go. Do you honestly think I could've swayed him?'

'And yet he's mysteriously changed his mind.'

'You can't blame him for wanting to be well enough to keep you safe. He's only doing what your parents asked of him.'

I threw daggers at him; he had no right to talk about my parents.

'It's not easy out there, you know that better than anyone,' he prompted.

'He can take care of hi—'

'He isn't thinking about himself.'

'And you know that, do you?'

'I know only what he told me.'

'Which is?'

'That he's afraid of losing you. You mean everything to him.'

My jaw dropped; Gerrin would sooner jump off a bridge than discuss his feelings, even with me. 'He wouldn't lose me.'

'You're all he has left.'

'It's not going to get better out there in a month.'

'But he will be more prepared to face it.'

'Why doesn't he just talk to me?' I asked, more of myself than Cosbi.

'Because it's Gerrin,' Cosbi said.

I sighed. 'Maybe I was a bit hard on him.'

'He'll live,' he said, grasping my shoulder. 'I've a favour to ask of both of you actually, if you have a spare hour during your remaining time here?'

'What?'

'There's a family moving in a few doors down. They've been living in another part of the caves and it'd be good for them to get to know a friendly face. Would you check in on them, see if they need anything?'

'Whatever,' I said with a shrug.

'Appreciate it. Room nineteen.'

'Stop being miserable,' I said, lobbing a balled towel at him. 'It's got to be better than sitting in here all day.'

'Do one, Nic,' Gerrin said, frowning in annoyance as the bundle hit him in the face.

'Where did you get the fags from, anyway?' I asked.

'Cosbi.'

'Come on. It'll only take ten minutes.'

'I'm not in the mood.'

'Afraid you might have fun?'

'I said *no.*'

'God, you're hard work sometimes,' I sighed. 'Fine, I'll go on my own.'

I left him to sulk, grabbing a coat from my room on the way and running some water through my hair. Looking a bit more presentable, five minutes later, I stood alone outside room 19.

It was a comedy of errors. At exactly the same moment I knocked on the door, the girl inside opened it. Still talking to someone behind her, she hadn't anticipated finding someone on the doorstep and screamed, instinctively slamming it shut. Not getting my face out of the way quick enough, the wood smacked me full force in the head as it swung closed.

'*Fuck!*' I hissed.

Recovering from the shock and realising what she'd done, the girl dashed to where I was bent over and tried to prise away the hand pressed to my forehead. 'Oh my gosh, I'm so sorry! Are you OK?'

'I'll live,' I muttered.

'Come inside, please.'

'It's fine.'

'At least let me check you—'

'No, really—' I snapped, emerging from behind my hand to show her I wasn't in the mood, but somehow I forgot what I was about to say.

Crouched low and trying to peek up under my hand was a girl of around seventeen, her pretty blue eyes wide with concern.

I blinked in surprise. 'I... I... erm... what?'

'See, you're not OK—you don't even know what you're saying.'

I didn't have the courage to tell her it wasn't the head injury that had robbed me of words.

She tucked a strand of long, wavy blonde hair behind her ear, her cheeks flushing slightly as I stared.

'No, no, I'm fine really,' I said, trying to straighten up and banging my head on a low crag. 'Ow.'

Her giggle sent shock waves through my body.

'If you won't come in, then maybe you should tell me what I can do for you,' she said. 'Were you coming to see us?'

'Yes, you. Well, not you. I mean, not just you, though I did want to see you,' I spluttered and then sighed.

'Let's start again,' she said, and I could hear she was smiling at me. 'I'm Louisa.'

'Nico,' I said, managing to state my own name without embarrassing myself further.

'Nice to meet you, Nico. Now, will you let me see?'

Mortified, I let my hand drop so she could see just what an oaf I'd been.

'It's erm... not too bad,' she whispered, her eyes darting to her feet after briefly connecting with my spellbound gaze.

'It was only a knock,' I said with a shrug, dragging back the remains of my dignity. 'Cosbi asked me to come see you, check if you needed anything.'

'What's going on, Louisa?' a female voice called from inside.

'We have a visitor,' Louisa responded.

The woman emerged from the room, smiling easily at me. 'Pleased to meet you, I'm Constance. Did Cosbi send you?'

'Nico,' I answered, shaking the offered hand. 'Just to see if you needed anything.'

'That's kind of you, but I think we're good for now.'

'Oh. OK. Well, if you need anything, my room's just across there.'

'Thank you, I daresay I'll take you up on that,' Constance said.

'No problem,' I said, knowing that was my cue to leave, but my legs refused to budge.

'Thank you for coming,' Louisa said, catching my arm as I finally turned to go.

My thumping heart practically leapt out of my throat as her fingers connected with my body, electricity zipping up my arm. I paused for a moment longer than was comfortable, hoping against all hope that she'd ask me to stay.

My God, pull yourself together.

'Seriously, get a haircut,' I said. 'You'll have enough for a ponytail soon.'

Gerrin shrugged. '*You* get a fucking haircut. The girls here love it, apparently.'

'You need to stop listening to that Roxan—'

I stopped mid-sentence, Gerrin grunting as I slapped a backhand into his stomach, halting our progress down the corridor.

'Hey!' I shouted. 'Hey, Louisa! Louisa, over here!' I waved to get her attention, bouncing on the balls of my feet.

Gerrin snorted.

Sneaking in a swift side-punch to the ribs, I half ran, half jogged the distance between me and her, trying not to appear too eager.

'Oi, twat!' Gerrin shouted.

She'd just left her room, looking up and smiling as I approached. My stomach flipped a perfect somersault.

'Oh hey,' I said, thumbing behind me. 'Just saw you back there and thought I'd come say hi. Are you off somewhere?'

'I was going to ask Cosbi if we could go outside for an hour if it's clear,' she said. 'Go and read for a bit on the hill while Rae plays.'

'Ah, cool, cool. So... what're you reading?' I asked, pointing to the book she had clutched against her chest.

She held it out for me to see.

'Collins?' I said, reading the cover and frowning. 'Is it a, er... romance?'

'No,' she said, smiling and pulling shyly on her blonde ponytail. 'It's more a sort of detective story, about a stolen diamond.'

'Oh,' I said, realising I was out of my depth on this subject. 'I've been meaning to go out myself, you know. Get a bit of fresh air. Hey, maybe I could come with you. Keep you company?'

'Oh! Oh, I like to read alone. Thanks though. I mean, maybe next time?'

'Oh. Sure. Sure.'

She chanced a quick glance at my face and a brief smile, before practically sprinting off in the opposite direction.

Gerrin appeared at my side seconds later, unable to stop sniggering at me being left red-faced. 'Man, you just got well and truly friend-zoned. Who is she anyway? She'd be hot if she dropped the whole librarian thing.'

Six weeks after arriving at the caves...

'MORNING.'

I peeled my eyelids apart, blinking back the whisky grogginess gluing them together, somewhat confused that I seemed to be sharing a room with someone.

'Oh, hi,' I croaked.

Elena's floor, of course.

She was lying in bed with her head propped up on her elbow, staring down at me with piercing brown eyes. Sleep had tousled her dark hair and it fell messily around her chest, the nest of blankets cocooning her bare chest.

'Thanks for staying with me last night,' she said.

'No problem. But I'll need some practice before I drink with you again.'

We'd spent a good part of the night talking, doing cheap whisky shots and playing drinking games before collapsing into bed in the early hours. I'd hoped to take her mind off Ash, but found myself genuinely enjoying her company.

'Sleep well?' she asked.

'Well enough.'

'I told you I didn't mind sharing.'

'Oh, it's fine,' I said, smiling awkwardly. 'I don't think that would've—
oh shit, what's the time?'

'Lights have been on about an hour,' she said, pointing to the
illumination creeping under her door. 'Must be just after eight.'

I scrambled out of the blankets, grateful that I'd decided to leave my
trousers on. 'I have to be somewhere,' I said, stuffing my T-shirt and shoes
on. 'I'll come grab my mattress later, OK?'

'Last night was fun, Nico,' she said with a grin, two bare legs slipping
from under the covers as I made for the exit.

I swallowed and managed to keep my eyes up. 'Yeah, it was.'

That summer was a scorcher. The midday sun beat down mercilessly on
the grassy hillside, slow-cooking the cave inhabitants as they sunbathed,
frolicked and snoozed.

Camouflaged amongst tree branches and regretting not borrowing
Jean's binoculars, I pretended to loosen apples while my unchecked gaze
sought something far better than fruit. Cartwheeling children,
disapproving mothers and beer-bellied fathers passed through my field
of vision, distracting me from my search. Exasperated, I laid a steadying
hand on the top wooden rung and leaned out to get a better view.

Finally, I glimpsed her.

Sat in the shade of a large oak, back against the trunk, Louisa had
her nose planted in a thick book. Absentmindedly, she twirled a ringlet
around her finger, stopping occasionally to wipe her cheeks, eyes darting
across the page.

My longing gaze was, as ever, unrequited attention. I would've had to
be a dashing literary hero to catch the eye of the beautiful Louisa Hewson.
And she was oblivious to everyday Nico Jakes.

I sighed.

I was jolted back into reality as something came whizzing past my
ear, missing me by centimetres. Before I could react, another missile had
bounced off my head.

'Fuck off!' I yelled at my unknown assailant, waving my arms.

I heard the laughter of women.

'Language, Jakes. Children present...' a voice taunted.

I pulled back the branches and saw Elena standing below, flanked by two younger girls.

'Fuck off, Elena!' I yelled back louder, meeting with more laughter.

'Who're you stalking up there?'

'Just making sure everyone's safe,' I lied.

Louisa still hadn't looked up and the basket had been full of apples long enough to start looking suspicious, so I gave up and climbed down.

Elena passed me a glass of water.

'Thanks,' I said, drinking half and tipping the rest over my hair. I shook it out and cold rivers poured down my warm chest. I passed the basket of apples to the two younger girls to take to Cosbi.

'So who were you really looking at?' Elena said. 'The boring blonde over by the tree, or do you want to bat for *that* team?' Smirking, she nodded at a group of guys who'd struck up a crude game of cricket with a plank of wood and an old tennis ball.

'Not my sport,' I said.

Her front teeth sank into her bottom lip, a finger reaching out to trace a trail of water down my arm. 'In that case, how do you fancy another drink sometime? I've got something stronger in my room, stole it from the supply cupboard.'

'Sure, sounds great.'

But I wasn't really paying attention anymore. Over her shoulder, I'd noticed Gerrin had tired of the attentions of the captive female audience watching him strum an old guitar on the grass and had spotted Louisa sitting alone. Brushing grass from his jeans, he jumped to his feet and trekked towards the oak, his admirers begging fruitlessly for one more tune.

'Hey!' Elena said, snapping her fingers in front of my face.

'Sorry, got to go,' I said, darting around her. 'Do me a favour and just tell Chase that Cosbi's looking for Gerrin?'

I moved swiftly over to Louisa, throwing out various appeasements to people who tried to talk to me as I passed and trying not to seem too panicked. I couldn't lose this one to Gerrin.

Arriving at the tree, I found him lounging against the bark, hand in pocket, taking a long drag of a cigarette. Louisa was smiling politely at something he'd just said.

'What's so funny?' I said.

'Oh, I was just telling Library Girl here about that time Mum caught you trying on her lipstick,' Gerrin said.

The warmth from my bare chest crept up my neck and into my cheeks. I glared at him.

'Don't listen to him, Nico,' Louisa said, aiming a shy smile at me. 'Gerrin was telling me about how he'd been scouted by a football team when he was a teenager.'

'Yeah, third division!' I laughed.

Gerrin scowled. 'I'd still beat y—'

'Oi, Gerrin! Cosbi's looking for you,' Chase called as he jogged past.

Gerrin looked torn between obeying and not leaving me alone with Louisa. 'Save me a space, Library Girl,' he said, with a deliberate flex of his arms.

I rolled my eyes.

'He's a... confident man,' Louisa said, as he jogged off.

I dropped to the floor and sat cross-legged opposite her. 'Yeah, he can be real charming too, but he has a short attention span. I wouldn't want to see you get hurt.'

She looked down at her lap and fiddled with her hair. 'I'm sure he's nice, but I'm not really interested. Thanks for the warning though.'

'Best let him down hard then,' I laughed. 'He doesn't get subtle.'

She smiled at me. 'How would you do it?'

'Well, nothing would say no quite like him seeing you with someone else.'

'Like who?'

'I'm happy to help out,' I said with a hopeful grin.

She tensed and pointed to her book. 'Thanks, but I'm on the last chapter. Maybe another time?'

The sound of shouting drowned out the awkwardness of my second rejection, followed swiftly by the metallic clanking of the old bell at the cave entrance. I jumped to my feet, yanking the knife from the waistband of my jeans. I pulled Louisa up.

'Get inside, now!' I said.

'Not without my family!'

I scanned the hillside and spotted Constance holding Rae, caught up in the panicked crowd heading for the entrance.

'There, go!' I said.

Louisa nodded and took off as several people thudded to my side.
'What is it?' Elena said.
'Group of outsiders. Somewhere near the forest,' Parker said.
'Here!' Gerrin said, tossing weapons to everyone.
'You guys, this way. Chase, get everyone else back inside,' I said.

Two months after arriving at the caves...

'I've got to get back!' Louisa whispered.

I caught her around the waist and pulled her back into my arms. 'Already?'

'Mum'll think you're a bad influence,' she said with a smile, trying to prise herself from my hold.

'And she'd be right.'

'You'll come see me tomorrow though?'

'You have to ask?'

We walked hand in hand back towards the room she shared with her mother and sister.

'Mum likes you too much to think badly of you,' she said.

'She does?'

'Yeah, you can do no wrong.'

'If only Gerrin were as supportive.'

'He'll come round,' she said. 'It's been the two of you for so long, it must be difficult for him to accept there's someone new in your life.'

I stopped and stared at her. 'You're amazing, do you know that? Not many people would've put up with the way he's been with you.'

'I know how much he means to you.'

We weren't that far from her room, but I wanted to prolong the moment until she closed that door on me again.

A low murmuring sound greeted my ears as we walked.

'Hold on a second,' I whispered, pulling her against the wall.

'What's—' she began, before I put a finger across her lips.

We were outside Parker and Chase's room, which Cosbi seemed to have chosen as the location for his meeting. Having caught the second voice in the argument, I knew this was a conversation I couldn't miss.

'I don't understand, Gerrin.'

'You heard me.'

'I did, but I'm still at a loss.'

'We're staying.'

'Why the sudden change of heart?'

'It's unimportant.'

There was silence for a few moments.

'Did Nico change his mind?' Cosbi said.

Another pause.

'Did he give a reason?' he continued.

'He met someone, that's all.'

'Ah, of course.' There was a hint of amusement in Cosbi's voice. 'Who's the lucky lady?'

'She just moved in near us. Blonde.'

Cosbi laughed. 'Understandable. She is quite beautiful.'

'I just wish he hadn't gone and—' Gerrin paused. 'Wait, that's it, isn't it?'

'That's what?'

'*Her.*'

'Her what?'

'Very well played,' Gerrin sneered.

'What are you accusing me of?'

'Like you don't know—the timing is too coincidental. Or were you hoping I'd fall for it instead?'

'Gerrin—'

'Is she in on it?'

'Won't you sit—'

With a snarl, Gerrin made a beeline for the door.

'Quick,' I whispered to Louisa, pulling her into the safety of the hidden bend in the corridor.

But he was coming this way.

'Act natural,' I said and raised my voice. 'I've had an amazing afternoon.'

She laughed. 'Me too. Come for dinner tomorrow?'

'I'd love to.'

We rounded the corner again and found ourselves face to face with a visibly irate Gerrin. I pretended to be surprised. 'Oh, hey!'

'I want to speak to you later,' he said. 'Any chance you'll be alone, or do I have to make an appointment?'

I put my hand out as he went to pass and it collided with his chest. 'You're being a bit rude.'

He shoved my hand away and glared at Louisa. '*Alone.*'

I stared after him as he continued down the corridor.

'What did all that mean?' Louisa said.

'Gerrin thinks Cosbi moved you near me on purpose, to stop us from leaving.'

'And is he right?'

'It's possible, I guess.'

'*Are* you only staying because of me?'

'I can't leave you here. That's just not an option anymore.'

She frowned. 'I don't want to cause trouble between you two.'

'You couldn't even if you tried.'

'But you hate it here.'

'I can't hate anywhere that you are.' I stroked her cheek as she looked up at me with those beautiful blue eyes. It wasn't that I couldn't leave her, I just didn't want to.

'We're not fucking tourists, Nic,' Gerrin complained. 'And there are far more interesting things to do around here.'

His eyes locked on two young women walking towards us carrying bowls of water, and he shifted as they passed, to continue watching from behind. One of the girls turned and smirked, whispering something to her friend.

I grabbed the back of his hoodie, pre-empting him trying to follow. 'We're trying to fit in here. Make friends, talk, smile. Try it.'

He pulled a mock grimace of a smile.

A door ahead of us opened, and a couple exited, followed by Cosbi who stopped in the doorway. The woman smiled and took his hand, pressing it between her palms.

'Thank you,' she said.

'Appreciate the advice,' the man added.

'Always a pleasure,' Cosbi said, with a nod of his head. 'Let me know how it goes.'

The man put his arm around the woman's shoulders and led her away.

'Ah, gentlemen,' Cosbi said, smiling as he noticed us loitering in the passageway. 'Ready for the grand tour?'

'Like you wouldn't believe,' Gerrin said.

I kicked him in the shin.

Cosbi's mouth twitched in amusement. 'Right, let's see. Nothing but bedrooms that way. We have several lovely ladies who bring water twice daily to all the rooms.' He pointed to the two girls now far in the distance. 'There's an underground stream at the north of the cave system. Drinking and washing are upstream, toilet facilities are further downstream. If you're looking for the man who ensures everything here runs smoothly, then look no further than room two.' He nodded at the room across from his, where a large balding man was just visible through a thin opening in the door.

Idly, I wondered if he had moved since someone had wheeled him in there. The man dabbed at his sweaty head and scribbled on his papers.

'He rarely moves,' Cosbi confirmed, reading my mind. 'Follow me.'

'It's freezing down here. How do you all keep warm in winter?' I said.

'We just keep moving,' Cosbi said. 'Lots of duvets and blankets at night. Body heat helps a lot.'

'Not a problem,' Gerrin quipped.

'Medical bay is at the end of that long corridor,' Cosbi continued. 'Our doctor lives in room three and there are a couple of nurses here too. Store cupboard with medical supplies is down there on the right.'

He moved on quickly, leading us through a narrow corridor that weaved like a black river through the caverns, until cold fresh air cut through the stale water smell and flowed into my lungs.

'Cave entrance,' Cosbi announced as we stepped into a crossroads of the path. Air thick with moisture filled the space, the patter of rain audible on the ground outside. 'Jean and Robert here take shifts at keeping watch.'

'*Walk!*' the man on the left bellowed, as two children came racing through the tunnel, the leader squealing in anticipation of being tagged. 'Apologies, *monsieurs*,' he said, approaching to shake hands.

I'd decided to go barefoot, and that had consequences. The rocks were ridiculously slippery where water trailed across the surface, and excruciating when you caught them wrong. And my feet were freezing.

The Gerrin nightmare had taught me the way. Taking a left, I sensed from the shortening echoes that I was approaching a dead end. Striking a match confirmed my fear and I found myself practically face first in a stone wall.

And there were footsteps.

I dodged into a cocoon of darkness provided by the dead end and extinguished the smoking match in a puddle of water. After a few seconds, a figure emerged from a concealed opening behind a rock, her red curls bobbing along in the light of a candle.

The gloom was even more saturating in the next tunnel, pressing in on me, forcing itself inside my lungs. With little more than my hands to guide me, I followed the bend in the passage, the texture beneath my palms changing from rough rock to smooth, damp wood. I reached up to where I knew the number would be and traced it. A *1* came alive under my fingertips.

Cosbi's room.

My heart pounded as I moved quickly and silently away. The place was the exact image of my nightmare, only there were many more doors.

Eventually, I stopped. Room 19 was by my side and there was a noise coming from inside.

The child knew what it was doing. Its sobs were so pitiful whenever it was laid down to sleep that its carer seemed unable to resist and resumed the cuddles. Footsteps paced inside and a soft female voice issued noises of comfort; the baby cooed in delight.

I smiled and turned away.

I knew where I wanted to go, but I never got there. Something caught my attention before I could turn my feet towards room 23, something I found impossible to ignore.

The door to Elena's room stood ajar and the contents called to me, luring me in to investigate. In the tiny light of the match, the dilapidated wood surrendered its secrets, hanging haphazardly from its frame and no longer able to close because of a shattered hinge. Splintered oak surrounded a huge indentation in the middle—a boot print.

I pressed myself through the space without opening it further. Just

'Handover time, Jean?' Cosbi asked.

'*Oui*, all clear outside. Apart from runaway children.' He shook his head but smiled indulgently.

'They must've got away from Kay and Louisa. I'll let them know on my way past.'

My heart leapt at the mention of her name.

'Stop them bloody breaking shit as well,' a grumpy voice muttered from behind the two men.

I craned to see and noticed a middle-aged man hunched at a makeshift table, a brass bell lying in pieces next to some tools.

'The kids did not do that,' Jean said. 'It just fell apart again—Daryl is not in a good mood. Eh, Daryl?'

The man grunted in reply.

'We'll leave you in peace,' Cosbi said, retreating and motioning to us to follow.

We passed through another winding corridor and emerged into a different section of the caves, abuzz with people.

'Wash bins,' Cosbi said, pointing to a tub against the wall. 'There's one in every corridor—make sure you write your name in your clothes.'

Right on cue, a broad, grey-haired woman with deep frown lines hauled the basket into the air and marched off down the corridor.

'Stream is that way,' Cosbi confirmed.

'Cosbi, my man!' an American accent drawled as a slight man with freckles and light brown hair emerged from a large doorway ahead and pulled Cosbi into an elaborate handshake.

A second man followed close behind and repeated the gesture. 'Showing the new lads around?'

The men offered their hands to us in turn. 'Parker, Chase,' the first man said, pointing first to himself and then sideways at his friend. 'Cosbi, we're leaving in five. Anything else to add to the list?'

'See if you can find some more clothes,' Cosbi said. 'Gerrin and Nico will be needing more now that they're staying with us.'

'Any requests, lads?' Chase said.

'Jeans, hoodies,' I suggested.

'Underwear,' Gerrin added.

Parker laughed and saluted, and the two men headed off towards the exit.

'They scavenge for us,' Cosbi explained. 'They find what they can and trade for anything else.'

'It must be quite far to any towns,' I observed.

'They have bikes,' Cosbi said. 'Sometimes they're gone for days.'

'Cosbi?' a short woman called, tottering up to us, breathless and full cheeks glowing. 'Have you seen Charlie and Elsie?'

'That way,' Cosbi replied.

'Thanks!' she said, her short ponytail bobbing along as she took off again. She called back over her shoulder, 'Can we talk later about getting that lock put on the classroom door?'

Cosbi gave her a thumbs up as she jogged off.

'How many fucking people live here?' Gerrin asked.

'Couple of hundred at the last count,' Cosbi said.

'How do you feed that many?' I added.

He gestured towards the space Parker and Chase had emerged from. 'Community room.'

We followed him into the large room. The place was a hive of activity. Several men were playing a hand of poker on one table, a couple of scrawny teenagers were setting tables with plates and cutlery, two guys were strumming guitars in another corner. A section off to the left housed three cooks who were busy preparing food, which was being retrieved from baskets of fresh produce and tins stacked against a far wall. As we watched the scene, two men came through the door carrying a pig carcass, several rabbits and a pheasant.

'Jackpot this morning!' one of them said, lowering the pig to the floor and stretching out his tattooed arms.

'Excellent work, Dean,' Cosbi said before turning back to Gerrin and me. 'Gentlemen—this is where I leave you. Lunch will be ready in about thirty minutes. You have the choice to dine here with everyone or take food back to your rooms. There's a small passage just around the corner from here that's a shortcut back to your rooms. It comes out near room twenty.'

ABEL

Drip.
    Drip.

God, I wish it would stop raining.

Drip.

Against the searing pain at the back of my head, I forced my eyes open and confusion hit me like a brick to the face. I looked skyward to the moonless, starless ceiling. This couldn't be outside.

The caves.

I reached up to feel the back of my sore head, and I didn't need light to tell me that it wasn't just water making my hand wet.

'Ah, crap,' I groaned.

I rolled over and staggered to my feet, colliding with a wall as I tried to remember exactly where I was and why. Still ajar, Elena's door slid across my vision. How long had I been out?

Mumbling words of encouragement to myself, I lurched back towards my hospital room. My feet fortunately knew the way without direction from my brain, but my stomach threatened mutiny the whole way, unsettled by the movement and the head wound.

Relief washed over me as I reached my door without incident; the watch chair was still sitting there, strangely empty.

I collapsed to my knees at the water basin and tried half-heartedly to wash away the evidence. Every memory from my blackout was still vividly imprinted on my mind, and I realised with tired happiness that despite the injury, the night had been a huge success.

After all, now I'd remembered *her.*

And she was just beyond words.

It must've been close to dawn by the time I finally fell into bed, and my eyes definitely weren't closed long enough before Hanna made an enthusiastic entrance with the breakfast tray.

'How are you so chirpy this early?' I protested, dragging the blankets over my face.

'It's hardly early, Nico,' she said. 'And I went to see my father last night.'

I sat up with caution, gathering the covers around my waist and wishing that I could just go back to sleep. 'You did? That's great, I bet he's missed you.'

She beamed. 'Thank you, he has. I think he's really lonely all on his...' she began, but her sentence trailed away. 'Nico, your pillow is soaked in blood!'

'Oh... yeah,' I yawned. 'I hit my head, didn't realise it was that bad.'

'Don't touch!' she shrieked. 'Let me take a look.'

I was too tired to argue, so did as I was told.

'You're a mess,' she concluded. 'How did you do so much damage by banging your head?'

'You tell me,' I said, motioning at her cheek.

Blushing furiously, she dived headfirst into the medicine cupboard, not emerging until her face was several shades lighter.

'Turn around,' she said, kneeling next to me on the bed and ripping open a packet.

Another knock at the door sounded a few seconds later.

'Are you decent?' Gerrin shouted, entering the room regardless.

'Ow!' I hissed, as Hanna's hand slipped.

'Sorry,' she muttered.

'You know that only works if you wait for an answer, right?' I said to Gerrin.

'We used to share a room,' he said with a shrug. 'We have no secrets.'

It didn't take long for him to take in the scene. It couldn't have looked respectable, what with Hanna's dress around her thighs and the wrapped bed sheet, making it look like I was going commando.

'Wait, what's going on?' he asked.

Hanna froze.

'The wall and I fell out last night,' I said, with what I hoped was a casual smile. 'Hanna's making sure I don't die.'

He walked over to take a look. 'Jeez, Nic. You're supposed to be getting better here, not making yourself worse. Are you OK?'

'I'm fine,' I said. 'Hanna's doing an amazing job.'

'So...' he said, taking the chair opposite. 'Anything last night?'

'Nothing of use,' I answered. 'But I need to talk when you have five.'

'Hanna,' he said.

'This is finished anyway, Nico,' she said. 'Just take it slow, OK?'

I offered my hand to help her down. 'Thank you.'

As usual, Hanna took the furthest possible route around Gerrin on her way out of the room, head firmly tipped at the floor.

'Do you have that effect on all women?' I said.

'Yeah, they're intimidated by this,' he said, gesturing down at himself.

I shook my head in disbelief, knowing he wasn't entirely joking.

'So, what's up?' he said.

'It's something I wanted to ask—it's kind of personal.'

At that, he stood and went to close the door. 'Fire away,' he called over his shoulder.

I took a deep breath. 'Who's Louisa?'

He stopped dead in the middle of the room. Whether good or bad, I had his attention.

'Who?'

'Louisa.'

'Why do you ask?'

'I remembered her. And she doesn't seem like someone I could easily forget.'

He clicked the door into place and turned to face me, forcing the corners of his mouth into a smile. 'She moved in near us a couple of months after we got here.'

'And I wanted to stay for her?'

He nodded. 'The two of you were friends for a while.'

My eyes screwed up as I tried to recall my feelings for the beautiful blonde—they definitely weren't platonic. 'Really? Just friends?'

'You know this isn't what you should be focus—'

'Please, Gerrin.'

Sadness crept into his eyes and he sighed. 'Fine, more than friends.'

My heart did a victory leap. 'Why didn't you like her?'

'Come on, Nic, cut me a break,' he groaned, running a hand through his hair. 'Cosbi wouldn't want me encouraging this.'

'Screw Cosbi,' I snorted. 'This is my life. Why were you angry with her? Because I decided to stay?'

'Stop jumping to conclusions. That's not how it was, it's just that—'

'That what?'

'It was too much, too soon. You were nineteen, she was seventeen. Making a decision about where you wanted to spend the rest of your life, based on having known the girl for days, was just barmy.'

'You thought Cosbi had set it up to stop us leaving?'

'Yeah. I was angry, and I was wrong. I apologised to them both. So stop saying I don't like her—I was just looking out for you.'

'Hey, you said don't.'

'What?'

'You said, "stop saying *I don't* like her", not "I *didn't*"—she's still here!'

Gerrin rolled his eyes. 'I've got a meeting with Cosbi, so maybe you can take some time to focus on what's really important. I mean it—no more Louisa.'

'Sure,' I smirked, and before he left the room called out 'When can she come see me?'

'*Goodbye,* Nic.'

With a smug smile, I flipped my pillow and lay back down. She *had* been mine.

'Knew you'd come eventually, Nico.'

I froze mid-stride as Gerrin sat up to face me, tense, ready.

Of course he wasn't surprised; this was the only place left for me to go, and the only thing left for me to do. The persisting, poisonous hatred had come, and with it the need to find him. It was as natural as the setting of the sun for me to be here tonight.

My lip curled. 'Then you know how this is going to end.'

'I doubt that. Humour me, though—what do you plan on doing afterwards?'

'Afterwards?'

He took advantage of my pause, walking towards me and not stopping until the tip of the knife I carried rested on the unprotected skin of his stomach. 'After you've killed me. Do you really think it'll stop the pain?'

'It's worth a try.'

'So then, what're you waiting for? We've done all our talking—apparently forgiveness isn't an option.'

'*Forgiveness?*' I hissed. 'You're beyond forgiveness, even if you wanted it.'

He nodded and took hold of the blade of the knife with his bare hand, pushing against it so the point made a hollow in his abdomen. 'I'll make it easy for you. I'm right here, the knife is right here, all you have to do is move. Just move, Nic. Feels good, doesn't it? That power, that knowledge that you have someone's life in your hands. You're not so different from me.'

My eyes snapped up from the knife. 'I'm nothing like you.'

'Look at what you're doing.'

The adrenaline kick faltered, my hand trembling as it ebbed. I looked down to confront what he'd turned me into.

'You're better than this weakness, Nic. *Want it.*'

My shoulders slumped in defeat; I couldn't end his life in hate.

'You don't have the guts.' He sneered, shoving my hand away. 'You never did.'

'People change.'

'Sure they do,' he said. 'Now put it down before you cut yourself.'

My grip tightened around the knife until I thought the metal would snap under my grief. How could he mock me?

'Did you come to hear me say it, how it happened?' he said, so nonchalantly he could've been asking me what I'd had for breakfast.

'I remember everything,' I snapped.

'I can tell you how it really happened. Every last little *detail.*'

'I saw enough.'

'Even the begging?'

Like metal to a magnet, his taunting words drew my aim back to his body, and before I knew what I'd done, the knife was buried deep in his stomach.

I smiled; it was easier than I thought.

Gerrin's mouth fell open, staggered at my betrayal.

Consumed by the memory of that night, of *that room*, I jammed the knife into his body until it would go no further. 'You're right. Having your life in my hands *does* feel good.'

His body shuddered from the damage caused by the serrated blade, tremors rocking through me as he gripped my arms for support. Time ticked by as we stared at each other, his breathing becoming more difficult with the passing of each second.

'It was all for you,' he eventually wheezed.

'*Liar.*'

'No. Never. I'm... your brother.'

Light and life were deserting his eyes; he only had moments.

I made him look at me. I wanted the pain he would see there to haunt his final moments of life and his eternity in death. 'You're no brother of mine.'

Those were the last words he ever heard. Tears spilled onto his cheeks and streaked the scarlet at his jaw, his blue eyes clouding with unconsciousness. Gerrin's body slid from the knife and collapsed in a heap on the floor.

My boot found his ribs and I rolled him to face me, streams of blood trailing into his matted hair.

I felt no remorse for my crime. I felt no emotion for the body beneath my foot.

My eyes flew open with a start. Heart pounding, body sweating, I screamed into the darkness until my lungs could no longer feed my voice.

'I had the dream again.'

She was the only one I could tell, and the only one I couldn't hide it from. How the tables had turned.

'Was it the same?'

'Almost.'

'Killing him still felt good?'

'Even better than before.'

I could only blame desperation for what I did next.

Craving relief from the knot of guilt weighing down my heart, I dropped to my knees at her feet and buried my head in the dirty shreds of clothing. 'Tell me what's happening, Elena. I can't keep seeing that happen. I can't. I'm begging you. Please.'

Every muscle in her slim legs clenched at the unexpected contact. 'Only you can understand your dreams about Gerrin.'

'How?' I snapped. 'Can't you tell me anything? You can see what this is doing to me.'

She sighed, her tone of her voice softer and more sympathetic towards me than ever before. 'Imagine I'm reading you a story, only I decide to tell you the ending before you hear the beginning or the middle,' she said. 'Do you think you'd understand what I'd told you or why? Do you think your mind would survive it? You have to figure out your own ending.'

Until this point, I'd wanted that too, but murdering my brother several times a week was taking the fight out of me. As time passed, the dreams were becoming more vivid, more detailed, more full of hate.

'And if I don't like my ending?' I said.

'You can't take the light without the dark.'

I clung to her legs, like she was the only thing stopping me sinking. '*Help* me.'

10 IYAR

'*Help me.*'

I writhed and squirmed, material weaving between my limbs.

'I don't want... want to kill him.'

Sweat poured from my pinned body.

'No! Elena... help.'

The material stuck to my skin.

'I'm begging... your... begging help...'

'*Hanna!*'

The crash of something breakable hitting the floor tore me from the dream. I sat up in a hurry, sweating profusely, my heart beating so fast it felt like it was going to break through my ribs. The sheets were slick and tangled around me.

My room was frozen in a moment.

Gabriel was standing near my bed, gloves in hand, frowning heavily in Hanna's direction.

Hanna's hand was open, the vial of medicine she'd been holding in pieces on the floor. Her wide eyes and parted lips managed to make her look both horrified and concerned for me at the same time.

My gaze turned to Gerrin, who was also staring at me.

He was more angry than I'd ever seen him, nostrils flaring as heavy breaths poured in and out.

'What?' I said.

Gabriel cleared his throat, breaking everyone from their trance. 'Well. I'm, erm... I have to, need to see to another patient. I'll erm... yes.'

And with that, he ran from the room without a backward glance.

'Out!' Gerrin ordered, not even turning to Hanna.

'Do you have to talk to her like that?' I asked, as she fled.

'What do you think you're doing?' he snapped.

'Uh, sleeping?' I said.

'And asking Elena for help.'

'When?'

'You were talking in your sleep.'

'Was I?'

'Everyone in the room fucking heard you,' he spat. 'What were you asking her for help with?'

'I can't remember,' I said, starting to feel ambushed. 'Probably help with remembering something.'

'And don't you remember who she is? *What* she is?'

'Of course I do.'

'So are you wanting to be friends with her again, forgetting your family, is that it?'

'Oh, don't be ridiculous, Gerrin,' I said.

'Ridiculous?' he said, advancing on me. 'You're letting her in your head again. I bloody told you not to!'

'For God's sake, it was just a dream—it doesn't mean anything.'

'I had to watch her break you once before. You think I'm going to sit here while you fall for it again?'

'I know what I'm doing.'

'I hope you do, because if I hear you doing that again, I'll pull the plug on this whole thing and take you out of here.'

'Bu—'

'No, Nico, I don't want to hear another word.'

Completing the hat-trick, he too stormed out of my room, yelling as he went. 'Gabriel, get the fuck back in there and sort him out.'

'It's not working, Elena,' I complained.

'You won't remember unless you focus,' she said. 'Close your eyes, relax.'

I sighed impatiently but did as I was told.

'Let go.'

I fought back the overwhelming urge to start laughing, and instead tried to remember what I wanted, the person I needed to understand.

Slowly my surroundings became peaceful, still. Everything was irrelevant, everything except Gerrin. His grimacing yet satisfied face appeared before my closed eyes. '*I did it for you, Nic.*'

I staggered back.

'Don't be afraid of it.' Elena was somewhere behind me.

Unsure whether I wanted to know what was going to come out of his mouth next, I made my world dark and tried again.

Raucous laughter sounded in the distance, not in my head, but actually in the passageway. It grew louder until I could pick out individual voices in the din. A clap on the back jolted me to life and my eyes fell on my monster of a brother, standing at my side.

'Let's go take a look,' Gerrin said, indicating towards the circle of people that'd formed ahead.

'Know who it is?' I asked.

'Another outsider from that group. At least that's what Parker sent that snake to tell me.'

'Foley? Wouldn't trust him as far as I could throw him.'

'That's why I came to see for myself. How did you find out?'

'Jean,' I answered.

By this time, we'd reached the edge of the group, which parted to allow us through. At the centre of the commotion, Chase was attempting to wrestle a man past my room towards 23, and was clearly losing. The scruffy visitor had a physical advantage over the slight American in both height and build, and he wanted to be free.

'Sneaked past the guard,' Parker said, hovering on the periphery of the fight.

'Has someone gone for Cosbi?' Chase wheezed, turning a violent shade of red.

'I'm here.'

Gasps from the crowd sounded as their owners scuttled backwards. Through the space they created, I saw Elena had emerged from her room and was staring at the scene.

'Who is this?' Cosbi said, smiling at the man as though he was a welcome dinner guest.

'Outsider,' Parker answered. 'Found the way in.'

'Indeed?' Cosbi said. 'Well, mission finally accomplished. How do you like our home?'

The man spat in Cosbi's direction. Gerrin started forwards, but Cosbi halted his motion with a hand.

'This man is our guest, Gerrin,' Cosbi said. 'Where've you come from, friend?'

There was silence except for the continued sounds of the scuffle. I hoped someone would put Chase out of his misery soon.

'What's your name?' Cosbi pressed.

No answer.

'Are you seeking refuge?'

Nothing.

Gerrin stalked forwards, knocking Chase out of the way and seizing the outsider by the T-shirt. The crowd inhaled as a collective; Chase breathed a sigh of relief.

'*Gerrin,*' Cosbi warned.

'Talk!' Gerrin snapped. 'Your name.'

'Eli,' the man hissed, struggling pointlessly.

'Glad to meet you, Eli,' Cosbi said. 'So, are you going to tell me what you're doing here?'

'Go fuck yourself.'

Gerrin raised a fist, ready to strike.

Some way in the distance, Elena's face darkened. She sought me out with a glare, gesturing to me to intervene.

Dutifully, I walked into the middle of the fight and put a hand on Gerrin's arm. 'There's no need to beat him—he's probably just scared shitless.'

Cosbi moved towards the man. 'Is that true, Eli? Were you attacked? There's no need to be afraid. Speak—I swear you'll be safe.'

The man turned to the crowd with a sneer. 'I feel sorry for you all,' he said. 'Living under the boot of someone whose word means jack shit.'

'There's a home for you here,' Cosbi urged.

'I'd rather gouge my own eyes out.'

Cosbi sighed and turned to the gathered masses. 'Please go back to your rooms. I'm afraid so many faces may be a little overwhelming for our new addition.'

Seemingly disappointed, the captivated audience began to dissipate. As the crowd thinned, I spotted Louisa waiting for me, watching what was going on. As it turned out, Gerrin was also distracted, and his grip on Eli had unintentionally loosened.

Eli seized the moment, belting Gerrin across the face and yanking the hunting knife from Chase's back pocket. Running towards freedom amidst screaming, zig-zagging crowd members, he had his arm around Louisa's shoulders and the blade at her neck before we could get there to stop him.

'Louisa!' The word choked from my throat at the sight of my worst nightmare.

'Nico?' she whispered, looking first at me and then moving her plea sideways. 'Gerrin?'

'Get away!' Eli shouted, backing up towards the narrow path next to Elena's room.

Gerrin let out a low whistle. 'Bad move. Boy, are you going to regret that.'

'Not a step closer. It'd be a shame to have to kill something so pretty.'

'Get your fucking hands off her *now*!' I hissed. 'Or I swear to God I'll kill you myself.'

Eli's shoulders dropped as he realised he'd hit the jackpot with his leverage. 'The boyfriend, I assume?' he said with a smirk, planting a kiss on Louisa's hair. 'Lucky man, lucky, lucky man.'

'You're dead, you hear me?' I roared, launching myself forwards, before being restrained by Gerrin.

'Put it down, friend,' Cosbi said. 'I won't tolerate threats to my people.'

'I'm not your *friend*, pal,' Eli retorted, shoving Louisa in my direction and sending the knife whistling towards Gerrin, before sprinting past Elena.

Cosbi sighed and tipped his head in the direction of the fleeing Eli, and Gerrin broke into pursuit. Louisa flung herself into my arms and sobbed against my chest.

'Shh, it's OK, you're OK now,' I whispered, stroking her hair. 'I'll never let anyone hurt you.'

The feeling of being watched pulled my attention up. Elena was standing in her doorway, arms folded, penetrating glare piercing the moment.

Gerrin returned moments later, dragging a wheezing, choking Eli along by the neck of his jacket.

'Take him to room 23—let's have a chat in safety,' Cosbi said.

Gerrin nodded. 'Louisa, go back home.'

Louisa looked at him and then at me. 'What're you going to do?'

'Whatever it takes to keep you safe,' I answered.

'No, please don't. I don't want you to do that for me,' she whispered. 'Don't hurt him.'

'It's for everyone's safety,' Gerrin answered. 'Please, go.'

'Please don't trouble yourself, Louisa,' Cosbi said with a kind smile. 'He'll be just fine.'

I cut off Louisa's second protest with a kiss, using my thumb to brush away the tears *he'd* made fall. 'Please go inside,' I whispered.

Gerrin barely waited for her blonde waves to disappear out of sight before hauling Eli away. Now moving in the opposite direction to the exit, the intruder bellowed his rage, but the sound was quashed to a pitiful gargle with the tightening of Gerrin's arm around his neck.

Fortunately for him though, he had a defender. And she was standing right in the middle of the corridor between us and 23.

'I won't let you kill him,' Elena said.

'Kill him?' Cosbi almost laughed. 'That's very dramatic, Elena, I just want to talk to the man.'

'You think I don't know what you're really like?'

'I'm offering him a home, safety, a new family.'

'He doesn't want to stay, so just let him go.'

'My priority is keeping this community safe. I have to ensure that before I even think about letting him go.'

'He's not trying to hurt anyone!'

'Do you know this man, Elena?'

'Don't be ridiculous, of course not.'

'Then how could you know that?'

'He could've easily killed Jean, but he just tried to sneak past. He's clearly just looking for something.'

'Then all he has to do is tell the truth,' Cosbi said as he moved around Elena.

I pulled her back from the departing group. 'Leave it, Elena.'

'You can't seriously be condoning this,' she hissed, trying to escape my grasp and follow Gerrin.

'Condoning what? What fantasy world are you living in?'

'He's an innocent man!'

'Well, let me go ask him, and then he can go,' I said, backing up towards 23.

'Is she really worth it?'

'It's my job to keep her safe—she's my girlfriend.'

'Guess we'll just see about that.'

'I love her.'

'You stupid fool,' she sneered.

'Nico, get down here!' Gerrin shouted.

I shook my head and stalked off, just hearing her shout before I was out of earshot. 'I'll be waiting when you realise what a mistake you've made.'

I ignored her remark and turned my attention back to the problem, the problem that was currently being dragged through the entrance to 23. Eli was still fighting Gerrin's hold as I walked through the door, with Parker and Chase stood cautiously to one side. Cosbi stood at the small table in the corner, pouring two drinks from the bottle of scotch that stood there. He offered one tumbler to Eli.

'Drink. Let's talk this through.'

Eli didn't have much range of movement thanks to Gerrin, but he still managed to elbow the glass from Cosbi's hand.

Cosbi sighed and knocked the broken glass aside with his foot. 'So, if you weren't seeking help or shelter, may I ask why you felt the need to come inside?'

Eli's lip curled. 'Fancied a look inside this shit hole.'

'Watch it,' Gerrin snarled in his ear.

'Well, you've landed us both in a bit of a predicament, Eli,' Cosbi said. 'You won't accept my offer of refuge, but you know the way in. How can I let you walk free knowing that you could show up tomorrow with an army?'

'I don't have a bloody army,' Eli snapped.

'How can I believe you?'

The man scowled.

'I want to let you live,' Cosbi said. 'But I don't see a way out of this situation.'

'If I disappear, my people will know. You'll regret it.'

'I'm offering you one last chance. Please don't make me do this.'

Eli stubbornly held his tongue.

'Cosbi?' Gerrin said.

'He poses a threat to our safety,' Cosbi answered, and retreated from our arena. 'We have other no choice.'

Gerrin glanced at me. 'Want one for Louisa?'

I nodded.

With an aggressive shove, Gerrin released hold of his prisoner, sending him stumbling and tripping towards me.

I let him recover his balance and his focus before I drew my arm back and took aim at his face. There was a gratifying crunch as my fist hit cheekbone, and he staggered backwards with a howl of pain.

'You threaten her, you answer to me!' I roared.

Gerrin smirked and leaned up against the wall. 'Told you you'd regret it.'

Panting the rattling breaths of a smoker, Eli raised both fists and shook greying hair from his eyes. 'Real brave, five on one.'

'And hiding behind a teenage girl is? You want to make it fair, huh? Come on, hit me. Hit me if you can.'

I beckoned him towards me. With a crazed look, he hurtled forwards, obviously hoping to hit me hard enough that he could get past. Unfortunately for him, however, I'd had lots of practice at dodging Gerrin's fists over the years, and poor old Eli was nowhere near as fast.

I caught him mid-flight and launched him at the wall so hard that his feet left the floor. 'You kissed your life goodbye the second you laid a finger on her.'

Eli tried to laugh, but his crushed windpipe only permitted a choke.

'What?' I snapped.

'Nothing.' He wheezed. 'It's just... if you're going to kill every man... who touches that... piece... of ass, you'll have time for... nothing else.'

Gerrin howled with laughter. 'It's almost like he wants to die!'

I took a step back and in utter, blind fury, I hit him. Once, twice, ten times. Eli could barely stand by the time I threw him back to Gerrin, but he was conscious enough to feel everything that was about to happen.

'*Now* you can kill him,' I hissed.

'Don't want to get your hands dirty, huh?' Eli taunted as he prised opened his swollen, bleeding eyes. 'Not even for your stunner?'

Gerrin reached inside his boot and pulled out a silver pen knife, flicking it open on his knee. 'We're brothers, we share everything.'

He seized Eli's hair and jabbed the sharp edge of the blade to the side of his pulsing throat, the tip so sharp that a small bead of blood collected where it pressed against his skin. 'Any last words, scumbag?'

'Yeah, fuck y—'

Eli never finished his final, poignant sentence. With a movement so quick I barely saw it, Gerrin drew the blade sideways, slitting the man's throat.

Pointlessly clutching at his neck, Eli slumped to his knees, eyes wide and making the most horrible gargling sound. He slowly bled to death on the dirty, dank floor of the most depressing room in the caves. Everyone was silent, unmoving, as the man lay twitching and jerking in an ever-growing pool of his own blood, pupils rolling to the back of his skull. I turned my back, unable to watch, but powerless to stop the last gasps of life reaching my ears.

It must've taken a full minute for him to die.

I watched Gerrin as he stood powerful and expressionless over the body of the man, silently wiping the dripping blade of the knife on his T-shirt, and found it hard to believe that was the first person he'd killed.

Cosbi closed his eyes and whispered a few words under his breath. 'Wait until lights out,' he eventually said to Parker and Chase. 'I don't want to upset anyone.'

I wrung my sweaty hands. I didn't want to face her look of disappointment, but I had to get it over with at some point.

But any nerves disappeared as soon as I closed my door, looked up and saw Ash leaning against the wall outside Elena's room, with her trapped between his arms.

'Didn't I tell you I'd break every bone in your body if I found you here again?' I thundered, striding over.

'Dunna get yer knickers in a twist, Jakes. Ah was just havin' a wee chat with Elena here.'

'Get out of my way!' she hissed.

'Take it easy, darlin',' he drawled. 'Ah could go tell Cosbi you went fer me, if yeh fancy a night in the cells.'

'Say whatever you have to say and fuck off,' I said.

'Ah, she already knows,' he said with a wink, pushing off from the wall and sauntering away.

'What was all that about?' I asked.

'A not-so-subtle warning,' she answered.

I sighed. 'Can you *please* try to keep your head down a bit? There are people here who will turn on you in an instant if they think you have some kind of connection with anyone outside. Most of them want revenge for one thing or another, and you know that Ash is just waiting to spread that rumour.'

But as usual, she wasn't listening.

'I assume you went through with it?' she snapped.

'Can we go inside and not argue in the corridor?'

She pushed open the door and I followed her through. 'Your silence speaks volumes, Nico. You went through with it.'

I hesitated. 'He's dead.'

'You don't sound sorry.'

'I'm not.'

'Then leave. I have nothing to say to you.'

I stayed silent, stubbornly refusing to feel any sorrow for the death of a man who'd threatened to take Louisa from me.

'Cosbi never had any intention of letting him go,' she said. 'You just did his dirty work for him.'

'Cosbi is protecting us,' I argued. 'He offered him a home, gave him every opportunity to save his own life.'

She shook her head with a huff. 'You're being brainwashed.'

'Where has all this come from?'

'Watching, listening. He's using you all and you're thanking him for it.'

I rolled my eyes.

'You're blind when it comes to Louisa too,' she added.

'Why do you hate her so much?'

'She changes you, Nico. She just changed you forever.'

'Don't be so ridiculous,' I snorted.

'It's true,' she said, laying her hand on my chest. 'I know the real you when you're here, messing about, or just talking to me. You're a kind man, a loving man—someone who stands by Gerrin even when sense and reason tell him not to. That wasn't you today.'

I took a step back, and her hand fell uselessly back to her side.

She sighed. 'What are you even doing here?'

'I don't want you to hate me.'

'Does it matter if I do?'

'Of course it does. You're the best friend I have.'

'Friend...' she repeated with a tiny, cynical laugh.

My eyes shot up. 'Yes, why? You don't still... I mean, I thought we agreed?'

'Go back to her, Nico, she'll be wondering where you are.'

'She doesn't know I'm here.'

'Then go home,' she retorted.

'Elena—'

'*Goodnight*,' she stated, opening the door.

It was my turn to sigh. 'OK, but I'm coming back tomorrow. You can't stay angry with me forever.'

'Wanna bet?' she answered, slamming the door in my face.

I couldn't look at myself in the mirror. The disappointed face of Elena refused to leave my sight, and all I could feel was the most gut-wrenching shame.

'What's up today, Nic?' Gerrin asked.

'Hmm?'

'You've barely said a word since I got here. Are you still angry? I told you I was sorry for shouting about Elena.'

Elena had been right; that man had no more planned to kill Louisa than I had. But I understood my actions perfectly. The fear of losing her had crushed every rational thought into oblivion. I remembered the satisfaction that his death had brought me and shuddered. A man's life so I could feel safe in my own?

'No,' I muttered.

'Then what's wrong?'

And what'd been Gerrin's motive for what we'd done? He hadn't liked Louisa enough to concern himself with her life.

I sighed. 'Nothing, I'm just thinking.'

'You need to spend less time thinking and more time looking after yourself. Have you eaten today?'

I glanced down at the untouched tray on my dresser. 'I forgot.'

'How can you forget to eat?'

'I'm not hungry.'

Gerrin rubbed his face. 'Nic, whatever it is, it's in your past, and that's where you're lost right now. Don't forget you still have a future.'

'You wanted this,' I reminded him.

'Yes, to make you better, not to watch you waste away.'

I shook my head. 'That future doesn't exist until I understand who I was, before.'

He shot forwards and grabbed me by the back of the neck, forcing me to twist around to face the mirror.

'Look at yourself, Nico, you look like a fucking ghost.'

'I can't,' I said, struggling to get loose.

'Can't what?'

'Look at myself.'

'Why not?'

'Because people have died because of me.'

Gerrin's grip loosened, and the colour drained from the face behind me.

NIMUE

I T'S A TRICKY thing, forgiveness.

Elena had understood that. She'd known my nature well enough to recognise that once the impulsive anger had died, I'd be left with a heavy conscience and a guilt that I'd carry for the rest of my life.

Maybe that's why this time was different.

Expecting my memory to return me to the darkness and grey in which I'd spent most of my adult life, I was instantly floored by the dazzling ball of light in the sky. I sat with a thud on the warm earth and buried my sensitive eyes in my T-shirt.

I panted, gulping in the fresh, warm air like I'd been starved for days.

'Elena?' I called.

Alert and curious, my other senses had heightened with the loss of my sight, and I could feel that she was somewhere nearby.

'I'm right here.'

'We're outside?'

'Just like old times. It's a beautiful day, Nico.'

'Give me a minute,' I murmured. 'My eyes.'

Stretching out on my back in the overgrown wild grass, I shielded my pupils as the sun beat down on my bare skin, warm and wonderful. Every colour of the rainbow sparkled on the inside of my eyelids.

Ten minutes later, I pulled my T-shirt from my face and cast my eyes over the long-forgotten world outside the caves.

The sky was a crystal-clear blue, the sea of colour broken only by the blazing yellow of the sun and thin wisps of cloud playing chase on the horizon. A warm breeze in the air teased through the trees overhead, rousing the green leaves into a frenzy, before reaching down to gently ruffle my hair.

I reached out and tickled my fingertips across the wild grass. 'Incredible,' I whispered.

Then my eyes fell on her, lying at my side, just out of reach.

Words failed me.

Gone were the rags, the dirt, the wild-looking wretch, and in their place lay a beautiful young woman, her dark eyes watching me through long eyelashes, full lips pulled up in a smile. Smooth, tanned skin that'd been hidden by tattered clothes was now on display in a white summer dress. Her silky raven hair was fanned out around her in the grass.

'*Elena*?' I exclaimed. 'Wha— you— *how*?'

She grinned. 'My, my, speechless again.'

'I have plenty to say, but none of it would be appropriate,' I said.

'Even if we were friends, Jakes, that would be overstepping the mark.'

I smiled. 'Friends...'

'Shall I show you a secret?' she said, propping herself up on her elbow, her loose hair falling onto my arm.

'I love secrets.'

She jumped up and pointed in the direction of a thicket of trees lying at the bottom of the hill. 'That way.'

I looked at the descent and tutted. 'Looks too steep for you to walk.'

Before she could catch on, I bent down and put one arm behind her legs, scooping her up over my shoulder.

'Nico!' she screamed, slapping me on the back. 'Put me down!'

Her shouts and threats got louder as I jogged faster down the incline, the wind drawing warm tears from my eyes and whipping through my hair. The deafening noise only stopped when I reached flat ground and skidded to a halt.

'Anyone would think I was killing you,' I said, chest aching from laughing.

'You're in so much trouble,' she gasped, cuffing me over the back of the head.

I swung her down off my shoulder and raised my hands. 'I surrender. Please don't hurt me.'

She eyed me mutinously.

I sank to my knees at her feet. 'Would a piggyback do it?'

With a wicked grin, she took her revenge unexpectedly, hands grazing deliberately up my back as she climbed on. Adrenaline zipped through me like electricity, every hair on my body rising at the contact. I closed my eyes against the feeling, fighting to regain control of my traitorous body. Climbing unsteadily to my feet, I took a deep breath and wedged my hands under her thighs.

With Elena's arms hooked around my neck, I hiked through the field, all the while thinking of her. None of this felt wrong, yet wasn't this gorgeous, charming girl the very same one I'd despised just days ago?

'Over there,' she said.

I turned my feet towards a thick cluster of trees huddled in the valley, the path growing progressively darker as the sun failed to penetrate the canopy of leaves.

'Watch your head,' I said, ducking under vines and dodging branches.

We battled on for a few minutes before the mass of plants began to thin, and we found ourselves at the edge of a large clearing.

Nestled at the heart of the glade, so vast that the far side of it seemed to disappear into the foliage on the horizon, lay the most beautiful lake anyone could've dreamt up. As still as a millpond, the blue water shimmered in the radiant afternoon sun, the surrounding rocks and shrubbery jealously hiding its beauty from the rest of the world. To one side of it stood a large but derelict log cabin, its roof bowing from years of neglect.

I stooped and let Elena slip from my back. 'Your secret?'

'*Our* secret.'

Longing to feel cold water on my hot skin, I led the way to an old wooden jetty that lay exposed to weather and water. The ageing alder groaned under my weight as I lowered myself onto the edge and dipped my feet into the lake.

'I'd forgotten places like this existed,' I sighed.

'The light with the dark,' Elena said, slipping her toes in beside mine.

We sat in silence for some time, basking in the light wind breezing around us, its breath making little waves in the water that lapped at my ankles and sent the various flies hovering over the surface scurrying for cover.

As my gaze swept across the scenery, taking a mental picture to remember in darker times, it inevitably fell on Elena. Eyes closed and humming to herself, she was lying on the decking, dipping her toes playfully in and out of the water. She looked so unguarded that the urge to reach out and touch her was overwhelming.

'It's rude to stare,' she murmured.

Laughing away the embarrassment of being caught, I reached down and scooped a handful of water from the lake and threw it over her bare thighs. 'I was admiring the decking, actually. Amazing craftsmanship.'

'You idiot!' Pulling her best scowl, she shifted further down the jetty and resumed sunbathing.

'Elena?'

'Hmm?'

'What you were wearing before, what happened to it?'

'Burnt,' she said, inviting no further questions on the subject.

'Did you come here alone?'

'I came here with you, stupid.'

'Not *here* here. I meant the caves.'

'I was messing with you,' she sighed, rolling onto her side. 'And yes, by myself.'

'You don't have any family?'

'Not anymore. My mother ran away from my father when I was ten. We left Spain to come to England, paying for the privilege of being illegal immigrants. I cried the whole way here,' she said, shrugging off the memory. 'She died when I was fourteen.'

'I'm sorry.'

'It was a long time ago.'

'What happened to you?'

'I refused to go back to my father and I had no other family, so they put me into care. I was seventeen when the war hit, packed all of my stuff and left. I avoided most of the fighting by hiding in sewers. Took me two years to get here. I was sheltering just inside the cave entrance when one of the guards found me. Two days after I got here, some wimp was supposed to help me move room, but showed up late,' she said with a grin.

'Were we really that close?'

'Best friends. Not everyone was happy about it though.'

'Like who?'

'Well, your brother for a start, and a couple of girls. There was one, a small redhead, I think, who started following you around when she was a teenager. I think she was a bit smitten.'

'Hanna?'

'Yeah, I think that was her name.'

'She wouldn't hurt a fly.'

She looked at me quizzically. 'You're very different from him.'

I assumed she meant Gerrin. 'Everyone normally says how alike we are.'

'Physically maybe.'

'You don't like him?'

'No,' she spat.

Slightly taken aback by the aggression thrown into that one syllable, I felt myself almost leaning away, but I found it impossible not to stare at her eyes. The darkness in them when she was angry was utterly captivating.

'A lot happened in the past,' she said.

'I wouldn't know—he tells me as little as you do.'

'But for a very different reason.'

I tore my eyes from her alluring stare, sat up and stuck my feet back in the cold water, frowning at my reflection for a few moments before turning back. 'I'm sorry.'

'What for?'

'I should've listened to you. About Eli.'

She shook her head. 'Don't look at me like that.'

'Like what?'

'Like that, like you're doing right now.' She was agitated as she sat up, holding me back with a hand when I went to move closer. 'You could commit mass murder and one of those apologies would get you off the hook. It's no wonder half the bloody caves were madly in love with you.'

My face reddened.

'Every night I lay awake wondering if that man had a family somewhere,' Elena continued. 'Someone who loved him and was lying awake too, questioning when he was coming home.'

'I never thought of him having a family,' I confessed. 'It's a nice dream, huh? That there's someone out there who would love and wait for you no matter what.'

'It's foolish to love here,' Elena sneered. 'This is a world of broken hearts.'

'So you've never fallen in love... with anyone...?'

'Are you hoping I'm going to say you? Get over yourself.'

And there it was again—threat, excitement and shadowy fury all in one glare.

'Your eyes are stunning when you're angry,' I said, without thinking.

'Huh?'

'Your eyes right now. Stunning.'

'Stop making fun of me.'

'They're just getting sexier the more cross you get,' I said, getting to my feet and poking her repeatedly in the arm, as her mouth pulled into a tight line.

'Do you want me to hurt you?'

'As if you could, Sexy Eyes...'

I was full on belly-laughing as she sprang to her feet.

If I was expecting it, I would've dodged. But I was far too busy holding my aching stomach.

Planting both hands on my chest, she shoved with all of her impressive might, knocking me off balance. I teetered on the edge for a few uncertain seconds, arms flailing, windmilling, before succumbing to the inevitable and belly-flopping into the lake.

The water was freezing. What'd been a cool feeling for my feet was a shocking one for my body. My brain couldn't think of anything but numbness for a few seconds, before sense took over and I pulled myself up through the water. Surfacing in confusion, I spluttered liquid from my throat, and shook sodden hair from my eyes. Scanning the jetty for my unruly companion, I found her doubled over at the sight of me.

'Serves you right!' she called.

Like hell was she getting away with that. Catching my breath, I swam back to the wooden platform and used a beam to lift myself out.

'That's it, you've done it now!' I said.

Catching sight of me approaching to take my revenge, she blew me a kiss with a wicked smile and took off, racing the length of the jetty and around the silt at the water's edge.

Wringing out my shorts and slicking back my hair, I sprinted after her. 'Oh, you'd better run!' I shouted, grinning as the sound of laughter reached my ears.

I was near enough to hear the soft thud of feet hitting the floor. She made it no more than a couple of hundred metres before I caught up. Reaching out, I grabbed her waist and lifted her clean off the ground, whirling her around through the air.

'Get off, you're freezing!' she screamed.

'If I'm gonna be cold, then you are too,' I said, rubbing my wet hair across her bare shoulders.

Everything was fine until my foot hit a rock. Still holding Elena, I toppled dangerously off balance, lost control and pitched towards the floor. I did my best to save her from the brunt of the fall, but she landed heavily on top of me nonetheless, the momentum sending us rolling down the shore in a jumble of limbs.

The world righted itself before we reached the water's edge, but it was a good minute before we could both stop laughing long enough to realise how we'd ended up.

Underneath me, hair everywhere and arms abandoned at her sides like a beached starfish, Elena was lying flat on her back in the sand. I'd somehow ended up on top, enclosing her within the brace that my arms made on either side of her shoulders. She couldn't look away, she couldn't move.

The laughter died from her eyes at the same time I felt it leave mine. We weren't playing anymore.

I couldn't stop myself. Raising a hand, I stroked the length of her face with the back of my fingers. 'Are you OK?' I murmured. 'I didn't hurt you?'

She shook her head.

My weak eyes skirted downwards, over everything I was so desperate to look at but had been trying to ignore. It didn't help that water had soaked through the top of her dress.

Her hand found mine and guided it to her chest, encouraging the weakness.

I shook my head, trying to resist this insanity. But my hand ignored reason and allowed itself to be led.

Willpower crumbling, I grasped eagerly at her soft flesh, my mouth breathing warm air against her lips as my hand forced its way inside the top of her dress.

Her back arched. 'Nico...' she barely whispered.

The sound of her voice dragged me back to reality.

Snatching my hand away, I pushed myself back onto my knees, apologies tumbling from my mouth. 'Sorry. I'm sorry. I just... want... I don't know what I was thinking.'

'Don't be stupid, I want it too.'

'No. Please, let's just forget it happened.'

'OK,' she said with a shrug. 'If that's what you want.'

'I think it's for the best.'

I stretched out so that my legs were back in the shallow water. We sat in awkward silence for a few moments, before Elena laid her head in my lap.

'Your shorts are soaking,' she observed.

'Elena?'

'Hmm?'

'Earlier, you said "just like old times". Have we been out here before?'

She lifted her head. 'Of course. All the time.'

'But how? The fighting—'

'There hasn't been any fighting out here for a couple of years.'

My heartbeat quickened. 'But how did we leave? You said it yourself, the entrance is always guarded.'

She laced her fingers between mine and laid her head back down. 'There's another way out.'

TRIANGLE

'THERE'S ANOTHER ENTRANCE to this place.'

I'd thought long and hard about what I was going to say before I asked Hanna to fetch them. I decided that revealing mine and Elena's unapproved trips outside was unnecessary, but the other exit was another matter. It seemed like a major security flaw now the caves were under threat.

Cosbi nodded. 'We discovered it existed after she ran, but it's never been found. Have you any idea of the location?'

I shook my head. 'It wasn't a memory as such, it was just...'

'Just what, Nic?' Gerrin prompted.

'Like a dream. Someone told me in the dream. God, it's hard to explain.'

The backward glance Cosbi threw Gerrin didn't escape my notice, nor did how awkward my sibling looked when Cosbi left the room.

'Spit it out,' I said, rolling my eyes.

'Hey, this is coming from Cosbi. He just wanted me to do it more calmly than I did last time.'

'Elena again,' I sighed.

'Yeah. Elena again. It *was* her... who told you about the other entrance in your dream?'

I nodded.

He hesitated. 'We just hope you don't let any... *feelings*... you have for her cloud your judgement.'

'Feelings? For Elena?' I said, with a snort.

'I know you, Nic.'

'I think someone's been watching too many romcoms.'

He rolled his eyes. 'I'm being serious. I should've showed you yesterday, but just in case you're ever in any doubt of what that woman is capable of, remember this.'

He yanked the bottom of his T-shirt up, showing me his back. There, still slightly red and no more than a few months old, was a five-inch-long scar.

My jaw dropped in horror. 'She... did that...?'

'Turns out she'd been meeting the outsiders in secret after finding that other way out. Foley saw her outside one day and reported it back. They'd convinced her that we were the enemy and let's just say she decided to start with me when she came home. Didn't even see her coming.'

'Not even in self-defence?'

'Just attacked, didn't care about what killing me would do to you. You see what she is?'

It made no sense. This couldn't be the woman by the lake, the one I'd got so close to in my dream. But the scar was there, no mistake.

'Don't be fooled by memories of good times, Nic,' Gerrin said. 'I'm pretty sure Elena's feelings for you only went as far as trying to get you into bed. Several times. That woman isn't capable of love.'

I nodded. 'I'll be careful.'

'That's what I needed to hear. Gabriel's on his way over, I think, so I'll see you soon.'

I lay back on the bed. 'She really hated you, you know.'

'I know.'

'The reason we're all here, gentlemen,' Cosbi announced, a hush falling over the crowd as he began speaking, 'is to learn how to fight and how to protect ourselves, should the need ever arise.'

'You know something?' one man hollered.

'No, Karl. This is a precaution only. Parker and Chase have been sourcing weapons, and Gerrin and Nico will teach you how to use them.'

Someone in the crowd sniggered, and I knew instinctively who it was.

'Ash, would you like to prove you're the better man for the job?' Cosbi asked, raising his eyebrows. 'Gerrin was saying the other day he'd like to organise a bare-knuckle fight...'

The laughing ceased instantly. Cosbi grinned.

'Do we have a choice?' another man asked. 'I didn't sign up to fight.'

'None of us did,' Cosbi said. 'But we all have families and a home to protect. Should those foreigners ever get in, your wives and children would be fair game. I'm sure you'd rather learn to fight than let murderers and rapists near them.'

A few outraged whispers passed between the men.

'Any more questions?' Cosbi said.

'Is this an open invitation?' someone said.

Cosbi looked confused at hearing a female voice amidst the all-male group huddled together in the cave entrance.

Elena raised her hand.

'I was intending for this to be a... mostly male training group,' Cosbi said.

'Elena is probably one of the best fighters here,' I interjected. 'I can vouch for her.'

Elena beamed.

'Very well,' Cosbi relented. 'Everyone choose a weapon and follow your trainers.'

Nerves flooded my stomach as I knocked on the door of Louisa's room. This wasn't on. Three weeks after we'd met and the thought of seeing her still sent my heart rate stratospheric.

Third time's a charm.

'Stay cool,' I muttered to myself. 'Just play it cool.'

I shoved my hands in my pockets and kicked some stones down the corridor, just managing to pull myself together before the sound of footsteps ruined my composure all over again.

'Hi, Constance,' I said as a face peeped out.

'Nico!' she said, her face breaking into a warm smile as she beckoned me inside. 'Don't just stand there, come in.'

'Thanks.'

'Well, don't you scrub up well? Going somewhere?'

'Just over to the get-together thing, you know? The thing Cosbi throws every month.'

'Ah, you'll be wanting me to fetch Louisa then?' she said with a knowing smile.

'Umm, yeah, if you wouldn't mind?'

'It's kind of you to keep trying to include her. She's lucky to have found such a good friend. She's just a bit shy,' she whispered with a wink.

I smiled at her tact; we both knew that friendship with her daughter was the last thing on my mind.

Constance had already made me feel like part of her family, despite having only known me a few weeks. She had one of those personalities that no one could speak badly of, and that drew everyone instinctively to her. It was clear to see where her eldest daughter had got her looks from too. Aside from the slight greying of her blonde plait, there were no signs whatsoever that she was approaching her mid-forties.

'Mummy...?' a tiny, excited voice sounded from behind the partition wall.

'What is it, Rae?' Constance called.

'Is that Nico?'

'No, go back to bed.'

'Can I come say hi? Please, Mummy, can I?'

Constance sighed. 'You don't mind, do you?'

'Of course not,' I said.

'Come on then,' she shouted to Rae.

With a squeal of delight, Louisa's seven-year-old sister came hurtling around the corner in a blur of blonde curls and pink pyjamas and threw herself into my waiting arms.

'And what're you still doing up?' I said, throwing her up in the air.

'Can't sleep, Nicky.' She giggled. 'Have you come to see Louisa?'

'That I have. I've come to see if Louisa wants to go out tonight.'

'Ooooooh. Are you going to kiss?'

I laughed awkwardly.

'Mum, Nico's going to kiss Louisa...' she sang in delight.

Constance walked over and took Rae out of my arms. 'Leave the poor man alone, Rae—you'll want to kiss boys when you're older too.'

The little girl wrinkled up her pretty nose in disgust. 'Me, kiss a boy? Never, they're smelly!'

Both Constance and I burst out laughing while Rae beamed at her audience.

'She probably won't want to go,' I whispered to Constance.

'Oh, Nicky!' Rae said dramatically, putting both hands on her hips. 'Of *course* she will want to go! All she has said for weeks is "I really like

Nico" and "Nico is soooo gorgeous". She puckered up her mouth into a smooch.

Constance put a finger to Rae's lips. 'That's enough, little lady.'

Rae's eyes watered and her lip wobbled; she tucked her face in her mother's neck where her tears wouldn't be seen. But my heart leapt in hope.

'Tired...' Constance mouthed to me. 'Louisa! You have a visitor!'

'Be there in a sec!'

I looked up as she appeared from behind the same wall that Rae had. My breath caught in my throat; she looked so different. Away from the gaze of the community, she was clearly more comfortable. Her long blonde hair was loose and the worn jeans and jumper had been replaced by a pale blue dress, a tatty book no longer clutched against her chest.

'Oh!' Louisa exclaimed, stopping dead when she saw me. 'Er... hi, Nico.'

'Mummy, Nico's staring...'

'*Rae!*' Constance scolded.

I cleared my throat, realising it was my turn to speak. 'Hi. I just, er... came to see if you wanted to go to the get-together thing. It's normally good fun. I can just walk you there if you want to go, you don't have to go *with* me. I just thought it might be... good.' I stopped, realising I was waffling.

Louisa blushed at being asked out painfully badly in front of her mother and twisted a stray curl around her finger. 'Sure, OK, that would be nice. If you don't mind walking me there of course.'

'Oh, it's no problem!' The words tumbled from my mouth in my excitement to accept her acceptance.

Rae wailed. 'Can't I go too, Mummy? Nicky, take me too.'

'Come to dinner tomorrow, Nico,' Constance said, 'or I'll never get her to bed.'

'I'd love to.' I smiled.

'Oh, and do me a favour and give these to Cosbi when you see him,' she said, passing me a box. 'All the clothes he requested to be made and altered.'

I nodded. Louisa grabbed a cardigan as Rae managed to raise a watery smile. 'Bye, Nicky!'

Audible even from Louisa's room, the music bounced easily through the caves, deafened at times by the sound of raucous laughter. I snuck a sideways glance at my date.

My date.

'Are you OK?' I said. 'You're not cold?'

She seemed startled by me talking. Maybe I was boring her so much she'd started daydreaming. How depressing.

She stopped walking and I turned around in surprise.

'I do like you, Nico,' she said, so quickly it took a moment to understand what she'd said. 'I didn't mean to be rude before, it's just... I... I dunno, I'm not really used to this attention. I guess I just didn't want you to think I don't like you. Because you seem really nice.'

A delighted smile pulled at the corners of my mouth. I put the box down, walked back and put my fingers under her chin, dragging her mortified gaze from the floor until it met my own.

'Can I?' I whispered.

She swallowed and nodded.

My lips met hers within a millisecond, softly, barely there at all. I wound my hand into her soft curls and gave myself to it completely—as if I had any choice in the matter. Senses confounded, I could concentrate on nothing but her for several minutes.

Eventually, I broke from the kiss.

'I've wanted you to do that for a while,' she whispered.

Her words knocked the breath from my chest; she'd been thinking about me too. 'Be mine,' I begged. 'I'll do anything for you. Just... be mine.'

'Yours?'

'My girlfriend.'

She opened her eyes and smiled—a breathtaking, heartbreaking smile. 'Yes.'

And with one word, she became my everything. The girl who within a month had completely robbed me of all sense, who'd made me fall far too deep, far too quickly. The girl I didn't have to resist anymore.

An ear-splitting roar of laughter thundered down the corridor as I leaned in again, followed by the sound of a crowd chanting Gerrin's name.

I tore myself away and sighed. 'Come on, let's go keep an eye on him.'

'Sounds like he's having fun.'

'Yeah, that's the problem.'

Hand in hand, we walked into the community room, only to be greeted with a loud cry of 'Nico!' from a blind-drunk Gerrin. He was perched atop the shoulders of one man and supported by the hands of several others, slopping a large glass of home brew carelessly over their heads.

'Pumme down, lads!' he roared.

'It's only nine,' I complained as he dragged me into a bear-like man hug. 'How are you in this state already?'

'It's a talent,' he said, his grin slipping as his eyes fell first on Louisa and then on our clasped hands. 'Have we met...?'

'Gerrin, this is Louisa. You remember?'

'Library Girl?' he said, eyes widening.

Louisa shifted uneasily.

Gerrin reached for her hand and pressed his lips to the back of it, his dumbfounded gaze drawing her to watch the gesture. 'How could I forget?'

It was a look I recognised from my teenage years, when my crush on the stunning sixteen-year-old Bianca Russo had ended in heartbreak when I'd spotted Gerrin snogging her behind the cowsheds. It'd been a harsh awakening for my young self, in the throes of his first great love.

'Nice to see you again, Gerrin,' Louisa said.

I tugged on her hand. 'Shall we go get a drink?'

We made our way to a more secluded corner, past the dance floor, the store of home brew, a table laid with food, and what could ambitiously be described as 'the band'. Female eyes and male gapes from candlelit tables followed Louisa as we moved, wondering who the beautiful new arrival was. Little did they know she'd been there all along.

We chose some seats near Jean, the old Frenchman who took shifts on guard, and the two girls I'd seen under the tree with Elena, who I assumed were his daughters.

I pulled out a chair for Louisa, sensing eyes watching my every movement. The culprit wasn't difficult to spot, in skin-tight jeans and a low-cut red top, and she certainly wasn't hiding the daggers she was throwing at me.

The tattooed guy trying to hold Elena's attention was having trouble keeping his eyes up and his hands in his pockets. She nodded whenever his mouth stopped moving, but her unrelenting, penetrating gaze was fixed on me, not caring who saw. Our eyes locked and held like opposing magnets; a private, unscripted game of chicken. The guy made some joke that he found hilarious and Elena's lip curled into an almost sneer of a smile, aimed again at me. She broke eye contact first and turned to her admirer, who excitedly licked his lips when she moved closer and placed a hand on his chest.

I shrugged in bemusement, knowing there was no point in trying to understand Elena. Pouring two glasses of wine, I sat opposite the French family.

'Busy out there, Jean?' I said.

'Ah, *monsieur*,' he said, animated as he swilled home brew into his glass. 'You know how it is. Nothing for days, and then suddenly, boom! You have people causing trouble, complaining, wanting to go out, and I tell them, you must go to Monsieur Cosbi and wait until 'e says it is safe. Bah, I am getting too old for their whining.'

I smiled. Jean had a flamboyant style of speaking that was made a million times funnier by the wild waving of his arms. I often wondered if he did the same when speaking French, or whether he struggled to say what he meant in English with words alone.

He leaned in, dramatically inviting my confidence. '*Mais*, between you and me, I think there is going to be trouble soon. You mark my words, *mon ami*.'

'Why, what've you seen?'

'There have been a couple of *personnes* snooping round outside. And those two'—he thumbed over his shoulder at Parker and Chase—'always whispering.'

'That's nothing new,' I said. 'You'd think sharing a room would make them sick of each other, but apparently not.'

'Then call it intuition, *monsieur*. But trust me, one day someone will get in.'

A visitor to our table made it in time to overhear Jean's last words, and Elena's eyes narrowed slightly as she sat opposite.

'Jean, Coco, Lisette,' she said. '*Quoi de neuf?*'

'*Salut*, Elena,' Coco responded with a smile. '*Rien de beaucoup.*'

'Nico...' She greeted me next, pouring herself a drink and flashing me the briefest glimpse of that dangerous glare.

'How's it going?' I said.

'Not bad. Cosbi and I had a bit of a disagreement about my job here. He wants me to teach the kids fucking languages,' she said, rolling her eyes.

'And you want...?'

'To teach them how to defend themselves.'

'Why doesn't that surprise me?'

She nodded at Louisa. 'Going to introduce us?'

'Sorry,' I said. 'Louisa, this is my friend, Elena. Elena, Louisa.'

'Nice to meet you,' Louisa said, offering her hand with a smile.

Elena raised an eyebrow and reached out her hand too. She eyed Louisa for a few moments before glancing at me. 'It *was* the blonde you were staring at then.'

'Staring?' Louisa asked. 'When?'

'It doesn't matter,' I said hurriedly, keen to change the subject. 'I—'

'What's your deal then?' Elena interrupted. 'Are you starting a book club?'

'Louisa's my girlfriend.'

'Since when?'

'Just now.'

'I hope we can be friends, Elena,' Louisa said.

Elena bit back a laugh.

I scowled at her, but Jean rescued the situation by jumping feet first into the conversation with the grace of an elephant. 'You must tell me more about your companion, Monsieur Nico. *Mademoiselle*, I hope *mon ami* Nico knows how to take care of such a beautiful creature, although admittedly he is no French lover.'

Louisa blushed.

Elena rolled her eyes.

I shook my head. 'Nothing but peacocks those Frenchmen, Jean—all mouth and nothing in the trousers. Not a patch on the Italians.'

Before the Frenchman could blow up like a bottle of pop at my slight to the sexual prowess of his countrymen, Lisette diverted his attention by sloshing more booze into his glass.

I whispered to Elena. 'Any more trouble from Ash?'

'Nothing.'

Her abrupt tone put an awkward end to the brief interaction, and

I had no choice but to listen to the mindless gossip at the table as she turned her back on me.

'It's true,' Coco whispered. 'Another one on the way, they already have four.'

'Karl and Sammy? Jeez...' Louisa added.

'Those three girls over by *la porte* keep looking over here,' Lisette joined in.

'Who are they?' Louisa said.

'One is called Roxanne,' Coco said. 'I heard Gerrin was seeing the one in the middle.'

'Really?' Louisa sounded surprised. 'I didn't think Gerrin was really the dating type. From what Nico's said, anyway.'

'Ask him.'

'Nico,' Louisa said, tapping my arm.

'Hmm?'

'Do you know if Gerrin's seeing anyone?'

'Unlikely,' I laughed. 'Why?'

'Just a rumour.'

'You want to be careful,' came a soft warning from opposite. Elena was gracing us with her attention again. 'Whispers can do awful damage to a relationship.'

I was starting to think that sitting here had been an incredibly bad idea when Ash lurched into our party and made things a whole lot worse.

'This seat taken?' he slurred at no one in particular.

Elena heard rather than saw him, flinching at the sound of his voice.

My hands slammed onto the table, my chair hitting the deck as I left it quicker than its balance would allow. The unreasonable reaction drew a gasp from Louisa.

'*Yes.*'

'Did it look like I was askin' you?'

'You aren't welcome here.'

'Why? One slag not enough for yeh, Jakes?'

Elena's hands balled, and I moved.

An inebriated Gerrin started running across the room. 'What's going on, Nico?'

'*Him,*' I spat.

With all eyes on me and Ash, no one had thought to watch Elena, who shoved me aside and had something sharp pointed at Ash's throat. The whole room gasped, the music died, and Ash staggered backwards in surprise.

'Some people don't *learn*,' Elena seethed.

With the drunk Scot far enough from the weapon, Gerrin yanked him back by his arms and propelled him towards the door. 'Go sleep it off, dickhead.'

'Elena, what the fuck is this?' I said, snatching a sharpened toothbrush handle from her grasp.

She didn't move an inch.

'Hey, you OK?' I tried again, touching her arm.

She turned furiously and for a second I thought she was going to lamp me too. 'Go fuck yourself,' she hissed.

And with that, she stormed across the dance floor and out of the party.

'What was all that about?' Louisa whispered.

'I'll tell you later,' I muttered.

'Fancy a lads' night in tomorrow, baby bro?' Gerrin asked as he surfaced from the bottle of wine he was drinking without the aid of a glass. 'Some of the guys are coming round for poker, drink, cigarettes... You game?'

'I can't tomorrow. I've promised to go for dinner with Louisa's family,' I replied.

He said nothing, but scowled and shrugged.

'You can come too if you like, Gerrin,' Louisa said.

'No thanks, Library Girl,' Gerrin said with a grin. 'I can think of other things I'd rather do with you.'

Louisa flushed red.

'Ignore him, he's beyond drunk,' I said.

'Elena is pretty,' Louisa whispered.

'Pretty crazy,' I muttered.

Gerrin caught sight of the group of girls by the door, just as they were gawking in our direction. With a grin, he rose from the table and grabbed his bottle. 'If you'll excuse me.'

My eyes followed him across the room, where he kissed each girl on the cheek, whispered to them, and exited the room with all three. Unbelievable.

❖

At a guess, I'd been asleep less than fifteen minutes when a gentle tap at the door shook me from the bizarre dream I was having. Half asleep, half drunk, and knowing that the knock didn't belong to either Gerrin or Cosbi, I paid no attention and flipped restlessly onto my back.

But the request seemed to be a courtesy, and my would-be visitor had no intention of being ignored. Through the fog of returning sleep, I heard the door open and close with a soft click and footsteps approach my bed. I was too tired to care.

The ageing mattress dipped at the side as someone crawled onto the bed, putting a knee on either side of my body, pinning down my pelvis. The weight was slight and gentle. She leaned forwards, her long hair tickling across my body, and my nose filled with the musk of her perfume. She smelled so good.

'Mmm,' I mumbled, my hands instinctively running up the thighs of whichever beautiful woman was astride me.

A moan escaped her lips as her fingers crept up my chest, playing, teasing. Sleep was becoming more impossible by the second.

'Louisa...' I groaned. 'Don't start this unless you're sure.'

'*I'm* very sure,' a voice purred inches from my ear.

It was the answer I wanted, but the words didn't belong to Louisa, and neither did the accent.

'Elena?' I asked tentatively, one eye cracking open.

'Yes, Nico?'

Like someone had dumped a bucket of ice water over my sorry head, I was awake and sober in an instant.

'Jesus fucking Christ! What're you doing?' I yelled. I tried to pull myself out from beneath her weight, but in my hurry misplaced my arm and fell back onto the pillow with a thud.

She laughed. 'I would've thought it was obvious, but if I was being too subtle...'

She grabbed the bottom of her red top and started dragging it up over her head.

'Whoa!' I said, grabbing both of her hands. 'You know that's not what I meant.'

'We're both adults. Tell me to stop.'

'Have you considered seeing a psychiatrist?' I said. 'Your Jekyll and Hyde tendencies are getting a little out of hand.'

'Are you scared?'

'A little,' I admitted. 'A couple of hours ago you were the last person I would've expected to be sneaking into my room, and now you're... we're... look, I don't even know what this is.'

'This is me satisfying my curiosity.'

'Curiosity about what?'

'Us.'

'And earlier?'

'You made me angry.'

'Well, somehow I gathered that much.'

'I've never wanted anyone more than when I walked away from you at that party.' She leaned down to kiss me and I had to bite back my physical need, hands snatching at the bed sheets as her body stroked across my groin.

Somewhat distracted, I still managed to dodge her lips. 'Elena, I have a girlfriend, remember?'

'Oh yes,' she said, rolling her eyes. 'The blushing bookworm.'

'Watch it.'

'You surprised me tonight. I never thought in a million years that'd be your thing,' she said, unbuttoning her jeans as she studied me. 'Wouldn't you rather see what you're missing out on before you decide Hermione Granger is the one?'

'That's enough, Elena,' I snapped.

'I know you want me too.'

'It's— Look, it's irrelevant.'

Her teeth nipping at her bottom lip, Elena's fingernails dragged back down my chest to where she was sitting until they were playing just along the waistband of my boxers.

'I can feel you need this,' she said with a smirk.

'Oh, come on, that's hardly fair,' I complained. 'You've woken me in the middle of the night by getting on top of me and offering me sex. Exactly how do you expect a man to react?'

'I didn't expect, but I hoped. And besides, it might be more than just sex. Let's find out.'

I shook my head in confusion, wishing that her hand would either stop or move north so I could concentrate. 'How long have you felt like this?'

'Since we met.'

'So why are you telling me now?'

'I didn't think there was any rush. But before you line up a little wifey, I thought I'd point out that you're attracted to me.'

'Look, Elena... Can we sit up?'

'Well, I'm comfy here, but if you insist... OK, OK,' she said, rolling her eyes at my seriousness.

She retreated gracefully, leaving me to scramble for some bed clothes to wrap around my middle before I could sit beside her.

'Of course I'm attracted to you,' I said. 'I'd be mad not to be. But—'

'But let's just be friends, let's not complicate things, yadda yadda.'

'But I'd met Louisa before I even clapped eyes on you,' I corrected.

'It's just one night.'

I shook my head. 'I'm not that guy.'

'Don't you think you'll get bored with Little Miss Perfect?'

'And I wouldn't with you?'

She grinned, the promise of danger sparkling in her eyes.

I swallowed. 'Point taken.'

Running a finger down my leg, Elena vacated the space on my bed and sauntered to the door. 'You'd better hope I'm still single when you change your mind.'

I smiled and fell backwards across my bed as the door clicked closed, trying hard to focus on remembering the first thirty numbers of pi.

VICTORY

An enthusiastic fire was burning in the hearth of the forgotten log cabin, the kaleidoscopic flames repeated in the grimy, cracked windows. I'd noticed the plume of dusky chimney smoke rising above the trees the second I'd returned.

She was waiting. It was night-time in the sleepy valley and an eerie calm had settled across the landscape. The grass and trees had been robbed of their bottle green by the pure silver of a full moon resting above the horizon, while the lake looked as smooth as polished black glass.

Hidden crickets chirruped in the long grass as I approached where she stood, her back to me as she watched the scene. Dark hair tumbled down her pale back, nature's evening colours making her appear ghostlike.

'I love the night, don't you?' she said.

'I guess, I've never really thought about it.'

'You should. There's such beauty in life, I think you can only appreciate it when you look at the stars and realise how small you are.'

'What's wrong?'

It took her a few moments to recognise I'd said something before she shook herself from her thoughts. 'Nothing, it's just that people never take the time to look up and appreciate that there's always a way out.'

'I'd like to believe that.'

'One day you will.'

'I almost do when I'm out here. This place looks even more stunning in the dark.'

'It really does.'

'How often did we come here?'

'Whenever things got on top of us. We ran from our troubles, sat and chatted, swam, fought...' she said, laughing at her last word.

'Always through the exit you told me about?'

'Yes,' she said, before an uneasy expression settled on her face. 'Well, apart from once.'

'Didn't anyone notice?'

'Sometimes. You had trouble keeping the secret—you're such a bad liar.'

As we resumed our silent contemplation of the scene, my thoughts were full of something even more intriguing than paradise. Elena was utterly fascinating to me; so angry yet so gentle, so serious, but such fun, so explosive yet so patient. She was impossible to read.

'What were you like as a kid?' I said.

'What kind of question is that?'

'Just interested. I can imagine a headstrong little brat, the type that used to stamp on the boys' feet in kiss chase.'

She grinned. 'Sorry to disappoint, but I was really shy.'

'I don't believe that for a second.'

'I had a hard time trusting people,' she said. 'When I was sixteen, I got close to a boy. He taught me that not everyone treats women the way my father did.'

'A boy? Who?'

'His name was Jackson.'

'Was he your boyfriend?' The question slipped out, but I didn't care. I wanted to know.

'After a while, yes.'

'Where is he now?'

'We ended it as friends when I left.' She snuck a sideways look at me. 'It's a shame, because he was just dreamy, blonde hair, dimples, tattoos...'

'Sounds like an idiot.'

'Don't get jealous, you wanted to know.'

'Jealous? Of someone with dimples? Please.'

She punched me in the shoulder to shut me up.

'You said we used to swim in here?' I asked.

'On hot days. Wouldn't stick a toe in there in winter.'

'It's still quite warm.'

She looked down and snorted. 'I'm hardly dressed for it.'

I walked backwards down the jetty, unbuttoning my shirt. 'Who said anything about being dressed?'

'What're you doing...?' she said, her mouth pulling up into a smile.

I scrunched my shirt into a ball and threw it at her. 'I'm game if you are.'

'I bet it's freezing in there.'

'Are you chicken?' I yanked at the zip of my shorts, pulled them down and threw them at her too.

'Nice underwear,' she said.

'Bet yours is better,' I retorted.

'Wouldn't you like to know?'

'I would actually.'

She smiled as I jogged to the end of the jetty and did my best cannonball into the cold, black water.

'Staying out there then?' I called when my teeth had stopped chattering. 'Chicken!'

If there was one way to push Elena's buttons, it was to call her a coward. Glaring, she threw down my clothes and turned her back. Her hands glided down the zip of her dress, the material slipping to the floor and falling into a puddle at her ankles.

Wearing only dark underwear, she dropped to the floor of the wooden platform and slid into the water with a small cry of protest at the temperature. 'Have I ever told you how much I hate you?' she called.

'Stop being a wimp. Start swimming, you'll warm up.'

I ducked into the water and started towards the centre of the lake. It was far deeper than I expected; even though I wasn't that far from shore, my feet struck nothing solid when I stopped to tread water.

Elena was at my side in a couple of minutes.

'Took your time, slowcoach,' I teased.

'Thought I'd let you get a head start. It's important for a man to know he's the best at everything, right?'

Droplets of water glistened like diamonds all over her skin; the sleek wet shine of her hair made her skin paler and her lips redder than before.

'You look better with your clothes off,' I said.

'Oh, really?'

'Yes, really.'

'They're not all off though.'

'Pity.'

'Shame you'll never get to see, Jakes.'

It really was.

'Care to put your money where your mouth is?' I asked.

'Meaning?'

'A race. Whatever stroke you want. Loser strips all the way.'

'And if I win?'

'I'll get out of the water to take mine off.'

She grinned. 'You've got yourself a deal.'

We shook on it, competitive eyes psyching out the opposition.

'Where to?' Elena said.

My eyes scanned over the shadowy lake. 'Those rocks over there?'

'You're on. Get ready to lose everything, the race, your dignity, your boxers...'

'Dream on,' I snorted. 'Ready?'

'Uh-huh.'

'OK, on the count of three. One... two...'

She didn't wait for me to get to three. With a wicked peal of laughter and a sweeping backhand, she sent a wave of water crashing over my head and dived into a practised front crawl.

'Cheater!' I yelled.

I kicked off, pulling myself quickly through the water to chase down the charlatan, who was already a few feet in front. About halfway to the rocks, I drew alongside and she turned her head to see me take a slight lead. I grinned at the fury on her face.

But no sooner was I past her, did I feel a hand clasp hold of my foot. With impressive strength, the hand yanked downwards, dragging my legs and then my head beneath the water.

'Elena!' I roared, spitting out a mouthful of lake.

'Catch me now,' she sang, dangerously close to the finish line.

I broke the surface and dived downwards, cutting smoothly through the reed-strewn lake. I threw everything I had into the last few yards; my arms and legs were screaming at me, but I refused to lose.

Vast, dark objects loomed in front of me through the murky water, and I veered upwards, emerging from the depths and slamming my hand blindly forwards, hitting the rough crags a fraction of a second before her palm smacked on top.

I dashed water from my eyes and broke into a jubilant laugh.

'Dammit!' she fumed, punishing the rock with a frustrated slap.

My heart was beating ten to the dozen. I couldn't breathe quickly enough, and my cold body ached from top to toe. But I'd won my prize.

'So, you know losing...?' I said. 'How does it feel to *lose*, loser?'

Her eyes narrowed. 'No one likes cocky, Nico.'

'It's better than cheating.'

'I don't do losing.'

'Well, you made a pretty good job of it for a first-timer. And now, it's payment time.' It was shallow enough to stand at the edge, so I backed up a few steps to get a better view and gestured to her body. 'Whenever you're ready.'

Something changed in Elena's manner. No longer sulky, she winked one of those smoking eyes at me, water lapping at her chest, and pulled her fingers through her hair, smoothing it down and flicking it behind her. 'You don't know what you've started,' she whispered.

My heart quickened.

Seeming to sense my reaction, she trailed her fingers down her neck, across her chest and out of sight below the level of the lake. Ducking down so that the water was kissing her lips, she raised an eyebrow, and I knew that her hands were busy with their task.

Sure enough, a few seconds later, a hand bearing a pair of black knickers emerged, which she paraded through the air for my approval, before throwing them onto the rocks behind.

I folded my arms, partly to show expectation for the next bit, but mostly to conceal how fast I was breathing. Elena had an incredible body and was fully aware of the effect her sexuality was having on me. The once simple dare was evolving into my own private striptease.

'More?' she asked.

'All the way.'

Her hands teased across her chest, following the curves of her soaking bra and moving around her back, unhooking the clasp. With everything risqué hidden safely beneath the surface, she pulled the straps from her shoulders and held the garment up high like a trophy before it too got discarded backwards. 'Payment in full, I believe.'

Words failed me. I just stood there and stared.

'And now what?' she said.

It was the most provocative thing I'd ever seen. She knew exactly what she wanted and how to get it.

I stood there in the freezing water for a few seconds, desperately trying to fight every physical instinct that my body was screaming at me. Needless to say, I lost.

It took me a matter of moments to wade through the water that stood between me and what I wanted. My hands refused to be restrained anymore and eagerly skimmed the length of her body, with no underwear in the way. I pressed my head to hers and sighed. 'Apparently I can't keep my hands off you.'

She closed her eyes. 'Apparently I don't want you to try.'

She was a siren, a temptress in human form. But if I could be allowed to kiss her, touch her just this one time, then maybe this intoxicating lust would subside and leave me in peace.

I pushed every objection firmly to the back of my mind, and just let go.

But I knew the second that my lips met her neck that one kiss would never be enough; just one time with her could never satisfy the appetite she'd awoken. This was a one-way ticket to hell, and I had absolutely no power to stop myself from jumping headfirst into the abyss.

I broke away to see victory written on her face. Race or no race, I'd won nothing that night. She pressed herself against my body.

'Kiss me, Nico,' she whispered. 'I know you want this.'

I nodded and wound my hand around the back of her neck. 'I do.'

My mouth was close enough to hers that I was drawing in the air that she was breathing out; there was no difference now between where one body ended and the other began.

'You're so beautiful,' I said.

Unable to resist anymore, I sacrificed myself and leaned in to seal my fate.

CONFABULATION

SEVERAL THINGS OCCURRED to me as my fingers closed on a handful of hair at the nape of her neck, pulling her to me in desperation. Several things that included the kiss not feeling as I expected it to, that her hair was no longer wet, and that the girl I'd just locked lips with had let out a small exclamation of surprise.

I opened my eyes and found myself looking not into the triumphant, beautiful face of Elena, but into the bewildered eyes of Hanna.

Oh, dear God.

I released her immediately. 'Oh shit, Hanna, I'm so sorry, I didn't mean to do that.'

'What?'

'I'm sorry,' I repeated, completely mortified.

She didn't reply, but absentmindedly traced her fingers along her lips.

'Hanna?'

'You kissed me.'

'I know, I'm sorry, it wasn't—'

I didn't get to finish my sentence. A dangerous spark had caught fire in her eyes and before I could stop her, she'd thrown herself forwards, returning the kiss I'd never intended to give.

Trying not to offend her, I pulled gently backwards, but she just followed. I took hold of her shoulders and forced her back. 'Hanna.'

'Hmm?'

'Stop,' I whispered.

Her eyes flickered open, confusion troubling her freckled face. 'You kissed me.'

'I didn't mean to. I thought you were someone else.'

'Someone else? Like who?'

'I... don't... never mind. What were you doing leaning over me anyway?'

'I came in to check on you. You were talking in your sleep so I tried to wake you, but you just grabbed me.'

'Oh,' I said, cringing. 'I'm sorry.'

'Don't keep apologising. I've wanted this for a long time, surely you must know.'

'Well, I...'

'Of course you know,' she said, seeking my mouth again.

'Hanna,' I said, pulling back more sharply. '*Stop.*'

Despite my best efforts, bluntness was the only way.

She flinched, tears forming in her eyes. 'But I love you.'

I groaned. 'No you don't, Hanna. Love comes from time, not a fantasy.'

'Don't patronise me.'

'I'm just trying to stop you getting hurt.'

'So you don't like me at all?'

'Of course, but as a friend.'

'I can't help the way I feel.'

'Neither can I,' I said. 'I'm in love with someone else.'

'Still?' she cried, tears streaking down her face.

Grabbing some tissue, I threw off the covers and went to her, but she backed away.

'I've made a complete fool of myself!'

'No, Hanna,' I said. 'No, no, I'm very flattered—'

'Flattered? Oh God!' she squealed, and ran from the room.

Collapsing back onto my bed with a heavy sigh, I rubbed my hands across my face and allowed the guilt to seep in. In the space of a few short hours, I'd got much closer to two women than I'd ever expected.

Elena. I had no choice but to admit it. I was drawn to her and it was getting out of hand. My mind was constantly inventing scenarios in which I almost won her. Yet, as much as I wanted the fantasies to reach their conclusion, something was holding me back. Or rather someone.

Louisa. She was the key to figuring this one out.

I had to know what the obstacle was. Figuring from the deathly silence that it was still the middle of the night, I lay back down and squeezed my eyes shut, preparing to have a very awkward conversation with Gerrin in the morning.

Dressed and ready ten minutes before we needed to be, two uneasy men lined up in front of the mirror, wearing matching dark trousers, white shirts and ties under waistcoats, all handmade by Constance.

'Listen. I just wanted to say thanks for doing this.'

'As if I would've missed it.'

'Still, it means a lot to me. And to Louisa.'

'I know.'

'I know we've been through this, but you are OK with it, right?'

'Everything is in the past. I'm happy for you guys. Genuinely.'

'I do love her.'

'I wouldn't be here if I didn't believe that.'

We both huffed an anxious breath.

'Nervous?'

'Bricking it.'

We both laughed.

One reflection offered a glass to the other. 'Here, get this down you.'

Two glasses clinked in celebration and two men downed their two drinks.

'Almost time to say "I do". Ready?'

'Lead the way, Best Man.'

There was an atmosphere of excitement and childlike joy in the caves that particular day. Parker and Chase were the heroes of the moment, having finally sourced some Christmas decorations in the attic of an old town house five miles from the caves and a viable tree from the local forest.

No one could remember the last time we'd celebrated this time of year, and the entire population had gone giddy for glitter, Santa resurrected after years on ice, as parents told the old lie to their children.

'That end needs to go up a bit,' Elena said, directing my end of the tinsel garland as I teetered on the top rung of a ladder.

I hooked the plastic around a higher crag and tied the knot. 'Cool, what's next?'

'The star needs putting on the tree, but we have to wait for team A to finish putting the baubles on. You can help me blow up balloons while we're waiting.'

'Balloons won't last long in here,' I snorted.

'You were a child once!' Elena chided. 'The first time you accidentally pop a balloon is a terrifying but necessary rite of passage.'

I laughed. Christmas was never really my thing, but even I had to admit that the cheer was infectious. I grabbed a balloon and started blowing, slowly going purple in the face despite the thing remaining flaccid.

Across the room, Gerrin and Louisa had been allocated to team A and were busy re-stringing baubles and finding branches high enough to hang them where the loitering children wouldn't just pluck them back off for their own private collections. Louisa was perfection, as always, in a festive red jumper and was singing along with a crude interpretation of Jingle Bells. Gerrin watched her every move, obligingly shouting out the particularly rude bits of the song, much to the annoyance of the parents hovering nearby.

Cosbi was engaged in a heated debate somewhere behind me, and I tried to eavesdrop as I kept half an eye on Louisa.

'You really think this is a fair price?' an unknown male voice said.

'I think it's how your family can best contribute to our society.'

Louisa laughed as Gerrin wrapped some tinsel around his head.

'I won't let her do it.'

'It's up to her, surely.'

Louisa reached for one of the top branches, almost falling over as she stretched onto her tippy toes.

'I'm not happy about this, Cosbi.'

'Take a couple of days, cool down, and we can talk about it some more.'

Catching Louisa just before she toppled over, Gerrin scooped her up and swung her onto his shoulders. Able now to reach her branch, Louisa placed the bauble and upside-down high fived him. The pair laughed as she climbed awkwardly back down.

Overinflated to the point of no return, the balloon between my lips popped with an impressive bang that reverberated around the room several times. A few people screamed. Children ran for the door. Everyone in the room turned to look at me.

'Sorry,' I muttered.

'I thought I asked you to focus on what was important here, Nico,' Gerrin said.

I could sense his agitation as we slowly walked laps around the medical bay. He was trying to keep his temper on his least favourite line of questioning. 'Louisa is *not* relevant right now.'

'Look, I really didn't want to ask,' I said. 'But it's getting in the way. Help me out here and I can get back to the important stuff.'

'What else do you want me to tell you? You know you dated her. Cosbi will have me fucking lynched.'

I stuffed my hands in my pockets. 'I just... The way I can remember feeling about her, it feels deeper than that, more intense. Like she was everything.'

He stopped and rubbed a hand over his forehead. 'Nic, I'm begging you, please don't do this again.'

'Do what again?'

'This. Using those words. Intense, everything. Just stop it.'

'I'm just telling you how I feel.'

'Calm it down. It's obsessive, and unhealthy.'

'It's a simple question, Gerrin,' I said.

'She's not relevant!'

'Well, she is to me,' I snapped in response. 'And if you want me to concentrate, you're just going to have to answer me.'

He sighed and shook his head. 'I can't tell you any more without talking to Cosbi. So you'll just have to wait until later.'

'This has nothing to do with Cosbi.'

'Later, Nico.'

She caught my eye, enclosed in a group of girls who were all fawning over her left hand as she held it out for their inspection. The whole room seemed to gravitate towards her, wanting to talk, to see, and it wasn't difficult to understand why. She'd been a beautiful girl two years ago, but as a woman, she was absolutely devastating. She accepted everyone's congratulations, while her eyes shot more than the occasional mischievous glance in my direction.

I finished my drink, noticing through the glass-distorted image of the room that she had finally broken away from the eager attentions of her friends. She smiled nervously as her eyes met mine, and I knew that we were both thinking the same thing. After two long and frustrating years, we were both impatient for our time alone.

Without waiting another moment, I set down my glass and made my way to the exit, dodging wayward dancers. With a knowing smile, I noticed her sneaking behind the backs of various guests on the other side of the room.

I seized her hand the second she was close enough to reach. Laughing like children, we ran down the corridor and didn't stop until we'd reached the safety of my door. *Our* door now.

Reaching down, I swept her and several armfuls of fabric up into my arms and carried her over the threshold. Taking out my cigarette lighter, I lit some candles around the room and shut out the rest of the world. It was just us now.

'Cold?' I asked.

'Nervous,' she corrected.

I reached up and silently pulled the knot from my tie, dragging the bind from my neck and casting it aside. Following my lead, Louisa drew a pin from her hair, releasing a torrent of curls around her shoulders.

'I'm nervous too,' I said, popping the top button on my shirt.

'Why?'

'I want to make you happy.'

She smiled. 'You already do.'

I went to her, running my fingers down her soft cheek. 'Trust me?'

'Always.'

My intentions of being a patient lover didn't last long; she ignited a fire in me that I couldn't hold back after such a long time. The tenderness of the first kiss I laid on her lips as her husband was forgotten as soon as she pressed her body up against me.

I dived for the fastenings of her dress, the complicated web of fabric coming apart under my keen fingers. The dress slid easily down her body, falling to the floor and leaving my beautiful wife in nothing but her underwear.

The pulse quickened in her neck when my hands skimmed around to her bra clasp, her heart thumping in anticipation beneath my lips. I slipped the lace straps from her arms as my mouth grazed the top of her ear. 'You're perfect.'

'You're not making this easy.' She giggled, breaking from my persistent lips so she could focus on the buttons of my shirt.

'Mmm,' I mumbled, my hands ripping the fastenings from their sockets.

The chair was wearing my shirt within moments, my breath catching as her hands moved onto my chest, branding heat into my skin as she traced every contour, nails dragging through the line of hair running from my navel.

I guided her backwards, and she sank down onto the mattress, watching as I unzipped and discarded my trousers. Her eyes swept low.

We were all mouths until I broke away, my lips dragging down her neck, across her collarbone, tongue licking the warm skin of her breasts. Blood flushed up her chest as I hooked my fingers inside her underwear and pulled.

My mouth lingered at the top of her thighs, her back arching off the bed when my fingers followed. She ground against my hand, craving the friction.

'You're my world,' I whispered, moving my body over hers.

She kissed my nose.

Taking hold of her chin, her stunning blue eyes found mine as I edged my body into hers, pushing forwards again and again, completing the physical union of our marriage.

Taking her hand, I encouraged her to explore, and she responded eagerly, smiling as she found ways of touching me that produced irrepressible sounds. Gradually I felt her body calm, the tension leaving her muscles.

I forced myself into her, harder, deeper, quicker.

'Oh!' she gasped, breaking involuntarily from my kiss and grabbing two handfuls of pillow.

I loved it, that sound.

'Do you need me to stop?' I teased.

'Don't you... *dare.*'

With a grin, I grasped her thigh and pulled her leg into my chest, picking up the pace. Heat flared in my stomach as my body yearned for the release she offered. My breathing became ragged, the noises slipping from my mouth getting more and more feral.

A light sheen of sweat had broken out across Louisa's skin. Eyes screwed shut, she whispered something beneath her breath. Nails carved chunks of skin from my back, pulling me to her in desperation.

Completely in awe, I watched her lose control.

'Good *God*,' she breathed. '*Please...*'

Wanting nothing more than to make her come, I abandoned any care, forcing her body to the brink.

Her blue eyes flew open, wild and out of control. Every emotion, every thought that passed through them in that moment, I saw it all.

The sound of my name, formed in a moan on her lips, obliterated my self-control in an instant.

I drove my body into hers one last time, hearing her gasp at my unexpected force. Every single muscle in me tensed and pulled as her body drew me in deeper.

Gasping at breaths, my braced arms trembling from the unpractised exercise, I hunched over her. Laying a kiss on my slick forehead, she drew me into her burning chest, stroking my hair until my breathing slowed. Several minutes passed before either of us could say anything.

'Oh, Nico,' Louisa whispered eventually.

'Fucking *hell*—'

The gasp and my movement happened simultaneously, my body folding in two like I'd been electrocuted. Dragging in breaths, drenched in sweat and ridiculously turned on, I fought to remember where I was. Or when.

Through the confusion, my hand reached out into the darkness to check the space next to me. She was gone.

'I'm married?' I choked.

Girlfriend had become wife, I was certain of it.

Fumbling beside me, I struck a match and lit the candle on my bedside table, examining my left hand in the flickering light.

A knock at the door caught me off guard and my hand swiped through the flame, knocking over the candle and burning my skin.

'*Fuck!*'

I scrabbled to set the thing back upright before it set fire to my dresser, clawing at the sheets to cover the dream-related problem I was having. 'Give me five minutes!' I shouted.

Footsteps moved away from the door as I tried to focus on the most mundane things imaginable, rather than the memory of Louisa naked. Five minutes later, and suitably frustrated, I pulled on some jeans and went to the desk, splashing cold water all over my sweaty body.

I didn't answer the second knock and Hanna entered uninvited, her red curls making a fleeting appearance in the mirror just as I'd stupidly got my hopes up that my visitor was Louisa.

Hurrying to set down the tray she was carrying, she fled from my sight before I could think of how to excuse my previous behaviour.

'Bye, Hanna,' I sighed under my breath.

Cosbi came next.

My reflection raised its eyebrows at him. 'Somehow knew you'd be paying me a visit.'

He smiled and took a seat. 'Gerrin tells me you've been asking questions.'

'*Private* questions.'

'You'll have to forgive him. He's worried about you and asked my advice.'

I huffed. 'What did he say?'

'He explained that you're a little fixated on Louisa right now.'

'You mean my wife?'

Cosbi glanced up and there was a brief flash of surprise on his face. 'Gerrin mentioned you remembered having dated her.'

'And now I've remembered that I'm married to her.'

'Nico, are you sure what you saw was corr—'

'I want to see her. Now. Or I don't help you anymore.'

He sighed. 'Which leaves us with something of a problem.'

'Why?'

'I must ask you if there is anything, absolutely anything else that you can ask of me instead of this.'

'I want nothing else,' I snapped.

'I feared as much. I can offer you many things, Nico, but as to you seeing Louisa, I'm afraid it's impossible.'

'Why?' I demanded again.

'I'd rather spare you that explanation.'

'I'd rather you didn't.'

'I really think it would be best if you just trusted—'

My frustrated snarl interrupted his well-planned speech, and I strode in the direction of the exit. 'To hell with this, I'm going to find her.'

I threw open the door.

'Nico.'

'No.'

Behind me, I heard the chair scrape back. 'She doesn't want to see you, Nico.'

I came to an awkward, involuntary halt. 'What?'

'She doesn't want to see you. I've been to speak with her on your behalf, but there was nothing I could say.'

My upper body crumpled under the weight of his words and I laid a steadying palm on the rocky wall, hurt scorching through my chest.

'I'm sorry. I wanted to save you this pain.'

'You're lying—she loves me,' I said through gritted teeth, not sure which one of us I was trying to convince.

'She did,' he corrected.

Hurt turned to anger. 'Do you mean to tell me that I've been in here all this time, and she doesn't even care?'

'It's not that she isn't worried, rather that it would be too painful to see you right now.'

'Painful? What on earth did I do?'

'I think it best that you find answers to that question yourself,' he said.

'Is she... certain?' I could hear the desperation in my own voice.

'I'm afraid so.'

My heart dropped into my stomach. 'I need to be alone.'

He nodded. 'Take some time to yourself, collect your thoughts. I'll drop back in later.'

Numb and confused, I shut him and his hurtful words out of my world, my back slamming against the door. As though they knew they could no longer function without her, my legs wouldn't hold me and I slid down the damp surface until I hit the floor.

All the times I'd remembered her, I'd never once considered why she'd never been to see me. Drifting along on my cloud of happiness, I'd been content with the memory of her, knowing in my heart she would be there waiting when the time came.

And now, knowing that she no longer felt the same somehow made me miss her a thousand times more. The more I thought of how I'd felt with her in my arms, the more intense the physical ache became, until, after an hour of brooding on the floor, I could no longer bear to be inside my own head.

I scrambled to my feet and pulled on a T-shirt, deciding that going for a walk had to be better than this.

Loose stones and the occasional discarded piece of rubbish felt the force of my miserable wrath as I walked. I was so preoccupied that it took some time for me to realise that the place was deserted and the door was again open.

No one would ever have to know.

My feet pounded down the low passageway as it stretched out invitingly, hope coursing through my body. I would see her, I'd be able to change her mind, she'd tell me Cosbi was lying. I... I...

I slammed on the brakes, tripping over my feet to stop myself hurtling into the middle of the conversation that was happening in the corridor beyond.

Clamping my hands over my mouth to stop my panting being heard, I flattened myself tight against the wall just two metres from where they were arguing.

'We have to stop this. Now,' Gerrin said, fury saturating his words.

'You're uneasy this evening, Gerrin.'

'This isn't a fucking joke, Cosbi. He's not going to let this go.'

'You mean Louisa?'

'He's not stable enough for this.'

I was surprised at how rattled Gerrin sounded; the cockiness was long gone from his voice.

'What are you worried about?' Cosbi said.

'He's not just going to roll over and accept that she won't see him. Couldn't you have thought of *anything* better?'

'He's heartbroken. Go and speak to him.'

'Heartbroken or not, he'll try to make her see sense.'

'And if he won't stop, then you know what you have to do.'

'It'll break him,' Gerrin said, almost pleading now. 'He'll hate me.'

'It's better than the alternative.'

Gerrin paused, inhaled a deep breath, and then spoke with more purpose. 'I'm scared about the obsessiveness. It's just like last time. It'll make him more determined to get out.'

'Agreed. I'll increase security outside his room.'

'Promise me he won't get to nineteen.'

'For the sake of everyone's safety, you have my word.'

Up ahead, two sets of footsteps moved in opposite directions as the conversation ended.

Alone again, I prised myself from my awkward position. With the way now blocked, I stalked angrily back down the pathway, closed the heavy oak door, and sat down against the wall outside my room. I dug a stone from under my leg and tossed it repeatedly against the wall, getting more furious every time I replayed the conversation in my head.

They were keeping secrets and people from me.

I hurled the stone down the corridor.

For the first time since waking, I felt like a dangerous man.

I held her tight and stroked fingertips down the smooth skin of her naked back.

'I love you more than anything,' she whispered against my chest.

Goosebumps leapt to attention across my skin in the wake of her breath.

I looked down. 'You're different tonight.'

'Can you guess?'

I breathed her in and a wave of affection warmed my chest. She was happy. So very happy.

She lifted her head and laid a hand on my cheek, warmth melting into my skin. She smiled, a sweet, bashful, beautiful smile.

'Tell me,' I whispered.

She shifted onto her back, her blonde curls falling on my body. Her hand sought mine, picking it up and placing it across her bare stomach.

My eyes widened.

She nodded. 'I'm pregnant, Nico.'

I couldn't stop the ridiculous grin that spread across my face. 'You mean... it's true? You're... we're... *baby*?'

She laughed. 'Yes!'

Our baby.

I scooped her back into my arms, trying to hug every inch of her being. I felt that my heart could explode. 'You've made me the happiest man alive.'

'Happiest... man...'

'Nico.' Gerrin snapped his fingers in front of my face. 'Nice power nap?'

I winced as my spine cracked, and I squinted up at him.

Jagged rocks from the wall dug into my back.

'Come on, back in,' he said, grabbing my hand to haul me up.

Adrenaline and anger stirred in my body. I was ready for this fight.

'I've been waiting for you to come back,' I said, revelling in his discomfort as he took longer than necessary to close the door.

'So... Cosbi mentioned that he stopped by,' he said, moving to the desk and picking at my food tray to avoid making eye contact.

I dropped onto the chair and folded my arms. 'Yeah, Cosbi *stopped by*.'

He glanced up. 'I hear he, um... explained about Louisa.'

'That she won't see me?'

He nodded. 'I hope... I mean, I don't want you to be too upset.'

'Well, I'm really touched, Gerrin.'

'Nic—'

'I'll get over her in a day or two. No worries.'

'Well, yeah, you need to.'

'You think you can stop me getting there?' I sneered.

His head snapped in my direction. 'I'll do everything in my power to stop it.'

'She's *mine*.'

'Stop this. Now. I mean it, Nico.'

'No, *you* stop lying to me. Her, this, Elena, it's all just one big lie.'

'She can't see you, that's no lie.'

'Where's my wedding ring? You stole it,' I said.

His jaw dropped, a string of vulnerable emotions passing through his eyes before icy anger banished the thaw. 'Don't speak to me like that.'

'Or what?'

'You of all people should know better than to ask that.'

'Never knew what a bullshitter you were.' I sneered. '"*Sure, Nic, you were more than friends...*" She's my fucking wife!'

'She's nothing to you anymore.'

'Is she there, room nineteen? I want to see her—you have no right to keep her from me.'

'I have *every* right,' he said. 'Why the hell do you think there's a guard at this door every night? And don't look at me like that, I know you know about it. Ever thought it's not for your benefit?'

'Go to hell.'

He stood there looking thunderstruck for a few moments. 'I said don't you fucking *dare* speak to me like that.'

'Or *what?*'

I understood Gerrin well enough to know that he wouldn't refuse the fight. Eyes burning with anger, he strode to me, thudding a balled fist into his waiting palm.

I was more than happy to oblige. My hands smacked into his chest as I stalked forwards to meet the challenge.

'That all you got?' I said, pressing forwards, shoving him until his back collided with the wall behind. 'Come on, Gerrin, come and shut me up. Stop me asking the wrong questions, stop me being with my wife just because you don't like her.'

He laughed in my face, he actually laughed. 'You really think she's not here because I don't like her?'

'Explain then, dickhead.'

He ripped my grip from his shirt and hurled out a hefty punch, catching me on the jaw. The force of it threw my balance, and I stumbled back into the medicine cabinet, scattering its contents with an almighty racket.

'Happy now?' he snarled.

Tasting blood, I wiped my split lip on my hand. 'Where's my wedding ring?'

'You don't have one.'

'More lies?' I spat. 'I know the truth.'

'The truth?' His tongue almost tripped over the words. 'The truth is that you couldn't keep her!'

I launched myself at him, grabbing his throat. 'She was pregnant. There was a baby too.'

'Don't you even—'

'Where's my wife? Where's my kid?'

Gerrin flipped. With barely any effort, he lifted me clean off my feet and slammed me down on the floor, pinning me there with a huge arm. He thrust his left hand in front of my eyes. 'You stubborn prick. Louisa is *my* wife. *Mine.*'

COGNATA

M Y DAZED EYES slowly focused on the gold band on his fourth finger.

'Why do you push it?' he said. 'Why force me to hurt you?'

Confusion hit me, my ears ringing as blood left my brain. I blinked. 'There was a baby...?'

Gerrin sighed and released me. '*My* baby, Nico. My son.'

'But... I saw, I saw, it was real.'

'I don't understand what you're seeing, but it's not real,' he said. 'Maybe there's a part of you that still wants this stuff, that's guilty about letting her go.'

'Letting her go?' I whispered.

'Goddammit, Nic, you're not well enough for this!'

'She was my girlfriend! You said so!'

'She was once. But she broke it off. She... caught you with someone else.'

'Someone else? I wouldn't do that.'

'Honestly, I never thought so either.'

'Who?'

He raised his eyebrows at me.

And there it was.

I'd spent enough nights dreaming of that someone else to understand how I could've been too weak to resist. My chest sagged, and I let my head drop to the ground with a thud.

'Oh God,' I moaned, fighting the urge to cry.

'I'm so sorry, Nic, please forgive me. I didn't want you to find out like this.'

I covered my eyes with my arm. 'It's not your fault.'

'I got your blessing to marry her, I swear.'

What a complete idiot I was, obsessing over my sister-in-law. No, it was worse than idiotic, it was sad. I was all alone, the idiot who'd messed everything up.

I couldn't help the sob that escaped from my throat. 'I have nothing to carry on for now.'

He snatched my hand, clasping my fist in his. '*I'm* still here, Nic. *Me.*'

CARNALITY

GERRIN WAS WRONG; he was no longer enough.
The brief taste of having my own family had ruined me forever. I still yearned for it, craved Louisa, and it was eating me up from the inside like a parasite, forever unsatisfied.

There was nothing left for me here.

I would fulfil my promise and then start again as best I could.

I threw myself into the anaesthetic experiment. The sooner I remembered what they wanted, the sooner I could leave this place behind.

There was unfinished business. I could think of nothing else as the cool liquid from the syringe flooded up my arm, swirling clouds of anaesthetic fogging my vision.

I found her alone, studying the spitting embers thrown up by the brooding fire in the cabin as she held out her hands to be warmed. I just stood there wondering, watching, until she realised I was there.

'Hi, Nico.'

'Hey.'

She reached for my hand, winding her warm fingers between mine and guiding it to her cheek. The temptation to ignore my dilemma was so overwhelming that it was all I could do to say, 'I need to speak to you.'

But she was already too close. 'I want you.'

'Elena, I really need to—'

We moved as a pair; she leaned in to kiss me as I pulled back, turning my head before she could change my mind.

'Nico?'

I couldn't bring myself to face her.

Taking hold of my chin, she made me do what I could not, her furious dark eyes searching mine for a problem that I didn't want to confront. And I knew what she saw there. Amidst the guilt, the confusion, my desire for her, she saw a heartbroken Louisa staring right back.

'What we did to her was wrong,' I whispered.

'Got to you, did they?' she sneered.

'I've still got feelings for h—'

'Then I can't help you right now.'

'What? Elena, what do you mean? Where're you going?'

'You need to choose.'

'Choose? Choose what? Elena, please...'

Her face softened momentarily. 'There'll be a time when you need me again. When that time comes, I'll be right back at your side. Like always.'

And with that she abandoned me, running from our refuge and disappearing back into the depths of my memory.

'If that's everything, gentlemen,' Cosbi said.

I yawned in response; I wasn't remotely interested in the workings of this place.

'*Un moment, s'il vous plaît*, Monsieur Cosbi,' the Frenchman piped up.

'Jean? Problems outside?'

'Nothing wrong out there,' Jean answered, his hands dancing unnecessarily through the air. 'But I did tell you about the young girl I found hiding nearby, yes? Elena.'

'So you did, Jean. Where is she now?'

'She is sleeping on our floor.'

'Daryl, room twenty is free?'

'Yeah,' came the gruff reply from a man sitting opposite with a grey beard and yellowing eyes. 'Door sticks though.'

'Would you be able to fix it within the next couple of days?'

The man didn't look up from picking at the hard skin on his knuckles, but nodded.

'Then it's settled,' Cosbi said. 'Gerrin, Nico, would you spare me five minutes of your time, please?'

We lingered while the group of men trudged towards the exit.

'Come with me,' Cosbi said, leading the way from his room and past both of ours. 'There's one other room down here. Go ahead.'

He pointed into the darkness beyond room 22, which now belonged to Gerrin.

Taking a lamp from its bracket on the wall, Gerrin led the way down the progressively narrower, steeper and damper-smelling path until we reached a door standing ajar. I wondered how I'd never had the curiosity to wander down this way.

I took a second lamp from outside the door and followed Gerrin inside, the flames falling on the hidden contents of the room.

Part of the large space had been blocked off by handmade brick walls and divided into two compartments, each with its own solid door.

A stale smell filled my nose, rising from stagnant water lying in puddles on the floor, no doubt fed by the relentless dripping noise that could be heard nearby, as regular and inevitable as a clock ticking. Three barrels filled with the same liquid stood rotting near an exhausted old bed frame, dressed with a stained mattress. A metal bucket holding multiple sizes of branding pokers sat in one corner.

'Neat!' Gerrin said, stopping to admire a collection of weapons hanging on rusting nails driven into the wall. Knives, more metal pokers, axes, and even an old rifle, protected from the elements by a plastic sheet stuck haphazardly to the wall.

'What the hell is this place?' I said.

'Room twenty-three,' Cosbi said.

'What's it's for?'

'The beginnings of a defence,' he said, a finger pointing skyward. 'Although we need much more to survive against them. For everyone here, it's for show—a reminder to keep the peace.'

'Clever,' Gerrin said.

'What's with the bed?' I asked.

Cosbi shrugged. 'Occasionally, we have to send someone down here to cool off. So many people living in close proximity is precarious at times.'

'And where do we fit into this?' Gerrin said.

'I would like you two to uphold the rules here, and help locate more weapons and train people to use them.'

I couldn't help laughing. 'Are you preparing for war?'

'If it comes to that,' he replied, without even a hint of a smile. 'The group outside are animals and we need to learn to defend ourselves. And correct me if I'm wrong, but as you were both interested in that rifle, my guess is that you know how to shoot.'

'What do you think, Nic?' Gerrin said.

'It all seems a bit dramatic,' I said.

'We've had trouble before with the wrong sort of people trying to get in, Nico,' Cosbi said. 'Someone who can hit a target serves as a good warning to them not to try. Like it or not, the threat is very real—I'm sure you want to be able to protect Louisa.'

'And none of this ever gets used on people here?'

'For show only.'

'It was my decision to stay—I'll leave this one with you,' I said to Gerrin.

Gerrin held out his hand to Cosbi. 'Throw in a supply of tobacco and you have yourself a deal.'

'Excellent,' Cosbi said, shaking the hand. 'One more thing. It's likely there will be a young girl moving in near you soon. She's the same age as you, Nico. I'm sure a hand with the packing boxes wouldn't go amiss.'

I jolted awake with one of those shocks that feels like you've been forgetting to breathe. The precious final moments of the drug had been long enough for Mum and Dad to visit my dreams. Squeezing my eyes shut, I tried to the relive the memory before it was lost to me again...

'Square your shoulders to the target and move this leg,' Oliver Jakes said as he smacked my right leg back a few inches and positioned the butt of the rifle into my chest. 'It gives you a greater range of movement to track a moving target when you stand like this. Try putting your weak hand further down the forestock too—it'll give you more control in aiming until you know what you're doing.'

At that point, the rifle next to me went off, startling me into lowering my own gun. Gerrin had fired at the first tin can lined up along a wall in the distance and missed by metres, putting a hole instead into a nearby water butt, which immediately sprang a leak.

'Squeeze the trigger gently, Gerrin,' my father directed. 'If you rush and snatch at it, you lose sight of what you're shooting at. And Nico, please remember you're holding a loaded gun. I'd like to keep my feet.'

Gerrin took aim again, slowly and steadily this time. Seconds later, the gun discharged, releasing a bullet that nicked the top of one of the cans, but didn't knock it from the ledge.

I set myself in the position my father had shown me and lined up the target before taking my own shot. With a satisfying crunch, the bullet bit metal and carried the can to the floor.

'Yes!' I shouted.

'Well done, Nico. First try too,' Dad said, ruffling my hair.

'Beginner's luck,' Gerrin said.

'It's not a competition, Gerrin.'

'What sort of thing will this take out anyway?' Gerrin asked, ignoring him completely.

'It's a point twenty-two, for shooting small game, rabbits, that sort of thing. Once you get the hang of this, I'll let you try something bigger, something we use to take down deer and wild boar.'

'How soon will that be?'

'Not until I say you're ready. You need to learn responsibility if you want to come on this winter's hunting trips.'

'Do I have to go?' I asked.

'Not if you don't want to, but you should still learn this. Any farmer should know how to shoot a rifle, and any man should be able to protect his family.'

I nodded and lined up the next victim, stopping when another voice reached my ears.

'Dinner's ready, boys!' my mother called from the doorway of the old farmhouse, the wind tangling her long chestnut hair as the delicious smell of fresh bread floated out on the air. 'Time to stop shooting holes in all of my things!'

'Coming!' we shouted in unison and abandoned the rifles, jogging back across the field. There was always foul play in our races, particularly from Gerrin. Objecting to me edging past him, he sent both of us crashing to the floor by launching himself at my back.

'Smells good,' my father said as he won the race and pulled my flour-covered mother off the porch and in for a kiss.

'Gross...' Gerrin said, going past them to wash his hands.

'Get a room,' I added, following.

My mother laughed, chiding my father with a playful smack to the chest and returning to the kitchen to dish up dinner. 'I think our boys are embarrassed by us, Oliver.'

'I'll tell you something, lads,' my father said, going to help her. 'If you ever find a woman as beautiful as this, marry her, and don't ever let her go.'

I snorted with laughter. At the know-all age of fourteen, football was still my first love, and girls were an unnecessary, annoying addition to life.

'Just you wait a few years, Nico, just you wait.'

'*Il mio cuore ti appartiene*,' my mother said, setting down my father's plate and kissing him on the cheek. 'So then, Gerrin, Nico, which of you needs to fix the water tank?'

I stuck out my finger.

'Grass...' Gerrin hissed.

... I opened my eyes and smiled. That was exactly how I wanted to remember my parents, happy, in love. Not the poster couple for domestic violence.

'Damn, I love it when you do that,' I rasped, throwing my head back as I sucked in a breath of ecstasy.

We hadn't made it to the bed. She'd walked in on me changing my T-shirt, and seemed to have completely forgotten about handing over my birthday present. Clothes and sheets were just in the way, and we'd ended up on my desk chair with her dress around her waist, but not before she'd slipped to her knees to show me exactly what she could do with her mouth.

'Happy birthday,' Louisa said.

'Better than any present.'

'Hope I didn't break it.' She threw a glance at the discarded parcel, lying in a tangle of ribbon in the corner.

We burst out laughing.

'Can you wear the bow next time?' I asked.

'Next year, if you're lucky.'

Kissing my nose, she climbed off my lap and went to the mirror to correct her makeup.

I zipped my trousers back up and grabbed a T-shirt. 'We need to be there in ten—I think Gerrin has something planned.' I paused halfway through putting it on. 'In which case, maybe it's better to be late.'

'I can help you be late.'

The hairs on the back of my neck pricked up.

I finished dragging the T-shirt over my head and turned slowly, glancing briefly at the empty space in front of the mirror.

'Let me show you...' Elena backed up to the wall with a grin, her red dress swallowed by the shadows. Out of the darkness, a finger beckoned me.

My lip hooked up.

Like the weak fool I was, I obeyed.

'Isn't this better?' she murmured in my ear. '*Forget her*, Nico.'

I seized her wrists and pinned her against the wall. Her smile widened; she knew she had me.

'Go on then,' I whispered.

'You want me, not her. Say it.'

I grabbed her leg and hooked it around my waist, pulling her body into mine.

'Say it.'

'*Yes*,' I whispered.

The door flew open.

'Nico? Are you ready, I've been waiti—' Louisa was halfway across the floor when the words stopped.

We froze mid-air, Elena's teeth wrapped around my bottom lip.

Louisa's face fell, her beautiful eyes filling with water as they moved between the two entwined, motionless figures in front of her. With a sob of horror, she was gone amidst a trailing cloud of blonde hair, her footsteps and tears fading down the corridor.

'Fuck!' I spat, trying to remove myself from the tangle.

'Oh, leave her,' Elena said, snaking her arms around my neck and pulling my face back to hers. 'She knows now.'

The dream slid out of focus.

'Stop it!' I hissed, smacking my palm on my forehead with each syllable. 'Stop it, stop it, *stop it.*'

I had to stop thinking about her that way.

Why wouldn't my brain accept that she was Gerrin's wife now?

'Accept it!' I whispered louder, with an extra hard smack to the head.

I'd like to be able to look her in the face when I eventually saw her again, and not feel ashamed that every time I closed my eyes, I was dreaming about how good she was in bed.

And I was pretty sure Gerrin was only going to be understanding of this infatuation for so long. Certain things were strictly off-limits between family, and my sister-in-law was most definitely on that list.

'Concentrate,' I instructed my brain for our next outing. 'Focus on what's important. No more Louisa.'

CONSUMING

'GETTING SOME STRENGTH back?'

Gerrin had found me jogging laps around the cramped medical bay and fell into step alongside me.

I shrugged.

Truth was, I was just trying to release some tension. With the object of my affection a locked door and a wedding ring away, my body was developing a substantial, unfulfilled appetite. And not of the food variety.

'Good idea,' he continued. 'It'll help your mood too.'

'Well, there's nothing else to do around here,' I panted. 'Gabriel won't let me increase my time in the experiment.'

'You're doing enough,' he agreed.

I slowed to a walk, more sweaty than I ought to be from a five-minute jog. 'I'm not. I'm not doing enough. I can't focus on the right things. I keep thinking about... I dunno.'

Gerrin stopped running too. 'You keep thinking about Louisa?'

I sighed. 'Yes.'

'You're worried I'll be angry?'

'Yes.'

'Nic, this isn't a normal situation. You're living out your past again, you just haven't reached the part where you got over her. You'll get there.'

'If I got over her, Gerrin, why do you need a guard at my door?'

He stopped completely. 'You got there in the end, but for a while you got a bit... intense with it all. When she broke it off, you had trouble accepting it. Found you sitting outside her door more than once, begging her to listen. You were a bit...'

'Obsessive,' I finished with a disheartened nod. 'Yeah, I can see that.'

'She got a bit scared. That's why I can't let her come see you, and why I can't let you go to her. Until you're past those memories.'

'Does she hate me?' I asked.

He put his hand on my shoulder. 'She hopes you get better soon. She asked me to pass that on. We want you back in our family as soon as you're well enough.'

I smiled a sad, hopeless smile. 'I'm not sure that will work.'

'It will, in time.'

'I'd never hurt her, you know.' I felt the need to say it.

'I know. Come on, let's do a few more laps, get that mood up.'

'Only a couple more. Gabriel will be here soon.'

RESTRAINT

'**G**ERRIN, STOP,' I said, slapping a hand on his shoulder. 'It was only a drunken argument.'

'He broke the rules,' Gerrin said, seething with rage. He pulled the struggling man's head out of the putrid barrel by his hair.

The man gasped in a spluttering breath, water sloshing down his front.

I'd sprinted down to 23 as soon as Elena told me that the unwitting brawler had laughed in Gerrin's face when told to stop. Turned out I was right to be worried.

The pure anger that seeped from Gerrin was getting a little too familiar for my liking. Far from life here allowing him to move on from the past, the power given to him had gone to his head, resurrecting an ugly, resentful side. The pain of Italy never seemed to be far from the surface these days, and he was all too willing to make other people feel it.

'Yeah, so give him a warning.'

'I dunno, Nic, given that he couldn't keep a straight face, I just didn't think a warning was going to cut it.'

'Is that any reason to be drowning him?'

'Well, if you were around more to help out, maybe I wouldn't have to be so tough on them.'

'We can discuss that later,' I said, knowing his jealousy of mine and Louisa's relationship wouldn't help this situation. 'Has Cosbi agreed to what you're doing?'

He paused. 'No.'

'Then let it go. I think he's learned his lesson.'

He looked torn between listening to reason and giving the man another dunking.

'Hey,' I said, holding out my hand.

Gerrin's breathing calmed as he straightened up. With a swift movement of his arm, the man flew through the air and landed in a heap, and Gerrin slapped his hand into my grasp. But his eyes were still betraying the inner torment, the decision between humanity and doing what he knew would momentarily ease the trauma of his past.

We exited the room together, but not before Gerrin had delivered a swift, hefty kick to the face, knocking the man out cold.

'Consider *that* your warning,' he hissed.

'I hear Nico interfered when you were dealing with someone today.'

I stopped just short of the door, seconds away from knocking.

'Said I shouldn't go ahead without your say so,' Gerrin said. 'He doesn't like it when I get that angry.'

'And do *you* like it?'

Gerrin paused. 'I guess. It's the only thing that makes me feel something sometimes, if that makes sense.'

'You must also feel some guilt, or you wouldn't be here asking my opinion.'

'He makes me feel guilty.'

'You and your brother are different men, Gerrin. You're dealing with the past in different ways.'

'I feel like I'm letting him down, like all the fucking time,' Gerrin said.

A twinge of responsibility pulled at my heart; was I putting too much pressure on him?

'Pain needs a release, one way or another. Physical anger is your outlet—you just need to learn how to pull it back,' Cosbi said.

'I'm glad someone understands. I swear Nic thinks I'm a fruitcake sometimes, the way he looks at me...'

'Don't judge him for it. Our experiences shape the men we become and you shielded him from the worst of it—you found your parents and you had to bury them. The pain might not be quite so raw for Nico.'

'I don't want this to drive a wedge between us, though. Maybe I should talk to him.'

'I'm happy to speak to him on your behalf, if you like—it might be better with a mediator to begin with.'

'Yeah, maybe.'

There was silence for a few moments, apart from the sound of liquid being poured.

'Tell me, how goes his relationship with the blonde?' Cosbi said.

'He does fuck all else.'

'You're feeling a bit sidelined?'

'He barely knows I exist anymore and he's getting so hung up on her. He goes on the defensive whenever I say anything remotely negative.'

'He's young, he's in love. Do you have anything against the girl?'

'Not really. She's not right for him though.'

'And perhaps he will realise that in time. You just need to spend more time together.'

I backed away from the door, hearing some people around the corner. Gerrin and I clearly had a lot to work on if we wanted things to go back to how they were.

'*Ow...*' I hissed, wincing as I underestimated the height of the rocky ceiling for the fourth time in as many minutes. I rubbed my sore head. 'Elena, where the hell does this go?'

'Don't you like surprises?' she shouted back.

'You aren't six foot tall.'

I had no recollection of the path we'd taken through this maze. Elena had given me no choice but to follow when she'd ambushed me outside my room, dragging me along and declaring she had something 'really important' to show me.

'Have you found a den of animals or something?' I said, pausing as a high-pitched whine sounded somewhere to my right.

'What the fuck are you on about, Jakes?' Elena said.

'You didn't hear that?'

'Hear what?'

'Sounded like something was being tortured.'

'And it wasn't you singing?'

I rolled my eyes and listened again for the sound. After a few seconds of nothing, and starting to believe I'd imagined it, I huffed 'come on then, what is this big surprise?'

'Right, before I show you this, you must swear never to tell anyone about it.'

'Not even Louisa?'

'No one.'

'Why not?'

'Let's just say I don't think Cosbi would be too happy about what I intend on using it for. Can I trust you, Nico?'

'Always.'

Satisfied with my promise, she scrambled up a steep incline where the ceiling became even more impossible for me to negotiate. About halfway up, I realised the flaming torch in my hand was no longer necessary. Natural light pricked through the black, catching a million dust particles red-handed in its beams as I sucked in fresh, clean air.

Handing her torch to me, Elena stepped a foot over a ledge in front and dropped out of sight, reaching up seconds later for me to pass back the light. Fumbling for the edge, I found my footing and copied, thudding down into a stream of water and soaking myself in the process. Elena was already inspecting the apparent dead end in front and beckoned for my help. With our combined strength, we succeeded in rolling back a huge rock that was keeping nature from entering hell. With an indignant creak, it surrendered its post, and pure daylight, along with the roar of falling water, streamed through the hole.

I gaped. 'How did you find this?'

'It's taken a while to figure out the path.'

'But I never saw—'

'I know, don't you think it's incredible? Sat there in my room every night and we never even noticed?'

I nodded. 'What *do* you intend to use this for?'

'For now, to get out of this dump for a while. In the future, who knows?' she said, grabbing hold of my T-shirt. 'Come on, let's go see where it comes out.'

'Are you sure we're looking in the right place, Nic?' Gerrin complained after half an hour of searching Elena's old room had yielded nothing.

'Positive,' I answered, scraping around the charred wall on my hands and knees. 'It's in here somewhere, we just need to keep searching.'

Some serious thought had gone into whether to confess what I knew to Cosbi. I wasn't sure who or what to trust anymore when even my own memory didn't know. And there was the old promise I'd made to Elena to keep my mouth shut about the second exit.

In the end, my decision had come down to purely selfish reasons. More than anything, Cosbi wanted to know the location of that second exit, almost as much as I wanted to walk past Louisa's door again.

I was slowly losing my fight against the part of me that desired her above anything else. And now there was an inexplicable urgency in me to know that she was safe. I knew I could barter; the location in exchange for allowing me to tag along.

Cosbi had agreed without question, on condition that the search was to be made during the night.

I don't know what I was expecting to happen. The frantic pounding of my heart, which had steadily built to a crescendo at the approach to the door, quickly sank back into a glum, despondent rhythm at the deathly silence as we marched right past. I didn't even dare look in the direction of where she was undoubtedly sleeping at that very moment.

What a terrible bargain I'd struck.

'Take your time, Nico,' Cosbi said.

I surveyed the wall for what felt like the hundredth time, yanking away loose stones to reveal the same unyielding rock face behind.

Maybe I *was* wrong.

'It should be here,' I said.

'Nic, stop and look. If it was here, it'd be obvious,' Gerrin said.

I froze.

And there she was at the lake, clear as anything, haunting my dreams on the darkest of starry nights. *'It's just that people never take the time to look up and appreciate that there's always a way out.'*

Slowly, I got to my feet and tipped my head up. There in the ceiling, barely distinguishable from the surrounding gloom, was a large chasm, big enough surely to allow a grown man through.

I pointed skyward. 'There.'

OMNISCIENCE

I OPENED MY eyes.

I was the shadowy figure.

I stood before her, jealousy and hatred coursing through me.

She had to go.

She tore her terrified stare from me and bolted for the exit.

I smirked and followed her to the door, producing the key from my pocket to show her.

I grabbed a fistful of her long hair and dragged her back to the wall.

She fought me, pathetic gasps of fear sounding every time she punched my arms.

I reached up and wiped tears from her cheeks.

He shouted from across the room.

I'd forgotten he was there.

I paused, savouring the moment.

I knew this would change everything forever.

I knew it would get better eventually.

My hands found their home at her throat.

I pressed, harder and harder.

She choked.

She clawed.

He screamed at me.

I wasn't listening.

I was sweating, shaking with the effort.

But she had to go.

ASTRAY

LYING IN BED, I turned my hands over. I looked at my palms and then at the backs, over and over. There was rough skin, some faded marks on my right knuckles, and a slight uncontrollable tremble. But nothing else.

I reached out and made a circle with my fingers, tightening my imaginary grip.

My hands trembled more.

Could I do it?

I shook the thoughts from my head, terrified that my immediate answer to that question wasn't no. I sat up.

'What do you think, Nic?' Gerrin asked, apparently unaware of my grim daydream.

He thrust a piece of paper into my hands.

'Looks like Braille,' I said, tracing my fingers over the series of drawn dots.

'We thought so too. Do you have any idea what this means?'

'None.'

Turns out Elena was a clever cookie. The only solution to the labyrinth of tunnels above her room was a code written in chalk. Ash had got lost twice before Cosbi had called time on the search and tasked Parker and Chase with finding some maps.

In the meantime, he'd turned his attention back to me, overruling Gabriel's request to stop the experiment, in the hope that I would remember both the path and my past.

'What an amazing day,' Elena said as she lifted herself out of the crisp, cold water. She slicked back her hair and reclined on the creaking jetty, body sparkling as the midday sun hit a thousand drops of water.

'Here,' I said, throwing her a dusty towel from the nearby cabin.

'Thanks.'

I ran mine over my face before collapsing onto the baking decking for a sunbathe. I watched Elena wring remnants of the lake from her underwear, understanding as always why the guys talked about her. Besides the obvious physical appeal, there was something behind those eyes, a spark, a mystery. But I guessed the greatest draw was the fact that she said no to them, every single time.

'I feel bad,' I said.

She smiled like she did every time I said that, knowing I wasn't comfortable that we were out here and everyone else was in darkness.

'I mean, I agree with not telling Cosbi, but maybe some of the others wouldn't—'

'Tell?' she finished. 'Whatever Cosbi wants, he finds a way of getting. And if he suspects what we've found, that'll be the end of that exit. Besides, at least this way we're only risking ourselves.'

I rolled my eyes. 'You're being melodramatic. We'd get a disapproving look and a slap on the wrist at best.'

'He's dangerous.'

'He's harmless. And this isn't fair.'

'Nothing will be fair while things stay as they are.'

I frowned at her. 'We should at least cut down the trips then. People are starting to notice that you and I disappear for hours on end.'

She shrugged and flipped onto her side. 'Maybe they'll think we're having an affair.'

I squinted at her under my hand. 'I don't think anyone would believe that.'

'People talk... especially bored ones.'

'If anybody had an affair, it would definitely be Gerrin.'

We lay there for hours, chatting, making pictures out of the trailing clouds, so drunk on the warm air that we forgot time and our troubles.

Elena had fallen asleep by the time dusk settled in the valley, and I earned a bad-tempered grumble as I tried to shake her awake.

'Hey, it's time to go,' I whispered.

Gathering our clothes from beside the cabin's smouldering fire, I returned to find her wide awake and throwing me a questioning look.

'What?' I said, stopping dead.

'Do you know what was up with Louisa the other day?'

'Huh?'

'Louisa,' she prompted. 'Stormed out of her room, slammed the door. I think it's the most personality she's ever shown.'

'Oh. Gerrin.'

'Now why doesn't that surprise me?' she said, rolling her eyes as she pulled up her shorts. 'What was your lovely brother's problem this time?'

I smiled. Elena was no fan of Gerrin's and she'd never made a secret of that fact, not even for my sake.

Fully dressed, we made our way back out to the fields, keeping close to the treeline.

After a few minutes she spoke again, cautiously, as though weighing up whether her next words would start a row. 'What do you think of all this, Nico?'

'All what?'

'I mean, do you really trust Cosbi? We've been coming out here for weeks now and we've seen nothing. No people, no fighting. And what about Eli?'

'Eli was necessary.'

'See, that's what I'm talking about. You got played.'

'For everyone's safety, it was necessary—he could've told anyone where we were. I was there, Cosbi had no other choice.'

'Then what about Gerrin?' she challenged.

'What about him?' I stopped and glowered at her, folding my arms.

She sighed and started to walk. 'You're not there yet.'

'Not where?'

'I understand, Nico. He's your brother, and I love that fierce loyalty in you, but he isn't the same man you used to know.'

'What does it have to do with you?' I snapped as we reached a break in cover and passed within sight of the main entrance to the caves.

'Nothing, of course,' she said. 'I'm just trying to be a friend.'

I said nothing, silently bristling in defence of my brother.

She carried on regardless. 'There are... a few of us, some friends of mine, who feel the same way and we've met up—'

But movement behind her had caught my eye.

'Get back!' I hissed.

Grabbing her arm, I pulled her into the dense cover of the trees, hoping to God that whoever had been standing guard hadn't seen.

'Who was it?' she breathed.

'Jean, I think.'

'I hope so.'

We remained in our hiding place for a few minutes, but night-time was fast approaching and soon we had no choice but to try our luck again.

'Come on,' I said.

'Jean wouldn't tell,' Elena panted, keeping pace with me as I jogged towards the waterfall.

'How do you know?'

'I just do. But it would be better if he hadn't seen—I don't want him to have to lie for us.'

'Beautiful, isn't she?'

Jean appeared at my shoulder and caught me watching Elena. She'd been accosted by an admirer, a guy by the name of Dean. Tall, shitty tattoos and hair shaved close. He was clearly in love with himself, oozing smug overconfidence as he lounged one-armed against the wall. Elena was laughing away at some joke he'd made.

'That she is, Jean,' I muttered back. 'Fancy your chances?'

Jean laughed. 'Ah, *non, mon ami*, but there is nothing wrong with appreciating a handsome woman. You were doing it yourself, *n'est pas?*'

I raised my eyebrows. 'I was just waiting.'

Out of the corner of my eye I saw his sceptical smirk, his lip twitching in amusement as he watched first me and then Elena.

'I would not worry about that one,' he said, tipping his head at Dean. 'She wouldn't settle for that.'

'Who was worried?' I said.

'I'm glad I've caught you on your own anyway, *monsieur*, I've been wanting to speak with you.' Jean's voice dropped low, his eyes skirting the corridor.

'Oh? What is it?' I said, my mouth pulling into a tight line as Dean rolled up his sleeve, revealing a large tribal tattoo across his bicep. With a smile, Elena traced her fingertips over the design.

'I need your help to keep someone out of trouble.'

'I'll do what I can, Jean, you know that.'

He hesitated before selecting his words. 'What is the term you English use? Hypothetical. Yes, hypothetically, Nico, what would you do if you saw two people doing something that could cause trouble? And it's not wrong about the fun they're having, *non*, but maybe one of the people doesn't realise the danger he's putting the other in.'

Shit, he did see us.

'If both parties agreed, I can't really see what could be done, Jean,' I said. 'Maybe it's no one else's business.'

'And maybe you are right. But consider that certain old men might have become rather attached to one of these people, might even regard her as a daughter. And headstrong though she is, this old man doesn't want her to get hurt. What would you do?'

I sighed and turned to meet his gaze. 'I guess I'd be standing right where you are now.'

The Frenchman nodded, his greying brown hair falling around his face. 'Then we understand each other.'

'And if he can't stop her?' I added, my eyes darting back to Elena.

'Perhaps if the young man opened his eyes, he'd understand that she'd do almost anything he asked.'

The insinuation that I had any control whatsoever over what Elena said or did nearly made me laugh out loud. I bit my tongue.

'She really is beautiful,' Jean said. 'Take the advice of this old man, Nico—stay home and leave well alone.'

I gave a tight nod and watched him go, preoccupied with his warning.

'What did Jean want?' Elena said, jumping in my line of sight and waving for added effect.

'Nothing much,' I said and tipped my head at where Dean was now glaring at me. 'What was all that about?'

'Nothing much.'

'He looked real happy that you had your hands all over him.'

Elena's expression transformed. 'I told him I like tattoos.'

'So that's what he wanted to talk about?' I said, failing to repress a snort of laughter.

'No, he wanted to ask me out,' she bit back. 'Not that it's any of your business.'

'And what did you say?'

'That I'd think about it.'

'I don't want you going out with him,' I snapped.

Raising her eyebrows, Elena turned on her heel and flounced back down the corridor. Throwing a defiant glance over her shoulder, she reached up and whispered something in Dean's ear, hooked her arm through his and lead him away.

I only realised I was digging my nails into my palms when I broke through the skin, having caught sight of the arrogant grin Dean had flashed my way.

Like fuck would she listen to me.

GOTCHA

'WATCH IT, JAKES!' Elena laughed as we collided outside my door. 'I was just coming to see you, are you going somewhere?'

'Just to see Gerrin,' I answered. 'Wait, why do you have your coat on?'

The rebellious glint behind her smirk told me all I needed.

'*Elena.*'

She rolled her eyes. 'Don't look at me like that. It's been five months and I miss it like hell. You game?'

'No, Jean was right—it's selfish of me to let you go.'

'You're not *letting* me do anything. Now, are you coming or not?'

'No.'

'Well, I guess I'll see you later then.'

She winked and turned on her heel, coming to an abrupt halt when I didn't let go of her arm.

'I can't let you, Elena, I promised Jean.'

'Promised Jean what? That you'd take care of me?' she scoffed. 'I guess if you want to satisfy that fragile male ego then you'd better come protect me, oh hero of mine.'

I glared at her, flummoxed by her quick wit.

'You impossible woman.' I grabbed my coat.

'Are you ready to talk about Gerrin yet?' Elena said, going straight in for the kill.

We were sitting on opposing tree stumps, eating wild blackberries. The light drizzle that dusted through the trees made for a damp picnic, but it didn't matter, it was enough just to be back out here.

I frowned and shifted my gaze from the woodland floor. 'What about him?'

'You need to ask?'

'What do you want from me, Elena?'

'There's no point burying your head in the sand. He's out of control and he's getting worse.'

My face fell. It was true; Gerrin was fast getting a reputation for cruelty in the caves. People knew him as someone you didn't cross if you valued your life.

Elena reached over and grasped my hand, her ebony ponytail falling over one shoulder. 'I'm sorry.'

'I saw him with Cosbi the other day.'

'And?'

'It was on the anniversary... you know... of when our parents died. He was crying. Cosbi had his hand on his shoulder.'

'And?'

'Well, it's wrong. Why didn't Gerrin come to me? Why couldn't he talk to me?' I stopped before everything I felt came pouring out of my mouth.

'You might need to make the first move,' Elena said.

'I've tried to speak to him. He shuts down as soon as I do. He's afraid I'm going to walk if he tells me what's really going on in that head of his.'

'He's that vulnerable?'

'Ever since Italy. Something broke in him that day and he's never dealt with it.'

'What would he do if he lost you too?'

'I don't even want to think about it.'

'How about anyone you get close to?'

I glanced up as she shrewdly hit on my worst fears. Gerrin's feelings towards anyone new in my life were unpredictable. He saw them as intruders, unworthy and unwelcome in our broken family. I worried there would come a time when he'd show the people who I loved the same malice he showed anyone who crossed him. 'He'll only get one chance.'

'He wouldn't even get that from me. He's unstable. It makes him dangerous, even to you.'

'He'd never hurt me.'

'Not physically maybe, but if what you say is true, then he's too damaged to be understanding of your feelings.'

This was too difficult to hear; we'd come out here for a break from things, not to air all my heart's worries.

'Enough, Elena.' I pulled my hand from under hers.

'No, not enough. You have to act now.'

'I said drop it.'

'God only knows what he'll do next if you don't do—'

'Do something? You think I don't know that?' I said, making her flinch as I sprang to my feet. 'You think I can't see him disappearing? I can't stop it, Elena.'

'You're wrong. You're the only one who can get through to him— before he hurts someone. And I mean *really* hurts someone.'

'And if I can't?'

The silent response was answer enough. Either talk him round or stand against him.

'You know what you're asking, right?'

'Yes.'

'Then you know you're out of order.'

Leaves crunched and twigs snapped as she moved behind me, a hand on my jacket urging me to turn around. Her hand was on my cheek before I could even say anything. 'For me?'

'You're taking advantage of our—'

'Of course I am. It's the only hold I have over you.'

I frowned, not appreciating her tactics.

'Say you're with me on this.'

I sighed. 'I'll speak to Cosbi, get his advice.'

'That's absolutely the last place I'd look for hel—'

'Shh!'

'Don't shush me, Nico.'

'*Here*,' I whispered, backing into a shadowy shelter between some dense shrubbery and beckoning her to join me. 'I heard someone.'

Within a second, she was in my arms, camouflaged from sight by foliage and gloom and breathing heavily against my chest.

'That truck must be around here somewhere,' a distinctive American twang complained.

'I'm beat,' a second voice answered. 'Let's go back.'

Parker and Chase.

I clapped my hand across Elena's mouth as she gasped audibly.

'What was that?'

The voice was alert, certain, aimed in our direction.

'What was what?'

'Quiet, would you? Who's there?'

Trousers rustled as he moved closer, feet meeting crisp undergrowth as they crunched slowly across the glade, measured steps carefully placed so the owner would catch any further sound.

There were no flies on his hearing. Judging by the slight shake of the forest canopy, he was approaching where we were standing. Hands appeared in front, prising back the branches in their path. As one being, Elena and I shrank further back into the shadows.

'Who's there?' he repeated.

'Do you realise how stupid you look right now, man?' Chase mocked from the clearing.

Backed into a corner with nowhere to run, there was nothing to do but make it look like we weren't hiding. Elena clawed in alarm at my clothes as she tried to stop me. I took a tentative step forwards and my boot unexpectedly met with something soft and furry rather than the leaf-littered forest floor.

With an indignant screech, the squirrel took flight from under my foot and made a bid for freedom, streaking past Parker and into the undergrowth.

'Shit!' he hollered in surprise, aiming a kick at the escaping animal and missing entirely. 'Fuckin' squirrels!'

A loud roar of laughter erupted from the vicinity of the logs as Chase no doubt caught the look of astonishment on his friend's face.

'Shut it,' Parker muttered.

Covered by the howls of amusement, I felt safe to breathe again. Elena relaxed in my grasp, her release of breath warm against my hand.

'Come on,' Chase gasped eventually. 'There's no one there—we haven't seen anyone in over a year.'

'Cosbi'll be pissed if we get back earlier than we said.'

Chase groaned. 'Fine. One more hour.'

'It drove north.'

'North is that way, you idiot!'

Laughter faded as the two men abandoned their post, their direction cutting off our return path.

'Let's go,' I murmured, pulling twigs and a beetle from Elena's ponytail. 'We have to find another way.'

'That's our way back in, Nico.'

'And they're going to be hanging around it for at least another hour. If we're not back for dinner, people are going to notice. We'll have to take our chances with the main entrance.'

'Our chances?'

'Hope that it's Jean.'

'We can't put him in that position.'

'We have no choice.'

Breaking into a jog, we left the clearing, thudding softly across the wet grass. We reached the hillside in no time at all and crept up the incline to where the main entrance was set snugly in the mountainside.

Crouching behind a rock large enough to conceal both of us, we waited and we watched, craning to see who was on guard. Ten minutes later, a man stood and flexed his limbs, rubbing cramp from his legs.

'Jean...' Elena breathed.

She was on her feet before I could stop her. Leaving the safety of our cover, she'd taken two steps towards the Frenchman before the movement caught his attention.

Slowly, barely perceptibly, he moved his head from side to side. A warning.

'Elena!' I hissed. 'Get back, he's not alone.'

And just like he'd heard me, the balding, greasy head of Foley came into view behind Jean. Elena gasped and dived for my outstretched hand, landing face down across my lap. Daring to peek around my side of the rock, I saw Foley's greedy weasel eyes alight with satisfaction as he stared at where Elena had disappeared.

I watched until he left the entrance. Jean stayed momentarily, throwing one last look of dismay in the direction of our rock before accompanying Foley inside.

'Hurry, the other entrance, *now*,' I urged.

'But Parker and—'

'We'll find a way.'

The Americans were nowhere to be seen as we skidded to a halt in front of the waterfall. Red-faced and sweating, we dragged the rock aside and collapsed in relief as we sealed ourselves back into darkness.

'He saw,' Elena panted.

'Yes.'

'He'll go straight to Cosbi.'

I scrambled to my knees. 'I told you, it'll be a slap on the wrist and a telling-off. But we deny everything—he probably didn't even get a good enough look at you.'

She nodded. 'Together?'

'Together.'

Dropping down into the cool shadows of Elena's room, we immediately made our way to the entrance to face the music.

'Jean? He left about fifteen minutes ago,' a hairy man grunted in answer to our query. 'I got sent here to cover him.'

My sense of dread deepened as we thanked him and made our way back to my room.

'Nico, Gerrin's been looking for you,' Louisa said, her eyes sweeping across my scruffy state as we passed her in the corridor. 'He said to tell you he needs you in twenty-three.'

'Thanks, see you later,' I said to Louisa, who was busy frowning at the woman behind me.

Neither of us said a word as we walked down to 23, throwing our coats into my room.

'Wait here,' I whispered when we reached the door.

'No, Nico. This was my idea.'

'Gerrin asked for *me*, not you. This might not be what we think.'

'No.'

'I'm not arguing with you, Elena, stay here.'

'And neither am I—I'm coming with you.'

'It'll look suspicious if we both go. They aren't expecting you. Let me go and find out what's going on.'

'Nico—'

'Nothing will happen to me, I swear.'

She looked mutinous, but sensing she wasn't going to win this battle, she conceded. 'OK, but promise me you'll shout if something's wrong.'

'I promise.'

She drew back as I opened the door and stepped into the middle of the largest group of people that I'd ever seen in the depressing room.

All eyes fell on me as I closed the door with a loud clunk. Scanning the space, my gaze dropped first on Cosbi, standing with his hands behind his back, smiling at me. Parker, Chase and Ash hovered nearby, looking somewhat confused.

Movement to my right caught my eye; a twitching Foley lurked in the shadows next to the door, eyeballing me with a disturbing smile.

My heart dropped as I noticed the last group, huddled tight, flanked by Gerrin. Jean was defensive, shielding his two daughters behind him who both looked on the verge of tears. His face was deathly white as he stared long and hard at me. I could barely look him in the eye.

'Nic, you got my message,' Gerrin said.

I nodded, trying to keep my face impassive despite my rising apprehension. 'What's going on in here?'

'Come in, Nico,' Cosbi said. 'We have a situation, one might say.'

'Oh?' I said, moving to stand beside Gerrin.

'Indeed. Now, I believe we are just waiting for one more person.'

And right on cue, Elena burst through the door, evidently unable to keep her word. I glared at her.

'Ah, Miss Martinez,' Cosbi said, smiling appreciatively. 'I was hoping you would find your way here.'

Turn around and go...

But, of course, she didn't. Blanching as she caught sight of Jean's family, she stepped forwards and met Cosbi's eyes with a look of determined, defiant expectation.

'Wonderful,' Cosbi said. 'Now, I think we should all have a chat, don't you?'

REVELATIONS

COSBI WAITED, SEEMINGLY studying the effect that his words had on the atmosphere in the room, and on the faces of its occupants. With a curious smile, he appeared to bask in the silent discomfort.

This wasn't the kind man I knew.

'Papa...' Coco whispered.

There was a scuffling of feet as Jean moved to reassure and shush her. I understood his fear; the tension in the room was growing so charged that it seemed like the slightest noise was going spark an inferno.

Everyone was afraid to speak.

Cosbi's dark eyes narrowed slightly as Elena fell under his scrutiny. As though satisfied by something he'd seen, he strolled to the door, twisted the key in the lock and dropped it in his pocket.

Fuck.

The room bristled. Opposite me, Parker shifted from one foot to the other. Elena threw me a look that asked for reassurance. I couldn't give it.

'What's this all about, Cosbi?' I said.

Even Gerrin seemed surprised that the first noise had come from my mouth, flinching from his trance to stare at me.

Hands clasped behind his back, Cosbi paced the circumference of the group, circling us like a patient predator. 'As I said, Nico, we appear to have a situation.'

'A situation that involves us all?'

'It affects us all,' he said, passing behind Elena; a barely noticeable flinch told me exactly how close he'd got. 'But only involves *some* of us.'

My skin crawled as I heard Foley's delighted titter from the shadows.

'Gerrin,' Cosbi said, calling his favourite to attention.

I felt Gerrin jump to life defensively, as though wounded that Cosbi could think he'd done anything wrong.

'Kindly remind everyone of the rules we put together for the safety of our community.'

'Erm, sure. No fighting, killing, stealing, cheating, putting anyone in danger, or helping those dickheads outside,' Gerrin recited.

'Much obliged,' Cosbi said as he wandered behind Ash. 'Now that we are aware of how to break our laws, is there anything anybody would like to say?'

Silence dropped like a dead weight in the absence of his voice, interrupted only by the continued, calculated footsteps.

Catching Elena's eye, I shook my head ever so slightly. Everyone was silently expecting, accusing, waiting to see which of us had caused the problem.

Allowing a full minute for any admissions, Cosbi spoke again. 'No one? Well, I am disappointed. For the security of everyone, a place such as this requires unconditional trust. We seem to have a breach in that unity.'

Still, no one said anything.

'Then nothing remains but for me to tell you a story,' Cosbi said, sauntering into the centre of our crude circle. 'Imagine, if you will, a young person. Independent, spirited and highly intelligent. This person is popular in certain circles, but given their temperament, has a little difficulty with authority.'

I didn't need imagination; I was looking at that very person right now.

'One day they witness something they do not like, the necessary removal of a threat posed by an intruder, who is likely an enemy. They resolve to do something about it. So they spend days, weeks, months testing the waters, finding like-minded people and bringing them together.'

Cosbi wandered out of the circle, and to my dismay, right towards the array of weapons nailed to the wall. He selected one of the branding irons and ran his fingers almost tenderly up the length of cold metal, then fed one end into the heart of a fiery wall torch. 'The purpose of this secret group is unknown, but, assuming some misguided notion of needing to save others from the *tyranny* of a safe home, one presumes that they intend to make a stand.'

A few stunned whispers floated through the air and a low whistle came from Gerrin's direction. I couldn't quite believe what I was hearing; was Cosbi accusing Elena of being responsible for some band of radicals?

Cosbi prodded at the torch with the poker, thrusting it time and again into the smouldering heat. 'Now, the leader of the community cannot allow this to happen—cannot allow the safe haven he has created to be destroyed in the name of one meaningless outsider. For some time now, he has suspected that members of the group have been leaving on a regular basis and colluding with the filthy gang outside, and that others in a position of responsibility have been facilitating it. This has put our community in danger.'

Jean's breathing faltered as my gaze shot to an ashen-faced Elena.

'I'm sure you can see the predicament the leader is in,' Cosbi continued. 'I would like your opinions. Chase?'

The American froze in surprise as everyone's eyes found him, and he spluttered something incoherent.

'Quite. Parker?'

'Negotiate, reunite the group,' Parker said, impressively calm.

'How very diplomatic. Jean?'

'I have no opinion,' the Frenchman said, not even attempting to hide the contempt in his voice.

'As you wish. Ash?'

'Kill the traitor,' Ash sneered.

I'd expected nothing less. But his hands would go nowhere near Elena while I was still breathing.

'Nico?'

'Violence would only cause more problems,' I retorted. 'If this person is as well-liked as you say, killing or even punishing them is going to make you unpopular.'

'A fair point,' Cosbi said. 'Gerrin?'

Ignoring my imploring stare, Gerrin ventured his opinion. 'I agree with Ash. Make an example of the traitor. Without someone there to stir things up, the group would be lost.'

He refused to acknowledge my disappointment, remaining stoic and impassive, like a soldier ready for inspection.

'Cosbi, whatever is going on here, do you really want this to be somewhere that people are afraid to speak freely, where we kill people who disagree with us?' I said. 'Think carefully before it's too late.'

'Killing has the potential to create a martyr,' Cosbi said, ignoring my plea. Removing the iron from the flame, he wandered back into our midst, blowing on the metal and making it burn from sultry amber to incandescent yellow. 'I pride myself on seeing people. I learn their ways, thoughts, their weaknesses.'

He circled again, quicker this time and with purpose. 'Foley, for example,' he said, aiming the poker in the direction of the exit, 'is motivated by what he can get, money, possessions, secrets. And Ash over there has a penchant for attractive women, especially the ones who say no.'

My stare flickered first to Ash, who was looking undisturbed by this incredibly public revelation, and then to Elena, whose mouth had fallen open and who was evidently thinking the same as me.

He knew. Cosbi knew what he was like.

'And this young lady...' Cosbi said, stopping well within the realms of Elena's personal space. My fingers twitched. 'Independent, spirited, highly intelligent... but what makes you tick, lovely Elena?'

Up until this point, Elena had been standing assured, gaining strength from our eye contact. But now she turned to meet him, staring him out with such fearlessness.

What a woman my best friend was.

'Oh, I see,' Cosbi said. 'Your weaknesses have been difficult to find, pretty girl, but you can't hide when you look me in the eye.'

He turned to address the room. 'She has no regard for her own life, and I daresay she would tolerate pain better than any man. You might think this would make her difficult to punish. Not so.'

Scanning the room, inspiration seemed to hit when he saw me. 'I wonder what would happen if I were to hurt Nico...'

Gerrin stirred, and for a moment I thought he was going to jump in front of me for the second time in his life. But he held his place.

Cosbi was behind me with one arm around my neck before I knew anything about it. My eyes were trained on Elena as he brought the still glowing branding iron up the length of my chest to within inches of my throat. Gerrin followed the movement like a hawk, ready to react if needed.

Sweat beaded on my neck from the blistering heat, but I didn't move an inch, I wouldn't give him the satisfaction.

The fire in Elena's glare cooled several degrees as Cosbi threatened my life. With one action, he rendered her fiery spirit helpless, drawing out deeply private fears and parading them for ridicule. It was one of the cruellest things I'd ever witnessed.

Cosbi laughed and lowered the weapon, releasing hold of me. 'Yes, I thought so. Dear, dear, Miss Martinez, feelings like those can really complicate a friendship.'

The cheap shot was as sudden as it was unexpected. Unarmed against the assault, she must've caught the look of surprise on my face before mortification took hold and she jerked her head away.

After all this time, she still wanted us.

'Does he know?' Cosbi said, tasting blood as he glanced back at me. 'I think he probably does. Does it just *kill* you that he doesn't feel the same way?'

Studying my expression with unpleasant intensity, he brought his lips to her ear, whispering something that the rest of us couldn't hear. Startled by whatever it was, Elena swallowed hard and dragged her wounded eyes up to meet mine.

Holding her gaze was pure torture.

'Remind me in the future, Miss Martinez, that should it be necessary, punishing you will be all too easy,' Cosbi said, finishing his attack with a flourish of the iron.

'Do you have a point to make?' I spat, seething with him for hurting her in such a way that I could offer no relief.

'Your concern is touching, Nico,' Cosbi answered, arching an eyebrow in amusement. 'As it happens, I do have a point. I am aware that harming the guilty party is likely to be an unpopular idea, however, their crimes are of such a nature that they cannot go unpunished.'

Ash sniggered.

'Earlier this evening, a member of our community was spotted outside, trying to get back in through the main entrance,' Cosbi said, pacing again. 'This was done *without* permission.'

'How do you know it was someone from here?' I said.

'I have no concrete proof. My informant unfortunately didn't get a close look, did you, Foley?'

'Only the hair,' the weasel squeaked.

'Oh yes, the hair,' Cosbi said. 'That beautiful long, dark hair. Difficult to miss.'

Elena looked resigned to her fate, pale and in need of a friend. I longed to walk across the room and be that person, but to do so would certainly give Cosbi the confirmation he needed.

'In a society such as ours, we must learn how our actions affect others,' Cosbi said. 'Therefore, as punishment for such selfishness, the blame will be shared.' He strode past me, his footsteps stopping at Jean.

Gerrin and I both craned to see.

'You were on duty this afternoon, were you not?' Cosbi said.

'I was,' Jean muttered.

'Did you let anyone out?'

'I did not.'

'Who did you see outside?'

'I saw no one, *monsieur*.'

'Indeed? I believe your words are lies, *monsieur*,' Cosbi said.

'Think what you want, you can't hurt me!' Jean burst out. 'I am an old man—I do not fear you.'

'I don't doubt you, Jean. But there are other things you care about.'

Slow enough that everyone could watch, Cosbi slid a lone finger down Lisette's cheek. Gerrin threw out an arm as he correctly anticipated Jean launching himself forward.

'Leave her alone—she's done nothing wrong!' Elena shouted.

'Oh, I know that,' Cosbi said, smiling and lifting a handful of mousy-brown hair to show Elena that it was the wrong colour for his criminal.

'Stop this, Cosbi,' I warned.

Jean struggled against Gerrin's hold on his shirt.

'Well, Gerrin, Nico...' Cosbi started.

'It was me!' Elena yelled. 'You fucking know it was me! If you dare touch them...'

I opened my mouth to declare my involvement too, but Elena's frantic glare made me close it again. She needed me to stop this, not add to the trouble.

'You've quite the mouth on you, Miss Martinez. Pity you couldn't have used it ten minutes ago,' Cosbi said. 'Ash, please remove Mr Moreau from my sight.'

Ash took the key from Cosbi's outstretched hand and seized hold of Jean's jacket.

'*Non, non, monsieur!*' Jean shrieked, his heels scrabbling across loose stone on the rocky floor, trying to gain some traction. 'Not my daughters. No, you can't! Please, take me, take me, don't hurt them, hurt me!'

Tears rolled down Elena's mortified face as she watched Jean being manhandled from the room. There was nothing I could do without giving myself away, so with a pained heart, I stood there and watched with everyone else.

Jean was sobbing, a despairing man who knew he wasn't strong enough to protect his children. 'No! *Non!* Please, I am begging you, please, *monsieur*, I'll do anything, *please!*'

But Ash had Jean at the door and his pleas had fallen on deaf ears and a cold heart. We all stood in silence, listening to the desperate cries fading as he was heaved down the corridor. Cosbi gestured to Chase to close the door, which emphatically deadened the last traces of begging.

All that could be heard through the room was the muffled tears of the two young girls, now without the protection of their father.

'Gerrin, Nico,' Cosbi repeated.

I tried to keep the loathing from my expression as he looked at us in expectation.

'Well, take your pick,' he prompted.

'Huh?' Gerrin said.

Cosbi gestured at the two girls. 'Their punishment, on behalf of Miss Martinez. They're yours.'

'I don't understand,' I said, thinking I probably didn't want to.

'I'll leave them in your capable hands. I'm sure you can think of something suitable.'

'You mean you want us to...' Gerrin said.

I was relieved to hear that he was unable to finish that particular sentence.

'If that's what you want to do,' Cosbi answered with a shrug.

'Are you insane?' I said in horror. The necessity of the bed in room 23 had just become frighteningly apparent.

'They broke the rules and put our community in danger, Nico. Fair's fair.'

'*Fair?*' Elena cried. 'What the hell is wrong with you?'

'On second thoughts, Nico, maybe I should offer your charming friend to you instead. But I fear she would enjoy it too much.'

Elena's face flamed as he took another shot at her heart, humiliating her and debasing our friendship in the process.

Amidst the horrific atmosphere radiating from the opposing sides in the room, Ash returned, ready for his next instructions.

'Won't be hearin' from him fer a while,' he said with a grin.

One of the girls gave a shriek of alarm and sank to her knees. 'Oh, Papa.'

'Wonderful. Now, if you don't mind, Ash, I do believe Miss Martinez has also overstayed her welcome,' Cosbi said. 'If you would be so kind.'

Ash licked his lips as his eyes found his old adversary. 'With pleasure.'

My legs were moving before Cosbi had even finished. 'Over my dead body,' I snarled, throwing out a backhand that caught Ash clean across the cheek and putting myself firmly between them. Elena seized my hand like it was a lifeline.

Ash was up in my face before he could even see straight. 'Reckon tha' can be arranged, sunshine.'

'A little overprotective tonight, aren't we, Nico?' Cosbi said.

'She goes with me or not at all,' I snapped.

'Oh, I see,' he said with a knowing smile. 'Your admirer is immune to a little Glaswegian charm.'

I said nothing, but my jaw tensed as Ash cracked his knuckles.

'Well, given that I need you here, perhaps you would agree to a compromise? Would you allow Parker and Chase to escort her instead?'

Looking like they were desperate for a reason to leave, the two Americans stirred. I looked Parker in the eye and was surprised to see a glimmer of sympathy there. Appeased, I nodded.

'Then it might be helpful if you could let each other go,' Cosbi said.

'I'm going nowhere,' Elena yelled as Chase tried to prise her from my side.

'Stay here an' yer mine, darlin',' Ash said.

'Elena, please,' I said.

'Keep your hands off me!' she screamed at Parker, who had dared approach.

'I can't guarantee your safety, should you remain,' Cosbi said.

'Elena,' I whispered, taking hold of her shoulders. 'Please. You're in danger here and you mean too much to me. Go, Jean needs you now.'

At the mention of her friend, she stopped and a resigned tear slid down her cheek. She brushed it away.

Out of Cosbi's line of sight, Parker peeled Elena's fingers from mine.

Physically separated from her, my hand was empty only momentarily as I felt a wooden object squashed into my palm and pressure forcing my grip to close around it. I ran a finger up the handle until it reached cold steel. Quicker than lightning, I tucked the knife into the back waistband of my jeans.

Looking tormented as she backed away from me, Elena mouthed, 'Be careful.'

Having fulfilled his nasty purpose, Foley slunk from the room after the trio.

'Well, you must want some privacy, gentlemen,' Cosbi said, like he was leaving us to conduct a business meeting.

'You're actually serious?' I said.

Like he'd been expecting my resistance, he turned before my sentence was even finished. 'Why so horrified, Nico? Try not to offend the young ladies.'

I stole a glance at the two girls, my heart aching when I saw what a morbid shade of grey they'd both gone. '*Offend* them?'

'Indeed. You two are the talk of our female population, are you not? I daresay you'll find them quite amenable.'

'I'm not interested.'

'So that's your problem, is it?' he said with a patronising smile. 'Just think of it as doing your job, if that helps with the attraction issue.'

'You know that wasn't what I meant, you sick bastard.'

The smile widened. 'Am I to understand that you're refusing to uphold my decision?'

'Wasn't that clear enough? Go fuck yourself, and your rules.'

Gerrin coughed uneasily.

As calm as ever, Cosbi strolled to me. 'I strongly suggest you watch how you speak to me—don't ever suppose for a minute that you are indispensable.'

'And who put you in charge?'

'Nico,' Gerrin warned.

Through the haze of anger, I realised that for the first time ever, he wasn't backing me up.

'It's perfectly alright, Gerrin,' Cosbi said. 'He's just exercising that keen temper I admire so much. Think what you like, Nico, but our rules work and I expect you to enforce them.'

'And what made you think I'd *enforce* this?'

'I wonder, Nico, have you ever considered that your precious Elena might be a little less excitable if Ash had, shall we say, broken her?'

Ash sniggered. I saw red.

I ripped the knife from my waistband and hurled myself at Cosbi, aiming for nothing specific.

But another member of the group was a step ahead of me. A huge arm seized me around the chest. Fingers dug into a pressure point in my wrist until I was forced to drop the weapon, which fell with a clatter of metal to the floor.

'Whose fucking side are you on?' I snarled at Gerrin, the words constricted against the pressure he maintained against my lungs.

'I'm stopping you doing something you'll regret.'

'I won't regret it.'

'It stays with you forever, you know, killing a man,' Cosbi said, bending to collect Parker's knife. 'If you have the guts to do it. Now, Nico, for Gerrin's sake, I'm going to pretend I didn't see that, and I'm going to offer you one last chance.'

I shook off Gerrin's hefty arm. 'Come on,' I said to him. 'I'm not listening to any more of this. Let's get them back to Jean and go home.'

I hadn't taken five steps towards the two girls before I realised he wasn't following me. Praying that my instinct was wrong, I turned to find them all staring at me. 'Gerrin?'

'I'm not coming.' He sounded so different.

'You can't seriously be considering doing this.'

He blinked at me, as though waking from a daydream.

'Gerrin...' Cosbi said.

'This isn't you,' I implored.

'Remember who our enemy is...' Cosbi coaxed.

'Shut your fucking mouth!' I shouted, going to my brother and grasping his face. 'You're scaring them, look. Do you really want to be a man that women are afraid of?'

'They broke the rules, Gerrin...'

'They did nothing, Gerrin,' I said. 'It wasn't them.'

Gerrin looked troubled, his eyes flitting between Cosbi and me as we spoke to him, each trying to win him around.

'He can't understand. He hasn't been through what you have...' Cosbi said.

'What do you know about what we've been through?' I snapped.

'She changed him. Look in his eyes—he thinks you're a monster. Show him you don't need his pity.'

So this was the poison Cosbi had been feeding Gerrin in private for so long, picking at old wounds, encouraging the monster while pretending to help him.

'Don't listen to him, Gerrin,' I begged, tears pricking at my eyes as I watched him battle the conflict. 'Please don't let him come between us.'

'He hates you now, you know...'

'Never, *never*,' I said. 'Look at me, what would Mum and Dad think of you right now?'

And for a moment, one sweet, brief moment, my brother came back to me. His eyes came alive again, shamed by my words. But it was short-lived.

'You know Elena's guilty, she admitted it,' Cosbi said. 'She's been helping *them* get in, and don't forget what people like that did to you. Deliver this punishment on her behalf.'

And at that point, all conflict disappeared. Gerrin drew himself up to his full height and turned to face the petrified girls. I knew I'd lost him.

'Gerrin,' I warned.

'Go home, Nico.'

'If you choose this path, it's the end for us. Do you hear?'

He kept his back to me, shoulders bunched defensively.

In desperation, I threw my open hand in front of him, waiting for him to reciprocate.

Losing patience, he whipped around and swatted my hand out of his way, shoving me with such force that I fell hard to the floor. I scrambled back to my feet, only to see him circling Coco and Lisette, watching, thinking. For the first time, I'd failed to bring him back from the brink.

His eyes darted to Coco, now stock-still on the floor; something he saw there made him frown, before he turned his judging gaze on Lisette. Flinching from him as she chewed on the nails of trembling fingers, she happened to look up through damp eyelashes and caught his eye.

'This one,' Gerrin said, stroking a finger down her damp cheek.

The girl broke down, screaming, crying, begging anyone who would listen.

Recognition of her hysterical pleas didn't even register on Cosbi's face. 'Well, Coco, it appears you aren't wanted. Nico, take her home if you can manage to do as you're told. You and I will speak tomorrow.'

I stayed put, staring at Gerrin. 'You know I'm going to have to stop you? Brother or not.'

Cosbi nodded at Ash; permission to see to Coco himself.

'Back the fuck off,' I warned. Gently, I took hold of her arm and pulled her to her feet.

'Lisette... *que dois-je faire?*' she whispered.

Lisette seized her hand and kissed it. '*Laissez-moi, allez, aider notre père. Tout va bien se passer.*'

Coco nodded and clung to my jumper as I led her from the room. I stopped just outside the door, speaking slowly so that she understood.

'Listen,' I whispered. 'I have to go back in there. Do you understand? To help your sister. Are you OK to get back on your own?'

She nodded and turned, fumbling her way along the wall, using it to hold herself up. I watched until she was out of sight.

'Well, Nico,' Cosbi said from behind me. I spun around in surprise. 'That was an eventful evening, was it not? I sincerely hope we can put this unpleasantness behind us.'

He smiled and nodded, but not at me, I realised, but at something behind my shoulder. Before I could even wonder what or who it was, a sharp, searing pain radiated through my head as a blunt instrument collided with my skull.

I sank in a heap to my knees, my eyelids flickering open and closed in confusion, as a warm, sticky stream of blood trickled down my forehead. Cosbi crouched down beside me, still smiling away as I toppled backwards.

Through the fog of approaching unconsciousness, I heard him talking. 'You think you know pain now, Nico? I can turn anyone against you in the blink of an eye. You put another foot out of line and you know who'll be next.'

And with that, he stood and opened the door to 23. 'Nico's taken Coco back to Jean. I want to see you in the morning,' he lied to Gerrin. 'Leave him there,' he added to my faceless assailant.

His footsteps had faded into the distant darkness before I sensed a second person bend over me. 'Reckon ah'll leave this here door open a wee bit, so you can hear. Sweet dreams, sunshine,' the voice mocked, and a booted foot struck me hard in the chest, knocking the breath from my lungs.

Blackness was closing in and the smell of blood filled my nose.

'Stay away!' a woman screamed.

Through the swirl of confusion, I knew I had to help her. Panting, I tried to stand, but my eyes rolled and spots dotted across my vision. I collapsed again.

'Are you afraid of me?' a man said.

Silence.

'You should be.'

I tried to sit again, but nausea knocked me off balance and my head hit rock once more.

Footsteps paced.

Whispered sobs.

Unconsciousness closed in as two voices became faint mumbles.

INNOCENT

Today, I didn't want to open my eyes.

Usually, my state after waking from a drug-fuelled night was euphoric, peaceful; the unparalleled relief of an addict who'd got his fix. But today, not even the chemicals in my body could take me back to a time when I didn't know about that horrific night in room 23.

'Anything today, Nico?' Cosbi said.

'Just childhood stuff.'

Opening my eyes, I sat up and swung my legs off the bed. Hanna removed the needles and dressed the wounds, leaving without saying a word, as usual.

Gerrin was eyeing me warily from the other side of the room. For a while I'd been trying to understand that look, with no success. Until now. In the last few weeks, he'd regained the brother he wanted, no one in the way, the slate wiped clean. And now every time I woke, he was terrified that something had put a stop to this lovely charade we had going on.

'I do hope your focus is where it should be,' Cosbi said.

'Where else would it be?' I snapped.

'I couldn't possibly imagine.'

'I'm doing my best.'

'Of course you are,' he said with a smile. 'I know you would never knowingly endanger anyone.'

His parting words left me furious, but gave me the courage I needed to ask for the truth, knowing the answer could change everything forever.

Uncharacteristically unsure of himself, Gerrin lingered for a few seconds before moving to follow.

'Stay where you are,' I said.

He stopped and looked over his shoulder, reluctant, terrified, and looking like he wanted to run before I ruined everything.

'It was me,' he said, forcing a smile onto his face.

'What?'

'The cricket ball through the car window. I tried to blame it on you, but it was me.'

'What are you on about?'

'You said you only remembered childhood stuff today, and you have a face like thunder, so I figured that was it. It was... a joke, Nico,' he added, quietly.

'Read the room, Gerrin.'

He bowed his head and moved reluctantly to sit on the chair, balancing his forearms on his legs, hands clasped, looking at the floor. Waiting.

'Tell me you didn't touch her,' I said.

He stayed focused on the floor. 'Who?'

'The young girl, the French one. Lisette.'

'Funny childhood memory.'

'Did you touch her?'

'You really think I'd cheat on Louisa?'

'Apparently you'll do anything Cosbi tells you to.'

He finally looked up. 'Nobody tells me what to do.'

'"*Our rules work and I expect you to enforce them,*"' I repeated. 'Does that sound like free will to you?'

'He's kept this place safe for years.'

'By killing men and raping women? And using you to do it.'

He shifted uncomfortably. 'Nico, I've never—'

'You know he's the one who told Ash to take me out, right?'

'We both know that Scottish fucker would've jumped at any opportunity to hurt you.'

'I nearly died, that's what Cosbi wanted.'

'Ash admitted that it was him, and *only* him, right before he lost a couple of teeth and spent a week in this room.'

I sighed in exasperation.

'Everything I've done, I've done to keep you safe,' he said.

'Did you touch her?'

He shook his head. 'I can't believe you're even asking me that.'

'Did you touch her?!' I yelled.

'No!' he shouted back. 'No, I didn't fucking touch her, OK? I wouldn't *want* to fucking touch her. And like I'd have to force anyone anyway—there's enough women around here giving it away for free.'

I snorted in disgust. 'Lucky Louisa.'

'I haven't been with anyone else since we got married.'

'I don't believe you. I don't believe that you've been faithful and I don't believe that you walked out of that room innocent. And I don't want anything more to do with you.'

I made for the door, needing to put some space between us.

'Nico,' begged a broken voice behind me.

I yanked the door handle.

'Please don't leave.'

Against my better judgement, I glanced over my shoulder.

He looked crushed, emotionally broken. Tears spilled from his eyes.

'I didn't do it,' he sobbed. 'I let her go as soon as Cosbi wasn't watching. Please, *please* believe me. Don't go.'

I'd never seen him like this.

I released the door handle.

He dropped to his knees. 'I couldn't. She ran. I found you straight after—you would've bled out if I'd been in that room for a long time. That should show you, right? I couldn't have done it. I let her go.'

I went back. 'You swear to me?'

'Yes! I swear. I swear... on Louisa's life.'

I shook my head. 'Don't swear on anyone's life.'

'I promise,' he said. He raised a hand and it lingered in mid-air, shaking, waiting.

I put my hand inside his and gripped it tightly.

'What's with all the secrecy?'

It'd been a week since the showdown in room 23 and I'd barely seen Elena until she'd turned up on my doorstep, looking worried and declaring she had something to show me.

Standing now outside her room, nervously fiddling with her messy plait, she was looking at me like I was a coiled snake.

'Swear.'

'Why? You know me,' I said, smarting from the distrust.

'I trust you with my life, but it's not just mine at stake here.'

I sighed, too intrigued to argue. 'Fine, I swear I won't tell anyone.'

With a flick of her plait, she took my hand and knocked on the door, a calculated pattern of short raps, before dragging me inside.

Illuminated only by several naked candle flames, the glassy eyes of everyone seated in Elena's room sought us out.

'He's here,' Elena said.

Eyes straining in the darkness, I tried to identify the people present. There were a few faces I recognised but didn't know well enough to acknowledge. Jean was there, his daughters on either side. Parker and Chase were seated at one side of the circle, appearing to be in the minority of people who were happy to see me there. Dean was sitting next to them, his sulk at my arrival transforming into downright hostility when he noticed my hand in Elena's.

'What is this?' I said.

'This is called making a stand,' Jean said.

'You're fighting?'

'We're leaving,' he corrected.

'Then, the son of a bitch was actually telling the truth?'

'To a point,' Elena said.

I glanced around; all faces were perfectly serious. 'How long?'

'A while,' she confessed, gripping my hand tighter.

'And you,' I said to her. 'You organised this?'

She nodded.

Wrenching my arm from her grasp, I turned on my heel and stalked away from the gathering, Dean's delighted laugh chasing me.

'Nico!'

'No!' I cut across her plea.

But she hadn't ever been one to give up easily. She caught hold of my sweater, slowing my thundering steps long enough that she could duck under my arm, pushing me to a halt with two hands firmly on my chest. 'Running away isn't going to solve your problems.'

'No, but it'll get me away from you.'

'You're being ridiculous.'

'Elena, *move*,' I snarled, knocking her hands away only to have her replace them immediately.

'Don't touch me like that,' she snapped back.

'Then get out of my way.'

'You want me to baby you, huh? Beg forgiveness for leaving you out of this? Let you ignore what Gerrin is so you can go back to your cosy little life?'

'If you don't like it, let me leave so you can go back to playing goodies and baddies with your new boyfriend.'

'Oh, stop being such a bloody selfish child.'

'*Me,* selfish? I had to find out what you were planning from Cosbi. I learned—in front of a room full of people – that he knew you better than I did. Now what kind of a friend does that make you?'

For a moment, she looked wounded, before deciding to let my insult lie. 'I had my reasons.'

'Such as?'

'Up until a week ago, you would've done anything for him. Your loyalty was conflicted. We couldn't take that risk.'

'I'm the last person you trusted with this. Parker, Chase, fucking *Dean,* I mean really?' Anger stopped my words, wrapping its thorny fingers tight around my throat.

'Think about it,' she implored. 'Would you have supported me if I told you we were against him? Would you have kept your mouth shut, Nico, or would you have broken my trust out of some misguided sense of loyalty?'

I scowled down at the expectant look on her face. She knew me far too well. 'So why are you telling me now?'

'You learned which side you're on. Regardless of how much you love him, you care too much to just stand back and watch. That's why now.'

'And everyone in there agreed with that, did they?' I said, tipping my head at her door.

'Some of them took a bit of convincing, but we took a vote. You won.'

'Lucky me.'

'Please, Nico. I've wanted to tell you for ages. Living with the status quo just wasn't an option for some of us—I've been getting veiled threats ever since I publicly defended Eli—'

'What threats?' I interrupted.

'Subtle warnings, notes posted under my door, the occasional person waiting in my room to intimidate me into behaving. Why do you think I had a sharpened toothbrush with me at that party years ago?'

'Why didn't you ever tell me?'

'I tried. You didn't believe me about Cosbi.'

My head dropped; I'd been wilfully blind, and others had paid the price for it.

'Don't be angry with me,' she pleaded.

I could never be cross with her for long. Our arguments were always fiery, intense, but notably short-lived. But the consequences of this one would linger.

'Do you even know what you're asking of me?' I said.

She nodded. 'And it'll be the hardest thing you ever do. It's time to choose.'

Old family or new family. Blood or heart.

'Are you with us, Nico?'

'I have a favour to ask of you,' Elena said tentatively.

'Oh? Go on.'

'Don't shout at me again,' she said, 'But would you consider going back to your job tomorrow?'

I stopped, the stool in my hands frozen mid-air. 'Come again?'

'Job. Back to.'

'Have you lost your mind?'

'No, Nico,' she said, sighing at what I assumed was my predictable reaction. 'I've not lost my mind.'

Realising the stool was still awkwardly airborne, I set it down. 'You want me to see him again, pretend nothing happened?'

'Yes, stop anyone else getting hurt.'

'Even if I could, he wouldn't believe me. I threw everything at him in that room.'

'Lie,' she said. 'He won't want to lose you—he might be more gullible than you think.'

'Elena...' I sighed, rubbing a hand over my face.

'For me?'

I raised my eyebrows at her. 'Again?'

She laughed. 'Yes. You'll do it?'

'Is there any point in me saying no?'

UNHOLY

LAUGHTER PEALED DOWN the corridor as I walked home to my room, weary after covering yet another of Gerrin's training sessions. But it wasn't a pleasant sound that met my ears.

I stopped before I reached a point where I would become visible to the group, in no mood today to become a pawn in their silly games. With no regard for my masculinity, I felt no shame in diving close to the wall and hiding out until they'd moved on.

'Say it again!' one girl squealed, taking a break from choking on her fake laugh.

I pulled a face as her wail went straight through me.

The laughter erupted again as a small voice mumbled something I couldn't decipher, obviously obeying the order.

'Yeah, right...' one teased.

'As *if*...' another jeered.

My heart went out to their victim, whoever she was. There was nothing deadlier than the venom of a pack of simpering girls all competing for the title of Alpha Bitch. I felt incredibly glad to be standing where I was.

''Fess up, Hanna—you're lying,' one pack-member piped up. 'You're just saying that to make us like you.'

Hanna, the nurse? The voice mumbled again, this time getting a few heckles amongst the cruel sniggers.

'There is no *way* Nico Jakes asked you to go to his birthday tonight,' the leader sneered.

I frowned as my name got dragged into their 'fun'.

'He's not even single, silly little girl.'

'Hot though,' a new voice giggled.

Urgh.

'Only as friends!' a nervous voice burst out, sounding close to tears. 'And he only mentioned it the other day, you know, just to be nice. I don't know if he meant it.'

I realised what the girl had set herself up for. She'd only wanted to be accepted, but they'd sussed her little white lie and run with it. I had no idea girls could be so pointlessly nasty.

'Come on, girls, carrot-top isn't worth our time,' Alpha Bitch simpered, much to the delight of her co-bitches.

My blood boiling, I made a decision.

I stepped out from my hiding place of shame, jammed my hands in my pockets and sauntered around the corner, whistling as though I'd never stopped walking.

The retreating teenage girls stopped their progress as I looked up in mock surprise at finding the group of them there. The familiar redhead was standing alone, her previous hurt morphing into absolute mortification at my appearance. And her concern was not unfounded. A look of delighted malice lit Alpha's face as she prepared for the ultimate humiliation.

She strutted towards me with the prowess of a catwalk model, hand on hip, a flirtatious smile painted on her red lips. 'Well, look who—'

'Hey, Hanna,' I said, cutting off Alpha Bitch with the loudness of my greeting.

I gave her such a huge smile that anyone would think we spoke on a regular basis, and planted a kiss on her cheek. Her already warm skin flamed beetroot red at my unexpected enthusiasm, and she regarded me with all the gratitude she could muster with one expression.

'We still good for tonight?' I asked, revelling in the fact that the girls' jaws had just hit the floor in my peripheral vision.

'Um... yeah, sure, of course,' Hanna stuttered.

'Cool, pick you up at seven?'

She nodded.

'See you then,' I said, adding a brisk, *'ladies...'* to the dumbfounded tribe as I walked past.

With a smile, I heard them all clamour and shove their way back to her, their hushed, incredulous whispers reaching my ears.

'Oh my God, Hanna, how did you manage that?' Alpha said, resentment dripping from her every word.

'His eyes are so dreamy...'

'Never mind his eyes, Naomi, did you see his body through that T-shirt...?'

'He'd look better with it off.'

A chorus of giggles sounded behind me.

'I prefer his brother.'

I didn't know whether to grimace or laugh as I left Hanna to her newfound 'friends', glancing down to check my T-shirt wasn't actually see-through.

'Off home are we, dreamy eyes...?'

'Knock it off, Elena,' I laughed, finding her leaning against the wall behind, grinning at me. I got the feeling she was doing exactly what I'd been doing two minutes ago.

'Going soft in your old age, Jakes?'

I shrugged. 'Can't stand girls like that.'

'You and me both,' she sighed, rolling her eyes.

'Still coming later?'

'Of course, the birthday boy owes me a dance.'

I'd decided to tell Gerrin first.

It transpired he'd had a heavy night and was sleeping it off in his room. I heard him surface at midday and gave it an extra half hour. His mood after waking up wasn't cheerful at the best of times.

He opened the door in torn clothes with his long hair stuck up in all directions, scratches raw and fresh down the side of his face.

'Good night was it?' I said.

'Too good,' he said. 'Feeling it now.'

'I can see that.'

I shut the door behind me, pulling a disapproving smile as he lurched across the floor and face-planted back onto his bed. Stale whisky hung like an invisible cloud in the air.

'Is Cosbi looking for me?' he said through a mouthful of pillow.

'No.'

'You come to take the piss then? Believe me, I feel sorry enough without being laughed at.'

'No, tempting as it is, that's not why I'm here.'

He turned his head to squint at me. 'Sounds serious. Oh shit, what did I do?'

'I don't know and I don't want to. I came to tell you some news.'

'What news?'

'Here goes,' I said, taking a deep breath. 'I asked Louisa to marry me last night.'

He stared at me for what felt like forever before shoving his face back into the polyester.

'Well, say something,' I said.

'You stupid fucking idiot,' he growled, the material's muffled distortion of his words failing to hide the anger behind them. 'That do you, Nic?'

It was pretty much the reaction I'd been expecting. I sighed and stood to leave. 'We wanted you to be the first to know.'

'What the fuck were you thinking?'

'I was thinking I want to spend the rest of my life with her.'

'I forbid it,' he spat.

'You can try. I want your blessing, but if you force me, I will do it without.'

He glared at me through bloodshot eyes. The spite in that expression was almost unbearable to look at. Where had my brother gone?

'You're too young,' he said.

'What're you afraid of, huh? That I might actually be happy? That I might not need you anymore?'

'I'll prove she's not right for you,' he said, an icy calm in his promise.

'You OK to cover my training session tomorrow? Nic?' Gerrin said, waving his hand in front of my drunk eyes.

'Sure, whatever,' I mumbled.

I managed about half of the community party before I knew I had to talk to her. I needed to know why she was shutting me out.

I found our room empty and the bed cold.

Wandering over to 19, my fist was raised and ready to hammer down the door in the inconsiderate manner of a drunk, when I heard Constance's soft voice from inside.

'You have to tell him sooner or later, Louisa. Even if you're not happy, he's your husband and you owe it to him. At least then you can sort out what you want to do together.'

My blood ran cold; it was exactly what I'd been dreading. She wasn't happy anymore. Then, from inside the room came one of the most devastating sounds I'd ever heard: the sound of the woman I loved in pain. Her wretched sobs drained me of all anger, and in that second I wanted nothing more than to have her back safe in my arms.

'I know, Mum, I'm not afraid of telling him, it's just... just...'

'What is it you're not telling me, Louisa?'

There was a pause before Louisa responded. 'Nothing. I'm just afraid it's not the best thing for us.'

'How can you know that when you haven't given him the chance? And if you want my opinion, I think you're wrong.'

Enough. I refused to be the only person that my wife couldn't talk to. One way or another, I was going to get some answers, even if I didn't like what I heard. Raising my fist again, I pummelled on the door and didn't stop until Constance opened it.

'Can I speak to Louisa?' I asked, too preoccupied to observe the niceties.

'Nico,' she said with an apologetic smile. 'Yes, I think that's probably a good idea. I'll give the two of you some space.'

The walk to her side was the longest I'd ever had to make. She didn't stop me, nor did she say anything, but there was an air of resignation radiating from her as she stared at the floor.

I took the chair at her side but made no attempt to greet or touch her; it would be all the harder to let go if I did.

'You've been drinking,' she observed.

'I thought it might help,' I admitted. 'This can't go on, Louisa. I don't know what I did to deserve this, but you must know you're killing me.'

'I'm sorry,' she said, tears falling from the tip of her nose. 'I didn't mean to hurt you, but I know I have been.'

She stopped as emotion threatened to flood her voice.

I couldn't help it any longer. My hand reached for hers and clasped it. 'I don't need sorry, I need to know why.'

She shook her head.

'Louisa, I love you, but keeping me happy isn't worth this pain. If it's easier for you that I say it, then so be it. You're done with us, right?'

Her head snapped up, swollen, tear-streaked eyes wide in disbelief. 'Nico—what? You think I don't want to be with you anymore?'

'I don't know what to think.'

She laid a hand on my cheek, her warmth melting into my skin. 'You're my world. I love you more than anything.'

My heart leapt out of the pit of my stomach and thudded back into its rightful place, my shoulders slumping in tired relief. 'Then what's wrong?'

She tensed and shook her head again.

'Tell me, please,' I begged. 'We're in this together, right?'

She had nowhere left to hide. With a sigh of utter exhaustion, she told me just what was causing the problem. 'I'm pregnant, Nico.'

My mouth fell open.

Of all the things that could've been making her cry with such desperation, the knowledge that she was carrying our child would've been the last thing on my list. I jumped up like someone had lit a fire beneath me.

'Are you sure?' I said once my jaw would work again.

'Positive.'

'But... we've been careful.'

'Obviously not careful enough,' she said, a residual sob choking her words.

I sank down at her feet, allowing the revelation to filter into my brain, turning it over in my mind. Our baby.

A smile transformed my face, erasing the lines of hurt etched there from the last three weeks. I pulled her hands from her eyes. 'I'm going to be a dad?'

'It looks that way.'

'Wow,' I whispered. 'That's incredible. Why have you kept it to yourself all this time?'

'It wasn't planned, I... I wasn't sure what you'd think.'

'You thought I wouldn't be happy? Louisa, I've always wanted this.'

With an angry cry, she threw off my hands and stood, fresh tears flowing down her face. 'Please don't talk like that.'

'Like what?'

'Like it's everything to you.'

'But it is.'

'I don't want this child, Nico!' she shouted. 'I never did. It was a mistake. Nothing more than a mistake.'

And with that, she fled from my sight, leaving me on my knees.

'Morning,' I whispered, sinking into the mattress and lowering the breakfast tray onto her legs. It'd taken me two hours to find the will to wake her; she looked so bloody beautiful when she was at peace.

Louisa's long eyelashes fluttered open.

'Thought you might be hungry,' I said.

'Nico,' she muttered, pulling blonde curls from her face. 'God, what time is it? I need to see to the kids.'

'Don't worry about that, you needed to sleep.'

Letting me rearrange the pillows behind her, she reached for a piece of apple from the bowl, brushing it along her lips before daring to chew it.

'There's something I've been wanting to ask you,' she said, after the experiment with the apple proved successful and she hadn't brought it straight back up.

The distracted way in which she picked at the fruit suggested she'd been working up the courage to say this for a while.

'You know you can say anything to me, right?' I said.

She nodded. 'I want to go, Nico.'

'Huh?'

'I want to leave this place.'

I stared at her in confusion. 'Louisa, we talked about this a few years ago, remember? You didn't want to leave your family.'

'They could come too.'

'Your mother wouldn't risk it with your sister.'

'Then just us.'

'You'd be willing to do that?'

In answer to my question, she finally looked up, showing me the grief that'd been aimed at the bowl of food.

'I'm so sorry I didn't want this baby,' she said, the pools of her eyes not deep enough to contain all the sorrow. 'What right have I got to hate something that's so innocent?'

I recoiled. 'Please don't say "hate", Louisa.'

'No,' she said, seizing my hand. 'I promise I don't. I was just afraid. I want us to have a chance at a normal life, Nico—our child can't be born in this hellhole.'

'I don't want that either, but—'

'No "but"s, let's just go.'

'You know Gerrin would never let us.'

'To hell with Gerrin. This has nothing to do with him.'

'Louisa—'

She turned her head and snatched back her hand. 'Oh, just don't.'

I removed the tray from her lap and took its place, pressing my mouth to hers before she could resist. She gave in after a few seconds, succumbing to my wordless plea for intimacy with a muted sob.

Breaking the kiss, I pulled back so that our noses were touching. 'You know I'd do anything to make you happy. I want that life too, just us, away from here.'

'But?'

'I have to keep you safe. You're nine weeks pregnant and you shouldn't be running from whatever's going on out there. Maybe after the baby's born we can think about it again, but until then, I won't do it.'

'I knew you'd say that,' she said, sadness shading her voice. 'You're a good man, I don't deserve you.'

A boy.

I smiled in astonishment, water blurring his features as tears swelled into my vision. There'd been a piece of my heart missing all this time. I glanced up to find Constance and Louisa watching us with tears pouring down their faces too.

'Look at you, making girls cry already,' I said, laying a kiss on his forehead.

The little devil stopped crying the second I passed him to his mother. Watery, ice-blue eyes opened wide and stared in wonder at the owner of the voice he knew so well.

'Hello, little one,' she whispered, wiping away his tantrum tears. 'You have your daddy's eyes.'

❖

'Thank you for walking me home,' Hanna whispered, glancing up at me, only to flush bright red and look at her feet again.

'I couldn't well invite you and leave you to walk home alone, now could I?' I laughed.

We'd been amongst the last to leave, Hanna giggling with her so-called friends and Elena and I playing a volatile game of beer pong. When Elena was barely able to stand anymore, she'd stumbled off home, leaving me to wonder where the hell everyone had gone.

'Goodnight,' I said as Hanna disappeared through the door, waving to the sour, ill-looking face behind her shoulder who I assumed to be her father.

Remaining on two feet after the amount of whisky I'd drunk was no simple task; the walls came in useful more than once. Heading down towards the appropriately named Eli's Way, my fingers found Elena's handmade gift tied to my wrist. I twisted the plaited leather band and a wave of affection warmed my chest.

Distracted as I was, I didn't hear the muffled sighs and kissing sounds until they were loud enough to burst the cloud of alcoholic nostalgia. I stopped when Gerrin's voice reached me from further down the path and rolled my eyes as I realised he was with a girl.

Great, this meant I had to walk the long way round.

Reluctantly turning my feet back the other way, I screwed up my mouth in distaste as the new conquest gasped in uncensored pleasure. It was the sort of sound that every man wishes he could draw from his lover.

At least this one sounds like she wants to.

I was about to jam my hands over my ears when his companion also spoke. Her plea for him to stop was breathless, anxious, but nonetheless dripping with unbridled desire. After the events of room 23, I understood enough about Gerrin to know that words would not stop him when he could hear such want in his partner.

Quiet though she was, the caves were deserted enough for the echoes to carry to my hearing.

'Gerrin, please, someone might see.'

Five little words was all it took for my world to stop turning.

Dread flashed through me as my feet took it upon themselves to turn once more. My eyes needed to see; my heart had to witness.

In the absence of any lights along that stretch, Eli's Way was lit only from the corridors it adjoined at both ends. But it wasn't difficult to spot the conjoined silhouette once I was far enough down; her dress and hair were as striking in the darkness as they had been in the community room.

Pressed against the wall, the woman in Gerrin's arms had one leg around his waist and both arms around his neck. His fingers dug into the soft flesh of her thigh, pulling her body into his. Lost to lust and all earlier protests left strewn by the wayside, her fingers tore at his hair, lips moulded to his. It looked more like they were trying to climb inside each other's mouths.

Breaking from him, she tossed her head to the side and flipped her long hair over her shoulder, begging him to move his attentions lower. It was all the evidence I needed. The clear shot of her face had indisputably proved her identity.

It was a car crash. Slow motion, tragic, impossible to stop.

I could do nothing but stand there and stare, watching my brother with his filthy hands all over my wife.

But... they hate each other. They can't stand one another.

Well, obviously not...

Oh good, my brain had re-joined the party.

'Gerrin, stop,' Louisa tried again, doing a terrible job of convincing anyone that this wasn't exactly what she wanted.

I needed to run, as fast and as far as my legs would carry me, but the urge to stay and smash his face in had an equally strong hold over me.

'*Gerrin.*'

'What?' he murmured, breathing the word against her neck.

'I can't do this,' she said, eyes on the floor as she pulled her leg from his hold and wrenched her dress back down.

'Why? Because of him?'

'He's my husband, Gerrin. He's your brother. I won't do this again.'

Again? Oh fuck no.

He pulled back, resting his hands on the wall either side of her. 'And where was he tonight, Louisa? Did he kiss you? Did he hold your hand? Did he even notice you were there waiting for him?'

'It's his birthday.'

'And? He might be my brother, but he's bang out of order—he didn't say a word to you all night.'

'He had lots of people to catch up with.'

'Lots?' Gerrin snorted. 'He spent most of it playing fucking beer pong with Elena.'

'They're best friends.'

'Is that what he calls it?'

'Oh, don't start that again.'

'He's still disappearing for hours on end. No one can ever find the pair of them.'

'He's working, Gerrin. Out training the men like Cosbi asked.'

'Those men are almost ready—they need an hour or two a week, tops.'

'What are you trying to say?'

He sighed. 'Nothing. You know Nic best, and if you're happy with how things are, then I'll keep my mouth shut.'

I glanced up from the floor as a muted sob came from Louisa, mirroring the teardrop slowly sliding down my cheek. I dashed it away with the back of my hand.

'Hey, hey,' Gerrin whispered, tucking his fingers under her chin. 'Don't cry. I'm sorry, I just hate to see him hurting you like this.'

'Nico wouldn't hurt me.'

'Maybe not on purpose, but he's too young to see how he's neglecting you. If you were mine, how could I ever want anyone else?'

Anger rushed through me. How I didn't kill him in that moment, I'll never know.

'You want that, don't you, Louisa?'

Tears poured down Louisa's cheeks as she shook her head at the floor. 'I... I...'

Gerrin caressed his fingers up her arms and back down over her neck, breasts, stomach, over everything that was mine, eyes devouring every inch.

Louisa dodged as he tried to steal another kiss, but she couldn't stop the finger that traced up her thigh, or the gasp that escaped her mouth as it staked its claim.

'Feel good?' he murmured in her ear.

Louisa's eyes screwed shut and her teeth bit down hard on her bottom lip, stifling a moan.

My brother. And my wife. I had to stop myself from being physically sick.

Taking advantage of the incapacity his hand was causing, Gerrin grasped her chin and claimed her mouth once more.

'I need to get back...' she protested as her lips broke free.

With a sharp movement of Gerrin's concealed hand, Louisa's back arched, and she cried out, grabbing two fistfuls of his T-shirt.

'Look at me, Louisa,' he said.

Confused, breathless and losing control, Louisa did as commanded.

'I'm in love with you,' Gerrin whispered.

Unable to muster enough self-control to refuse, Louisa abandoned her objections and submitted. Breathing furiously, she scrambled for the button of his jeans.

Gerrin slammed their weight hard against the wall, and they were a jumble of tongues and lips again before I knew I could watch no more.

Enough.

Silently, numbly, I dragged my gaze away and retreated from my position. One last look down the corridor saw two eyes gleaming in the distance. Two brown weasel eyes, in fact, ogling at the forbidden tryst in the corridor.

Foley.

I took a step towards him and his piercing stare shot instead to me. Pulling a sinister grin, he responded with his own backward movement, unseating several pebbles with his foot.

Gerrin and Louisa broke apart at the sound.

'What was that?' she whispered.

Foley slipped away unseen with much-practised stealth, and I pressed myself back into the concealing shadows of Eli's Way.

'Ignore it,' Gerrin muttered, licking his lips and winding his hand back around her neck.

'No, I have to go.'

Shoving his hand away, she hurried down the corridor in my direction, pulling at her dress and blindly checking her makeup. Gerrin huffed his frustration and smacked the wall, taking off after her and calling for her to return.

Like my feet were stuck in treacle, I plied myself from the shadows and trudged unthinkingly home to await her arrival.

GHOSTS

I DIDN'T KNOW what I was seeing anymore. Memories, dreams, lies, I couldn't separate them.

Was she my wife?

Was he my son?

Was *she* the one who'd cheated?

I couldn't possibly have invented all of that.

I didn't waste another second before dressing, knowing that Hanna would arrive in moments to attend to her morning ritual of re-bandaging my bruised, needle-tracked arms. I ignored the dark circles under my dull eyes, now set deep in my drawn, pale face. I just needed to put some weight back on, that's all.

I offered up my customary greeting at Hanna's predictable arrival just seconds later, and as usual she ignored me.

'You took these out yourself?' she said, wiping away the beaded blood with a tissue that reeked of alcohol.

I winced as it caught broken skin. 'You were late.'

She didn't bite. Stuffing the tissue in her pocket, she set to winding a cotton dressing around my forearm.

'How long are you going to keep this up for?' I said.

Chewing her lip, she backed up, planning to leave without answering. I caught hold of her arm.

'Oh!' The exclamation jumped from her lips as she shied from my unexpected touch.

'If I ask you something, will you answer me honestly?'

After a few seconds, she whispered, 'Will you let me go if I do?'

'Jesus, Hanna,' I said, releasing her immediately. 'You really think I'd hurt you?'

'No, Nico, I...' she began and then thought better of it. 'Ask then.'

'Did you help deliver a baby boy?'

'Erm...'

'Is he mine?'

'I... I don't know.'

I grabbed a hoodie, realising in my haste that I'd put my T-shirt on backwards, and forced my feet into shoes without undoing the laces. 'What about Louisa?'

'No, Nico, I can't do that. I can't talk about Louisa.'

'You don't have to. Just tell me where she is.'

'You can't get down there.'

'Where? Room 19?' I said, snatching at the key fob hanging from her pocket.

'Nico!' she squealed. 'Give them back!'

'I won't be long—cover for me.'

Not listening to Hanna's protests, I ripped open the door of my room and unlocked the big oak door to the main cave system.

I wonder what his name is.

Not for the first time since my imprisonment did I find myself sneaking around, trying to get somewhere I was forbidden to go.

She'd said he had my eyes.

I flew past Cosbi's room.

And how old was he?

A jumble of declarations were jostling through my mind, in no particular order and making no sense.

Definitely less than a year old.

'Where is he?' Gerrin shouted, his footsteps booming up ahead.

Without thinking, I dived into the nearest room, briefly noting the *18* carved into the wood. So close.

'I only went for a glass of water,' Chase complained.

'Fuck your excuses. You find him now.'

'I'll get Parker—we'll start searching rooms.'

'I suggest you start with nineteen and twenty,' Gerrin snapped.

I scanned the contents of my asylum. It was immaculate, and mercifully deserted. Two single beds lay side-by-side in the corner and the walls were adorned with wilting posters of the Vancouver Canucks.

'What's up?' Parker shouted.

'Keep it down! Nico's gone walkies, stole Hanna's keys,' Chase said.

To my surprise, Parker laughed. 'So that's why Goldilocks is pissed.'

'Damn straight. You start in twenty, I'll take nineteen. We can work our way down.'

'If he's in nineteen, it's already over.'

I waited until they'd gone to check their respective rooms and ducked out of my hiding place, hoping to take refuge in my old room until they'd moved past. But the footsteps of another searcher were already approaching from that corridor. Blocked in, I had no choice but to run back the way I'd come, frustrated that my attempt at reaching Louisa had ended so quickly.

I'd almost reached the long corridor that led back to the medical bay before a thought occurred.

There was another way around.

It wasn't late enough to kill the lights. Unreliable surges of electricity flushed through the weak bulbs dangling from the ceiling, fuelling a mechanical buzzing. The artificial bluish tinge battled with the roaring orange of the wall torches for the award of most fearsome shadow.

The occasional feel of cool, fresh air glancing off my cheeks told me I was nearing the entrance, and the need for stealth became even more pressing. I would have just one chance at getting past the guard and into the other half of the cave system.

Flipping up my hood and barely daring to breathe, I edged towards the corner concealing the exit from view, digging my fingers into natural crevices in the rock to allow the tiniest glance into the space beyond.

Hunched on the floor beneath a cast metal bell hanging from a rusting nail, the guard was sitting cross-legged and shrouded in a huge overcoat. An old grey blanket lay soaking up moisture beneath him and another was pulled over his knees to protect him from the elements whistling through the cave entrance. Shivering from the cold, he craned his face into clasped hands, blowing warmth into the material of his fingerless gloves. An old flat cap pressed his unkempt greying hair around his face, obscuring his identity. A rusting axe lay dormant but ready at his feet.

Pulling back, my heart sank. Unless the old man was deaf, my chances of not disturbing him were slim at best. But I hadn't come this far not to try.

Keeping my stare fixed on his movements, I inched my foot out into plain sight.

I knew it was a mistake the second I committed my weight to it.

My damp shoe made contact with a mildew-covered stone and promptly slipped off with a clumsy thud, my ankle snapping awkwardly in on itself.

'Shit!' I hissed, the shooting pain up the side of my leg causing my mouth to react before my brain could have a say.

The guard was on his feet in a flash, the clatter of metal dragging over stone telling me the axe had gone with him.

'Who is there?' The uncertain words stole through the vacuum.

My breath faltered. The accent was strong, it was unmistakeably French. I held back only momentarily to question the loyalty of the man who'd been a friend to both Elena and me, before my desire to see him again overtook any concern I had.

Stepping from the shadows, I pulled my hood back, letting the intermittent light of the torches reveal my face. 'Jean,' I whispered.

'*Mon Dieu!*' he gasped, the weapon falling from his slack clutch as he staggered backwards in his attempt to get away from me.

I'd never seen a man closer to a stress-induced heart attack. Transfixed green eyes were wide in his white, panicked face, and a shaking hand drew upwards and made the four-point sign of a cross over his heart.

'Nico.'

'Hello, Jean.'

He'd aged since I'd last seen him. The face beneath the cap was weathered and demoralised, a soul beaten into submission. New evidence of the consequences of flouting Cosbi's rules was written into his features, not least a heavy scar running from above his eyebrow to his cheek.

Pressing my index finger across my lips, I approached, which only served to startle my old friend further.

'Why so afraid, Jean?' I asked.

He looked me up and down as though it were irrational that I should be speaking. His mouth opened and closed several times, the protruding lump in his throat bobbing about as though his larynx was trying its damnedest to fight his incapacity. Licking his raw lips, his brain eventually put one word onto his tongue. 'Dead.'

'Dead?' I asked.

'Both dead,' he confirmed with a nod.

Two words, it was an improvement.

Jean rubbed his hands down his weary face and blinked. He seemed disappointed when he re-focused and found me still standing there.

'It was bound to happen eventually, my father warned me this happened when you hit fifty.' He snorted, bending to collect his things.

'Who's dead, Jean?'

'You and Elena,' he said, chuckling to himself as he folded the blankets in half and rolled them into a neat, fat sausage. 'Ah, Jean, talking to ghosts—if you ever had the plot, it's finally lost.'

'No, I'm real,' I whispered, laying a hand on his shoulder.

He froze, one hand on the blanket bundle and the other halfway through stuffing the handle of the axe down the middle of it. Composing himself, he exhaled and shrugged off my hand.

'Jean, look at me!' I said, attempting to shout in a whisper and dragging him to face me by the scruff of his coat. 'What do you want, dammit? Proof?'

He threw me a look of scepticism. Moments later, the silence was interrupted by a furious voice and our attention jerked simultaneously towards the direction where Gerrin was ranting.

'You want this rammed up your arse? Now fucking find him!'

'For God's sake!' I hissed, releasing Jean and pulling my hood back up, searching around for my escape.

'*Commandante...*' Jean called as I began my retreat. '*Vous êtes en vie?*'

I looked at him blankly.

'You're alive?' he obliged.

The anger booming through the caves had brought my old friend to his senses; Gerrin only ever sounded that panicked when I was involved.

I nodded.

Without warning, Jean dropped all of his belongings and threw himself across the cavern, clasping me in a tight embrace. Slightly taken aback, I patted him awkwardly on the shoulder.

'*How, mon ami?*'

'Take it easy, Jean,' I muttered.

'They told everyone you died. Your *sale con* of a brother even did a pretty convincing job of mourning you.'

I stared at him in confusion. 'I've been in the medical bay.'

'All this time?'

'All this time.'

'Why didn't you come to find me? I could've helped you, we could've—'

'I couldn't remember anything,' I interrupted, knowing time was running out. 'I woke up and didn't know who I was or what I'd done.'

'And now?'

'Parts. It's coming back to me in pieces.'

'You know how it happened?'

'They said Elena attacked me.'

'Elena,' he whispered, his voice swelling with emotion. 'Don't listen to a word of it. She loved you, probably more than you deserved at times.'

'Past tense, Jean. Quit talking about her like she's dead.'

He drew back like I'd slapped him across the face. 'You mean, she's not... not... just like you?'

'They told me she's alive. That's what they want from me, to find out where she went and what she knows.'

'*Ma belle fille...*' he whispered, his body creasing in half, the fate of the girl he held so dear in his heart pushing him past breaking point.

I backed up as the approaching footsteps got ever closer. 'Look, I have to go, but I'll be back real soon. Don't tell anyone I was here.'

'Nico?'

'Yeah?'

'Where were you trying to get to?'

'Louisa and the baby.'

'Them?' he said, sounding surprised. 'Nico, don't you—'

'Bye, Jean.'

I'd barely made it around the corner when Ash burst into the cave entrance behind me, not bothering to whisper. 'Has anyone come past you?'

'Not a soul,' Jean said. 'Why, who are you looking for?'

I smiled to myself as the Scot made some poor excuse about why people were shouting and chasing their tails at this time of night. But my amusement didn't last long.

A realisation almost tripped me as I briefly forgot to pick up my feet.

Of course, Louisa thought I was dead too. Why would she ever think of coming to check for herself if that was what she'd been told?

I imagined her crying for me, explaining to a child who wasn't old enough to understand that his daddy was never coming home.

What had I done to deserve that from my own brother?

Gerrin was breathless and seething from fear when he eventually returned and found me sitting on my bed. 'Where were you?'

'Around.'

'I couldn't find you.'

'It's not my fault you can't look properly.'

His eyes narrowed in anger, but I guessed he was too relieved at being back in control to do anything about it.

'I want to sleep now,' I said. 'Get Gabriel.'

MATRIMONY

S TUMBLING INTO OUR room, booze and a numb heart unsettling my balance, I threw myself headfirst into an obliging bucket. Retching and heaving, my body forcefully dispelled the contents of my stomach as though that could mend what was now broken inside me.

When there was absolutely nothing left to give, I grabbed a towel and plunged my face into the freezing basin of water on the dresser, sobering instantly. Positive that being drunk had suited me better, but needing a clear mind for whenever she returned, I sank down on the bed in wait.

It must've been past two by the time she finally arrived, and I tried not to torture myself with thoughts of what had taken her so long. Lighting a candle, she proceeded to search through the baby's things, not noticing me until several minutes later.

'Oh!' She jumped back with her palm across her heart. 'Nico, you scared me. What on earth are you doing sitting in the dark?'

'Sit down,' I said.

'I really have to go feed the ba—'

'Fucking. Sit. *Down!*'

Flinching, she dropped onto the desk chair. I'd never raised my voice to her before, but now felt like a good time to start.

'What?' I sneered. 'Not neglecting you anymore, am I?'

She stilled, and even by the light of the candle I could see the blood had left her face.

'How long?'

She looked at me blankly.

'How long have you been fucking my brother?' I obliged.

A startled cry escaped her lips. 'Nico, don't say—'

'Answer me, damn you.'

'*Twice,*' she gasped, tears spilling from her eyes. 'Just twice, I swear.'

'The first time?'

'A year ago.'

'Oh dear God,' I groaned, my face falling into my hands.

With the screeching of chair across rock, she was in front of me, trying to peel my hands away while she knelt, begged and sobbed for all she was worth.

'Please, Nico. It was just a stupid mistake, I'm so sorry. Nico, look at me.'

'Get away from me!' I snapped, ripping her hands from mine and stalking across the room.

'It was a mistake!' she screamed.

I rounded on her and shouted back. '*Two* mistakes? Did you have to go back to him just to make sure, huh?'

'I tried not to!'

'Who started it?'

'Baby, don't do this to yourself.'

'Louisa, so help me God,' I said through gritted teeth, glaring at her make-up-streaked, but still impossibly beautiful, face.

'Gerrin.'

She could easily be lying, but I could believe it of Gerrin; he'd been jealous from the beginning. Anger built in my chest, a small bubble at the beginning, a blazing ball of fire as it reached my throat. With a roar of fury, I threw out my fist and struck the mirror on the wall, an innocent bystander to our argument.

The glass cracked clean down the middle as my hand sprouted streams of blood from several shards lodged in my knuckles. Adrenaline wasn't nearly enough to mask the pain.

'*Fuck!*'

For a few seconds, Louisa's pitiful sobs behind me were the only remnants of the wreckage of our relationship.

'You're hurt. Let me help you,' she begged.

I shook my head, seeing her face crumble in the distorted reflection.

'Nico, say something, please.'

I faced her, with only one thing left to know. 'Do you love him?'

My question caught her like a deer in headlights. 'I... I... don't... not...'

'You fucking *love* him?' I choked out. 'Gerrin. You love Gerrin.'

Louisa threw herself across the space between us and flung her arms around my neck, new tears soaking into my shirt. 'No. I love you, you're the one I want. Please forgive me.'

It killed me, not returning her embrace. 'Then why? Weren't you happy?'

'I... I don't know... I guess I was lonely. You were always away.'

'Lonely?' I snorted. 'What a great reason to end our marriage.'

'End? No, Nico, no, please don't say that. I don't want this to be the end of us. Tell me you don't mean it.'

I backed out of her arms. 'I don't know what I want.'

Her blue eyes widened in alarm. 'Oh God, please... don't... for the baby...'

And there was me thinking she'd hit rock bottom about two hours earlier. 'Don't you even *try* to use our son—' I snapped, furiously pointing a finger.

But I never finished that sentence. My heart went ice cold as I put two and two together and unfortunately came up with four.

Our son. Conceived a year ago.

I looked at her in horror, and she recoiled, hands flying to her mouth at what she'd unintentionally given away.

'Whose?' I demanded.

She backed up until her legs hit the chair, dropping heavily into the seat and burying her head in her hands, the last and very worst lie crumbling around her. 'I don't know,' she whispered.

I didn't move an inch. Two hours ago I'd had it all and now my world was fast imploding. 'That's why you wanted to leave when you found out you were pregnant,' I said. 'Why you didn't want to keep my child, his child. Whose fucking kid even *is* he?'

She couldn't see me cry. I took off towards the door and didn't look back.

'Nico!' she screamed. 'Don't leave me! Please...'

'The two of you were all I ever wanted, Louisa.'

My voice cracked as I walked out, leaving my wife behind, hysterically calling my name. There was only one place I could go right now, only one person who would understand.

Moments later, I was hammering on Elena's door. It took my bleary-eyed, messy-haired best friend a good couple of minutes to open it, but I couldn't feel bad for waking her.

'Do you know what time it is, shithead?' she yawned, pulling hair from her face.

'Can I come in?' I panted, clinging to the door frame like it was the only thing stopping me from hitting the deck.

She was awake instantly, seizing my hand and pulling me into the familiar refuge of her room. 'What's happened?'

'Louisa.'

'What about her?'

The tears finally came. I needed the release, so I slumped on the bed, put my face in my hands and just didn't care anymore.

'Nico...?' she whispered. It was the first time she'd seen me cry.

'Louisa and Gerrin.'

'Yes, what about...?' she began, before her ever-keen perception kicked in. 'They've been...?'

Head down, I nodded.

'Oh, Nico.'

All credit to her, she never once said those dreaded words: 'I told you so'. She sympathised when I cried and listened when I needed. She was just there.

'That hand needs looking at,' she said when I'd talked myself silent.

Collecting several towels and filling a bowl of water, she gestured across her lap. 'Lay your arm flat. What did you hit?'

'A mirror,' I said, flinching as she removed glass fragments from the gouges in my skin.

'That temper of yours.'

The last piece of mirror clinked into the waiting bowl and she wrapped a freezing, water-sodden flannel around the swollen wound. Dampening another, she gently wiped the dried blood from my arm, her fingers pressing lightly up and down my skin.

I looked at her. Engrossed in her task, she swept her hair to one side, out of the way. Even sleep-tousled, she was a stunning woman.

Her touch brushed close. My hand snatched hold of her fingers, my wayward thumb stroking across her knuckles. She said nothing but just watched the movement, anticipating what I was about to do.

She flinched when I tipped her chin upwards, watching in doubt as my eyes lowered to her lips. The temptation to do it was too much. I reached for her with no thought for the repercussions.

'Stop,' she whispered, pulling away at the last second.

'I thought this was what you wanted.'

'Not like this.'

'Does it matter how it happens?' I said, licking my lips as I leaned in again.

She pushed on my chest and shifted away, putting physical distance between us. 'You're not being fair on either of us. You can't use me to make her feel what you're feeling.'

Stung by the rejection, I abandoned my clumsy advances as the mortification of trying it on with my best friend quickly caught up with me. 'I'm sorry, that was really stupid,' I muttered, clambering to my feet.

'Where're you planning to go, Nico?'

I stopped. She had a point; I was fast running out of places to sleep.

'Come back, you idiot. You can stay here.'

I relented after a brief argument, but insisted on sleeping in the armchair, much to Elena's amusement.

Exhausted but unable to switch off, I lay awake under a musty blanket, watching drips of water splash reliably onto the floor until the early hours.

I pulled off my blood-spattered top, an unwanted relic of the worst birthday ever, and tossed it into the bin.

'Take it you didn't sleep well.'

I turned to find Elena watching me, propped up on her elbows.

'Sorry, I didn't mean to wake you,' I said.

'You want me to get you some spare clothes?' she asked as a timid knock sounded at the door.

She jumped out of bed and pulled on a top over her underwear, although the garment was so see-through it was pretty pointless. For a few seconds, I genuinely thought it was a guy at the door, given the apparent desire to flaunt her half-naked body. But then I heard my name.

I lit a cigarette and joined her.

'What do you want?' Elena said, with a flick of her long hair.

'Is he here?'

Louisa.

With a glare that would've made any man run a thousand miles, Elena pushed the door wider to reveal that I was standing next to her.

Louisa's eyes skirted up Elena's lack of attire before they transferred to me, lingering on my shirtless chest and unbuttoned jeans. An unimpressed scowl settled on her pretty face.

'What?' I said coldly, taking a drag on the cigarette.

'Can I speak to you?'

I shrugged as Elena and I both stayed put.

'Alone...' she added.

Elena flashed me a dazzling smile. 'I'll be right over here if you want me,' she said, laying a hand on the bottom of my torso and dragging her fingers through the hair on my chest as she sauntered past.

Trying not to laugh at her audacity, I looked expectantly at Louisa, who looked like she was about to pitch a fit on the doorstep.

'Does she have to walk around dressed like that?' she hissed.

Overhearing, Elena called back, 'He's seen me in a lot less, sweetie.'

Seeing me trying to bite back laughter, all the jealous rage blazing in Louisa's eyes died stone cold.

'Nico,' came the crushed whisper as she nodded over my shoulder at Elena. 'You didn't... did you?'

'That's none of your business,' I said, but seeing her on the verge of tears, I rolled my eyes and added, 'No.'

Exhaling a relieved breath, she took my hand. 'Come home.'

'I can't do that.'

'He's missing his daddy,' she said, trying to appeal to my better nature. 'You'll always be his daddy, it doesn't matter what's happened.'

'Can't you hear how stupid you sound?' I cried. 'Of course it fucking matters!'

I ripped my hand away and was about to slam the door in her face.

'I'm so scared, Nico.'

The bottom dropped out of my world again. Even after everything she'd done, it still hurt to hear that she was in pain. And now that I'd taken a moment out of wallowing in anger, I noticed how troubled her face was.

'What's wrong?' I said.

She hesitated. 'You saw... everything that happened, in the corridor last night?'

I nodded, wincing as raw screenshots flashed through my head.

'Did you... did you notice anyone else?'

'Foley was there,' I said.

'Oh.'

It took me a few seconds to understand, before I remembered what Foley dealt in. 'What did he ask for to keep quiet?'

'The locket my father gave me for my thirteenth birthday.'

Its absence from around her neck told me that she'd caved to his demand, probably too frightened to even try resisting. She'd bought herself some time, but I knew that Foley wasn't likely to meet with such readiness when he tried the other culprit.

'I'll sort it,' I said, looking uselessly around me for something to wear.

'Shoes!' Elena shouted, before my trainers came cartwheeling through the door.

Leaving the two women in my life eyeballing each other with distaste, I took off at a jog, calling back, 'Stay with Elena, she'll make sure you're safe.'

It had to be true.

If she *was* my wife, then that meant that Gerrin had been lying through his teeth.

It was early morning when my guard nearly fell from his perch as I emerged from my room.

I guessed from the smell of the man that the uncontrollable shaking of his hands was more down to alcohol withdrawal than any fear of me. He was nothing, obeying any order if it meant someone would sort him out. As a fellow addict, I almost felt sorry for him.

A faded shell of a man though I was, it only took one weighty punch to the face and he was out cold. I dragged him inside and heaved his body into the bed, stabbing the propofol line into his arm. Beneath the sheets and in the dark, I was satisfied that he could be mistaken for me.

For weeks I'd been hoping that this dream would never come true, and now its realisation was all I wanted. Strange how life works.

Everywhere was quiet, no one was stirring. I paused at 19, but no, things needed to be done before I could speak to her again.

The potent smell of ethanol seeped from the open mouth of a neglected bottle near the bed, its remaining contents guarded by a lolling arm, fingertips skimming absently across the rim.

Cavernous snores resonated back and forth between the stony walls as his face-down form came into view by the light of a candle. Half-naked, with splayed blonde hair curtaining his face against the pillow, Gerrin looked like he'd passed out exactly where he'd fallen.

He was so untroubled; the lies didn't disturb his sleep.

Swooping low, I plucked the bottle from under his reach, earning a splutter of interrupted breathing, and settled myself on a chair at his side.

I took a long swig from the stolen container, calmness sweeping over me as the heady fumes hit the back of my nose and the tasteless sterility of vodka washed down my throat.

Gerrin restlessly flipped onto his back, spitting a clump of hair from his mouth and throwing a hand over the crotch of his cargo shorts. I necked the spirit, spinning the handle of a knife I'd grabbed from his dresser between my fingers.

The anger that'd so often coursed through this scenario was absent. He'd polluted my marriage, stolen fatherhood from me, and lied through his teeth about the lot. I felt numb to it all.

My eyes were sore when he began to stir around twenty minutes later. My mind had been lost in a chasm of empty thoughts, cheeks itchy from the salt of dried liquid.

Setting down the depleted vodka, I took up a glass of stale water and hurled the contents at his face.

Spluttering and thrashing like a man possessed, Gerrin was awake in moments. With a loud roar of anger, he tossed sopping wet hair from his face and used his palm to dash streams of liquid from his eyes.

It took a few seconds for him to recover before he could focus on me. Eyebrows shot north, jaw dropped south. There was a brief moment of vulnerability in the armour before his gaze took in the knife, and my opponent was back.

'Nico.'

He knew my purpose.

'Found your way here eventually, I see,' he said.

'Sleep well?' I asked.

"Til about two minutes ago.'

'Sober?'

He nodded. 'Having a freezing glass of water thrown over you kinda sorts that out.'

'Normally, I'd apologise, but...' I trailed off with a shrug.

Keeping wary eyes on the sharp steel point, he stood and selected a T-shirt from the chair, the water staining odd patches on the cotton. 'Out with it then.'

'Tell me about your wife.'

'You're going to have to be a bit more specific.'

'How is she?'

'She's fine.'

'Why isn't she here with you?'

'She's staying with her mother tonight.'

'Can't imagine she's happy that you've taken your wedding ring off.'

He glanced at his hand. 'It was Dad's ring, it's a bit big. I take it off sometimes so I don't lose it.'

I shook my head in disbelief. 'What's her favourite colour? Her favourite book? What does she do with her hair when she's thinking?'

'What's that got to do with anything?'

'I just want the truth.'

'You're pointing the knife, Nic, maybe you should explain what I've done wrong.'

'You wrecked my marriage!' I shouted.

He flashed me a look of surprise, and after a few moments, nodded and reached into a drawer in his desk. He flicked a shiny object through the air. 'Here, it's yours. You took it off when you left her.'

I looked down at the metal, branding a cold circle on my palm. I still needed to hear it. 'She *is* my wife?'

'Unless you decide otherwise.'

'And you slept with her?'

'Yes.'

'Twice?'

'Yes.'

Uncertainty gave way to anger. 'You could've had anyone in this place. *Anyone.* Why couldn't you let me be happy?'

'I tried, Nic. But I wanted her, and she wanted me.'

The chair toppled sideways as I hurled myself at him, the knife swift to find a home at his throat.

His teeth bared in a grimace, quickened breath whistling between them. 'Not bad, didn't think you had the strength these days.'

'For this? Always.'

'Then do it,' he said. 'Put me out of my fucking misery.'

He dropped his hands to his sides, shunning any resistance, and tilted his head back to give me full access to his exposed neck.

As the steel tip pressed against his raw skin, the artery began to hammer furiously, as though it sensed the threat to its existence.

I hesitated, absorbed by the movement.

'What're you waiting for?' he goaded.

Was I the man to kill my brother?

'What about the baby?' I said.

'What about him?'

'Is he yours?' I asked, the words sending a fresh wave of tears crashing through my defences.

'Mine?' A laugh erupted from his mouth. 'Shit, I bloody hope not.'

'How do you know he isn't?'

'How do you know he *is*? Kid has blonde hair,' he said with a shrug. 'Could've got that from her.'

'You don't want either of them?'

'Christ, Nico. We fucked around behind your back a couple of times— it was hardly the romance of the century.'

My jaw trembled as I tried to force my hand into pushing the knife forwards. But it shook out of control, tremors rocketing up my arm, into my shoulders.

'You lied to me,' I said. 'You broke my heart.'

'What we did to you was wrong, and I've wanted to take it back every day since you found out. You think I wouldn't tell any lie to avoid tearing your world apart again?'

'I—'

There was a smart rap at the door. I whipped around, realising I'd forgotten to close it.

'My, my, Nico, your focus really wasn't where it should've been, was it?' Cosbi said, leaning against the wooden frame. 'We'll have to see what we can do about that.'

'How long have you been there?' I said.

'Long enough.'

'You think I'm going to carry on helping you?'

'Of course.'

'You're delusional. I'm leaving, and I'm taking my family with me.'

'I'm afraid I cannot allow that yet. Unfortunate though it is that you remembered this little escapade before you kept your promise to me, it doesn't alter our end goal.'

'Meaning?'

'Renegotiation.'

'I know what kind of man you are. Any secret of ours is going nowhere near you.'

'Oh, come now, Nico, let's not fall out,' he said, smiling. 'Our mutual friend, Miss Martinez, you remember her, don't you? We both know she will come back for you. After all, how could she leave behind the man she loves?'

'And if she does?'

'*When* she does, the two of you will be free to leave, with your family, provided I have my answers.'

'You think I trust anything you say?'

'What choice do you have?'

'And if I say no?'

He shrugged. 'Then as soon as she steps foot inside this place'—he raised two fingers and pressed their tips to his temple—'*Bang...*'

I had barely taken a step forwards when Gerrin seized me around the chest. The tip of a needle pierced through the material covering my bicep, burying itself in my flesh. The anaesthetic in the syringe emptied into my body as Gerrin squeezed the plunger, and I instantly felt my world get a shade darker.

'Gabriel hoped I wouldn't have to use this, Nico,' Gerrin said.

Eyes rolling to the heavens, I felt Cosbi smack my cheek.

'Have a think about it...'

SECRET

'I FOUND SOMETHING the other day,' Elena said, beckoning for a leg-up.

I finished moving chairs and cushions, removing any trace that a gathering had taken place. 'Oh?'

'I need to check it out properly. Will you come with me?'

I hauled myself up through the gap after her and stood hunched in the passages above her room, not even vaguely interested.

'Are you going to tell me what these stupid dots mean yet?' I complained as I stumbled along behind her, hitting my head more often than I cared for.

'It's Braille,' she said. 'You know the way outside without it.'

We trudged on a while longer, before Elena ventured off the known path and I noticed different patterns of dots appearing above new paths. This was unexplored territory.

I was studying the drawings on the rocks when I heard a strange noise—a quiet howl that rode the gentle breeze passing through the corridor.

I looked up. 'Wait, did you hear that?'

'What now?' Elena called, on her hands and knees some way in the distance.

'You must be deaf if you didn't hear it this time.'

'Bugger off, I'm concentrating.'

'*Shh*, listen.'

I heard her stop up ahead with an exasperated sigh. We waited in silence for a few seconds before the sorrowful yowl pealed out again.

'Oh yeah!' Elena said. 'I wonder what it is.'

'Animal of some sort,' I said. 'Are there wolves around here?'

Elena shrugged. 'Come on, we don't have much time.'

'What does this symbol mean?' I asked.

'Braille for "P". "*Peligro*" in Spanish means danger.'

'What danger?'

'Some passages have unstable ceilings or floors that drop away,' she said. 'Come on, we're nearly there.'

My legs moved but my face was stuck gawking; the things I didn't know about her after four years were innumerable. Like Braille and cave exploration, and the fact that she had far too much time on her hands.

'In here,' she said, after a few more twists and turns brought us, bizarrely, to a door.

'What the...?'

I had to admit, my interest was finally piqued. Nobody had been down here before, and yet there was a huge handcrafted piece of oak in our way.

'I've only managed to sneak a look through the gap there,' Elena said. 'I wanted you with me when I went inside.'

'Why?'

'I think this is a dangerous place.'

'And how do you plan on getting in?'

Reaching up to her hair, she removed the hairpin holding together her bun and straightened it. I held both torches as she twisted and turned the metal grip in the lock, and with a sharp yank to the left, relieved the catch of its duty.

Add lock-picking to that list...

'All yours, big guy.'

Taking possession of the torches, she stood back as I slammed my weight into the bulky wood, shoving it back with a squeal of aged hinges.

Even through the dense darkness, I knew the room was vast. Searching around for a better source of light, my big toe soon met with the perils of blind cave exploration.

'Ow, bugger!' I hissed.

Hopping on my uninjured foot, I swiped the flame downwards to see what metal object had tripped me. Jutting out from the wall, a large blue device sat amidst a thick layer of dust.

'Looks like a generator of some sort,' I said, bending to inspect the machine.

'Sounds like running water,' Elena said, pressing her ear to the wall.

'Might be hydroelectric, like ours.'

I ran my hands over the filthy casing, searching for a mechanism that might kick-start the contraption. At length, I found a rusting flip switch and forced it into the opposing position, and a deafening engine stuttered to life.

'What's it meant to do?' Elena mouthed, hands clapped firmly over her ears.

'Lights, I hope,' I mimed back.

It took a good few minutes, but one by one, flickering like they were props in some cheap horror movie, bulbs around the cavern sprang to life with a telltale electrical zap.

'Holy shit,' I mouthed.

We were standing on a balcony that encircled the room; a loose chicken wire fence was secured around the brink in an attempt to prevent fatalities. In the centre of the floor, a good thirty feet below, proudly sat a vintage Triumph Bonneville, standing guard over the more sinister contents surrounding it.

The grotto was filled from floor to ceiling with every type of weapon imaginable: semi-automatics, revolvers, knives, grenades, axes. The place was stacked with enough ammunition for an army.

'Are they... explosives?' Elena shouted over the generator, pointing across the room to a pile of stacked cylindrical tubes.

I nodded. 'And petrol.'

She glanced at me, looking as horrified as I felt.

With a tip of her head, she indicated that we should leave. I turned off the generator, restoring peace to the forbidden cavern, and Elena closed the door behind us.

Not a word was uttered as we scrambled back to safe territory.

Peering down from the lip of the passage entrance in Elena's ceiling, I checked that the room was as deserted as we'd left it and dropped silently from the height, reaching up to help her down too.

'Cosbi must never find that,' Elena said, getting the obvious out of the way.

I nodded. 'What was that place?'

'Must've been used as some kind of storage during the war, but I wish I'd never found it. Christ, what he could do with that lot.'

'There must be another entrance to it somewhere,' I said. 'How else would you get a bloody motorbike in there?'

'I don't think I've ever seen so many guns,' she said.

'Or explosives.'

The moment that followed our worried silence was disrupted by the strangest of sensations, one I was certain I'd felt before. I crept to the door and inched it open. The corridor was abandoned, even when I brandished the torch in both directions.

I shrugged at her.

Paranoid.

RUN

'DO YOU EVEN know what you're asking of me?' I said.

She nodded. 'And it'll be the hardest thing you'll ever do. It's time to choose.'

Old family or new family. Blood or heart.

'Are you with us, Nico?'

Several seconds passed before I could vocalise my decision. 'Yes.'

'Will you come back?'

'If it'll wind Dean up.'

'Nico,' she chided, with a playful slap to my chest.

'Slight misunderstanding,' she announced to the dubious, blatantly eavesdropping members of the group as we returned.

'He shouldn't be here,' Dean said.

'We agreed, Dean,' Elena said.

'Some of us didn't.'

'She is right,' Jean piped up. 'He gives us an advantage.'

'Advantage?' I said.

'Over your brother. You are his weakness.'

'I'm not so sure anymore.'

'It's true,' Elena said. 'In his own twisted way, everything he did was for you.'

'Then I should've been able to get through to him.'

Elena shook her head. 'There're other things motivating him now.'

I frowned as I remembered Cosbi's poisonous words in 23. 'Jealousy, revenge...' I murmured.

Jean nodded. 'Precisely.'

'That's how Cosbi works,' Elena said. 'His strength comes from the weakness of others.'

I frowned. 'I didn't have a weakness.'

'Exactly, that's why he needed Louisa.'

I didn't fully understand the emotion in her voice, but my heart called it sadness. She realised now that without Cosbi's scheming with Louisa, things could've been so different for us.

'So he did do it on purpose,' I muttered.

'He fooled us too, Nico,' Parker said.

'We did things out there that we're not proud of because of promises he made,' Chase continued. 'Said that he'd be able to help us get home if we stockpiled supplies for a while. He's been saying it for years, but I guess the lie only really hit home when we realised that other people were being made to do stuff too, that night in 23.'

I glanced at Parker. 'The knife?'

Parker nodded. 'I don't know what I was hoping you'd achieve, but I didn't know what else to do. We came to Elena straight after.'

'We haven't seen anyone outside in ages,' Chase said. 'There's no reason for us to still be hiding out down here.'

'Then why are we?'

'Because it's what Cosbi wants,' Elena said.

'Why could he possibly want to live down here if there's another option?'

'Control,' Jean said. 'Down here, he has it all.'

I listened as the talk turned to Cosbi's motives. Smiling at Elena, I felt a part of something bigger for the first time in ages. We weren't settling for this.

'So what's the plan then?' I said.

'Get everyone out of here,' Elena said.

'Why don't we just tell everyone what he's like? They'll soon leave,' Dean said.

'Most of the people here are happy to be looked after,' Elena said. 'Even if they believed us, the security he offers might be too much to resist.'

'Then there is the safety of our families,' Jean said. 'We have seen how far he is willing to go. We must act in secrecy for now.'

'No one can know,' I said.

'"*Junta*" means meeting...' Elena said, as I glanced over her shoulder.

She scrawled the date beneath the first word. The names of the group were jotted beneath as they were volunteered by each member of the circle.

'Any flashes of inspiration?' she said.

'We need to start stockpiling,' Jean offered. 'Food, blankets, medicine. Anything we can get our hands on.'

Elena nodded. 'I've somewhere I can store it all. Parker and Chase should be able to help get things.'

'Weapons too,' I said.

Uncomfortable looks passed between the group at the suggestion that we might encounter violence.

'Yes, you never know what we might come across,' Elena said, scribbling away.

'A time frame would be helpful,' someone piped up.

'What does everyone say to three months?' I said. 'Gives us time to prepare, and my wife will have had the baby.'

A general rumble of consensus stole around the room, and a flash of excitement. Giving it a date made it real.

My hand refused to knock on the door. There it was, raised in the air, poised to complete the action, and yet nothing.

I couldn't believe what I was about to do. There were some things in life that only Elena could've talked me into.

Move... my brain urged my hand.

You don't want to see him... my muscles objected.

True enough, but I'd made a promise. Overruling my arm and straightening the curl of disgust from my lip, I pounded my fist into the ageing wood.

'Come in.' Gerrin's glacial tone cut through the silence.

Too late now.

My entry to the room was wary. No amount of psyching myself up or rehearsing my words would've made it any easier.

'Nic!' he exclaimed, my name breathing life into his black heart.

Scrambling to his feet, he scraped unruly blonde tresses behind his ears as the cigarette hanging from his mouth carelessly dropped ash onto his jeans. The place stank of stale, cheap whisky.

'Here, have a seat,' he said, digging his fingers beneath the pile of discarded clothes, papers and the odd cigarette packet that sat on his desk chair and negligently launching the debris across the room.

He gestured hopefully to the cleared spot when I didn't make any move.

'Thanks,' I said, doing what was required of me.

An awkward silence, vast and unpredictable, settled between us as we both avoided the inevitable. He occupied himself with twiddling his fingers, shifting his weight between the two forearms that rested on his knees. Occasionally, he would open his mouth, only to shut it again. I stared at the wall.

'I've missed you.'

It hit me hard, like five knuckles right to the gut. Feeling something was not what I'd had planned here. 'I needed time.'

He swallowed hard and nodded. 'Cigarette?'

'Please.'

He stood and removed the packet from his jeans, selecting one and passing it to me with his lighter. 'I'm glad you came, I honestly didn't think you ever would.'

'Neither did I.'

The returning silence hit the room like a car slamming into a brick wall, filled only with exhaled smoke and anticipation. Gerrin was again the first to break it.

'What changed your mind?'

'Perspective.'

He glanced at me.

'The closer Louisa gets to having the baby, the more I think about their safety,' I explained. 'And what those guys did, it was dangerous for us all.'

Elena had known what that sentence would cost me. She'd pleaded, appealed to any selflessness that lived within me; she'd made me practise it until the words didn't mean anything anymore.

His head jolted up, the most desperate look of hope plaguing his features. 'You mean you understa—'

'I don't want to talk about what happened in that room, Gerrin,' I snapped, before he uttered anything that would ruin my poker face. 'But I understand that something had to be done.'

His face fell, like that of a scolded child, and he took a long drag on his cigarette to hide his disappointment. Seconds later, he found his voice again. 'Do you think you can forgive me?'

'In time,' I conceded, having left him to stew for a few seconds.

'Then, you'll come back to work?'

'I'll come back to work. But you swear to me that nothing like that will ever happen again.'

'I swear,' he said instantly.

'Then I guess I'll see you tomorrow,' I said, stubbing the cigarette out on the wall and standing to go.

He rose too, his hand outstretched and ready for mine. I complied.

'What about Elena?' he said.

'Awkward as hell,' I answered with a shrug. 'What Cosbi said kind of ruined our chances at staying friends.'

He nodded. 'Thought it might. I'm sorry.'

'Don't be,' I said. 'She wants more. I don't. End of story.'

He held out the packet of cigarettes for me to take another.

'Oh, shit, forgot something,' he said, diving into the now scattered pile of junk lying across the floor. He selected something and brushed off some dirt before presenting it to me. 'For the baby.'

I stared down at the soft white bear in my grasp and locked my fingers around its stuffed neck. 'Thank you, Louisa will love it.'

'Oh, one more thing—have you got some time tomorrow? Can you cover my training session?'

'Sure, whatever.'

Anger heated my face as I strode back to my room. I hated him and I hated what I'd just done. Tossing the toy bear straight into the bin, I slumped on the bed and confronted the real reason behind my fury.

Whatever happened, the unalterable truth remained that one day soon would be the last time I ever saw him. And I hated myself for being sorry.

The night of the escape…

'YOUR FAMILY WILL be in my group,' Elena said. 'The sooner they're gone, the better—it'll leave your head clear to take care of the second group.'

I nodded. The joint leadership thing was a farce; I deserved no credit for getting us to the position we were in that day.

'I'll take care of them, I swear,' she said.

'There's no one I'd rather trust them with,' I said. 'You're the most incredible woman I've ever met.'

She beamed at the compliment before realising it contained a goodbye of sorts. Huffing in frustration, she threw herself into helping the Moreau clan rearrange the room.

'There were a few missing today,' Jean observed.

'Parker and Chase were called to Cosbi,' I said.

'And nobody's seen Dean all day,' Elena added.

When no evidence remained of a meeting, Elena and I left the family and meandered home, the silence between us thick with nervous anticipation and worry.

We were to meet at eleven that night. Several of the men would block off the main entrance with debris we'd been stockpiling in a disused passageway for weeks, while Chase and Parker locked the doors of all those likely to oppose us. If all other preparations failed, at least the obstructions would slow them.

As plans go, it was flawless. And who knows, it might just have worked.

'*Go!*' Parker bellowed as he barrelled down the corridor.

Elena and I were just about to enter Eli's Way, completely oblivious to the world, when we froze.

'Huh?' I said.

'Get out of here!'

'Parker—'

'Someone blabbed,' he panted. 'Cosbi knows everything. I've just heard it from his own mouth. He knows the plan, the time, where we're going. *Shit!*'

'Who told him?' Elena said.

'He wouldn't say. Whoever it was blamed the whole thing on you, Nico, but Cosbi knows Elena's involved. They're coming for you both.'

I clapped him on the shoulder. 'Thank you, we owe you.'

'Hurry!'

Matching each other's pace, Elena and I took off without wasting another second. Slamming and locking her door behind us just a few minutes later, we stood facing each other, fear pumping our chests.

'Lighter!' she demanded.

'What?'

'Give me your lighter, quickly!'

I tossed it over, and she set fire to the corner of two pieces of paper, flames licking at the scrawled Spanish words as she threw them into the corner, on top of some clothes and wood.

'I can't believe it,' she whispered.

'Fucking grass,' I seethed.

'They're blaming you, when it was all my idea.'

'It doesn't matter anymore. You need to go.'

'We can't leave everyone.'

'I'm not suggesting *we* do anything.'

She paused, looking frightened for the first time since room 23. 'You think I would even consider leaving you here alone?'

'You have no choice.'

'But they think it's your fault—'

'And they've figured out it's yours too. Which of us is most likely to survive down here? Gerrin won't let me be hurt too badly, you know that, but he wouldn't think twice about killing you after what you said the other day.'

'I won't do it.'

An invisible force from outside rattled the door handle.

'Yes, you will,' I said, taking her by the shoulders. 'You know where you're going, find help and bring it back.'

Our eyes shot to the door as the rattling ceased.

'Nico... Elena...' Cosbi sang. 'There's nowhere left to run, make it better for yourselves and open up.'

'I can't leave my family,' I said. 'And I can't lose you. Don't make me watch that, Elena, I'm begging you.'

For only the second time in our eventful relationship, her emotional dam broke. She took hold of my face. 'Stay safe,' she whispered. 'I'll bring help, I swear.'

Patience had exhausted on the other side of the door, and a huge force shook the wood in its fittings, pounding mercilessly, steadily. Gerrin, undoubtedly.

Fearing in my heart that this would be the last chance I ever got, I mirrored the hold of her hands and memorised the molten brown of her eyes, the smell of her hair, the perfect line defining her full lips.

And then they were mine.

We kissed. Urgently, out of sheer necessity, years of mutual want exploding as gunpowder met naked flame. The embrace happened more naturally than I could've ever imagined, desperate mouths taking us far beyond the limits of friendship.

With a sob of torment, she pressed herself into my arms, not wanting to let go. The salty taste of sad tears broke through our kiss as I pulled back and grazed my lips across her nose.

'*Run...*' I begged.

'I promise I will see you again,' she whispered, climbing onto a chair and hoisting herself upwards with my help. Wiping new tears from her eyes, she peered down at me one last time.

And then she was gone.

REUNITED

'Nico...' Elena sang.

She had such a beautiful voice, soft and sensual as it rippled through the afternoon air and into my waiting ears, that unique smoky texture of her Spanish roots sending shivers up my spine.

The sunshine speckled across my closed lids, tinting them a warm, squintingly bright pink as her falling hair tickled across my cheek.

'Time to wake up, sleepy head.'

Acutely aware of a dull pain in my bicep, stabbing and aching in alternating peculiarity, I lifted my arms around her and rolled to the side so that she was beneath me. I forced open my heavy eyes until her face came into focus from the jumble of colour the summer sun was throwing down.

Loose dark hair was everywhere, entwined in the buttercup-strewn wild grass, and two pools of molten chocolate blinked up at me.

'You came back,' I whispered.

'I told you I would, when you needed me again.'

'God, I've missed you.'

I hadn't realised how much until now.

'Are you ready for this?' she said, running her warm fingers through my hair.

'Ready for what?'

'The end, Nico,' she said. 'You're so nearly there.'

'Will you stay?'

'Forever.'

She put her hands on my chest, gently pushing my weight so that I sank back onto the grass. A palm brushed like silk over my face, pushing my eyelids to a close in the wake of its path. Laying a kiss on my cheek, she leaned close and whispered in my ear.

'Go back. Go back to that day.'

HUNT

Gerrin was through the door less than thirty seconds later.

'You aren't welcome here. Fuck off,' I said, not taking my eyes off my book.

'A little birdie tells me you had more pressing plans for today, Nico,' Cosbi said, stepping out from behind my brother.

'Listening to the gossips?'

'Oh, more than gossip,' he said. 'It appears you have a rat.'

A figure was thrown into the room, landing on its knees and keeping its bloodied face tipped at the floor. But I didn't need to see his traitorous face. Dean avoided my eyes meticulously, concentrating only on his wheezing breaths. The pain he was in suggested that Gerrin had broken one, if not more, of his ribs.

'And he is...?'

'The one who wanted you out of the picture,' Dean panted. 'Game's up, dickhead.'

Anger had flashed across my face before I could feign indifference.

'A declaration of guilt if ever I saw one,' Cosbi said, looking at me with a smile. 'Now, are you going to tell me where your lovely accomplice is?'

'Wait, you promised you wouldn't hurt her!' Dean cried.

'I lied,' Cosbi said. 'Get him out of here.'

Ash silenced Dean's protests with a few knuckles to the face before dragging him away.

'You won't find her,' I said.

'We'll just have to see about that, won't we?' Cosbi said.

'Where should we start?' Chase said, avoiding eye contact with me.

'Outside?' Cosbi enquired, studying my expression. 'Mmm-hmm. Bring him, he will see what happens to traitors.'

Gerrin took up the challenge of making me comply, exercising his full, unsurpassable strength against me. Strong though I was, my body was no match for it.

Cosbi smiled. 'Gentlemen, let's go catch ourselves a vixen.'

> *'Blow thy horn, hunter,*
> *And blow thy horn on high!*
> *There is a doe in yonder wood,*
> *In faith she will not die.'*

Cosbi lead the rousing chorus to cheers of appreciation from the group of men parading through the tunnels. With the old rifle hanging from a strap around his neck, Ash joined in heartily, encouraging the two Americans with a hefty thump on the back.

Parker threw an edgy sideways look at Chase, and then aimed it over his shoulder at me when no one was looking. A quick jerk of my head told them to go with it.

People left their rooms to see what all the commotion was about, eyes widening at Cosbi heading an outdoor expedition of men carrying weapons and baying like werewolves.

The titanic struggle at the back ensured that Gerrin could neither sing along nor cheer. I was the only one strong enough to make him break a sweat, and he grunted and battled for control of our dysfunctional duet.

Familiar, allied faces fell when they saw he had the better of me. It was a clever move to make a spectacle of my capture, and Cosbi watched with immense satisfaction as every clap, holler and booted stomp beat the hope from their eyes.

> *'As I stood under a band,*
> *The deer shoff on the mead;*
> *I struck her so that down she sank*
> *But yet she was not dead.'*

Ash pounded his fist into his palm as he chanted and pranced, all the way up to a flabbergasted Jean, standing guard at the entrance.

Seeing that something was wrong, Jean took a step towards me, hoping to achieve God knows what. The singing instantly ceased and Ash darted between us, knife poised.

'Back off, old fella,' he said. 'This is none o' your concern.'

I shook my head at Jean.

The Frenchman reluctantly obeyed and backed up to the wall, letting the company pass out of the caves.

The evening was dreary, the typically British weather teeming from a dark sky. Under normal circumstances, I would've been relishing the cool sheen of rain on my skin, but my fears for Elena were eating at my stomach.

Where was she?

My bravado back in her room had been just that. I had no idea which way she'd run, or how far she'd gone. I just hoped it was enough.

Cosbi inhaled a mouthful of wet air. 'Nobody returns until she's found.'

He'd taken three steps down the sodden hillside when Parker called. 'She must be long gone by now. Cosbi, is this really necessary?'

Cosbi turned with a look that brooked no back chat. 'She's coming back for *him,* probably with help,' he said, jabbing a finger in my direction. 'She knows the way back in, and she's created holy hell down there that I'll have to calm. Any more questions?'

All mouths remained shut; all legs followed.

'How do you do it, Nic?' Gerrin mocked, steadying me by the collar of my T-shirt as I skidded down the grass. 'They're all just tripping over themselves for you.'

'I find consent helps,' I said, provoking him into delivering a harsh shove.

Reaching the bottom of the hill, Cosbi addressed the group. 'Our young couple have been overheard discussing a lake. It may be worth our while to find it.'

'*You* were out here too?' Gerrin hissed in my ear.

I remained silent, forbidding myself to react to either accusation.

'Quite the double life your brother has been leading, Gerrin,' Cosbi said. 'Parker, Chase, you head over there. Lee, Shane, Dan, you can start in there. Ash, Gerrin, with me. You find anything, use the flares.'

My troubled heart sank as I realised the group that was to be led by Cosbi was bound for the heart of the woodland territory Elena and I had claimed as our own.

Cosbi led our ramble along the field as Gerrin propelled me onwards, while Ash smashed enthusiastically through the woods. Trying to stall for time, I threw my weight into making a nuisance of myself.

'Do I detect panic, Nico?' Cosbi said. 'Am I getting close?'

'You underestimate her,' I spat.

'Well, we'll soon see, won't we?'

Fear weighed heavy in my stomach; he had to be wrong this time.

'There's a path through here,' Ash called. 'Looks recent, no footprints.'

Hopes that our well-trodden route through the forest would've grown over in the rain-soaked weeks since we left it were dashed. But if she had come this way, at least she'd been smart enough to cover her tracks.

'We follow it,' Cosbi said.

Hacking indiscriminately at nettles and low-lying branches with a serrated hunting knife, Ash led the way down the familiar track, eating into the half-mile distance to our lake. Midges were rampant in the air around our heads, accompanying our journey like nosy, microscopic predators, the occasional swatting sound of palm meeting skin foretelling the end of another winged life.

Gerrin manoeuvred me from one end of the path to the other, admirable given my continuous fight. Both of us emerged from the canopy fifteen minutes later considerably worse for wear, huffing from the effort and covered in all manner of scratches and bites.

'Well, well, well,' Cosbi said. 'What a beauty.'

All eyes sought out the majesty of the wooden cabin sitting adjacent to the lake and it stared impassively back, refusing to spill its secrets. It was mercifully unlit, a grey shell without our jokes by the crackling fire.

A sliver of moon sat low amongst the treetops, battling with clouds and impeding leaves for the limelight. When it shone out from its competitors, it lit nature's stage a magnificent silver and sent regal shimmers across the living surface of the black water.

Raindrops rebounded as liquid hit liquid, miniscule drops of mercury permeating the water with a celebratory dance of ripples.

It was striking.

'The flare,' Cosbi said.

'I don't know about this, Cosbi—she had a decent head start. Why wouldn't she just keep running?' Gerrin said.

'She left him behind. She associates this place with him. She'll come here to grieve for it,' he said. 'The flare.'

Obediently, Ash struck the flare. A jet of red light swooshed into the sky, sending showers of blood-coloured sparks cascading over the monochrome scene.

Cosbi tipped his head at the cabin. 'Eyes open, this isn't your average woman.'

Gerrin threw motion into our conjoined form, propelling me down onto the pebble-strewn shore. I repeated the same mantra over and over in my head, too scared now to rebel.

Please don't be in there.

Ash was all too eager to be the first inside. Knife held high, he turned the handle of the wooden door and it swung open without resistance, ricocheting off the wall behind from the force.

The single-roomed lodge greeted us with a cold welcome, wooden perimeter stoic and smelling of damp, the moonlight highlighting several weaknesses in the rafters as it caught bright drops of rain in the act of breaching the defences.

I released the breath I was holding; judging by the contents of the burnt-out fireplace, it looked as though the place had remained ownerless since our last visit.

Gerrin selected a packet of matches from his jeans pocket and set fire to a sheaf of yellowing newspaper, throwing it in the fireplace to warm our refuge. 'You still reckon she's around?'

'Of course,' Cosbi said. 'We just need to do a little coaxing.'

Reaching into the backpack of tricks that Ash had set down, Cosbi tossed a pack of cable ties at Gerrin's feet. 'To leave your hands free,' he explained.

Although briefly reluctant, Gerrin overcame his concern at shackling his brother a little too easily. Having to rely on Ash to hold me still as I lashed out at the prospect of being bound, he dragged my wrists together in front of me and threaded the tie through the head, pulling it tight. Jagged plastic teeth bit into my skin when I tried to prise my hands from the bindings.

At a quick nod from Cosbi behind Gerrin's back, Ash swung down the rifle and used the butt to cave in the back of my legs. Hit by surprise, my weight had nowhere to go but down, and my shins thudded into coarse oak.

Gerrin whipped around; he would not tolerate anyone else hurting me.

'Coaxing,' Cosbi placated, before speaking to Ash, who'd retrieved a length of grubby white cotton from his pocket. 'Leave that out.'

So I was to be bait.

Pain concerned me no more than my life did, not anymore, but Elena... she mattered. If she *was* here somewhere, I hoped to God they killed me quick before she acted the martyr.

'What a way to treat your brother, Nico,' Cosbi said, performing the circling, pacing act again.

I ignored him.

'Do you just lack respect, or do you actually despise him now?'

I didn't even have to see Gerrin's face to know how he was reacting to the goading. Cosbi and I both had a strong hold over his conscience, but the silver tongue licked at known wounds.

'You need to be taught not to betray your own blood.'

'Nico?' Gerrin sounded depleted, issuing my full name as he did only in times of utmost seriousness.

'Do what you want, Gerrin,' I dismissed.

Cosbi crouched down in front of me. 'You've been sneaking out here with her. Confess.'

I smirked. 'For ages, shithead.'

A palm lashed out the second the words had been uttered, the large hand managing to strike the entire side of my face in one fell swoop. I heard Gerrin's sharp intake of breath.

Blood flushed to my skin, heat spreading like wildfire in the aftermath of the smart slap, and I blinked furiously to keep the flow of water within my eyes.

I reset my face to its original position and stared up at him, waiting for the next.

'You were leading this ridiculous plan?'

'What do you fucking think?'

The back of the hand caught me this time, swiping a path across my other cheek to return home. The power behind his arm almost knocked me off balance, and I widened my knees to withstand the coming assault without giving him the satisfaction of having to pick me back up.

Gerrin's boots moved. '*Stop it*, Cosbi,' he snapped.

Cosbi held up a hand. 'Do you realise what damage you've caused down there?'

I grinned again. 'Great, isn't it?'

The fist balled before it hit out, sinking its energy into the flesh around my eye socket. My skull screamed in agony, angry swelling tissue forcing my eye to close.

'*Stop!*' Gerrin half shouted, half begged. 'I'll... I'll get the answers you want.'

Out of everyone's sight, Cosbi winked at me. 'As you wish.'

Slowly, Gerrin made his way to where I was kneeling, one agonisingly measured clomp of boot at a time. Jaw twitching, he cricked his neck from side to side.

I looked up in resignation; here we were at last.

'How long have you been plotting behind my back?'

'Since you turned into a dickhead.'

Before I even saw him move, a solid fist had flashed out and thumped me in the stomach. Excruciating pain shot out from the nucleus of the blow. My diaphragm contorted awkwardly, stopping all airflow into my body for a few seconds, shock waves pulsing through my stomach. It was a good job I hadn't eaten.

'You hurting yet?' he said.

I made no sound; he wouldn't hear any hint of physical pain from my mouth. I could take this, and I would do it in silence.

'Are you done with me, Nico?'

'I hate you.'

A laugh from Cosbi told me that this was going exactly as he'd wanted.

Gerrin's face fell. He'd been hoping to see anger when I said that; it was the only way he'd know I still cared. But there was nothing he could salvage from apathy.

Pacing around, he snatched a handful of my damp hair and yanked my head back so far that I was looking up at him behind me. 'You need to realise how much damage your words do.'

'Words?' I laughed so hard I started choking from the strain on my neck. 'You're hurt by *words*? After what you've done to me? I hope my words fucking destroy your life, if that's all I have.'

Ripping his hand from the strained roots of my hair, he completed his circle and stood before me, a killer where Gerrin had just been. There could've been no one else in the room.

'Did you really disown me because she asked?' he said.

'Yes.'

A cry of wounded rage, and Gerrin lost all self-control. His arms flew out one after the other, hitting any part of me he could reach.

I felt my nose break and skin shred, blood pooling to feed bruises, my mouth filling with the metallic taste of iron as my jaw took a pounding. He ripped into me with every ounce of his hurt before he could find the discipline to pull back.

'Why?' he gasped.

I pulled my head up from its slump, just making him out through my swollen eyes and smiled with a mouthful of blood. 'Because I love her.'

In spite of his rage, he couldn't help but grin. He clamped his hand around my bruised jaw, bringing his nose within millimetres. 'And we all know what happens to the women you love.'

There was only one way of hitting him. I pulled my face back and rammed my forehead into his nose. His broke with as much blood as mine had, but he was significantly less happy about it.

He wound his fingers around a length of my blood-stained top and lifted me up. 'On your feet.'

It was easier said than done after the abuse my body had taken, and I staggered around my designated spot for a few moments before I found my balance.

Gerrin held out his hand, shouting, 'Crowbar,' at whoever would listen.

Looking fearful for his life should he take too long, Ash scrambled to offer one of the many weapons he'd crammed into the backpack. Gerrin snatched it from him, slapping the end of the metal bar into his waiting palm as he prowled, looking for a weak spot.

At length, he found one. The weighty iron strip flashed out and buried itself in the solid muscle defending my abdomen. My body buckled, air surging up my throat and ejecting streams of blood from the corners of my mouth.

Gerrin didn't let me recover long enough to stop choking before the weapon smacked into my back, finding my kidneys with perfect aim.

It was too much. Back on my knees and gasping for breath, I braced myself for the blow that would be one too many. I knew he wouldn't stop; I could never leave if I was physically incapable of moving.

Dazed, I stared at the floorboards and watched the blood dripping from my chin form gruesome reservoirs on the pockmarked surface, dropping through gaps in the boards.

Hollow.

The floor wasn't solid.

A fraction of a movement caught my eye through a larger gap left by misaligned timber, my heart breaking at the sight of the lips I'd kissed not two hours ago.

My bruised eyes squinted at the gap and I saw tears flashing on her cheeks as the firelight stole through the fissure, and hands reaching up to cover her mouth.

I knew what she was about to do.

The microscopic shake of my head was interrupted by the swift movement of Gerrin swinging the bar up again. I jammed my eyes shut.

But it didn't come at all.

I found Cosbi holding Gerrin's arm mid-action when I was brave enough to peer up. Shaking his head, he pressed a finger to his lips and then pointed it at the floor.

He'd seen.

Gerrin set down the bar without a word and yanked the rifle from Ash. Inspecting the magazine, he held up the spread fingers of his right hand twice, indicating that he had ten rounds with which to end my friend's life.

From behind, the icy skin of Ash's grass-stained hand snaked around my face, sealing itself across my mouth. Breath streamed through my nose as my frantic eyes scanned the ground, needing only a glimpse to warn her.

'Well, Nico, I hope you've learned your lesson,' Cosbi said.

For a moment, I was puzzled about the volume he'd used, until I realised he was covering for the noise, as Gerrin loaded a magazine into the rifle and cocked it.

I mumbled in panic against Ash's fingers, which tightened their grip.

Rifle primed and ready to fire, Gerrin squared his stance and lined it up with the dark gap, one eye closed in concentration. A finger discoloured with my blood inched towards the trigger, squeezing it the way our father had once shown us.

Slender fingers reached for the floorboards near my knees, so close, but not quite able to say that last goodbye. She was there again.

I bit down hard on Ash's finger, not letting go until my teeth hit bone.

With a screech of agony, the Scot snatched back his hand and I hollered with all the voice I could muster. 'Elena, *move!*'

The shot fired as the figure in the cellar vanished. The bullet clipped the board as it made its way through to the floor below, splintering the wood and audibly hitting stone.

'Shit!' Gerrin hissed, swiping the rifle butt at my face.

I keeled over, darkness pooling in my brain. Through the buzzing, I heard Gerrin raging and swearing, discharging the gun at random points through the floor, thick wood absorbing each metal round and fracturing on impact.

I counted them in my head, praying that he would run out before one thudded into flesh.

Seven.

Eight.

Nine.

The firing stopped; the rifle smoked.

'One left,' Cosbi said. 'Use it wisely.'

'What do you suggest?'

'There's more than one way to smoke out a fox.'

Gerrin laughed and tossed the rifle aside. Footsteps were followed by the ripping of paper, the floor shaking underneath as numerous heavy items were dropped by my feet.

'Get him out of here,' Cosbi said.

I managed to force the slits of my eyes open a few millimetres, wide enough to see the stack of kindling piled up in the middle of the floor and Gerrin standing over it, cigarette hanging from his mouth, box of matches in hand. Reaching into his pocket, he flipped open the cap of a silver hipflask and doused the composition with its contents.

'Completely worth it,' he said, smiling at Cosbi.

'No, don't!' I gasped.

But my plea was ignored as Ash seized my arms and dragged me backwards, his lack of care a sure sign of the damage I'd done to his finger. In the last moment before my head thudded over the doorstep, I saw Gerrin drop the lit cigarette into the ready-made bonfire. Pale blue flames peeled across the rivers of spirit and ripped into the pile of wood, warming my face before I hit cold grass.

Ash pulled me away from the jetty, the rain lacing the grass slowly soaking through my bloodied clothes.

I phased out momentarily, the damage to my body sending waves of pain through me, pulling my pupils back inside my head. But even against the shroud of my eyelids, I could sense the colour of my surroundings was changing. What had been deathly dark was lightening like it'd been hit by the rising sun.

I had to stay awake.

My eyes opened to hell in paradise. Warmth streaked through the air from crackling flames licking their way up the cabin walls, the damp wood no match for the flammability of the whisky.

The entire hut was alight and with her still inside. I watched on in groggy helplessness as blazing heat shattered the windows, glass exploding in all directions. Mother Nature was merciless, relentless, indifferent to my friend.

'Stay sharp, Gerrin,' Cosbi instructed.

The rifle swiped up to ninety degrees. Gerrin's eyes never rested, scanning the cabin perimeter for signs of movement.

It was the worst wait of my life.

'There!' Ash shouted.

All heads whipped to where his bloody finger pointed. A shadowy figure emerged from the side of the hut, coughing and spluttering as it threw off material engulfed in flames. Catching sight of Gerrin, Elena turned and sprinted for the jetty.

'What's going on?' Parker shouted as he and Chase burst from the trees.

They distracted Gerrin long enough for me.

Fighting the need to be sick, I rolled towards him and struggled to my knees, trying to focus on the middle of the three blonde men I was seeing. Everybody was too busy looking at Parker or Elena to notice. Mustering all remaining energy, I wrenched out the knife that Gerrin kept in his boot. I flicked it open and slashed wildly across his back with my bound hands.

'Motherfucker!' he roared, clutching at the wound.

Hearing the shouts, Elena stopped and looked back.

'*Run!*' I hollered.

His back pouring with blood, Gerrin threw out an arm and struck me to the ground, the side of my head thudding heavily into a blunt rock.

Through the black spots in my vision, I saw him pick up the rifle and track the running figure. With a squeeze of the trigger, the last round burst from the carriage, carrying faster than the speed of sound towards the water.

Now nothing more than a spectator to her fate, I watched as an invisible force struck the running woman as she was about to throw herself into the water, her silhouette contorting with the impact.

Horror drove the scream from my throat.

Lifeless and limp, she fell into the waiting depths of the watery grave, pulled beneath the surface by its greedy black arms.

BROTHER

'You heard it too, right, little shadow?' Gerrin said.

I nodded. 'Monsters?'

'I've told you before, there's no such thing. Right, kiddo?'

'But maybe we should get Daddy.'

'I want to look.'

He crept forwards as I shuffled behind, clinging to the toggles of his anorak. He was so brave.

There was nothing around that could have caused the crash. All the animals were in the fields. I was sure it was the work of the rascally monsters.

'Who's there?' he called. 'You'd better come out now before I call the police.'

I whimpered.

A giggle.

A girl?

I wrinkled up my nose; girls were no fun.

A dirty face peeped around a bale in the top loft, her yellow hair knotted with muck and hay needles. 'Who are you?'

'I live here,' he said. 'And you're not allowed to be up there. Wait 'til I tell my dad.'

'Oh no, don't! I wasn't doing no harm, it looked fun in here.'

He stuck his hands on his hips. 'Come down, or else.'

The little girl's face screwed up in dislike, but she stood and climbed down the wooden ladder. Her dungarees were ripped and muddy; she looked more like a boy to me. Girls were supposed to like playing with dolls, not hay.

Like the rabbits my daddy hunted, she stood in front of us with really wide eyes.

'What's that?' he said, jabbing a finger at the rectangular bulge in her pocket.

'My camera. My mummy bought it for Christmas.'

'I want it.'

She scowled. 'Well, you can't have it.'

'Give it to me.'

'No.'

He lunged for it and she jumped sideways, knocking me to the floor, a nail on the wall cutting my skin.

I tried to be brave like him, but my arm started leaking blood and it hurt bad. My chin wobbled.

'You hurt my brother?' he shouted. 'Don't you fucking *dare* hurt my brother!'

She flinched at the noise and the naughty word.

His hand hit out and smacked her across the face.

I squealed and hid my eyes.

She was crying.

'It's mine now. And if you tell anyone, I'll come and find you, you understand?'

There was a fight and running steps; they were too quiet to hear after a bit.

He crouched in front of me and peeled my hands from my eyes. 'Where does it hurt, little shadow?'

My bottom lip stuck firmly out, I pointed to my arm.

He tore his T-shirt and wrapped it around the cut, kissing his lips to the bandage, just like Mummy did. 'Better?'

I looked at him, interested but afraid. 'Daddy told us never to hit girls.'

'She was a naughty girl though, huh, kiddo? She was trespassing.'

'Chess-passing,' I repeated with a nod, pretending I understood.

'And you won't tell Mummy or Daddy, OK? Because if they knew, she'd get in trouble, and we might have to move house.'

I nodded.

'Pinkie promise?'

I held out my little finger. 'Pinkie promise.'

'Let's go get you some ice cream.'

He was the best big brother.

'Find the body.'

He spoke those words like he said them every day.

Blood beaded and dripped from my eyelashes as I focused on the scarred man with the grey hair.

'You got her?' another one said.

'Of course I fucking did,' a blonde giant leered. 'One bullet, problem fucking solved.'

Grey Hair turned to a shorter, slighter man. 'I mean it, I want proof.'

The man mock saluted, happy to be given the task, and took off towards a nearby lake. Several more bodies rushed into the circle, clapping fists and celebrating as they learned of the death of the woman.

'What about him?'

Through severely hindered vision, I saw every man in the clearing glare at me like I'd committed treason. They didn't like me.

'They have to think he's dead,' Grey Hair said.

A growl of dissatisfaction rumbled from Blonde.

'They *must* think he's dead,' Grey Hair continued. 'We start the rumour, but confirm nothing. With both her and him gone, nobody will continue with this ludicrous plan. And once I've stamped out all rebellion, then everyone can be informed that he lives.'

'And how are you going to manage that?' one man piped up.

'He stays in twenty-three for now.'

'I won't allow it,' Blonde snapped.

'A temporary measure only, until we figure out the best course of action. You've a simple choice, Gerrin, it's that or I must leave him out here to die.'

Blonde looked mutinous, but seemed to know that his hands were tied.

'Parker, Chase, you wait out here. I will remove the guard and make sure everyone is in their rooms in one hour.'

Grey Hair then turned his attention to the general audience. 'Gentlemen, be vocal in our success as we walk back through, and watch the sheep come back into the fold.'

Murmurs of assent stole around the group, numerous pairs of boots clomping from the clearing. They hadn't been gone a minute before the two remaining men skidded to my side.

'Fuck my life,' one said. 'What've they done to him?'

A damp handkerchief was pressed to my face, putting agonising pressure on bruised and broken bones. A hand gently lifted my head a few centimetres and the circumference of a bottle opening was guided to my lips.

'Drink,' he instructed.

My jaw cranked open a fraction to allow the cooling liquid to swill into my mouth, washing a torrent of blood down my throat.

'Can you hear me, Nico?'

'Not me,' I mumbled. 'Her...'

'Don't think about that,' he whispered.

'Explain.'

Silence.

'*Explain.*'

'She's gone.'

Gone.

I rolled onto my side and pushed myself onto my knees, ignoring every sickening crunch from my body.

'Whoa, slow down!'

'Yeah, lie back down, bud.'

'Who are you?' I snapped. 'Get out of my way!'

'Take it easy, Nico, we're your friends. Remember?'

'Parker and Chase,' the man on the left said, pointing at himself and then his companion.

Grimacing and panting, I looked from one to the other and back again. Pain scorched through me.

'What's wrong with him?'

'He can't remember us. That bastard's really done a number on him.'

'Then what do we do?'

'We got no choice—we take him back in.'

I passed out.

BACKTRACK

'JESUS CHRIST, COSBI!' a plump man said as his round glasses tottered to the end of his nose. 'You need to learn to call off your pit bull.'

He opened a black satchel, still shaking his head and shone a bright torch in my eyes. 'What do you remember?'

I could neither shrug nor move my head, so I just stared.

'Do you know what happened?'

'Leave me alone,' I mumbled.

'Do you need to sleep?'

'I need to get back to the farm.'

He straightened up with a frown and turned to Blonde, who was looking horrified. 'The Americans were right, his cognitive function is impaired.'

'What caused it?' Blonde said.

The plump man shrugged. 'It could've been a blow to the head, or severe emotional trauma.'

'Severe emotional what...?'

'Trauma. Post-traumatic stress disorder. The mind shuts down to prevent painful memories from causing harm. You might've pushed him too far.'

Blonde took a step forward. 'You speak out of turn, friend.'

'You asked for my help.' Plump dismissed him with a wave of his hand. 'That's my professional opinion.'

'Blame me again and it'll be your last opinion.'

'You did just kill his lover, if reports are to be believed.'

'She wasn't his lover,' Blonde snorted.

'It's true, then?' a delighted voice squealed.

I could sense the surprise; this new speaker was both unexpected and unwelcome.

'Much as I appreciate your talents, Foley, I do not care for you using them on me,' Grey Hair said.

The creature stepped into a beam of light; I say 'creature', because I could never in all honesty describe it as a man.

'But that part's not true,' he said, pointing a crooked finger at me.

'But we'll say nothing about that,' Grey Hair said.

'Oh no, no, course not,' the creature soothed, his face breaking into a grin of cracked, yellowing teeth. 'Least you got 'er before she could tell anyone outside 'bout that cave, eh, Mr Cosbi? Doesn't look like he's telling no one, neither.'

His snigger was cut short when he noticed that his audience was looking ominously curious.

'Gabriel, leave,' Grey Hair instructed.

Plump obeyed the command and closed the door behind him.

'Cave?' Grey Hair prompted.

The creature gulped. 'Y'know, Mr Cosbi, what the pair of 'em found when they was using the other exit.'

'*Other* exit?'

'Sure, I um... heard 'em talking about it.'

The briefest of glances passed between Blonde and Grey Hair before Blonde conjured a knife and had its tip lodged just millimetres from the creature's now terrified beady eyes.

'Wait, wait, I can tell you anything you need to know!' he squealed.

'Talk!' Blonde said.

'For a small pri—'

'I said, *talk.*'

'Whoa, OK, Mr Jakes. Guess I could forgo the usual price. Few days ago, I was passing 'er door when I heard 'er saying that Mr Cosbi must never know what they'd found.'

'Which was?'

'Only caught a few words, I did, sir. Storage, guns, explosive... I heard 'er say she wished she'd never found it, and "Christ, what Mr Cosbi could do with that lot."'

I could imagine the expression on Grey Hair's face even though it was hidden.

'And... the location of both the exit, and this place of storage?'

'Oh, I don't know that, sir. Only her and him, I think.'

Deathly calm enveloped the room.

At length, Grey Hair spoke again. 'And you didn't think to tell me this *before* I had her shot?'

'Kinda thought that's *why* you had her shot, sir. That and their plotting to leave, of course.'

'You know that too?'

'Know everything, I do. But you 'as been too busy to see me the last few days, Mr Cosbi.'

Grey Hair laughed. 'You are intelligent, Foley. So perhaps you also know what must happen next.'

The creature seemed momentarily confused, his face only displaying understanding a split second before Blonde had driven the steel knife point through his eye socket.

I closed my eyes against the gruesome spectacle as blood peppered the room and I heard the former creature drop to the floor like a sack of potatoes.

'Dear, dear, my thieving friend,' Grey Hair said. 'That admission was practically suicide.'

Blonde laughed; metal scraped against cotton as he wiped away the evidence of murder. 'This is what we've been waiting for, Cosbi. We could take them out.'

'Without a doubt. But the question is whether it can be found without help. Our only remaining informant appears to be one card short of a deck.'

'He wouldn't tell us even if he could, not in a million years.'

The door opening and a gasp of shock told me that Plump had spotted the sinister turn in events. 'I want none of this, Cosbi. I ask only protection for my family in exchange for my services.'

'If you wish to guarantee the safety of your family, Gabriel, I suggest you do exactly as I ask. Gerrin's brother, I want your prognosis.'

With a sigh, Plump gave it. 'I suspect it's only temporary. Post-traumatic stress.'

'Treatment?'

'You say he'd drawn on the walls of his cell in twenty-three?'

'Ramblings, but relevant ones. In there if you want to take a look.'

'Then I suspect the medication I gave you to knock him out helped his memory, relaxed his conscious mind enough to break the barriers he's put in place.'

'Can he have more?'

'Certainly, if you have the resources. I would suggest the induction of a medical coma for a few weeks. Let him heal.'

'He'll need twenty-four-hour care, Gabriel. Ask around for a discreet, trustworthy individual.'

Plump left soon after, leaving the other two to their plotting.

'What happens if it doesn't work, Cosbi?'

'We earn his trust, keep trying with the drugs and guide his memories in the right direction. Until then, we search for this cave ourselves,' Grey Hair said.

'But as soon as he remembers how... how he ended up like this...'

'Then we'll have to see what your brother is willing to sacrifice for the lives of those he loves, won't we?'

'And Elena?'

'She attacked him. If he believes she's still alive, he'll hate her enough to want to help us.'

'It could work, I guess.'

'Best remove his wedding ring, Gerrin. I'm sure your history with Louisa won't help our case. And hurry, we need to get him over to the medical bay before sunrise.'

Boots thumped across the rock and coarse fingers lifted my left hand from the bed, wrenching a heavy something from my fourth finger.

'Belongs to me anyway,' Blonde said.

GEMELLI

WAS IT POSSIBLE this was the one thing they *hadn't* lied to everyone about?

She just couldn't be. Not Elena. Not my fearless, impetuous Elena.

But the refusal of my tired heart to summon any optimism told me that this memory was as true as the rest. The pointlessness of everything I'd been through was just excruciating.

It was so dark in here, the room, my mind, both as black as each other.

The cell in room 23 was too cramped, not nearly big enough for a grown man, cold and damp. To stay here for any length of time without heat would definitely result in hypothermia.

The dose that Gerrin had injected into my arm was high, but I'd now been without for twenty-four hours, the longest stretch since we'd begun the experiment. Despite the sub-zero temperature of the caves, a light sheen of sweat had broken out across the surface of my skin, salty drips discarded as tremors took hold of my muscles, my body twitching violently whenever sleep tried to claim me.

I hyperventilated on an hourly basis, the need for a hit magnifying the claustrophobia, sending my body to the brink of panic and back.

After two days, lack of sleep brought hallucinations. Curled up on the floor, soaked in my own piss, it didn't take long for the incarnations of Elena to tip me over the edge.

Tears pouring down my face, I grabbed a rock and pressed it flush with a vein in my wrist. I welcomed the pain and the blood that pooled around the jagged edge. I could still feel.

There was only one thing that stopped me. Well, two actually, if you count what I noticed on the wall behind me.

Shifting to my knees, my fingers picked over chalked pictures, scrawls—diary entries of a sort—inscribed on my cell wall. Hundreds of them.

I traced words, letters and pictures before my fingertips came to rest on two elaborate, entwined letters: *N* and *E*.

I'd been locked in here before.

I picked at the rock in my hand with my filthy fingernails; it was chalk-like inside. I reached up an arm, weakened from lack of food and water, and carved one further word amidst the rambling tirade.

SUR-VIVE.

It was what she would've wanted; there was no better way to honour her memory.

No sooner had I thudded an emphatic full stop into the end of the word than the door to my prison was thrown open, bright firelight streaming in. I shied away, scrambling for the corner.

'Enough of this,' Gerrin said. 'Get him out of there.'

A reluctant Gabriel crept forwards with a syringe. Aghast at the conditions, his hand flew to shield his nose from the putrid smell, baulking and retching and unable to do his job.

Gerrin wrenched the needle from his grip. 'Fuck off, I'll do it.'

Looking dead ahead, I held out my arm. Resistance against these people was apparently futile, and besides, I was going batshit crazy without what I needed.

Seeming surprised at my compliance, Gerrin gently lowered the tip into my upper arm, waiting for the sedative to kick in before turning to his unknown assistants.

'Take him back to his room.'

Leaving the two women in my life eyeballing each other with distaste, I took off at a jog, calling back, 'Stay with Elena, she'll make sure you're safe.'

Hoping to find Foley lurking around room 23, I headed in that direction, and didn't get very far before my hypothesis was proven right. I flattened myself into a shadowed nook in the wall.

'You think I care?' Gerrin snorted.

Knowing he had dirt on such a favourite of Cosbi's was clearly delighting Foley. The beady brown eyes glinted eagerly in his sagging face as he scuttled alongside Gerrin.

'Not yet, Mr Jakes, no. But Mr Cosbi will be wanting to know about this. He's been looking for an excuse to punish your brother, after all.'

Gerrin waved his words away. 'So, she's the one in trouble, so go pester her.'

'I've already paid the lovely lady a visit, of course, sir,' Foley said, with a grin and an emphatic jangle of the gold chain in his coat pocket.

'Then you have what you want. Take a hike,' Gerrin said, losing patience and striding away.

But Weasel wanted more, and I wondered if he valued his own life at all. Panicking, he scampered after Gerrin, walking backwards in front of him so that my now seriously irked brother had no choice but to acknowledge him.

'I guess Mr Cosbi might let you off with breaking the rules, if he gets what he wants. After all, you is one of his favourites. But why take that risk, Mr Jakes?'

Gerrin stopped and glared at him. 'How much did you see?'

'Enough. And I wasn't the only one.'

Gerrin took a threatening step forward. 'Have you got people spying on me?'

'No, no. The other Mr Jakes was there, sir. In the shadows, sir.'

'Come on, Foley, you can do better than that. He didn't see anything I didn't want him to see, and he won't say anything.'

Weasel Man gawped. 'How did you know he'd be there?'

'Keep your nose out,' Gerrin warned. 'And stay away from Nico—this is between me and him.'

'And if I did tell? You think he'd let you be after she's punished?'

'You're either very brave or very stupid,' Gerrin said, deathly quiet. 'Where exactly do you think blackmailing me is going to get you?'

'Mr Cosbi really doesn't like rule-breaking. And you know people will pay well for what I know. But I like you, Mr Jakes, so just a small donation and you don't have to worry about a thing. My lips are sealed.'

As expected, Weasel was met with an unenthusiastic response to his demands. Gerrin grabbed a fistful of his musty coat, lifting him clean off the floor.

'Shall we play a little game, Foley?' Gerrin said and shook his victim until his teeth rattled, making his legs flail through the air. 'Let's just forget this conversation ever happened. You go crawl back into whatever hole you came from, keep your mouth shut, and I will let you live. Deal?'

Foley nodded, turning an odd shade of purple as he was slowly being strangled by his own jacket.

'Glad you've seen sense,' Gerrin said, lowering him to the ground and smoothing his ruffled coat with the back of his hand. 'Nice doing business with you.'

Foley screwed up his sly little eyes as he scowled at Gerrin, before taking off down the corridor as quickly as he could.

'Halfwit,' Gerrin muttered, smirking as he breezed past my hiding place in the direction of Elena's room.

I matched his pace until he realised someone was following and stopped. Intuition must've told him it was me, given that he issued a stiff greeting of 'Nico' before he even turned around.

I like to think that the last thing he saw before he was airborne was either the thundering hatred in my eyes or the desire to rearrange his face.

I charged at him, my head colliding with his stomach, lifting him clean off his feet. The two of us landed in a pile of limbs on the floor.

The door of 20 flew open several seconds after; the sound of our combined weight falling to earth almost creating seismic activity. Louisa and Elena burst into the open just in time to see me burying my knuckles into his smug face.

'You *worthless* motherfucker!' I roared.

My fists wouldn't stop, expelling the pain from my heart with every single, satisfying blow. Rivers of scarlet erupted wherever my hits landed, flesh swelling and tearing beneath my rage.

'Nico, Nico, don't!' Louisa screamed, and through the red mist I saw Elena seize her arms as she attempted to throw herself between us.

He did nothing but lie there and take it until my blind fury had ebbed and I was just sat there panting. Trickles of sweat ran down my bare chest when I staggered to my feet and slammed my foot into his stomach, earning a pained grunt.

'Get up,' I hissed.

Louisa was crying now, still held back by a conflicted-looking Elena; the desire for retribution against him warring with her concern for me.

Using the floor as a prop, he hoisted himself up onto his knees and then unsteadily onto his feet. He spat a mouthful of blood on the floor.

'Feel better, Nic?' he said, rubbing his jaw.

'Nowhere near. She said it was a mistake. That true?'

'Me fucking your wife?' he said with disinterest. 'No, there was no mistake.'

His words drew a startled gasp from Louisa. 'What? Tell him the truth!'

'I am. I knew exactly what I was doing, and so did you.'

'And what *were* you doing?' I said.

'I told you I'd show you she was no good. I swore it to you, Nic.'

Oh dear God. Squeezing my eyes closed, I sagged against the adjacent wall and buried my face in the blackness of the rock.

'I've been trying it since I saw you were serious,' he continued. 'You actually did half of the work for me—disappearing with that bitch for hours on end.' He nodded in Elena's direction. 'Throw in you covering some of my training shifts, and it was easy to convince her you were fucking around.'

I dragged my eyes from the wall and looked in despair at the two women staring at me. I saw disbelief and sympathy in Elena's face, while Louisa was silently pleading for our marriage, regret seeping from her eyes as she realised how brutally she'd been used.

'*Please,*' I whispered, my begging making Louisa sob even harder. 'Please tell me you feel *something* for her. Tell me you haven't ruined my life for some pointless vendetta.'

'I hate the bitch.'

Both women gasped at that one.

'Gerrin...' Louisa whispered.

But he just looked at her with contempt, like she was a piece of dirt on his shoe.

'Then why do it again?' I said. 'Why not once and then tell me, if that's all you wanted?'

'You needed to see it with your own eyes, Nico. Physically *see*. She got chickenshit after the first time and called it off before I could arrange for you to walk in on us. Then I had to wait for the fucking kid to be born. I made doubly sure we were in your way when I had her the second time.

And look how easy it was, Nico. All I did was swoop in like some fucking romantic hero and she couldn't keep her legs shut.'

I heard only the sound of Louisa's scream and more doors popping open in the distance as I threw myself back at him. Slamming him into the wall, I thumped him again. And again. And again.

Two sets of arms eventually dragged me off, an American accent in my ear urging me to calm down. The tunnel vision cleared, and I realised a stunned Constance was also stood watching.

Shaking off my restraints, I pointed a finger at his bloodied face. 'You're dead to me.'

Elena released Louisa, who ran immediately to her mother, too ashamed to look at me.

'Get Gabriel, or leave him there to bleed,' I snapped at the Americans. 'I couldn't give a shit.'

Leaving a mass of gaping mouths behind me, I stormed back to my room, throwing open the door and heading straight for the dresser. In the bottom drawer, underneath a pile of Louisa's clothes, I kept the old backpack that contained all of the possessions I owned when I arrived in the caves. Rooting around in the bottom, I found an old Rolex. It'd been passed down through our family and my father had given it to me before he died. It no longer kept time, but as belongings went, it was probably the most precious to me.

I eventually found Foley skulking down by the medical bay, listening for more secrets, finding more lives to trash. Seizing him by the throat, I threw him to the floor and amidst his pleas for mercy, slammed the watch into his filthy, grabbing hands.

'This ends here,' I said. 'You keep your mouth shut about what you saw. And if you threaten my wife again, it'll be the last thing you ever do.'

Sheathed out of sight beneath my sweatshirt, the two knives clacked with every strike of my running feet against the floor.

My record as a thief was improving. Within twenty-four hours, I'd managed to secure enough tinned fruit and soup to last the group a couple of days, along with four blankets, some paracetamol and now the two weapons from 23.

Hell bent on getting back before anyone caught me, I was racing down the path when the door to my room opened. My *old* room.

'Oh, Nico, wait!' Constance called.

Reluctant to partake in idle conversation with two pieces of steel jabbing into my thigh, I waved in her general direction and jogged on.

'I need to talk to you.'

Grimacing, I thudded to a halt and waited for her to catch up. 'Does it have to be now, Constance? I'm a bit busy.'

'Too busy to see your son?'

The dismayed tone in her voice caught me off guard; my mother had once spoken to me in that way when Gerrin had bowled a cricket ball through the car window and blamed me.

'Don't you mean my nephew?' I snapped.

She laid her hand on my arm, managing with one touch to offer her full sympathy while also telling me to grow the hell up.

'I mean *your son*,' she said firmly.

'Maybe you should save your disappointment for your daughter.'

'Believe me, Louisa is fully aware of my opinion on her behaviour,' she said. 'But there is an innocent little boy stuck in the middle of this, who needs both of his parents.'

'I'll let Gerrin know.'

'Your brother will never be anything to that child.'

The boy was fair-haired; he shared both mine and Gerrin's eye colour. I would never know if he was a product of the love Louisa and I had shared, or the result of a dirty affair designed to separate us.

'I can't,' I said, squaring my gaze at hers.

'I know you're hurting, Nico. I can see it in your eyes. Don't act like you don't care.'

'Oh, I care, Constance,' I bit back. 'I care so much that I kicked seven bells of shit out of my own brother. I care so much I can't sleep. I care so much that I'm afraid to look at that boy and feel something other than love.'

Pity dampened her eyes at my words, but that motherly censure was still winning out. 'Are you really going to punish him for the mistakes of others? I thought better of you.'

That one hurt. How was it that all women were so good at that?

'Don't make the biggest mistake of your life,' she urged.

I sighed at her tenacity, annoyed that she seemed to think it was my responsibility to fix this. 'I'll come tonight.'

'She still loves you,' she said before I disappeared, making me stumble as I forgot to watch where I was going.

I adjusted the cuffs of my shirt and smoothed a hand across the stubble running into my ruffled hair, fidgeting nervously like I had when we first started dating.

I suspected that the time taken to open the door was the result of her own final adjustments being made. And sure enough, when she opened the door, the picture before me was a far cry from the shy teenage girl I'd met years ago.

Immediately sceptical of her intentions, I swallowed quickly as my eyes swept downwards. 'Er, hi. Did Constance tell you I was coming?'

'Of course! Come in.'

I accepted the invitation warily, my eyes picking up on the muted, romantic lighting burning from scattered candles, blurring the cold angles of the room with orange warmth.

'Louisa...' I hesitated.

'You're looking really good.'

A tired yawn caught my attention. Lying in a puddle of blankets and dressed in one of Constance's handmade blue Babygros, a little boy was stretching his fists to the heavens.

An uncontainable smile tugged at my mouth. 'Hey, buddy.'

It was a relief to feel another emotion, having been stuck at bitter for the last two days. I scooped him up in my arms and kissed his chubby cheeks, breathing in that delicious baby smell. Chewing on the sleeve of the overlarge sleep suit, he wiped it affectionately on my shirt and giggled his delight at successfully evading bedtime.

'I've just fed him,' Louisa said. 'Would you like to put him to bed?'

'Sure... if that's OK with you?'

'More than OK,' she said, beaming in delight.

Launching into a fairy tale from my childhood, I tucked the yawning baby into the crook of my neck and rocked him to sleep as I paced the room.

Peaceful, gorgeous snoring reached my ears before five minutes had passed, which I put down to the comfort of my shoulder rather than a lack of storytelling prowess. I tucked the cot blankets around him, and an innocent soul drifted into a world of untainted dreams.

I could feel her eyes on me as I stood watching him sleep. She'd been transfixed by us the whole time, an emotional smile showing her relief that my resolve had softened. The movement of her chair started my heart stuttering; her arms wrapping around my body from behind almost stopped it.

I didn't dare move at the risk of encouraging her. Or discouraging her.

'You've still got your wedding ring on,' she whispered, her hand skimming across my unhealed knuckles.

I nodded. It hadn't occurred to me to take it off.

Obviously encouraged by this, Louisa snuck her fingers inside the front of my shirt, teasing her touch across my abdomen.

My palm shot out to still hers. 'I've come here to be a father, nothing more.'

'I want to be close to you again,' she murmured, kissing her lips across my back.

'Louisa...'

'Forgive me, I'm begging you.'

Tugging on my waist, she implored me to face her, and I found my traitorous feet responding. Her hands reached for my face, looking for a kiss.

A low grunt of annoyance came from my throat as I turned my head away and shoved my hands in my pockets, trying my hardest to ignore the temptation. I had to maintain this distance.

'You don't understand how manipulative he was,' Louisa whispered. 'The lies he told.'

'Did you never think to just ask me?' I said.

'I was scared I'd lose you. Whenever I was lonely, he was always there, saying all the right things.'

'How stupid do you have to be to believe Gerrin could ever fall in love?'

'It became easier to believe with the right persuasion.'

My heart sank; we'd played right into his hands.

'At your birthday, I was watching you and Elena playing games, and there he was again,' she said.

'I understand,' I snapped. 'It's all *my* fault.'

'No, it's his, Nico. Gerrin did this.'

'And you fell for it.'

'Please let's just talk, let me show you who I want.'

Her hands pressed up against my chest, watery blue eyes pleading for some emotion or softness from me. Anything.

I pushed her back.

Eyeing me determinedly, she reached up and unbuttoned her top, throwing it emphatically to one side.

'Stop it!' I said.

The jeans came next. The button popped open and denim teased across her smooth thighs, before joining the discarded top on the floor, the absence of any underwear betraying that seduction had always been an option.

Studying my scowling face, her fingers snapped open her bra clasp, and the last garment was thrown away.

Nobody said anything as the air bristled with an angry sexual tension. You had to admire her guts. She stood before me, naked and prepared to be rejected. And I was impossibly aroused.

I glared at her, unable to slow my breathing.

'I want to go to bed too,' she whispered, sliding my hands from my pockets and guiding them to her body.

'Jesus...' I groaned.

It was a valiant fight, but as pointless as it ever had been with Louisa.

Sensing my imminent defeat, she went in for the kill. Planting the softest kiss on my lips, she whispered, 'I'm yours.'

Before she could beg any harder, I'd snatched her up in my arms, pulled her thighs tight around my waist and forced my tongue in her mouth, desperate to shut her up. I fought for control, an iron grasp on the back of her neck.

Sweeping my arm across the wooden desk, I stripped it instantly of all possessions, clothes and pens diving for the floor amidst a rainstorm of fluttering paper.

I slammed her down on the cold surface, drawing a startled gasp, and ripped open shirt buttons. Her hands made light work of my jeans fastenings as I threw off my top and wrenched her pelvis into mine.

She bit her lip in anticipation, while I, panting furiously, summoned all the pain and anger of the last few days and heartlessly forced my body into hers.

I think that was the only time I ever regretted sleeping with a woman.

Lying there with just a sheet covering my modesty, a victorious Louisa sleeping across my body, it was also the point that I knew we could never get back what we'd had.

Things had changed beyond repair. Gerrin had wound himself inextricably around my heart like poison ivy, progressive and malignant, always there to keep her out. And now I had to leave, before I changed my mind.

Carefully and spinelessly, I peeled her arm from my chest and slid from the sheets. I had my boxers on and one leg in my jeans before a sleepy voice invited me back to bed.

'Stay the night.'

Stuffing my other foot in the denim, I yanked up the waistband and shook my head dismissively. I took an indulgent look at the sleeping baby, miraculous given the amount of noise we'd just made, and went in search of my strewn clothes, successfully locating my shoes and slinging my shirt over my shoulder.

'Then, come back tomorrow?'

I remained silent, guessing this was the price I was going to have to pay for giving her the wrong idea.

'Nico, I don't understand,' she said, dragging the sheet from the bed and crafting it into a makeshift toga. 'What just happened—'

'Was a mistake,' I cut her off. 'I told you that wasn't what I came here for.'

Her mouth dropped open in dismay, realising her plan had failed. 'Don't you love me anymore?'

'Louisa,' I groaned. 'I love you too much.'

'Then forgive me.' She put herself between me and the door.

Losing patience, I pushed her aside. 'Don't you understand what you've done to me? Every time I look at you, all I see is him, him with his fucking hands on you. Tell me how to forget that, Louisa, and I'll gladly try again.'

'Then let's leave, start again. We were going to do it anyway. Please, Nico, I'll do anything to get you back.'

I shook my head and sidestepped her in favour of the exit. 'It's too late.'

'Nico?'

'It's over.'

Echoes of desperate tears carried with me as I left her there, giving Gerrin exactly what he wanted. As luck would have it, they also caught the attention of the other inhabitant of that corridor, hovering in the distance. Someone had cleaned up his face, and I could see the confused frown at seeing me emerge from Louisa's room change to exasperated anger as he noted my state of undress.

Jamming my arms into the sleeves of my shirt, I glared at him and walked away.

'Hello?' The woman's voice rang out, becoming ever quieter in its successive echoes. 'What're you doing here?'

The panic in it never failed to disturb, as unsettling now as it had been the first time.

I groaned. As if it hadn't done enough damage for one day, my mind was now going to make me listen to this again.

Out of boredom and nothing more, I went to where I knew the man and woman would be fighting, him dominating, her cowering. I snorted in disdain; I really didn't need to see my father hit my mother again.

But something caught my eye as I went to leave—a flash, a blaze of brilliant red. I turned and walked into the middle of the fight.

This wasn't the same as last time.

She wasn't the same. Her tight red curls, the source of the colour in my peripheral vision, bounced wildly as she searched for a means of escaping him.

Hanna.

My gaze roamed to where the man stood, his imposing build exuding aggression. His ice-blue eyes and long dirty-blonde hair made him look exceptionally like my father, but not quite. The cold sneer on his face distinguished him from Oliver Jakes's kind features. The monster had come back out to play.

Gerrin.

'What're you doing here?' Hanna repeated in a low whisper.

He let out a horrible laugh. 'I think you know the answer to that. You were only supposed to watch and listen, not throw yourself at him, you silly little bitch.'

'*Shh!*' she gasped. 'Nico might hear—we've stopped the drug.'

And so I had heard. Subconsciously heard the fight that'd gone on in my room all those days ago, but never realised that my mind had mixed up who'd been involved.

'Couldn't help yourself, could you?' Gerrin taunted as he advanced, smiling in satisfaction as she tensed. 'I saw you. Holding his hand, all doe-eyed. Were you hoping to get in there quick, huh, before he remembered his wife?'

'I didn't! I wouldn't do that! I was only doing what I was told.' She broke down and sobbed. 'Please don't hurt me.'

Despite her protests, he closed in, goading her with the inevitability of what was coming, the gap between them down to a few threatening inches.

A hand as solid as iron shot out and caught hold of her throat, pinning her to the wall. Gasping for breath, Hanna's innocent hazel eyes screwed up in pain and her hands flew to her neck, instinctively trying to free herself.

There wasn't an ounce of pity in him as his mouth moved to her ear. 'You'd better figure out which side you're on.'

Gerrin's eyes travelled up and down her body and he seemed to sense an opportunity, a chance to show her the meaning of real fear.

She didn't have time to scream. His mouth silenced the sound when he forced her into a kiss, ignoring the look of abhorrence on her face and the muted squeals of protest.

'Don't you want to play the field, anyway?' he said. 'Girls here need to see there's more to life than my sodding brother.'

Either his words or the mention of me seemed to wake a dormant strength in Hanna. Realising she was all alone and in serious danger, she seized him by the shoulders and drove her knee full force into his crotch.

Taken down by the weakness of all men, Gerrin collapsed to his knees, clutching at his groin and bellowing his rage.

Shaking hands clutching at her bruised throat, Hanna seemed aware that she didn't have long to get out of there. Slowly, unsteadily, she clawed her way towards the exit, but the few seconds advantage weren't long enough to escape Gerrin. He caught her by the arm and spun her around to face him, a large hand cracking across her cheek.

The sound of the sharp slap resounded around the room, the strength he put behind it enough to snap her head sideways and send her crashing to the floor. She remained where she fell, sobs racking her body as he towered over her, strained and seething.

'Just remember what I can do to you if you don't start behaving!' he roared.

She flinched at the noise and curled herself up into an even tighter ball, begging to be left alone. Gerrin looked like he was trying to decide what course of action would hurt her most, when his eyes flicked up, seeking me out.

'Lucky for you he's waking up. I could think of a million ways to make you pay for what you just did,' he spat, striding past her.

After a couple of minutes of lying on the floor, motionless apart from the jerked movements of her back as she cried, Hanna lifted her head and reached a hand to her cheek.

The familiar wound was already beginning to colour an angry shade of red.

There was no one around when I woke in my room once again. No one to talk to, to grieve with, no one to hold me and tell me everything was going to be OK. I had no one left.

Alone was exactly the way he wanted me, with no one to rely on but him.

He had hit Hanna, broken my marriage, murdered Elena.

I recalled the slash wound to his back. The next time I had a knife, I would do the job properly.

But the door was locked and guarded.

I was a prisoner now.

I waited patiently for Hanna to arrive and lock the door behind her.

'You're afraid of me sometimes,' I said.

She looked up in surprise.

'You're afraid of me, because I look like Gerrin?'

Her startled gasp told me I was right before she could bolt for the exit. I got there first and pressed my back against it, refusing her the sanctuary that lay beyond.

'Let me out, *now*,' she choked.

'No.'

'Nico, please,' she begged. 'Don't make me answer you.'

'If there was any other way...' I said. 'The two of you argued in here, tell me how it ended.'

'What? How... you... but you were—'

'Asleep? Not asleep enough, apparently.'

'Oh, God,' she whispered.

'What happened?'

'... What he'll do.'

I put my arms around her. 'He will do nothing more, do you hear?'

Muted tears came from the vicinity of my jumper.

'Why was he so angry with you?' I asked.

'Cosbi told me to make friends with you when you refused to do what he asked. He wanted to know why you were so afraid, so...'

'So he asked you to find out.'

She nodded against my chest. 'I'm so sorry. Gerrin really doesn't like anyone else getting close to you.'

I could only imagine the blush that was going on beneath all that hair.

'It was a pointless plan anyway,' she said. 'In the end, Cosbi only needed Gerrin.'

'Huh?' I said, pulling back.

'That picture of your parents, it worked, didn't it? You remembered the only good thing he's done for you in years and wanted to repay the favour.'

'Well, shit,' I said, the last fragments of my shattered faith in Gerrin slipping away. 'The anniversary of their death?'

'He lied. It's not yet.'

I nodded my resentful acceptance and returned to sit on the bed. Anger was one thing, but he actually cared about our parents. I was certain of it. To lie about that, for someone like Cosbi, I had no words for someone who would do that.

'I'm so sorry, Nico,' Hanna whispered.

Everything I'd let them do to me had been to repay a man who no longer existed. The now incessant gnawing in the back of my mind, the stark pangs of a hopeless drug addiction, was all I had to remind me of a brotherly love I'd been willing to sacrifice everything for.

I swallowed. 'Did you know she was dead? Elena?'

'Yes. A lot of people didn't believe the rumours, but I overheard Gerrin say that Ash found a body in the lake.'

I knew too well what the lump in my throat was holding back, and that talking would only dislodge the deluge.

'I'm so sorry, Nico, I know what she meant to you.'

I sighed. 'Why would you be a part of this?'

'I did what I had to do. My father is diabetic, nothing's free around here. In fact, I got off pretty lightly compared with what Cosbi makes others do for safety, food and medicine.'

It seemed there was no one who hadn't sold me out for their own gain. I shook my head at the floor.

'I'm not proud of myself!' Hanna burst out. 'If I can do anything to make it up to—'

'You can,' I interrupted.

'What can I do?'

'I want you to make me a promise.'

'What promise?'

'Swear to do as I ask.'

She hesitated, reluctant to blindly agree, but her guilt threw the odds in my favour. 'I will.'

'What Cosbi wants from me, he must never have. A lot of innocent lives depend on that.'

'Innocent, who?'

'Those people outside, they aren't a threat.'

'Then why—'

'Cosbi and Gerrin want them all gone. I don't know why.'

'You mean we don't need to be hiding down here?'

'Exactly.'

She frowned at me. 'What're you asking me to do?'

'When the time comes, Cosbi will try to force me to give up what I know, and he'll use my son. I will get him out before that happens. But there's a chance I could get left behind, and I need you to give me a way out.'

'I don't understand.'

I raised my eyebrows, waiting for the realisation to hit.

'No!' she exclaimed. 'You can't, I won't help you do that!'

'Hanna—'

'Don't *Hanna* me!' she shouted. 'Why are you so eager to throw your life away?'

'Shh! There might not be any choice.'

'There's always a choice. I'll get you out of here, we can—'

'We can try,' I interrupted. 'But we have to be prepared to get caught.'

'But...' She started to cry, tears of despair. I pulled her into a hug to show my gratitude that she still thought me worth saving.

'My life next to all theirs is a no-brainer,' I said.

'And what happens to us when you're gone?' she challenged.

I sighed. 'I don't know.'

'And your son?'

'You saw what they did to me last time,' I said. 'Even if I could take that again, I can't promise the truth wouldn't slip out. Please, Hanna, I'm asking as a last resort, from a friend to a friend.'

She tensed, refusing to commit herself.

'Would you watch me suffer?'

But events of the last few weeks had toughened the usually compliant Hanna. With a look of disappointment, she pulled back. 'No, Nico. I would watch you live.'

And with that, she walked out, leaving me no assurances.

TRIGGER

Hanna could sulk all she wanted, it didn't change what had to be done.

And preoccupied Hanna had also forgotten to lock the door.

I threw one last glance around the room that'd been my home for the last few months, and left with the satisfaction of knowing that whatever the outcome of that night, I would never set foot in there again.

'Where're you going, bud?'

I spun around; I'd forgotten about the guard. I wouldn't let them stop me, even if I had to go through two old friends.

Parker and Chase were standing in almost identical arms-folded poses when I turned. It looked like I'd interrupted something pretty serious, given their closeness to one another.

'Are you trying to leave?' Parker whispered.

Chase used the distraction of his friend's question to get closer, something I'd learned to consider a threat.

'Stay back,' I warned.

'What's the plan?' Parker said.

Chase failed to heed any caution, inching closer even when I put up a hand to tell him he was taking his life in his hands. A strangled cry vibrated across the forearm I snapped around his throat, his hands flying up to relieve the pressure on his windpipe.

'Nico,' Parker said, palms raised high. 'We're on your side.'

'You've been working with them.'

'Only for appearances, I know it looks bad.'

'Too fucking right it does.'

'C'mon, Nico, you know us.'

'Why're you trying to stop me?'

'We not... idiot... trying to... help you...' Chase spluttered.

'All the times you've got out of that room, who do you think was supposed to be on guard? Who do you think left that door open?' Parker said.

My grip loosened slightly.

'We... supposed to be... watching you... now,' Chase gasped.

'Who warned you and Elena to leave?' Parker added. 'Trust us, you don't have much time.'

Against my better judgement, I launched Chase back at his friend; he rubbed his bruised throat with a reproachful glance and backed safely out of reach.

I thrust my chin upwards. 'Talk.'

'Cosbi's coming to see you,' Parker said.

'Why?'

'It was only a matter of time, especially after your performance in Gerrin's room the other night. If you don't know now, you soon will.'

'He thinks I've remembered?'

They nodded.

'Tough shit, I won't be here.'

'Wait, Nico,' Parker said, as I turned to go. 'If he finds your room empty or you up there, your family will be in danger.'

'All the more reason to get them out of here quickly.'

'I agree, but let us go. You can hang back a bit and take care of whatever business you need to. We can sort it without Cosbi knowing a thing.'

I hesitated. 'You can do that?'

'Easy.'

'Even easier if we knew the other exit,' Chase said.

I looked at the two of them, assessing whether to entrust the lives of my only remaining family to men who'd seemingly been loyal to Cosbi.

'Elena trusted us,' Chase prompted. 'That must mean something to you.'

His words were painful but true; Elena had been an excellent judge of character.

'In Elena's room, the hole in the ceiling. Follow the trail of two-dot patterns until you reach a long path with our initials written on the ceiling above it. That's the exit.'

'Well, I'll be damned. All those weeks we spent looking,' Parker huffed.

'You get them to some place safe, as soon as you can.'

Parker nodded. 'We'll go now, get them to pack up to leave.'

'I need keys for the bedroom doors too,' I added.
'I can get keys.'

The long passageway wasn't empty for once.
The approaching footsteps stopped.
'Hello?' a voice whispered.
When she was close enough, I clamped a hand over her mouth and dragged her into a nook in the wall. She squealed against my fingers.
'*Shh!*' I whispered.
'Nico?'
'Keep quiet, Hanna.'
'I've not got much time,' she said. 'I've been forbidden to come to you.'
'Then go. Don't risk your life to be here.'
'I had to see you, I've been thinking about what you said.'
'Forget it. It was unfair of me to ask it.'
'No, I was being selfish, I was only thinking about myself, about... about how I didn't want to lose you.' Her head dipped low.
'I understand,' I said, tucking two fingers under her chin. 'I care about you too.'
She heaved a disappointed sigh. 'I wish you looked at me the way you looked at her.'
'Who?'
But she shook her head and pressed her two hands around one of mine, contemplating a spot on the floor for several moments. Eventually, she drew back, and I realised that despite the absence of her fingers, my palm was not empty.
'Promise me you'll at least try to get out,' she said.
I glanced down at my open hand, where a large syringe rocked precariously.
'It's lethal,' she said, half looking like she wanted to snatch it back.
'Thank you,' I said, with a look that I hoped showed my gratitude. 'For everything.'
'Last resort?'
'Last resort.'

Frantically compiling a mental list of everything I needed to do before setting the cat amongst the pigeons, I ran from the medical bay one final time.

The first stop on my list was probably the most dangerous—getting my old backpack from my room. I wouldn't go anywhere without my memories. But I was heading straight for the corridor where I was most likely to encounter Gerrin.

I kept the hood of my sweater up and my face tipped at the ground, hoping anyone I passed wouldn't look too closely and cause a scene.

Arriving at the junction of the path that wound off towards 23, I stopped and peered around the corner, checking if the coast was clear, and trying to ignore the lure of Louisa's old door. First things first.

I ducked into the passageway and ran to my door, closing it behind me and exhaling the breath I'd been holding. I cast my eye across the room. Louisa's belongings were still scattered around the place, jumbled up with my own. I frowned. I'd assumed she and the baby were living with her mother, but maybe she'd decided to stay here.

I fished under the bed for my rucksack, where I'd hidden it prior to the planned escape. But there was nothing there. Looking around, I caught sight of it in a heap against the wall, like it had been carelessly thrown into the room. I frowned again; this wasn't adding up.

I opened the top of the bag and caught sight of the plaited brown leather band, engraved with an 'N', peeking out from under a shirt. I quickly sealed the bag before the emotion pricking at my eyes spilled over.

I stood and slung the weight up onto my back.

'Where are you going, Nico?'

I jumped in alarm.

'Saw you come in,' Gerrin explained.

'I wanted my things,' I muttered.

'I could've brought them to you.'

'I don't want anything from you.'

He sighed. 'I told you I was sorry about Louisa. We didn't mean to hurt you.'

'Didn't you?' I challenged. 'So you didn't pursue her deliberately, to prove I couldn't rely on anyone but you?'

His mouth pulled into a tight line. 'Ah.'

'*Ah.*'

'I did you a favour.'

'Did you do me a favour by hitting Hanna too?'

He pulled a face. 'So, I guess you're leaving?'

'Are you trying to stop me?'

'Go if you want, Nic, I'm done with you.'

Pain shot through my temple like a brick to the face. I staggered sideways, blinking against the bright spots in my sight. 'What did you say?' I gasped.

'Go,' he said with a shrug.

The imaginary brick hit me again. Behind the bright spots, I saw something, a flash of Gerrin with a glass of brandy in hand.

I blinked up at him. 'You've said that before.'

Something was wrong. Something was very wrong here.

The migraine beckoned with a familiar but more ferocious intensity. I held my palm to my head, pressing against the pounding.

'So this is goodbye then?' Gerrin said.

'Stop!' I yelled. 'Stop saying those things!'

'What things?'

Something was trying to get through, trying to break through a dam. I pressed hard against my temples, trying to keep it away. I didn't want this.

A stab of pain projected another image in front of my eyes. Gerrin prising Louisa's fingers from my hand.

I couldn't see this.

I cradled my head in my hands, my moans sounding like they were coming from underwater.

'No, no, no...' I groaned.

I didn't want to see this.

'*You'll never see me again after tonight,*' Gerrin's warped voice said.

The last brick to the face was the worst, and I lost control. I grabbed the nearest object—a pink vase—and swung it through the air, cracking Gerrin across the head.

He slumped to the floor unconscious and I fell beside him, the darkness of the looming memory pulling my eyes shut.

GO

SOMETHING DIDN'T FEEL right tonight.

A cold draught snuck up the back of my coat, icy fingertips tapping at each vertebrae before glancing across my neck. Shivering, I turned up my collar against it and hurried on, with three large bottles of stolen water tucked under my arm.

It was only ten, but not a voice could be heard anywhere. There was only the water, the ever-present water leaking from the ceiling, exacerbating the emptiness as it fell with an echoed splash.

Drip. Tick.

Drip. Tick.

Like it was counting down, ticking away the seconds.

'Nico, wait! Please stop!'

Whirling around in surprise, the water bottles slipped from my grasp with three dull thumps as I tried to catch a frantic Constance before her legs failed to hold her.

'Constance? What on earth—'

'Help me, help *her!*'

I propped her against my shoulder and returned her to 19, where apparently all hell had broken loose. Furniture had been uprooted, glasses were lying in smithereens on the floor, and the baby was screaming mercilessly in Rae's arms as she rocked him on her knee.

'You alright, Rae?' I said, cupping the youngster's chin in my palm and scooping the boy from her shaking arms.

She shook her head but didn't elaborate.

'Give him here!' Constance urged, practically snatching him from me. 'Go quickly, Nico, I'm begging you.'

My blank face would've been comical if everyone in the room didn't look so damn terrified. 'Huh?'

'Louisa!' she said.

'Constance, you're not making any sense.'

'He came for her,' she blurted out. 'Cold as anything, even when she begged him to leave us alone. Something about breaking rules.'

'Who?' I said, grasping her by the shoulders. 'Who came for her?'

She looked in my eyes with an all too knowing fear. 'Who do you think?'

I sprang to my feet, sprinting to where I knew Constance kept a couple of old bags. Either Foley had told someone or Gerrin had taken matters into his own hands after seeing me leave her room half-dressed.

I flung the bags at Constance's feet as I bolted for the door. 'Pack everything you need, we leave tonight.'

'Here!' Elena ordered, throwing me the occasional object that I was supposed to cram into the old backpack at my feet.

I was relying on her to take care of the details. I could only think of what might be going on in that room while I was here kicking my heels with the packing.

'You should have everything you need in there,' she said. 'Food, water, blankets, a change of clothes for you both, and this...'

She lifted the knife to get my attention and tossed it along the floor to me.

'Make sure everyone else knows,' I said.

She nodded. 'I'll go now. Get what you need from your room, and then go get her. If we see your sign, we'll know to meet you at the lake in two hours. Carve it into my door.'

I zipped the bag and claimed the knife, scrambling to my feet and eyeing her with frightened determination.

'Be careful,' she whispered.

Hurling the now heavy burden up onto my back, I pulled up my hood and left my room, heart pounding in my throat as I considered what scene might be playing inside 23.

The mechanism squealed in protest at the friction, metal squeezing over metal as my hand forced the key sideways, gauging the lock from its socket. I seized one of the dormant torches from beside the door and set it on fire with my lighter.

Everything was quiet.

I couldn't see anyone, hear anyone, feel anyone.

I aimed the flaming torch at the row of cells, sweeping the trailing embers through the air until the light fell on a lone closed door at the far end.

The door was locked, and Gerrin had the only key. Setting down the torch, I anchored my shoulder against the weakest part of the door and threw my weight behind it.

Once did nothing.

Twice rattled the bolt screws.

The wood groaned in objection as muscle smacked into it a third time.

Sensing weakness, I slung everything I had into attempt number four.

Rotting wood, heavy with water, splintered and tore as I practically took a dive into the confined space. Seizing hold of the light, I cast it through the pitch black until I saw a figure pressed close to the wall.

Petrified and shivering from the freezing cold, Louisa cowered from the sudden introduction of light to her bleak prison. She risked a peek of one blue eye through her sodden hair, ready to beg whoever had come to hurt her, and crumpling in relief when she realised that no such pleas were necessary.

She stumbled and fell into my arms.

'Shh,' I soothed, stroking her hair. 'It's OK, you're safe now.'

'Nico,' she whispered.

'Did he hurt you?'

She shook her head.

'Good, can you walk?'

She stayed put, not even acknowledging my question. 'I don't know what I was thinking. I had you and I lost you, for someone like him.'

'We'll talk later,' I said.

'We're leaving?'

I nodded and tugged at her hand.

'Only if you take me back.'

'What? Louisa, no, just come on.'

'I mean it, Nico. I'll only go with you as your wife.'

I could tell she wasn't budging without my word. Desperate to get her moving, I threw out the most difficult lie I'd ever had to tell. 'Fine, we can try again. Now will you please move?'

'Prove it.'

'For God's sake, Louisa!'

She shook off my hand in defiance. Knowing that Gerrin could be along any second, I took her face in my hands and broke our separation.

Her lips told me exactly how much she loved me—how much she craved my forgiveness. But for me, it was all a lie, and no amount of pretending could reignite that spark in my heart. It would never be the same.

'I almost believed you,' she whispered as she pulled away.

'I'm sorry,' I said, brushing a tear from her eye.

'I had to try.'

'Hurry,' I whispered.

It'd been an hour already; if I didn't get the sign to Elena soon, she would abandon the plan and we wouldn't get to end this tonight.

'How fucking *sweet*.'

The light of the flaming torch coloured his tied hair a brassy gold as he stepped from his hiding place behind the door, two replica torches appearing in the glassy blue irises.

He'd been listening to everything.

'Gerrin,' I said.

'Nico,' he mocked, cocking his head in amusement. 'Where do you think you're going?'

'Thought we'd go back to bed.'

'And you couldn't find anyone better than that cheating whore?'

I raised the knife between us. 'You're the only whore here.'

'That's what happens when the person you love most really couldn't give a toss,' he spat. 'Makes you desperate.'

'*You've* done this to us, not me.'

He said nothing but pushed the door to and walked across to the circular table in the corner, on which stood a half-empty bottle of scotch. Happier times had seen us sitting there, betting old money on poker.

Keeping his back to me, he removed the stopper with his teeth and poured liquid into two glasses. My grip remained tight on Louisa's arm.

'So you're finally leaving me, huh?' he said, taking an overly long time with the task.

'Are you trying to stop me?'

He shrugged. 'Go if you want, Nic, I'm done with you.'

It was a convincing act, but nothing more; Gerrin would sooner cut off my legs.

I wasn't sticking around to find out what he was up to. 'Come on,' I said to Louisa.

'So this is goodbye then?' he called, holding up one of the glasses. 'For old times' sake?'

'No.'

'Where's the harm in one drink?'

'*No.*'

'You'll never see me again after tonight.'

His words rekindled that same maddening regret I'd felt before at the thought of our parting ways forever. I sighed and strode to him, snatching the glass and knocking it roughly to his. 'Cheers.'

The sarcasm seemed to amuse him as he tipped the scotch to his mouth, watching me like a hawk over the glass rim as I drained the contents of mine in one gulp.

'Happy?' I asked.

'Fucking ecstatic.'

Hand in hand, Louisa and I were inches from freedom when he spoke again.

'She'll do it again, you know.'

I looked back, inviting him to explain himself.

Taking another sip of his drink, he smirked. 'Soon as some other poor fucker pays her some attention.'

'Ignore him,' Louisa urged.

'I wondered for a while why it was so easy,' he goaded. 'And then I realised.'

'Realised what?' I snapped.

'That she can't have been very happy with what she had.'

Louisa had to hold me back by my sleeve. 'Please, Nico, this is what he wants.'

'True though, isn't it, beautiful?' he said to Louisa. 'He's not enough for you.'

The temptation of improving my artwork on his face proved too hard to resist. Louisa's frantic calls were ringing in my ears when the room, and more specifically my target, lurched out of focus.

Knocked off balance, I staggered sideways and tried to shake the blurring from my vision. Each object in my line of sight trebled in number with the movement, each copy sliding past the original as my brain smacked uselessly into opposing sides of my skull.

It wasn't until I tried to take another step in his direction, still intent on delivering my parting gift, that I realised it was taking too much concentration to lift my foot.

Blood drained from my head at an alarming rate, fingers and toes tingling, with a buzzing in my ears that no one else appeared to be able to hear.

'Nico?'

Louisa sounded like she was far, far away.

Gerrin laughed and took up the stationary torch, strolling around the perimeter, lighting all of the other beacons until the room was aglow with fiery radiance. I flinched with every new flame, shying away from the sparkling embers, my pupils unable to constrict enough to contend with the dazzle.

A hand smeared across my forehead, trying to wipe the rapidly collecting beads of sweat leaking from my skin, but my palm was already too damp to make anything dry.

I aimed my feet at the stools by the whisky table. By the time I reached my goal, my muscles were so leaden it was like the gravity in the room had increased tenfold. The last hoist of my foot was so sluggish that my toes dragged across the rock, catching on an unfortunate crag and sending me stumbling headfirst into the furniture, the bottle of scotch and used glass taking immediate leave of the table.

'Dammit,' I muttered.

Louisa's hand was on my arm as she guided me to sit, her concerned voice telling me to take a minute. In a moment of impressive clarity, my eyes fixed on the still intact tumbler rocking in a floor crater.

'What the fuck was in that drink?' I hissed, adrenaline flooring the accelerator pedal in my heart.

I didn't need a full complement of senses to know that Gerrin was highly satisfied with himself. Nor did he answer me. That honour was left to the newcomer to our party, standing in the doorway.

'Ketamine,' Cosbi stated.

Louisa gasped as he closed the door and crouched before me with a smile. 'Best we could do at short notice, I'm afraid.'

'You...' I tried, but I was fast losing the ability to form a coherent word and the will to part from my seat.

Magnetism, that's what it was. The chair and I were drawn to one another.

'You drugged him?' Louisa cried.

My chair loved me too much. A small giggle bubbled up from my throat.

'Like I'd ever let him leave,' Gerrin snorted.

These lights were too pretty, like big eruptions of fairy stardust, golden glittery showers of sparks jumping through the air. I stared in wonderment.

'Now then, Louisa, what to do with you,' Cosbi said.

I looked down to see a large hand prise delicate fingers from mine. She didn't want to leave. Trying my damnedest to keep hold, I grasped for her, my hand clutching at thin air like one of those useless metal grabbers at the fair.

'She's mine now, Nic.'

This man was gloating at me. Mean man.

'Give her back,' I sulked.

'She broke the rules.'

Rules, yes rules. Those stupid bloody rules.

I dragged my eyes up to the two blonde figures, looking like they belonged on a damn magazine cover together.

'Yeah, with you, you sick son of a bitch,' I said, unable to contain my laughter. I looked over at the other man. 'Is he gonna get punished too?'

'He'll have the chance to redeem himself,' he responded.

Pressure slapped hard into my chest, knocking the air from me as my body plunged down an invisible ravine, leaving my stomach lingering and bewildered at the top.

A rollercoaster. I used to like these.

Hyper-speed, even around the corners.

But Louisa.

Fast, racing, exhilarating.

I couldn't let him hurt her.

The ride was heading straight for a yawning, spiralling vortex.
'I hate to see him hurting you like this, Louisa...'
I smacked my palms into my ears and screamed. Internally, externally, who knew?
'He's tripping.'
'We'll have to wait until he comes out the other side, if that's what you want.'
'It is.'

Everything has melted away.
No more heaviness.
It is floating, it is freedom, stretched from the beginning to all infinity.
There is light at the end of this tunnel. I have no means of reaching it, nor do I have any desire to. To leave would be ungrateful.
My body is irrelevant. I am a consciousness in the vacuum.
I like it here.
'What's happening to him?' she sobs.
'That's impressive shit, I might have to get me some of that.'
Someone switches on the gravity in my heavenly subway. Turns out I do need a body, and it hurts when you hit the ground. I run my hands through the earth. Gritty dirt, embers, ash. Quicksand.
I am sinking.
Not everything, just a me-shaped coffin-sized hole, pressed like a biscuit from a pastry cutter out of the tunnel floor. The earth tumbles in on me as I vacate the space, weighing me down. Flecks of dirt cling to my tongue, escaping down my throat, clogging up my nose.
Piles and piles more, scooping in on me. Suffocating.
I can't breathe.
I choke, I fight.
The last mound falls in, obliterating my sight.
I cry out as I smash through the ceiling and land on firm ground.
There are three people; I know them.
But more, lots more, flitting in and out of the walls like ghosts, as though they've come to witness.
Some smile, some sneer. None of them stay.

The walls are fascinating, wriggling, alive with life. I want a closer look.

'What's he doing?'

'Not a fucking clue.'

'Gabriel did say one seven five might be a bit much the first time.'

They are the most beautiful shade of red, a crimson sunset through the grey of the room's nothing. And the texture, incredible. I hold out my hand to touch.

It slips and slides beneath my fingers; a rich, oozy velvet blanket.

I pull my hand away—it is covered in blood.

Now I look, I know that they are not walls, but living, breathing human flesh, liquefying with blood before my eyes, squirming ominously as they threaten to subside.

Elena is here. With a devastating smile, she beckons me to her, only to turn and run when I obey.

Blood drips from the ceiling as the vast, squirming entrails claw higher above my head. A baby sitting cross-legged at the centre of the room squeals in delight and claps together his liquid-filled hands. Rich, ruby drops splatter all over his cheeks, clinging to angelic blonde curls.

And then I see them: tiny blue veins, intricately impregnated into the gory wall artwork. Each has a tiny black name written along its length.

I seek out my own.

Nico Jakes.

How long had it been?

I was on my knees and everything was normal once more. Everything apart from my lower body at least, which was seemingly paralysed in the aftermath of the high.

A fuzzy-looking Cosbi swam before me. 'Was that fun?'

Moments later, Gerrin dropped a chair down in front of me. Seating himself with a heavy sigh, he leaned forwards and positioned his face in such a way that I had no choice but to look at him.

'I need you to watch this, Nico,' he said, like a parent explaining a punishment. 'Remember every detail, just in case you ever think of leaving again.'

If only I could've reached out and caved his face in, but it would've been easier to uproot Mount Everest than to move my right arm. 'What… are… you doing?' I gasped.

'Only what I get told to do,' he said, smirking as he stood and kicked the chair away.

'Trust me, Nico, I know how much this is going to hurt,' Cosbi said. 'Still, if you'd kept better control of your wife, perhaps we wouldn't be in this situation.'

'I don't own her,' I said.

'And that, my friend, was your mistake.'

He turned, business-like, to the fallen angel shrinking from him. 'Beautiful Louisa,' he began. 'You know our rules, do you not?'

Louisa stared at him, blank-faced and terrified.

'Yes?' he encouraged. 'Then you understood what you were doing, and what the consequences might be. There can be no defence.'

'Can't be… or won't be?' I snarled.

'I do not tolerate whores, Nico.'

The stirrings of anger burnt in my gut, but with no physical outlet, it only ate away at me, tearing up my insides like a parasite.

'So…' he said, turning to Gerrin.

A smile snuck across Gerrin's face; he'd been waiting for this for a long time.

'Gerrin, I swear to God, if you lay a finger on her—' I raged.

'I already *did* lay a finger on her, Nic. What's one more?'

'One more means I kill you.'

He shook his head and offered out his palm. 'You don't have what it takes.'

Accommodating his request, Cosbi drew something from his pocket and placed it in the vacant space. Both Gerrin and I looked at the same time. A pristine silver-handled knife sat there, the sharpened point glinting in the light.

Terror streamed through my veins as I saw that Gerrin looked surprised by the order, but not entirely unwilling. Throwing twenty-three years' worth of memories into my mouth, I begged with every inch of my being. '*Please*, Gerrin, no.'

He floundered in shock, the emotional force of my words forcing him to stagger. He saw the tears in my eyes and I saw the decision being made in his.

'Not necessary,' he said, tossing the knife back to Cosbi.

I'd finally got through to him.

I exhaled and was just about to tell Louisa that everything was going to be fine, when the sound happened. It was the only time she'd ever screamed in fear, and it pierced my soul as it fell from her lips, long, drawn-out, spine-chillingly frightened. I knew right then that the sound would haunt my sleep for the rest of my life.

I opened my eyes to see him standing before her, all aggression and unanswerable dominance. Blood drained from my face. There was no greater drug than violence for easing Gerrin's own pain. I was powerless against such a pull. 'Louisa, *go!*' I bellowed.

Tearing her transfixed stare from him, she nodded and bolted for the exit.

Gerrin snorted in laughter as she wrenched at the stubborn handle, leisurely producing my key's twin from his pocket.

Sauntering to the door, he seized her around the waist and carried her back to the spot she'd just abandoned, grinning as frightened gasps of effort punctuated each thump of a small, balled fist against his flexed arms.

I launched myself onto my stomach, using anything my feeble arms could grab hold of to drag myself forward, one painful handful of stone at a time.

Smiling down at her distraught face, Gerrin pressed his body up close and tenderly took her chin between his fingers, stroking away the tears.

My clothes ripped and tore as I hauled myself across the space, craggy spikes clutching to slow my progress, my toes scrabbling uselessly against loose pebbles. Panting, I snarled in frantic annoyance, 'Come *on...*'

I had to reach her. I had to.

Like the most devoted lover in the world, he brought her lips to his, stoically ignoring her refusals, and kissed her.

'Get your hands... *off!*' I roared.

He smiled at my jealousy and dragged a finger up her chest, the tip coming to pause against the skin of her pale neck.

I grimaced and I writhed, baring my teeth in pain as I laboured across the rock. Done with my clothes, the sharp edges impaled my skin, leaving a glistening, bleeding trail in my wake.

He paused, I froze. The eye of the storm.

Like our movements were two opposing halves of a whole, my cry of horror rang out as his hands leapt to attention, fingers binding, tightly encircling, thumbs concentrating all of his almighty strength against her vulnerable throat.

'No!' I screamed.

The look in his eyes was an abomination; I had no answer to that kind of hatred.

Choked of all breath as he crushed her windpipe beneath his grip, Louisa grappled with his hands, legs thrashing in panic as she tried to kick him away.

'Louisa!' I shrieked. 'Gerrin, stop! Stop it, I'm begging you!'

But he'd blocked me out, engrossed in his task.

His face screwed up in furious concentration, Gerrin's lips pulled back across his teeth, turning vivid red with the effort of wrestling the life from my beautiful wife.

I hauled myself closer and closer, effort and tears choking the breath in my throat.

'Gerrin, please...' I sobbed, fingernails splintering as I clawed at the floor.

His arms were shaking as he forced more power into his vice-like grip, sweat clumping the loose strands of hair that'd fallen loose from his ponytail. Gasping and spluttering, Louisa clawed at the skin of his face, hands, neck, anything she could reach, leaving deep welts in his skin.

'No!' I cried. 'I lied! It's over, I'll end it. Just stop!'

But he was oblivious.

Unconsciousness was beckoning Louisa, hopelessness written in her pained eyes.

I shook desperate tears from my sight and watched her give up the struggle, reaching a shaking hand for me with one final effort.

'I'm going to fucking end you!' I screamed at him.

Body fading from lack of oxygen, the arm imploring my help and forgiveness fell limply to Louisa's side, her stare eventually leaving mine.

'Louisa!'

She was at blackout; I only had seconds.

With an almighty roar of determination, I dragged myself to his feet and heaved with all of my might, trying to knock him off balance long enough to let her breathe. Blinkered in his course, all emotion banished, a boot kicked out to silence the intrusion.

I saw stars as leather collided with my cheekbone, shooting pain flashing across my face, my world temporarily deserting me.

It was only moments later when I opened my eyes and saw.

Panting like a freed lion, his fingers relaxed around her throat and Louisa's body slid helplessly down the wall, slumping to the floor.

My scream was noiseless.

A bizarre, slow motion silence had invaded the room.

Gerrin's head fell against the arm resting against the wall, biceps shaking as he fought to drag in breath.

'No, oh no, no...' I sobbed.

My worthless body crawled to her side, hands trembling as I sought her pulse.

Nothing.

I dived for her face, leaning my ear across her mouth to hear the rhythm of her breathing, feel that precious air dispelling across my cheek.

There was none.

She couldn't be... I wouldn't let her.

Throwing myself into motion, my hands thumped into her chest, pounding away where I knew her heart was. Down and up. Down and up.

My mouth breathed life time and again into her lungs, my tears escaping down her face and trailing into her hair. It almost looked as though she was crying.

Pound. Breathe.

Again. Again.

Her blue eyes were wide and staring, fixed towards some point way beyond my face, pink lips already tinged with the purplish hue of cold blood. His brutality was already plain to see on her skin; deep plum bruising was spreading out from oval indentations.

'Don't,' I sobbed. 'You can't go.'

My hands worked for so long. I breathed for her until my chest ached.

'Oh God,' I whispered. 'Please stay.'

But she was gone.

She'd left before I'd had the chance to save her.

I laid my head on her chest and breathed her in. Disbelief gave way to grief, thinking no longer possible. Lying there, I cried an ocean for the lost girl cradled in my arms.

'I'll protect him. I swear it.'

It was the last thing she'd asked of me, with the reach of her hand. And my answer was a breath across her ear, for her alone and no one else to hear.

I brushed a kiss across her lips and slowly lost consciousness with her wrapped in my arms, my mind switching off to protect me from the unforgettable.

'Goodbye.'

NOTHING

Twenty-five days before the escape...

E VERYTHING WAS NOTHING for quite some time.
It would break me if I let it in.

Glass after glass of water stagnated at my side, bowls of soup congealed, fruit left exposed and rotting. Elena brought it, I wasted it. She knew it was all she could do and therefore she did so tirelessly, in the vain hope that I would start caring enough to live again.

Few people knew what'd really happened. Elena had got the truth from me in fragments, and she, in turn, had broken the unimaginable to Constance.

She had taken me in, changed my clothes and silently patched me back together.

And lying on her bed is where I'd been ever since.

The stubble on my face had grown into a light beard over time, my hair an unwashed mass of knots. I stewed in filth, my vest and jeans clinging like a second skin from grime and the sweat of endless nightmares.

Occasionally I would drag myself off the mattress to go to the toilet, but it was becoming less necessary as my body fought to hold on to what I was not putting in.

Often I felt her watching me, despairing as I slipped further and further away.

Twenty-three days before the escape...

'HOW IS HE?'

'Same.'

I hated their persistence.

I lurched onto my side, turning my back on the world before they could even try it. Elena's face would no doubt have fallen; perhaps she was shaking her head or silently mouthing concerns that I didn't want to hear.

'Nico?' Constance whispered.

Shit.

As if I didn't have enough guilt to be going on with, I had to listen to the voice of one of the strongest women I'd ever known crack clean under the weight of my name. Elena scrambled for tissue as sobs poured into the gulf between us.

She needed to grieve with me; that was her purpose in coming. I was the only person who could possibly understand.

But I couldn't be anybody's rock right now.

A slight weight depressed the mattress behind me, a little body having his impatient demand to be set down next to me satisfied. His tiny fingers scrunched the grey material of my sodden vest and resorted to smacking my skin repeatedly when I didn't respond.

A low howl of pain tore from my throat as I curled up, the first sound in days frightening the boy to the point of tears. I felt Elena scoop him from my side, prising his impressive grip from my clothes.

'There is more to live for, Nico,' Constance whispered.

Sixteen days before the escape...

JACKPOT.

Silently and gleefully, I offered up my thanks to whoever had dropped their store keys along my path to the toilet as the two dusty bottles of Talisker thudded onto Elena's bedside cupboard and I ripped the cork from the nearest.

It went down too easily.

With each mouthful, the memory faded; with every sharp burn of alcohol against my dry throat, my heart bled a little less.

I was halfway through the first bottle when she returned, freezing in the doorway as she caught sight of me necking a glassful.

'Where did you get that?' she demanded.

I dragged my eyes up to the blurred image of my livid best friend stomping towards me and managed to raise a bitter smile as I poured the next round.

'What's it to you?' I slurred.

'You aren't going to find the answer at the bottom of there.'

'I wasn't looking for one,' I said with a scowl, raising the glass to my mouth.

Losing patience, her hand lashed out and knocked the glass from my grip, dashing it and its contents across the floor.

With a snarl of fury, I was on my feet and in her face, spilled whisky dripping from my chin onto already stained clothes. 'Mind your own fucking business.'

Unfazed by my threat, she stood her ground and stared me out. 'Enough of this, Nico, snap out of it.'

Keeping my deadened gaze on her, I reached for the bottle and brought it to my lips, swallowing the smoky liquor with a wry smile that showed her glasses were only a courtesy.

'I won't watch you kill yourself,' she whispered.

'Then look away.'

'No,' she said, catching me by surprise as she snatched the bottle from my hand.

'Dammit, Elena!' I roared, making a drunken grab for the bottle, but was met with a harsh shove of her palm, pushing me back onto the bed.

'Sober up, have a wash. Stop using your anger to destroy yourself,' she said, throwing clean clothes at me. 'Drinking won't bring her back, but stopping might save others.'

Five days before the escape...

'ALL SETTLED THEN?' Elena asked.

One by one they nodded as her gaze moved over them. I was the last to give my permission to the arrangement, and I did so dutifully, a disillusioned inclination of my head giving Elena her unanimous vote.

The date was set. The plan had been laid down, due to be rehearsed to death in the coming days. Each member had their part to play, and it would be an intricate performance of correct timings if we were to pull the whole thing off.

'I think he should bring up the rear,' Dean said, tipping his head at me. 'Elena should lead both groups.'

'They're the only two who know the way,' Chase said. 'There's too many for one group, we've been through this. Elena will take the first lot, and Nic will take the second.'

My conscience prickled. What I'd failed to clarify was that I'd only lead the second group to the safety of the forest, before turning back to settle some scores.

'Why're you so interested in what Nic does, anyway?' Parker said.

'He's the strongest,' the handyman said with a shrug. 'If something goes wrong, he's the best one to have our backs.'

'I'm happy to do that,' I said.

Elena threw me a look that was either angry or fearful. I couldn't tell which. 'Nico leads the second group,' she reiterated.

Dean scowled but kept quiet.

'Same time tomorrow, everyone,' she said.

Her words were met with an animated scraping of chairs and all inhabitants exited as soon as Parker had inspected and cleared the way.

'Whatever you're planning, I won't let you go through with it,' Elena said, as soon as we were alone.

'I don't know what you're talking about.'

She glared at me, but knew that reasoning would be pointless.

'Here,' she said, beckoning for a leg-up. 'I found something the other day.'

'I don't want to see anyone,' I drawled, resorting to my well-practised trope for dismissing visitors.

But Jean came in anyway.

'Didn't you hear me, old man?' I said.

He looked around and frowned at the condition of Elena's room. It wasn't that bad today; there were only five plates of food on the floor, three spilled cups of water and a half-empty whisky bottle. I was only dressed because Elena had threatened to remove the alcohol if I hadn't shown some signs of life by the time she got back.

'Live this way if you wish, *monsieur*, or go stop Elena committing suicide. Up to you.'

He had my attention. 'What?'

'Community room.'

The teetering pile of plates beside the bed became the first victims of my haste, falling and cracking under my weight. I slipped on squished vegetables as I made my way to a viable pair of shoes and practically tripped past Jean in panic.

People stared and scrambled to let me through as I hightailed it to my destination, either surprised to see me after so long, or wondering who the bearded caveman was, reeking of alcohol.

It wasn't difficult to spot what was going on as I clambered against the tide of onlookers. Two individuals were ringed by a conflicted-looking crowd, one half of which seemed scared shitless about being found there and were leaving quicker than water through a sieve.

Barging through a gap, I found Gerrin and Elena practically nose to nose, screaming profanities at each other without stopping to listen to what the other was saying. They both were several shades redder than was healthy, unruly loose hair being tossed back, blonde against brunette. It was difficult to predict which one would hit out first.

My footsteps stalled as I caught sight of him; it was the first time since... since...

'Shut it, before I shut it for you!' Gerrin shouted.

Dragging myself from the oblivion of memories that'd been stamped from my conscious, I threw myself into the ever-decreasing gap between them. They barely noticed the intervention.

'Afraid they'll hear what you are?' Elena bit back and raised her voice for the benefit of her audience. 'Adulterer, rapist, murderer...'

'One more word, bitch!' Gerrin hollered, clouting me in the face as he tried to find a way through.

'And you'll what?'

'And you'll never see daylight again.'

She stopped struggling and eyed him mutinously. 'You want to kill me?' she goaded. 'You want to do to me what you did to her?'

'*Elena,*' I whispered, her tactless words stealing my breath.

Abashed at her behaviour, she stopped and frowned.

'Mighty tempting to send you the same way as that home-wrecking slag,' Gerrin said.

She drew herself up to her full height, proud, beautiful, a triumphant smile on her face. 'You still think it was Louisa who came between you? Please. He gave you up because I asked him to, weeks ago.'

'*No,*' I said, the word dragging behind me as Elena's perilous confession forced the turn of my head.

Gerrin stilled on my left, danger pulsating from his calmness.

'You're nothing to him now,' she said. 'And he did it for me. You hear me, you shit? *For me.*'

'Elena, no,' I pleaded.

A bellow of blood lust sent the remaining spectators running for the hills. My weight was just enough to stop him carving a path through to his target, rage making lumbering fists inaccurate as they swiped over my shoulders.

'Leave... leave her... *alone,*' I wheezed, managing to throw him backwards.

'Oh, I see,' he said. 'Didn't take her long to weasel her way in.'

'You'll have to go through me.'

He straightened up, accepting the challenge with a tight smile. 'So be it.'

Glaring at a still fired-up Elena behind my back, he lit a cigarette and stalked away.

I rounded on her. 'Of all the stupid, brainless, *idiotic...*' I spluttered. 'What on earth were you thinking?'

She grinned at me. 'Welcome back.'

'I mean it, Elena, what was that?'

'I was just explaining a few things... publicly.'

'And you think they'll let you get away with that?'

'If we protest in the open, they'll never guess what we're up to in secret.'

'Are you trying to get yourself killed?' I said. 'You couldn't have said anything worse to him.'

'It's about time someone took him on.'

'Elena,' I groaned. 'You know what he does to people who get close to me. It would finish me if he hurt you.'

Her amusement softened, eyes conducting a search of my face as my confession left us both exposed. 'It would?'

I squeezed my eyes shut against the unbidden image of her pinned against the stone wall under the pressure of Gerrin's hands. It was the first reminder I'd let in. My shoulders slumped. 'More than you know.'

She looked winded, not knowing what to do with what I was admitting.

MUTINY

I OPENED MY eyes to the bleakest new reality.
Sharp rock stuck into my head and cheeks, adding more pain to the throbbing migraine. My face was already soaking wet with tears.

'*Louisa...*' I sobbed.

I pawed at the floor, my entire body shaking, massive heaves of my chest forcing noises from my throat.

She was dead.

He murdered her for being with me.

Lifting my head slightly, I saw Gerrin just inches from my face, still unconscious and bleeding from the smashed vase. The brother I'd known was dead; I didn't want to save the monster that remained.

I rolled onto my back and howled into the air.

She never should've married me. If only I'd just left her alone. She'd been in danger the second I'd walked into her life, and I was as much to blame as the heinous creature beside me for not realising it.

I clambered to my knees, shaking as the migraine raged in the background. I shoved Gerrin onto his back and searched his person, taking the two knives I found.

I stared at him for several moments, wondering where it had all gone wrong. 'I should've left you out there to die,' I whispered.

Staggering from the room and shutting him in, I looked around for something to wedge under the handle.

'Nico, keys!' Parker yelled, as a large bundle of metal came whizzing towards my face.

I caught them and locked my old door. It would hold him for a few minutes.

Part two of the plan would now be the hardest of all.

I hesitated before I tapped on the old wood, becoming louder and more persistent as my arrival was ignored by those inside. Eventually, the door creaked open and a wary Constance peered out through the tiniest fraction.

Needing to get out of plain sight, I stuck my boot in the gap and pushed my way into the room, succeeding in frightening the living daylights out of her.

Dressed in mismatched clothes and surrounded by half-packed bags, her usually plaited hair loose, Constance pointed a pair of scissors directly at my heart. 'Whoever you are, get out,' she hissed under her breath.

'Not until I've got what I came for.'

She looked surprised by my response, perhaps half recognising my voice. 'Who are you?'

With a flick of my fingers, the hood came down.

The scissors clattered to the floor as her hands leapt to clamp in a scream. 'Sweet Jesus!'

'It's been a long time, Constance.'

'Nico... I... How are you...? Why are you...? Oh!'

Shock gave way to misery, and she dropped into a nearby chair, sobbing her sorrow into tightly cased hands.

I understood her suffering well. It takes a will of iron to keep the most damaging of memories buried under lock and key. And seeing me again brought it all back.

She was inconsolable for a solid minute, while I stared at the floor, broken and empty inside.

'You thought I was dead?' I said eventually.

She nodded and wrenched a handkerchief from her sleeve to shield her face from view. Its accessibility told me that these tears had needed drying frequently. 'I had no reason not to believe it.'

'He's done worse,' I agreed.

Green eyes encased in sore, red circles peeped over the top of the cotton, regarding me warily as though I might disappear. 'How?'

'I've been alone for months in the medical bay. I lost my memory. Everything was completely blank until a few days ago.'

'Then, you remember...?'

'Just now.'

A silence fell between us, an unspoken eulogy saturated with the mourning of a mother and a husband.

'What happened afterwards?' I whispered.

'It was covered up,' she said. 'They retreated into their bubble of righteousness, no remorse. Only you and I were allowed to attend when she was laid to rest.'

The confirmation was incontestable. Any hope I'd been harbouring of it being a bad dream fell silently away, along with the part of my soul that Louisa had owned.

'I couldn't cope with losing her, but my anger made things dangerous,' she continued. 'Cosbi turned his attention to Rae, not so subtly telling me to shut my mouth.'

I bristled. I'd earned the right to watch that man die.

'They had bigger problems keeping your friend Elena quiet though,' Constance said, a ghost of a smile crossing her lips. 'She knew how to make a nuisance of herself.'

'What do you mean?'

'Physical threats had no effect. I believe she was in the middle of sharing her opinions with a rather large audience when *he* went to stop her.'

I could tell by the tone of her voice exactly who the 'he' was.

'We tried everything to get you to respond again,' she said. 'But it took her being in danger to snap you out of it. Whatever was said between the three of you that day, getting rid of her became a priority for him.'

'And he succeeded,' I said quietly.

'I heard you'd been killed trying to protect her. It sounded so much like something you'd do,' she said, with a sad smile.

I shook my head. The web of lies was so intricate, so deceitfully spun.

She cocked her head at me in motherly concern. 'And you? You're much changed, Nico. Tell me they haven't hurt you.'

'What more could they do to me, Constance?'

'But you are reliant on something. Alcohol?'

Just like a typical mother, nothing got past her.

'They've been giving me something to help my memory.'

'Why?'

'Elena had a secret. They want it.'

And it had been my secret for a while now too. Mass weaponry and enough explosives to blow up Fort Knox; it was undoubtedly the location of the hidden cave that Cosbi wanted.

She laid her hand on my shoulder. 'No more of it, do you hear me? Give yourself the chance to heal.'

The conversation was interrupted by a muted wet 'pop', an item being dragged from a mouth before clattering to the floor.

Standing on legs that threatened to buckle, I made my way over to a dark corner of the room, scooping a plastic dummy into my fingers. My eyes blinked away the watery intrusion as I hauled myself up on the cot bars and prepared for the moment I'd been longing for.

He must've been just shy of a year old. Golden-blonde hair fell to his neck, long eyelashes fluttering against the dream he was having. His frown of concentration was a fitting tribute to his mother, but every other feature screamed that he belonged in the Jakes family.

He wriggled in his sleep as I wiped the dummy on my T-shirt and replaced it between his lips, Constance appearing at my side.

'What's his name?' I said.

'You don't remember?'

I shook my head.

'Luca,' she whispered. 'Luca Nicholas Jakes.'

I tried out the name on my lips; yes, it sounded wonderfully familiar. 'That's Italian, right, Luca?'

She nodded. 'Louisa wanted to choose something in memory of your mother.'

'He looks like Gerrin.'

The observation had been voiced before I could kick myself for it. Maybe it lay simply in the fact that he had blonde hair, but I could see my bastard of a brother in every line. The poor kid would never get away from the legacy of his looks.

'Through no fault of his own,' Constance berated. 'Don't forget how strong your family resemblance is. I can see you in him, Nico—look past your pain and you will see it too.'

But gazing down, all I could see was a beautiful reminder of someone that Gerrin had destroyed, in my name. The truth was, neither of us was good enough for him.

'I'm so sorry, Constance.'

'What on earth for?'

'I swore when I married Louisa that I'd protect her.'

'You lost as much as me that day,' she said. 'She was your wife just as much as she was my daughter. You never let her down.'

If only that were true.

I raised two fingers and met them with a kiss at my lips, pressing the tips to his soft forehead. 'Whatever happens tonight, promise me you'll take care of him.'

A horrified gasp accompanied tightening fingers on my arm. 'Get that idea out of your head right now.'

'Someone will be coming soon to help you get out. Finish packing your things and be ready.'

'Come with us.'

'I have to go.'

'Let it go, Nico,' she pleaded. 'For the sake of your son, he's just got you back.'

'It's because I love him that I have to go. I can't leave everyone else here, and I can't let Gerrin follow us.'

'He needs his father!'

'He needs to be safe.'

'I'm begging you.'

I shook my head, taking one final look at Luca to give me the strength for what I was about to do.

'Cosbi's locked in!' Parker yelled, as I emerged.

'Nineteen first!' I shouted back.

'On it!'

It was the image of Gerrin's smirk as he held Luca in his arms that drove my run; it was thoughts of saving my son from his mother's fate that was behind the force that kicked open each door, as I looked for people to evacuate.

There was only one man I could think of turning to for help with the shoddy, improvised plan forming in my mind. Jean. And I knew where I'd find him.

I threw open every door in my path, shouting instructions at numerous, faceless inhabitants to get to room 20 as soon as possible.

It occurred to me as I ran that this was the first time since I'd started sneaking out that the caves had been awake and operational. And judging by the excited, scandalised chattering that I generated in my wake, as people got an undisputable sighting of a man who was supposed to be dead, I knew it wouldn't be long before news of my escape reached those in charge.

By the time I got to Jean, people had already run ahead to spread the gossip, and my door-slamming was creating so much noise that he was already standing outside his room, looking baffled.

'Jean!' I called.

'*Commandante!*' Jean shouted, his face lighting up.

Waving to indicate that I was coming over, I managed to knock aside a stocky member of the milling pack. The man threw me an irritated look, doing an amusing double take when he saw who I was, and tripped over his feet while nudging his friend.

'Get your things, Jean, we're leaving!' I yelled as soon as I was within earshot.

'Yes, sir!'

The Moreau clan dived back through the door and I followed, pacing the room while they threw items into three already full rucksacks retrieved from the bottom of a broken wardrobe.

'I know what Cosbi wants,' I explained as they raced around me, shouting orders in incoherent French. 'I either have to get out or I have to—'

'You get out,' Jean interrupted sternly, throwing a blanket at Coco. 'Your son?'

'Parker and Chase have already taken him out.'

'Ah, I always knew they were trustworthy.'

It wasn't two minutes later when I had three escapees stood before me, dressed in everything they could lay their hands on for the wintery hills.

'We're going to find Elena?' Jean said.

The reminder stabbed at my beaten heart. 'No, Jean,' I said, trying to make further explanation unnecessary.

The poor man's face fell. But there wasn't time now to think about what we'd lost.

'Hurry,' I said.

'*There!*'

Gerrin's relieved holler met my ears the second I stepped from Jean's room, the sight of a five-strong stampede of men following soon after.

'Go that way, and take this,' I said to Jean, giving him one of the stolen knives. 'Get as many as you can to Elena's room. I'll distract him.'

'You dare fucking run from me, Nico!' Gerrin roared.

A huge crash rocked the surfaces around us, aftershocks knocking loose stone from the walls and scattering ripples across the puddles. Instinctively, everyone ducked.

'What the—' I yelled.

Another smash of rock beat down my voice, diminishing echoes followed by a delayed collective high-pitched scream from the crowd and shouting in the distance.

The remaining inhabitants poured from their rooms in various states of undress, flooding the corridor, eager to see what all the commotion was about.

'Out of my way!' Gerrin bellowed.

More precise, individual bangs sounded behind Gerrin, who was carving a brutal path through terrified onlookers, each followed by a distinct ping. Gunshots.

A universal moment of silence ensued, but there was no fooling the crowd about the source of the noise. Anarchy erupted. Screams. Stamping. Bodies colliding. Nobody knew where to go.

I shouted, I yelled. No one could hear me.

Looking around, I spotted an opportunity. Hauling myself upwards using rivets in the wall, my feet found a boulder half-embedded in the wall. It set me a good couple of feet above the crowd.

'Oi! *Oi!*'

A child standing at my feet tugged the hem of her father's overcoat and pointed up. Seeing who was calling for his attention, the man elbowed his neighbour, who elbowed his neighbour, until the message had been played like charades around the cave. A sea of white faces looked up at me.

'Listen to me—'

'Why the hell should we?' a man heckled. 'Where've you been the last few months?'

'Shut up, idiot!' a woman shouted.

'I've been dead,' I called, to a rumble of laughter. 'I know a lot of you have been forced to do things—things you hated, to keep your families safe. I have a way out for anyone who wants it. Follow Jean, head for room twenty and take only what you can't live without.'

'How do you know we ain't gonna starve or get shot out there?' a voice cried.

'It's gotta be better than this shithole!' another offered.

'The fighting stopped years ago,' I said. 'It's now or never.'

The last word had barely left my mouth before people started lunging into various rooms, emerging seconds later with bags and possessions.

'Out of the fucking way!' Gerrin hollered.

Jean waded to the front of the masses. I jumped down and darted for a random path.

'Nico, on my life, if you make me come after you—'

I flipped Gerrin the bird, a roar of fury chasing me down the narrow shortcut.

'*Duck!*'

I hit the deck, obediently throwing myself into the space where my corridor had emerged, somewhere back near the medical bay.

Milliseconds later, a bottle of spirit came somersaulting through the air, whistling past my head, the rag stopping its neck aflame. With the splintering of glass and the roar of ignition, the bottle delivered on its promise and set alight the three men running from it. They scurried away, howling in pain and trying to put each other out.

'Nice dive!' a man called as he raced past in pursuit. He was a stranger to me, but looked vaguely familiar as he pulled a mock salute and gave me his name. 'Shem.'

'Hey, thanks for the heads up!' I yelled as he flew around the corner, setting fire to another bottle.

It was like some kind of bizarre Armageddon.

More shots and bangs could be heard from a distant somewhere, teasing out screams. I scrambled to my feet and kicked open every door I came across, yelling exit plans at whoever might be inside.

LAURA J. SILLETT

'Nico!' I heard someone shout in the distance.

A thick-set man further up the corridor stopped thumping someone and looked around him, his eyes eventually falling on me. 'Are you Nico?'

I didn't know him, but he was cheerfully pummelling one of Cosbi's men. So I nodded.

'So, finally I meet the famous Nico Jakes.'

My jaw dropped. 'Do I know you?'

'You will. Not how I pictured you from the description—I've seen more meat on a sparrow's kneecap,' he called. 'But each to their own.'

I stayed looking gormless as I tried to think of a witty comeback.

'People'll be looking for you,' he said, before returning to beating up his prisoner. 'Stay safe.'

'Hey, Nic!'

'Thank Christ you two are back!' I yelled, as Parker and Chase jogged to meet me. 'All hell's broken loose.'

'I know, we started it,' Parker said.

'Huh?'

'We took your family outside—' Chase began.

'All safe, by the way,' Parker added quickly.

'Yeah, all safe. When we took them out, we saw a guy hanging round. Parker took him down, but the dude seemed real interested in knowing whether a woman down here was still alive. He asked about you too.'

'So, of course, we said you were still alive—'

'But that you might not be for much longer.'

'He panicked when we said that,' Parker said. 'Said he belongs to a group that live nearby, and they've been trying to find a way of getting people out—'

'So, of course, we told them the way,' Chase said.

My face broke into a smile. 'Then, you mean...'

'Yeah, we're under attack,' Parker laughed.

'He ran to tell everyone, and they came back with all sorts of shit,' Chase said. 'Guns, knives, alcohol.'

'And that's not everything,' Parker said. 'Wait 'til you hear this—'

I never got to hear it. A loud, long howl, the mimicking of a wolf-cry, peeled through the air, followed seconds later by Jean's stampeding herd of escapees hurtling round the corner.

I saw what was driving their speed. Ash had armed himself with a gun, undoubtedly stolen from one of the attackers, and was firing it indiscriminately from the back of the pack. People were dodging, screaming, running in zigzags to avoid his haphazard aim.

Laughing like a manic fool, he spotted us and raised the gun higher, aiming the next two rounds at my head. One hit the rock just to my right, and the other sank its smooth metal teeth into Chase's arm. With a yowl of pain, he slammed back into the wall and clutched at his bicep, which immediately started pouring blood.

'Go, get out!' I shouted. 'You can't help anymore. Go!'

With a slap on my back, Parker took off towards 20, propping up his injured friend.

'Follow them! Jean, go!' I hollered at the approaching throng, which gathered momentum at the instruction. 'He's mine.'

Ducking and diving, I scrambled along the wall, ranting at people to move. Ash only noticed me in time to quickly toss aside the gun. We collided with two grunts and a crunch of bones, straight into a wall. I raised my fist to strike.

'I think you'll find he's ours,' called a female voice.

I looked over my shoulder and saw a group of five young women, each with a weapon in hand, all glaring at Ash. My mouth pulled up into a smile.

'This your fan club?' I said to him, tipping my head at the group. 'Guess I'll leave you to it, *sunshine*.'

Ash caught sight of the blood-thirsty mob and his mouth dropped open. 'No, wait, don't leave me with them!'

I released hold of his jacket. 'All yours, ladies.'

A high-pitched scream sounded as I retreated, and I looked back to see that Ash had disappeared beneath a pile of arms and weapons.

No matter where I ran, whatever doors I opened, there were bodies lying on the floor. Unconscious, dead, friends, enemies, I couldn't think about it. The sound of scattered gunfire became less frequent as my search wore on, and only the occasional flaming object flew past me.

'That way!' I yelled at two women sheltering in a small nook.

They scuttled away as I took the corner and came face to face with an attempt by four men to bring Gerrin down. The whole area was on fire; explosives and spirits brought in by the outsiders had set alight the alcohol supply in the vicinity. It was a ticking time bomb, occasionally cracking and spitting with the promise of fireworks.

Heavily outnumbered, the bastard was still winning. The longer the fight went on, the more time it was taking each challenger to get back to his feet.

Looking about me, I saw a knife shining in the hand of an unconscious and somewhat burnt man. I lunged for it, took aim and sent the blade whistling through the air. It missed his arm by the smallest fraction, but the action didn't go unnoticed.

Rearing his head to identify his fifth attacker, Gerrin looked wounded that I'd thrown to kill.

'*Murderer...*' I mouthed at him.

The wheezing group of men took advantage of his distraction and each landed a punch—face, stomach, kidney, back of the knees. Gerrin grabbed a discarded plank of wood, knocking two of them out with a single swipe.

I was looking about me for something of more use when a hand tapped insistently on my back. The man was filthy and charred from the siege but was unmistakeably gaunt. His bones poked out through papery white skin, and his thinning curled hair was a familiar colour. His brown eyes, although they showed fear, had something inherently dislikeable about them.

I'd seen him only once before, looking out at me as I walked his daughter home.

'Mr Jakes?' he heaved.

'Mr Phillips, Hanna's father, right?'

The man nodded. 'I need... your help.'

'What's wrong? Is it Hanna?'

To my surprise, the seemingly insincere man began to cry. 'He hit her. He hit my little girl. Said he'd only let her go if you give yourself up.'

'Who said that?'

'Mr Cosbi.'

Hanna. How could I have forgotten Hanna?

'Where are they now?'

'Twenty-three, sir.'

'Come with me,' I said, pulling him along. 'I'll show you the way out, and then I'll go help her, I swear.'

'Oh, God bless you, sir. God bless you!'

It took us twenty minutes to travel a five-minute path; progress was impeded by bodies littering the blood-flecked rock, and snails moved faster than Thomas Phillips.

I pointed to 20 as I ran off. 'Go—there'll be someone in there to show you the way out.'

23 loomed before me, my own personal hell. Momentarily considering my empty hands, I remembered the second stolen knife in the back of my jeans.

Cosbi was most likely on his own; I'd seen the majority of his bodyguards either fighting or beaten throughout the caves, but I was clueless as to how precarious a situation Hanna might be in.

My hand found the entrance ajar, and I edged past the sodden door and whispered, 'Hanna?' into the torch-lit room.

The hammer on the revolver clicked as the barrel was jammed against my temple.

'Drop it.'

ADDICTION

'**I** SAID DROP it.'
   'Cosbi—'
'I am aware of how to use a gun, Nico. Do as I say.'
I raised my hands in surrender, dropping the knife. It clunked to the floor and bounced an unpredictable path, resting close enough to his heel that he could swat it out of reach.
'Where's Hanna?' I said.
He said nothing, but I could sense his smirk.
'I mean it, Cosbi. You have me, let her go.'
'Turn around.'
Making no sudden movements, I shuffled my feet so that I was facing him and the revolver was pointing at the centre of my forehead. Not wanting to stay there long, I manoeuvred myself until it was aimed at my other temple and I had a clear view of the wrecked corridor outside.
Thomas Phillips was standing a few feet away, a smile plastered on his face that finally matched the unpleasant look in his eyes. Broken teeth were bared with satisfaction at seeing me with a gun to my head.
'She'll be better without you around,' he said.
'She isn't even here?' I said.
'In the medical bay, *sir.*'
'My thanks, Mr Phillips,' Cosbi said.
'Always a pleasure, Mr Cosbi,' the man responded, tipping an imaginary hat in farewell before remorselessly leaving me to my fate.
Cosbi tapped the barrel of the revolver to my temple and indicated to the remains of his underground empire, devastated and aflame even all the way down here. 'Proud of yourself?'
'Like you wouldn't believe.'
'I've tolerated your disruptiveness for long enough,' he said. 'You're only still alive because of Gerrin. Now get over there.'

Keen not to anger him until I'd had time to think of a way out of this, I obeyed the order.

'Not going to save your own skin?' I said.

His aim was held steady at my chest, the eyes behind the gun glinting like polished black glass. 'Have you considered what your little stunt will mean for everyone who lived here?'

'It means freedom.'

'They won't survive without me. How will your juvenile emotions cope with that?'

I shrugged. 'There's no fighting out there.'

'Not for years, granted. But try taking rules and order away from people who know nothing else. Institutionalised, I believe they call it.'

'Were they ever a threat, the people out there?'

'For a time, until they fought themselves into extinction. The one group of foreigners left around here sent the odd person looking, hoping and failing to take back something that belongs to me. But a threat? No.'

'Something that belongs to you?'

'Something that needs to learn her place.'

'Wife?'

'Daughter,' he corrected.

I frowned, not recalling Cosbi ever mentioning family members. 'You have a daughter? Where?'

'Somewhere safe, where she will no longer be led astray.'

'You've been here for years—how could you possibly have kept her hidden all that time?'

'I'm sure someone must've heard her at some point—she did fight it for a while. But her room is secure.'

'What do they want with her?'

'*He* wants her back. But she understands now that she must choose a partner from among the men here, or not at all.'

'What do you have against the man?'

'It's unnatural!' he spat.

I pulled a face. 'What's unnatural about love?'

'It wasn't love,' he dismissed. 'Her mother was a whore too—it needs stamping out before it starts.'

'You'd ruin your own daughter's happiness?'

'She paid for disobeying me, and so will he.'

'Is that why you want what's in that cave?'

'Precisely. Not so much a *defence* as an *offence*.'

'You'd kill all those innocent people just to get back at one man?'

'Collateral damage, unless they choose to join me.'

'You're unhinged.'

He smiled, the gun held steady at my heart. 'My late wife said the same thing.'

'And what about Elena?' I said.

'As innocent as a traitor can be. Whether he admits it to himself or not, Gerrin was the cause of your memory loss. But it was necessary to convince you otherwise.'

'Why?'

'You needed to think she was still alive and a threat, or else there was no reason for speed in regaining your memories. You were to be persuaded that the whole place could be attacked at any moment, should she open her mouth. Those impeccable morals let you down, friend.'

'And I hated the memory of her—'

'Because I suggested that you should. The mind is so easily influenced, Nico.'

'But she hated me too.'

'In your mind, she had every right to. You showed me her hiding place that night, your own guilt did the rest.'

I hesitated, trying to force back the lump in my throat. 'Where is she buried?'

He licked his lips, a smile unfolding around the action. 'Somewhere in the hills, unmarked. I told Ash not to concern himself with the niceties.'

'You're sick,' I snapped.

He smiled as he rubbed at the greying black bristles on his chin. 'You know, when the pair of you first arrived, I genuinely thought Gerrin would be the tough nut to crack.'

'And yet you managed to crack him.'

He shrugged. 'You were as foolish in your youth as any man, so easily swayed by the charms of a pretty face. As such, there were things I could offer you. But your brother was a disturbed man, unpredictable, volatile. Probably incapable even then of unselfish love.'

My skin prickled as anger swelled to the surface.

'The one possibility I could see was in his unhealthy devotion to you.

But once you began to shun his company in favour of quenching your teenage hormones, I noticed that there were even stronger things living within him. Jealousy and the need for revenge grew and festered, with only one outlet. The violence, you see, provides a momentary tonic to alleviate the trauma he has suffered in his life. As addictive as your drugs, my young friend.'

'She'd still be alive if you hadn't put her between us,' I said.

'I must admit, even I was surprised he took such an exception to her being in your life. I never thought of it when I introduced you. Still, we all make mistakes.'

'*Mistakes?* People have lost everything—family, friends, their lives. There's only one way this ends for you.'

'And perhaps you will get your chance, Nico. Just as soon as you honour old promises.'

'What's your leverage this time?'

That was answered by Gerrin crashing through the door, bouncing off the door frame as the girl in his grip tried to stamp on his foot. He looked more dishevelled than I'd ever seen, clothes blackened by fire, messy hair singed and various wounds leaking blood. Her corkscrew curls bounced angrily as she fought him, a charred piece of cotton gagging her mouth.

Hanna.

'Boy was gone,' Gerrin huffed. 'Found this down the corridor, bickering with Daddy about betraying *her Nico*. Figured you could use it.'

'Right on time, Gerrin,' Cosbi said, pointing at the filthy rag preventing her from speaking.

'Kept trying to bite me,' Gerrin said.

'She must have learned her manners from your brother.'

Gerrin's hurt expression sought me out. 'Throwing knives now, are we?'

'You murdered my wife,' I said through clenched teeth. 'Next time, I won't miss.'

Cosbi nudged the revolver handle into Gerrin's arm, who pressed the barrel into Hanna's cheek. She whimpered into the gag.

'Consider this my leverage, Nico,' Cosbi said.

'It's going to be OK,' I mouthed at Hanna.

I moved my hand to my pocket slowly, deliberately, giving Gerrin no reason to get trigger-happy, and retrieved the syringe I'd convinced

Hanna to steal. I removed the cap with my teeth and pressed the needle to my forearm.

'Let her go,' I said.

They looked baffled by the threat.

'What's that?' Gerrin said.

'Lethal dose,' I said. 'You heard me.'

'Now, where would you get something like that?' Cosbi said, stroking Hanna's cheek with a finger. 'Was it you, sweetheart, did you give that to him?'

'Christ, they really can't say no to you, can they?' Gerrin said.

Frightened and disgusted, Hanna screwed up her eyes.

Cosbi backed away. 'She's guilty.'

Gerrin's finger moved to the trigger as he looked at me expectantly.

'Cosbi—' I began.

'Put it down, or she dies.'

'I'm no use to you dead.'

Gerrin rammed the end of the gun angrily into Hanna's cheek, making her scream into the material. 'You want this on your conscience too, little brother?'

I knew he wasn't bluffing. There would be other ways of making me talk, even without Hanna. I bent down and rolled the syringe into the space between us. 'Now the gun,' I said.

For once, Gerrin did as I asked and lowered the weapon. Hanna sank a few inches.

'Good,' Cosbi said. 'Now, the location of that store.'

I glanced at Hanna, who shook her head. Gerrin caught the gesture and used the gun to drag her hair back off her shoulder. She froze.

'You have no other choice,' Cosbi said.

'And Hanna?'

'Goes free.'

'Give me your word.'

'You have it.'

I had no reason to trust him; I only knew I couldn't face watching another innocent person die in front of me. 'The passage leading from Elena's room,' I started, watching arrogant satisfaction form on Cosbi's face. 'Follow the t—'

A stray bullet from outside ricocheted off the door frame and buried itself in the ceiling, inches from where the trio was standing. The ceiling cracked, the ceiling crumbled. Unable to bear the weight from above, the rock tumbled downwards and split the pack.

Hanna dived in my direction, Cosbi fell backwards, and Gerrin collapsed under a heap of masonry. More rubble cascaded near the door, sealing us off from our rescuers.

I scrambled to help Hanna.

Miraculously, she'd escaped without serious injury. I ripped the gag from her mouth and pulled her to her feet, shrapnel falling from her hair and clothes.

'We need to get out of here before they come round,' I said.

Hand in hand, the two of us struggled for the door, clambering over unsteady rocks, coughing out thick dust, knowing our lives depended on speed.

My shaking hands hauled stone and debris from the door, one load at a time. Progress was slow and wasn't helped by the frequent glances thrown backwards to check that we didn't have company.

I wanted to be free.

Within minutes, we could see torchlight and hands pulling debris from the other side. My excitement at the promise of a new life streaming through the door did not stop a regretful glance back at a wounded Gerrin, still lifeless on the floor.

'Leave him,' Hanna whispered.

Turning to abandon him one final time, a glint on the floor caught my eye. I glanced down at my trembling hands and then back at the full syringe.

'Nico...'

I licked my lips.

'Please, Nico.'

'I have to.'

Her eyes followed my line of sight. 'No, please, let's just go.'

'I need it.'

'You don't, you just think you do.'

But my mind was made up; where I was going, there would be no more of this. I needed that hit just one more time.

I pushed her in the direction of the door. 'I'm right behind you.'

Diving back towards Gerrin, I swooped for the syringe and ran for the exit.

The sound of rocks falling turned my head.

In slow motion, I saw a grimy, blood-covered arm emerge from the rubble, and this time the finger didn't pause on the trigger.

Without thinking, I threw myself in front of Gerrin's intended target.

'Nico!' Hanna cried as I knocked her to the floor.

I recoiled as the bullets punctured my stomach. One. Two.

FATE

I STAGGERED BACKWARDS, clutching at the sharp pain.

Blood soaked slowly through my top, dripping between my fingers.

I stumbled. My foot caught on some rubble, and I fell, inches from freedom.

'No!' Hanna cried.

Gerrin's face froze, complete horror visible beneath the blood-soaked grit on his skin, his teeth still bared from the rage that made him fire.

I grunted in pain, a wave of blood erupting over my fingers.

Furious tears streaked dirt into his beard as he yelled, 'What did you do that for, you stupid son of a bitch?'

'Oh, what have you done?' Hanna whispered, dropping to her knees and ripping her cardigan off, pressing it hard against the wounds.

I gagged and felt a dribble of liquid ooze from the corner of my mouth.

'This wasn't meant to happen!' Gerrin cried. 'I saved you, *I saved you.*'

'And now I've saved someone,' I said, creasing from the pain of talking. '*From* you.'

'*Damn you,* Nico! Damn you to hell.'

'Everyone OK in there?' someone called through the gap.

'Help me get him out!' Hanna cried.

I felt hands grab my arms, clothes and fingers, heaving me backwards through the half-blocked doorway. Hanna grabbed my feet.

'*Nico!*' Gerrin sobbed.

Every movement was agony. By the time I was set down on the other side of the door, I was fading in and out of consciousness.

'Get that doctor back in here!' someone yelled. 'Here, put pressure on the wounds.'

I retched as something heavy weighed down on my stomach. I dragged in a heavy breath.

The shadow of Cosbi loomed through the hole as he clambered to his feet. A hysterical, wild-looking Gerrin was already careering towards me.

'Live with what you've done!' Hanna screamed at the moving figures. I flinched at the noise.

The floor shook and a low rumble ripped through the corridor. Stone and rock crumbled as a large crack split the ceiling leading into room 23. The last thing I saw was the grief and remorse on Gerrin's face, before the roof gave way, burying everything and everyone in that torture chamber beneath tonnes of rock.

My head dropped back.

The lump in my throat finally gave way.

The tears fell.

It was done. He was gone.

Luca would be safe; it was OK for me to go now.

'What should I do?' Hanna said, tears rolling down her cheeks.

'I want to sleep,' I said, her face growing fuzzy. 'Let me sleep.'

She peeled back the covering on my stomach and paled, the tears now trickling slowly—resigned, accepting. Wiping her cheeks with the back of her bloodied hand, she reached up and removed the locket I'd seen her fiddling with weeks ago. Resting my head gently on her lap, she draped the chain around my neck and opened it so I could see the picture inside.

'This belonged to Louisa. The photo was taken on your wedding day,' she said. 'I took it back from Foley after he was killed.'

Trying to focus through stuttering movements, I looked down at the image in the locket, captured all that time ago. She was so beautiful; we looked so happy that day. I pressed her face to my cold lips and snapped the necklace shut.

Hanna laid a kiss on my forehead and whispered, 'Go to her.'

'Thank you,' I choked out.

I reached into my jeans pocket, twitching fingers eventually retrieving a crisp piece of paper. The charred edges of the burnt list I'd retrieved from Elena's fireplace crumbled as my finger traced along the letters her hand had made, tears blurring the image.

I wasn't alone in the grey place for long. Thoughts of her drifted into my quietening world to accompany my slowing heart, her voice lulling me into a last sleep.

So beautiful.

So peaceful.

US

SUN STREAMED INTO the clearing as I stood in the wild grass at the edge of the trees, sprigs of ragwort brushing past my legs in the breeze. A burnt-out hut stood to the left of a periwinkle-blue lake, the water deliciously tempting in the warmth of the perfect summer afternoon.

There was no mark on my skin; no pain prevented me from marvelling at the beauty of my favourite place in the whole wide world.

I was brand new.

But she was just the same.

She stood with her back to me, one hand held out at her side.

I obeyed her wordless call.

'You came back,' she said.

'I came back.'

My fingers brushed along her arm, pulling her hair back to reveal smooth, unburnt skin. I pressed my lips to her exposed shoulder, my fingers lacing between hers. I squeezed, to show her I was real.

'You won't leave me again?' she said.

'Never.'

'No one can hurt us anymore. We have a lifetime, Nico.'

I smiled at the promise and held the woman who had saved me, in so many ways. 'My Elena.'

Hands entwined, we walked down the embankment towards the lake shore, bare feet swishing through the weeds, the noise masked by rustling trees.

Here, no one could touch us.

THE END

To Be Continued...

ACKNOWLEDGEMENTS

PENGS. Where to even start. I wouldn't have had the courage or self-belief to make it to this point without your support, encouragement, and advice. I would probably still be floundering around on my 84TH draft trying to avoid taking the plunge, with a completely Hollywood-tinted view of how guns work. Thank you for agreeing to design my cover and somehow getting roped into doing all of my promotion materials too. I'm sure you get told enough times a day already, but you are so talented, which may come back to bite you for all my future books. Thank you for being you, the utterly wonderful human being that you are, and for loving me the way that you do. Lastly, thank you for being brave enough to read my book, knowing that you would have to be honest and tell me if it was terrible. I appreciate it more than you know.

TOM AND LUKE. Sorry for all the times I must have ignored you when I wrote this around 10 years ago. I hope you don't remember. Love you.

MUM AND KEL. Thank you for all your support over the years.

SARAH. Thank you for being the very first person to read my writing, chapter by chapter, giving me feedback at the gym every week. And thank you for not laughing—I probably would've given up if you had.

WRITERS UNITED. Love you, you fabulous bunch of weirdos. Anya, Bean, Carol, Caroline, Gareth, Helen, Jo, Joan, Libby, Lucy, Paul, Sue, Susan, Suzanne (and also Lydia & Sam)—thank you for all of your advice over the last few years. Thanks in particular to Carol, Helen, and Gareth for beta-reading, to Paul for the excellent self-publishing advice, and to Lucy for your brutal honesty when the book (and I) needed it.

Thanks to my editor, REBECCA MILLAR, for accepting the daunting challenge of editing for an editor, and for doing such an amazing job.

Thanks to my typesetter, PHILLIP GESSERT, for an outstanding job typesetting *Let Me Sleep*, having bowled me over with the very first sample.

And lastly, thanks to YOU, for purchasing this book and supporting an unknown indie author. Please keep doing it.

ABOUT THE
AUTHOR

R ESIDING IN CHESHIRE with (near) her partner, twin boys (now twin men), and four cats, Laura is a medical editor by trade, as well as a trained dancer, musician, and sometime artist.

Laura graduated from Keele University in 2012 with a somewhat strange dual honours degree combination of English and human biology. An avid and occasionally lucid dreamer, Laura is fascinated by the power of the unconscious mind and Freudian interpretation of dreams.

Many years ago, Laura had a dream, which prompted a thought, which led to an idea, which slowly formed into a plot over a summer of relabelling books in a library. And so, she became a writer, sixteen years after her teacher suggested it.

Let Me Sleep is Laura's debut novel.

Instagram/Twitter: @MsLauraSillett
Facebook: Laura J. Sillett / Author
www.laurajsillett.com

Printed in Great Britain
by Amazon